Second Time Around

Second Time Around

Darrin Lowery

www.urbanbooks.net

Urban Books, LLC
78 East Industry Court
Deer Park, NY 11729

ISBN 13: 978-1-60162-302-7
ISBN 10: 1-60162-302-X

First Trade Paperback Printing June 2011
Printed in the United States of America

10 9 8 7 6 5 4 3 2 1

Distributed by Kensington Publishing Corp.
Submit Wholesale Orders to:
Kensington Publishing Corp.
C/O Penguin Group (USA) Inc.
Attention: Order Processing
405 Murray Hill Parkway
East Rutherford, NJ 07073-2316
Phone: 1-800-526-0275
Fax: 1-800-227-9604

Acknowledgments

I would like to say thank you to Carl and Natalie Weber, Brenda Hampton, my readers, my colleagues at Hull House Association and the JTDC Phoenix Center, my friends from the block and my friends in the writing game, but especially K'wan who has been like a mentor to me, Monica Marie Jones with her Monday Morning Motivation, Michael Baisden, Eric Jerome Dickey, Travis Hunter, E. Lynn Harris (RIP), Lissa Woodson, Victoria Christopher Murray, Nichelle Walker, Ms. Toni, Shannon Holmes, Marc Gerald, Verl and Leesa from Da Book Joint, OOSA Online Book Club, Sugar and Spice Book Club, Readers Paradise Book Club, Reading Rendezvous Book Club, Nikki Woods, Common, Twista, Devonshe Person, Rawsistaz, Deon Cole, Donovan McNabb, Derek Rose, Karrine Steffans, The Ladies of RAGE Book Club, The Ladies of Dolce Vita, Linda Davis, Brandi Higa, Carmen Buick, Jo Oliver, Earl Sewell, Leslie Swanson, The Smith Family, The Gandy Family, Lisa Thomas, my TAGGED Friends, Facebook friends and everyone that has ever supported me in this writing game.

Chapter One

She and her closest friends, Eula, Jayna, Elise, and Tatiana were done with the final touches of her make-up. Her full-skirt wedding gown was only missing her veil. She looked at herself in the mirror one last time as her girlfriends helped her put it on. She smiled to herself as she looked at her own reflection. I'm ready. My day is here and I am finally ready, she thought to herself.

Her bridesmaids moved the long train to the rear so she could walk. Her dress gave balance to her ample rear end and her curves, while still accentuating her bustline.

Prior to today she practiced how to walk in her shoes, how to smile, how to hold back tears, and how to do every tip she had seen at every bridal expo and read in every bridal magazine. Practice makes perfect, she thought. She needed today to be perfect.

Her makeup was flawless. The makeup artist did a remarkable job. Her hair was tightly done in an up-do. Her neckline sported classic pearls with matching ear-rings. She tried her best to maintain her breathing and, at the same time, she resisted the urge to cry. It took forty-five minutes to apply her makeup and she didn't want to ruin it.

In a few minutes she would be at the chapel door. In twenty, she would be married to the man of her dreams. Tomorrow would mark the first day of the rest of her life.

She hugged her girlfriends a final time and they each took photos. They tried to hide their tears as well. Each of them wished they were her. Each one of them quietly wondered to themselves when their day would come. Each of her bridesmaids was beautiful. They were stunning black women. Their dresses complemented hers. Their curves rivaled hers, but there was no doubt about it: Today was her day. Not only that, but she was clearly the most beautiful of brides on her special day.

Her half of the wedding party smiled as the usher came to get them to tell them it was time. The ladies made the final touches on the bride before escorting her to the grand oak doors of the cathedral. Side by side they walked, like ladies on a mission. As they reached the doors they each took their places ahead of her and prepared to walk in.

"You ready?" Jayna asked.

"I am," she said.

The usher was told that the bridesmaids were ready to walk in. Slowly but surely each of her friends walked ahead of her toward the altar. She stood off to the side so she wouldn't be seen. The bridesmaids made their trek down the aisle. Jayna was the last to go. She whispered to the bride before walking down the aisle. Her best friend always had to have the last word.

"I'm proud of you and so very happy for you. I love you, girl."

"Thank you. I love you too. Thanks for having my back."

"That's what best friends are for. Now let's do this. We need to get you married," she said with a smile.

The doors closed a second time and they would only open once more. After that, she would be a married woman. These were her last moments of being single.

She couldn't wait for them to be over. She had grown tired of immature men, men who didn't work, men who didn't know their own potential, and she tired of the drama and games. She was ready to be married. She was ready to be happy. She was ready to exhale. She smiled to herself and thanked God that her day had finally arrived.

She exhaled as the doors opened again and once again she had to fight back tears. "Here and Now" by the late, great Luther Vandross was playing. She made her way to him. Each step was careful. Each step was graceful. Each step took her closer to happily-ever-after.

The cathedral was crowded and everyone stood in her honor. People gasped and whispered as she walked by. Many of her guests commented as to how stunning she looked. Other women held back tears of joy.

With each step she took she felt liberated, happy. She walked slowly and gracefully down the aisle and smiled at the man waiting for her at the other end. He was handsome and regal. Any nervousness she had was quelled at the very sight of him. His smile put her at peace. She was a vision of loveliness. She walked to him and took his outstretched hand.

He smiled at her as she made it to his side. He was the luckiest man in the world and he knew it.

"Are you ready to do this?" he asked quietly with a smile.

"I am ready. I'm ready to marry you."

She smiled so hard that her high cheekbones were flush red. Happiness was written all over her face. The doors to the cathedral closed behind them and everyone sat down as the ceremony began.

"Dearly beloved, we are gathered here this day to join this man and this woman in holy matrimony. They say that he who finds a wife finds a good thing and—"

His speech was interrupted by heavy footfalls on the tiled floors of the foyer. The sounds were so loud that everyone in the church heard them. The footfalls were as loud as the trot of a horse, but were clearly the footfalls of a man.

There was a sound of chaos on the opposite side of the closed doors. There was noise, as if someone was arguing with the usher. Soon after, the sound of a body falling against the cathedral doors was made. It was a sound that suggested the usher had been pushed against the door and out of the person's way.

Everyone in the cathedral had a shocked look on their faces. Everyone wondered what the source of the chaos was. Just as suddenly as the noise started, it stopped. The footfalls ceased.

The church was overrun with whispers and everyone looked from the doors back to the altar where she stood alongside her soon-to-be husband. There was confusion as to what would happen next, but her fiancé urged the clergyman to continue the ceremony.

She kept looking back at the doors. She didn't know what or who was on the other side. Whatever or whoever it was had her heart racing with fear. Something wasn't right. She could feel it in her heart. Still, today was her day. She turned to face the priest again. She turned and faced him so that she could be married.

Fearfully and with concern, the priest started again.

"He who finds a wife finds a good thing. We are here this day in front of friends, family and the almighty, to join this man and this woman in holy matrimony. It is said that—"

Again, heavy footfalls were heard. Again, the priest gave a moment of pause. The light beneath the door revealed the shadow of a man's feet on the opposite side. Someone was standing there. Someone who had no intention of leaving.

There was a knock on the church doors. It was a resounding knock that sounded as if God himself was on the other side. No one moved and the entire cathedral looked in the direction of the closed doors. Everyone looked back at her. She felt frozen in time. She felt frozen with fear.

The knocking stopped and then started again. It was three hard and loud knocks. They weren't knocks requesting permission to enter so much as they were knocks announcing one's presence.

When no one made an attempt to answer, the screeching sound of the doors opening again announced his presence. The doors were forced open and on the other side was a man with a look of defiance on his face. His looks reeked of defiance as well as anger.

Her ex-boyfriend was on the other side. He headed down the aisle toward her. His every stride was deliberate. His footfalls were heavy. The look on his face said that he was ending this madness . . . now.

Her heart skipped a beat. This couldn't be happening. His being here took her breath away. Her face was riddled with confusion and anger. The problem was, part of her was happy to see him. Part of her was relieved to see him. But he was too late; this was her wedding day. He had no right to be here. He had no right to interfere with her happiness. She turned to face her fiancé and the priest. His footsteps became louder as he approached them. She kept her back to him and said a brief prayer asking God to forgive this madness.

She turned to face her fiancé. She gave him a look that said he should do something. She wanted him to confront her ex. She wanted him to tell her ex to leave. She turned to speak to him; to direct him to stop him before her perfect day would be ruined.

Her fiancé was gone.

She turned back around and her ex was gone.

The church was empty.

The doors were again closed.

Her dress was all that she had left and it was old and in shreds. It had a yellowish tinge to it, as if to imply that it was ages old. She was alone. The man of her future was gone along with her ex, the man from her past.

She was alone. Alone in the world and, it seemed, trapped in the church. She sat at the altar alone and slowly began to cry. She no longer wanted to be alone. She wanted to be married. She wanted to be loved.

There was a second knock at the closed doors. She stopped crying and looked in the direction of the doors. The knocking was insistent. Someone was on the other side, trying to get in. Perhaps it was her fiancé, perhaps it was her ex. In either case, once she opened the doors she would no longer be alone. She ran to the doors as the knocking continued. She was just about to open them when a blinding light made its way into the church through the stained-glass windows.

Chapter Two

Korie Ann Dillon woke up at six in the morning to a thunderous knocking at her door. That was the knocking that she heard in her dream. She was happy to be awakened from her nightmare, but the dream was so vivid and so intense she didn't feel well-rested at all. Initially, she buried her head deeper into the pillows. When the knocking began again, she knew someone was at her front door and, whoever it was, wasn't leaving. She let out a few grunts and moans to express her displeasure.

Damn, it feels like I just went to sleep. And what was up with that dream?

Damn, that was weird. It can't be morning already, she thought.

She halfway opened her eyes and reached out for her cell phone, which was now buzzing. Now Korie was frowning. It was obvious that she wasn't going to get back to sleep, not that she even wanted to after the dream she just had. She did want to rest, however. She needed to rest.

She picked up her phone with one hand and moved the hair out of her face with the other. She looked at the small screen on her phone.

She struggled to focus on the picture and text on the phone, which said Jayna. She let out a groan and stretched a bit before picking the phone up just before it went to voice mail.

"Heifer, that better not be you at my door," she said in a groggy voice while stretching across her bed like a newly awakened cat.

Jayna laughed. "Yeah, it's me. Korie, get up, it's time for our run."

"We don't run for another hour or so. Why are you here so early?"

"Daylight savings time, princess; you must have forgotten."

Korie looked at her clock and then at the Post-it she wrote to herself that was sticking to the front of her TV screen in her bedroom. The note said daylight savings time, change the time. Korie shook her head as she realized her mistake.

"Aw shoot, I did forget. Come back in an hour," she said jokingly.

"Girl, get up," Jayna said playfully.

Korie got up out of bed like a restless child. She put on her robe and partially closed it. She walked as if she was slightly intoxicated. She reached again for her robe, and retied it as she headed to the door.

Her heavy footfalls sounded off the hardwood floor of her apartment. They were footfalls that reminded her of the dream that she had. She wiped the sleep from her eyes and closed the phone before opening the door. On the other side was her best friend, Jayna, but today she looked at her as if she was her worst enemy. Bad dream or not, Korie would have preferred to remain in bed a while longer to try and make sense of the dream.

Korie worked mornings, but she hated waking up early, especially on Saturday. Her first client wasn't until four o' clock in the afternoon. She would have rather slept in most of the day. She wasn't up for a run.

"Damn you look a hot mess! Did you get some last night or did you have a bad dream?"

Korie frowned at her best friend and scratched her head as she ushered her in. She wished she had some last night and started to lie, but Jayna would know better.

"I had a bad dream." In the back of her mind, Korie was trying to make sense of it all.

"Well, it's over now. Time to get up, sleepyhead," Jayna said, while running in place. "You wanna talk about it?"

"Nah, that's okay. You ready to run this morning?"

"Sure, can't you tell?"

Jayna did her playful mock-professional-runner's jog into Korie's apartment. She jogged around the living room a little bit like she was really ready to do something. Korie let out a half smile at her friend's playfulness. Jayna was running in place like she was about to audition for a Nike commercial.

Jayna wore jogging shorts that were a size extra-large. Although she was only a size eight, she needed the extra material to cover her perfectly round bottom. She tried her best to cover up her best asset, but there was nothing that could hide the fact that she had great hips and a butt that most women would die for.

She wore a headband and a sports bra that showed off her just-developing abs. Her long brown hair was up in a ponytail and she had a small backpack, which housed all of her personal belongings. Her legs were strong and powerful, and her arms were just beginning to tone up. In a few months time, Jayna might actually just be in good enough shape to do a commercial for Nike.

Korie hated getting up, but she was glad that her best friend was here. She was also glad that they vowed to push each other to get into shape. For four months now, they'd been watching what they ate. For four months they'd been going to the gym every other day and running on alternate days. Today was one of the days that they were scheduled to go running.

They were now up to two miles a day. This was a huge accomplishment because when they first started running, they could barely make it around the block. Now, they were considered "real runners" with the outfits, running shoes, and other such accessories.

They worked out in some way every day except Sunday. On Sunday they rested. Their excuse was it was the lord's day. The truth was by the time Sunday rolled around both women were often exhausted.

Korie looked at her girlfriend's progress and quickly became motivated. Before they started working out, Jayna and Korie were considered, by black standards, to be thick. The truth was they were both a few choice meals away from being fat.

Before they started working out, cellulite had begun to flex its muscle or lack thereof on their legs and perfectly round bottoms. They were both short of breath all the time, and they knew they needed to get in some type of shape. They were only in their late twenties, but they knew professional women in their forties who were in much better shape than they were.

Every white woman that they knew was in phenomenal shape, whereas both Korie and Jayna would sometimes be winded by a simple flight of stairs. They knew if they didn't get into shape soon, a heart attack, obesity or diabetes would claim them before there were in their mid-thirties. That's how out of shape they were.

A long, healthy life was the goal. The tight bodies they were getting were a bonus. Rather than continue to bitch and moan, Korie complimented her girl as she made her way to the coffee machine. She pointed her finger at her girlfriend with one hand and put her hand on her hip with the other as she jokingly took verbal shots at Jayna.

"I was going to curse your behind out for coming here so early, but now that I see how good you look, I know that we need to do this."

Korie rolled her eyes as she spoke, then smiled.

"Girl thanks," Jayna said. "Your hair is still a hot mess this morning, but look at you. You're in great shape too. Go jump in the shower, I'll finish making the coffee."

"That sounds cool. A hot shower might just be the thing that I need."

Korie retreated into her bedroom to gather her things and Jayna went to the kitchen to grab two cups for coffee.

At first glance, Jayna looked like a model out of a black men's magazine. She had long, strong hair, striking features, chiseled curves, and a beautiful smile. She was a woman whose main goal in life was to be the perfect woman and one day a wife. Jayna was smart, thick, and stunning: Three great qualities that black men loved in a woman. Men saw her and often paused. Many were captured with her smile and later mesmerized by her body. Jayna was a gorgeous black woman. Part of the problem was she knew she was a gorgeous black woman.

Just as beautiful as Jayna was, she was also very demanding when it came to men. They had to look a certain way, dress a certain way, and make at least six figures if they were going to speak to her. Aside from that, men were a waste of her time. She loved the attention that she got, but only if it was from the right kind of man. Average men were boring to Jayna and above-average men were often competing for her affection.

Jayna's standards were high. Some might say her standards were unrealistic. This was probably why at twenty-nine and a half, she was still single. She had proposal offers, but, for one reason or another, things never seemed to work out.

Jayna thought if she improved the outer woman, men would see her and offer her the world. She figured she deserved the world because of her looks. She often thought to herself that God made her so damned fine because he wanted someone to take care of her. She figured no man could turn her down and any man who would was a damned fool.

Korie loved her girlfriend but knew if Jayna needed to change anything, it was the woman she was on the inside. Jayna had strong credentials and experience, but that did nothing for who she was as a person.

Jayna was a financial advisor in a downtown Chicago firm. She could talk finances with the best of the best. Professionally, she was considered a beast. She was a true force to be reckoned with. But then there was the other side of the coin. Personally, Jayna was a bit of a bitch—or at least that is how most men saw her. Seeing her fueled their lust for her, but most men referred to Jayna as a bitch or gold digger behind her back.

Gold digger wasn't a fair assessment of her because Jayna had her own money and was quite independent. There was nothing a man could do for her that she couldn't do for herself. However, she demanded that the men she dated be either powerful or wealthy. The two things were almost always linked hand in hand.

To date her, the criteria were quite strict. If a man met those criteria, he would be given an open invitation as one of her suitors. Oftentimes, this also meant that he would be given an open invitation into her bedroom. Jayna was drawn to powerful men.

Jayna bedded many men who she came across. She was like a black version of the character Samantha Jones on Sex and the City. That was one of her major flaws. Sometimes she acted as if she were addicted to sex. If nothing else, she was addicted to the attention.

She was in therapy for her issues with men. She was also in therapy for being what her therapist called hypersexual. Let Jayna tell it, she simply liked powerful men and also liked sex.

That was her position.

The position of her therapist was that Jayna was having high-risk behaviors; behaviors that often had high consequences. Jayna had been blessed that she hadn't been raped, killed or given an STD. These were three very real things that could have happened to her at any time. Things she never thought about until after she had an orgasm.

Korie didn't think that Jayna was a whore or whorish, but she did think her girlfriend was sometimes too eager to give away her goodies. She knew that Jayna needed help, and was happy that she was seeing a professional.

Korie's worst nightmare would be for her longtime friend to come to her crying one day because she got the big disease with the little name. If that should ever happen, Korie was sure that Jayna would gladly trade places with their friend Eula, who recently lost her leg to a different disease—diabetes. Korie worried often about her friend. Every night she prayed for her. Even with counseling, that didn't stop Jayna from having the high-risk behaviors. It didn't stop her from inviting many men into her bedroom.

***

The more money and more potential stability a man had to offer, the greater his chances were of taking Jayna to bed. She'd slept with very powerful men around the city of Chicago. She slept with them in their offices, the homes that they shared with their wives, and in many of Chicago's best hotels.

All the men Jayna bedded were handsome and were all considered pretty good catches professionally. Some were clients, some were colleagues. All of them were men who could make things happen. The problem was none of them ever made anything happen with Jayna, outside of sex.

Nothing serious ever developed from any of those relationships and because of that, Jayna was down on herself. She would sometimes come to Korie complaining about how trifling men were, even the professional ones.

There were times that Korie would listen to her girlfriend and say to herself, what did you expect to happen?

When Jayna was upset about a man, she shopped. She bought the finest clothes, drove luxury cars, and traveled often. The thing was, many times she was doing these things alone. If not alone, then she would have one-night stands with men she barely knew. The men were always wealthy, but they were almost always married.

On the outside Jayna looked like she had everything together. She had a great job, two great cars, and great looks. On the outside she was damn near perfect. On the inside, she was a mess. Still, being friends means sometimes that you don't judge. That was the lie that Korie used to tell herself.

Korie loved Jayna like a sister and today the sisters were going running. When they ran, they weren't professionals, they weren't judged by the world and its shallow expectations. When they ran, they were just two women hanging out with one another. Two beautiful black women, hanging out with one another.

Korie grabbed her warm-up gear, which was always neatly folded on the edge of her bed. She grabbed her running shoes, her full-length outfit, bra and panties, and headed to the bathroom. She ran the shower and turned on her iPod.

Korie quickly got undressed, brushed her teeth, and examined herself in the mirror as she brushed.

Like Jayna, Korie too had made a considerable amount of progress in these past four months. She went from a size ten to a size six. Her abs were also beginning to show and her breasts, which were just beginning to sag a little, began to firm up.

With all the water she was drinking, Korie's beautiful Hershey chocolate–colored skin began to look flawless. Once upon a time Korie's butt rivaled that of Jayna's. Now, with the weight loss, she was beginning to look like a model; not like a music video model, but a model who you might see in a magazine. Korie had the killer looks and Jayna had the killer body.

She looked in the mirror and was satisfied with what she saw. Before stepping in the shower she quickly thought to herself, what would he think? What would he think about her body? What would he think about the changes that she made with her life? It had been quite a few years and still, Korie couldn't help herself thinking about him.

Just as quickly as she asked the question, she dismissed it. She jumped in the shower, lathered up with her favorite vanilla-scented body wash, and rinsed off.

When she stepped out from the bathroom fully dressed, Jayna was there with a small cup of black coffee in hand for her girlfriend. They each drank their coffee and talked about what was going on in their careers. Twenty minutes later, they were out the door and running the trail at the park.

As Jayna ran, she was looking for wealthy men at the park. As Korie ran, she tried to make sense of the dream that she had this morning.

Jayna knew Korie would judge her, so she never mentioned when they ran that she was also looking for men. Korie knew, but she also knew enough not to say anything.

Korie was preoccupied as they ran because the dream she had was so vivid and so real to her.

He must be out there thinking about me or talking about me and that's why he's on my mind, she thought.

Korie couldn't shake the feeling that something major was about to happen in her life. The question was, would the major event would be good or bad? She liked the fact that she was happy in the dream. Did it mean that marriage was around the corner or something else?

Chapter Three

Darren Howard awoke from a sound sleep. His alarm was set to go off and waken him to the sounds of "Struggle No More" by Anthony Hamilton as it did every morning during the week. Darren got up, stretched, and went to the bathroom to relieve himself. He then ran bathwater and stepped into the living room to boot up his laptop.

He made his way to the coffee machine and brewed some Exotic Coffee, checked the final tally of the stock market, and stretched his six-foot frame to its full length as he tried to get the last of the morning kinks out.

He was up this early because he had a full agenda of errands to run before seeing his first client. Darren was a therapist for Chicago's elite. He counseled pro athletes, R & B singers, CEOs, and other celebrities.

He charged 300 dollars an hour, which was nothing to his clientele. Because he made his own schedule, life was good. He worked when he wanted, made a great salary, and had a lot of the finer things in life. The only thing that was not complete was his love life. That was another matter entirely.

He grabbed the universal remote for his condo and switched the overhead speakers on. His favorite slow songs began to play. Darren went into the master closet and pulled out a pair of white-on-white gym shoes, blue designer jeans, and an equally expensive T-shirt.

He laid the ensemble on the bed and headed back to the bathroom.

The steam was billowing off of the water in his custom-made Jacuzzi. Darren slowly eased into the water and practically lay down in the water until it was at chin level. He sat in the tub and relaxed for about an hour, listening to jazz and neo-soul.

When he was completely relaxed and his mind was free, he got up out of the water and rinsed off. His mind was wandering a lot this morning and he couldn't seem to figure out why. He needed his music this morning to be a distraction. He had a lot on his mind. One of the chief things bothering him was how lonely he felt these days in spite of having just about every material thing that a man could ask for.

When he stepped out of the tub and onto the thick rug on the bathroom floor, he listened to "And I Am Telling You" by Jennifer Holliday. Jennifer Hudson's rendition followed as he began to shave and air dry. Most people Darren knew loved Jennifer Husdon's rendition better than the original. Darren thought the original was a classic. He playfully used the shaver as if he were singing the song himself. His cracking falsetto was horrible, but that didn't stop him from trying to sing the song.

As he trimmed his goatee, he thought about all the things he had to do today. He picked up his phone and added a few new entries to the notebook. He then began to apply body lotion and sprayed on his favorite cologne. He went to the bedroom and put on his boxers, put on his clothes for the day, and headed out to his car after turning off the stereo in his condo.

The first thing he wanted to do before starting his day was wash his car. He went down to the parking garage, chirped the alarm on his new sports car and hit the streets. His favorite hip-hop was blaring over the eight-speaker system.

Darren's first stop was the car wash. He went to the manual wash where he could give his car the attention that it needed. Like other black men who were washing their cars, Darren popped the trunk and had a host of cleaning supplies for his car, including a shammy, wax, degreasers, and Armor All.

He washed his car with the care all black men give their cars when they are new. He gave other men there the universal head nod. He also made note of all the beautiful women cleaning their cars as well. Many were scantily clad. Others were in jeans, gym shoes, and tops.

It was early in the morning and the sun was just beginning to flex its morning muscle. In spite of it being early, all the ballers, dealers, and anyone with a decent whip seemed to be at the car wash.

Everyone was gearing up for a beautiful Chicago day. The sun was shining, music from various artists were blasting over the multiple speakers of different cars, and those with chrome rims were shining them to a point where the sun's rays would bounce hard off the reflection of the rim tops.

Darren cleaned his car and dried it off slowly. He cranked his system back up as he gradually pulled out of the parking lot.

Next he went to get his hair cut by Big Gucci at the old barbershop in the hood. Darren slowly drove through the hood so women and men alike could see his newly cleaned car. He liked the attention, as did most men when their cars were cleaned. He checked out the women as they checked him out and smiled to himself as he thought about how all his hard work had paid off these past few years. He was already successful. His new goal was to be wealthy.

Many brothers rocked hardcore rap as they drove their cars in the summer. Darren rocked slow jams. Eighties music was playing overhead as he slowly pulled into the parking lot of the barbershop. He stepped out of his car and walked in the barbershop all smiles as he was greeted by the other men inside.

"Whaddup, playa?" one guy asked.

Darren gave the guy a head nod.

"What's up, D?" Gucci said to Darren. "I got two ahead of you, but I got you."

"Cool, cool. Thanks, Gooch."

Darren sat down on the bench and watched as the many men in the shop fellowshipped with one another. Some were playing basketball on video consoles as they waited to get their hair cut. Others watched music videos, which were playing on the monitors overhead, and others still were talking about current events, the economy, and the challenges that faced the first African American president.

Going to the shop was like being at an all-men's club. It was a place where men could go to be men, and freely talk about the things that affected them. From sex to politics, nothing was off limits at the shop. Men of all ages passed wisdom on to each other, from financial advice to advice on women. On Saturdays, the barbershop was the place to be and it stayed crowded every day that it was open.

Even though he made a high, six-figure salary, Darren still got his hair cut by Big Gucci. Gucci, whose real name was Guy, had been his barber for well over ten years. Many of Darren's colleagues and high-society friends went to salons in downtown Chicago to get their hair cut. Darren kept his money in the community. He always went back to the hood.

The successful brothers who didn't go to salons had their barbers come to their homes. The cost was often over a hundred dollars. Darren was considered to be bourgeois by some, but he was not too good to go back to the hood and get his hair cut.

A haircut in the hood was thirteen dollars; twenty with a tip. In addition to a haircut, there was always something going on that was entertaining at the barbershop. Whether it was a debate about who was the best ballplayer of all time, or a debate on what woman in Hollywood had the nicest body, the barbershop was quite an animated place on the weekends.

Darren knew that contrary to popular opinion, men gossip just as much as women. The men in the shop gossiped, talked about each other, and joked so loud you would have thought they were teenage girls.

Forty minutes passed and it was finally his turn. He sat in the chair and Gucci put the wrap around him to catch any extra hair.

"Bald fade, right, D?" Gucci asked. He had a deep voice like a late-night radio personality.

"Yep, you know it," Darren said.

Darren sat in the shop and looked at all the various hairstyles that were in the room. He looked at the brothers that were there to get a lining, brothers with bald fades, Afros, and one-level haircuts. Some guys were there to get razor-sharp fades and others were there to get their hair shaved off entirely. No matter what style they were looking for, Gucci could accommodate them.

Darren reached for his cell phone and turned it off as he sat in the barber chair. A lot of the dope dealers in the hood came in and got their hair cut, but stayed on their phones almost the entire time. All of them were chasing paper. None of them could pause long enough to properly get their hair cut despite the sign posted that said Please put your cell phones away.

Darren thought to himself, What's with niggas and their damned cell phones? He powered his cell phone off in hopes that others in the chairs would get the message.

They didn't.

Perhaps they didn't want to miss any paper. Perhaps they needed the attention. At any rate, the drug dealers stayed on their phones and looked at the exotic pictures they had saved on them. They were oblivious, it seemed, to common courtesy and manners.

"So did my guy come and see you?" Gucci asked.

"Yeah, yeah he did. Thanks for the referral, Gucci," Darren said.

Gucci was not just a barber; he was kind of a celebrity himself. He played two years of pro basketball until he blew out his knee. When he was playing ball, however, he had a reputation for cutting the hair of a lot of professional ballplayers on his team and the opposing team the night before a game.

Gucci stood six feet eight inches tall and was a force to be dealt with in his basketball-playing days. He was built like a pro wrestler. After he blew his knee out, he was devastated. He didn't know how he would make ends meet and his heart was broken because all he ever wanted to do in life was play ball. Like a lot of young black men, he thought sports were his only avenue out of the hood. But a good insurance settlement gave him some other possibilities. Even though the money wasn't enough to cover all the taxes he owed and the payments on his expensive lifestyle, he liquidated his assets, took the two million that he cleared from that, and invested with some brokers. As a result, he recently opened up his fourth barbershop and business was great.

When some pro basketball players were in town to play, many of them drove to the shop and Gucci cut their hair. For some players, he cut their hair during regular business hours and for others, he cut their hair after hours.

Gucci knew most of today's star players and put pictures of him and them up all over the shop. This was a major draw. Many men that came in the shop were proud that their barber was also the barber for many of today's pro basketball stars.

"So my guy called you, right?" Gucci asked again.

"Yeah, yeah he did."

"So D, what's going on with him right now?"

"Gucci, I really can't talk about it," Darren said, laughing.

Client confidentiality was a staple in counseling. Darren knew that Gucci was concerned about his friend, but he couldn't say anything. It would be a breach of confidentiality to do so.

Gucci had a friend named Bryce Irving whose game was slipping fast. He was a point guard from a West Coast team who went from averaging twenty-six points per game during the regular season to fifteen in the play-offs.

Gucci was cutting Bryce's hair a few weeks ago and noticed that the man was depressed. He also noticed that the man's cell phone was blowing up as he was getting his hair cut. It was obvious to Gucci that Bryce and his woman were having problems.

Bryce's fiancée was a famous R&B singer named Maurielle and Gucci couldn't believe that the guy's girlfriend and soon-to-be wife was giving him so much grief weeks before their high-profile wedding. While he was getting his hair cut, all he seemed to do was argue and get yelled at. Gucci couldn't hear all the particulars, but he knew the main arguing point was the upcoming wedding; a wedding that had been announced all over the news and television.

Everyone in the media figured Bryce's game was off because he was getting married soon. His coach, teammates, and sports analysts all told him that he needed to get married in the off-season because his lack of focus was affecting the team.

Bryce was in the last year of his contract with his current team and with such a major drop in production, chances were he was going to go from making tens of millions of dollars to possibly a one-or two-million-dollar-a-year deal with his next team. On top of that, Maurielle was giving him all sorts of grief on the phone—according to Gucci.

Gucci knew that his friend needed help. He knew that his friend needed someone to talk to. He also knew what it was like to lose millions of dollars. Gucci referred Bryce to Darren. It was not uncommon for Gucci to introduce customers to one another at the shop to network—for a finder's fee, of course.

Darren took the case and in just a few weeks the guard's numbers were climbing high again. His productivity was almost where it once was.

"You must be doing something magical, D. My man's point average is almost back where it was before he started having problems. You must have really had an impact on him. Either that, or he had some serious problems, huh?"

Gucci's voice was inquisitive, as if he wanted to know exactly what it was that Darren did, or what it was that was bothering Bryce.

"Gucci, I really can't talk about it," Darren said, laughing again.

"Oh yeah, right. That confidentiality thing, right?"

"That's right. Confidentiality prevents me from saying anything."

"But don't you think I should be in the loop? Shouldn't close friends of the person in question be privy to what's going on?"

"Nice try Gooch, but . . . uh, no."

"Yeah, but I sent him to you."

"And I'm grateful for it, brother, but really, I can't talk about it."

"Okay D, I understand."

"Cool."

"So did you get a chance to meet his fiancée yet?"

"No, not yet."

"Man, D, she's fine as hell, you know?"

"Yeah, I know."

"And she is sexy as an MF in those music videos."

"Yeah, she is."

"So tell me, she's the reason that his game dropped off, right?"

"Gucci . . ."

"I know, I know. You really can't talk about it."

Gucci winked at the other guys in the shop waiting to get their hair cut. Darren smiled and laughed a little because he knew Gucci wouldn't stop probing. That was how things went in the shop. Everyone was in everyone else's business.

Everyone in the shop laughed. Gucci was starving for gossip, as were all the other men. Gucci didn't mention the name of the ballplayer, but he did mention to everyone that Darren was seeing one of his friends who played pro ball.

He also mentioned that Darren was a therapist, and a good one at that. As soon as he mentioned that, women in the shop, getting haircuts for their sons, started to take notice of Darren. One minute he was off the radar. After Gucci let the cat out of the bag, he was on every woman's radar in the shop.

A lot of women came to Gucci's to get their sons hair cut. Many more dressed rather provocatively because they knew men would be there; men with good jobs, as well as the trifling ones and the drug dealers.

Some women came to the shop every week pretty much just to see who was there. Their sons' hair certainly didn't need to get cut every week. Some women came to try and meet the police officers or bus drivers that came. They just wanted a man with benefits. Others came scantily clad to meet the drug dealers. The real mothers that were only there for their children dressed regularly and were often in and out without any conversation with anyone.

One woman in particular, who was drop-dead gorgeous, looked out at Darren's car and then looked at Darren as Gucci was finishing cutting his hair. She looked at him as if she were trying to gather the nerve to speak to him.

The woman was at the shop getting her son's hair cut. She was a beautiful woman with implants so fresh they looked like they were about to pop like a balloon with too much air in them. They sat up so high they looked unnatural.

"Is that your sports car out there?" she asked Darren.

"Yeah, sweetheart, that's mine."

"You must be making some major paper to drive a whip like that. If you don't mind my asking, how much do you charge?"

Guys in the shop all started looking and smiling at one another. It was obvious to them that the fine young woman was smelling paper, and she was trying to screen Darren to see how much money he made. Darren cleared his throat before speaking.

"My fee is three hundred dollars an hour, love."

"Three hundred an hour!"

The woman's eyes bugged out some. Her expression didn't say that she was impressed by Darren's fee, but that it was very expensive.

"You can't talk to her in numbers that high, D," Gucci said sarcastically.

Gucci then spoke directly to the woman, whose name was Karen. She went by the marquee Special K at the local strip club.

"He makes fifteen lap dances per hour," Gucci said to Karen.

The barbershop erupted with laughter.

"Go to hell, Gucci! How could you say that? My son is right there." She spoke in a scolding tongue.

"My bad."

Gucci went back to cutting Darren's hair.

The woman was incensed. She began going off on Gucci.

"I don't know why I always come in here and give you my business, when all you seem to do is poke fun at me!"

She rolled her eyes and if looks could kill, Gucci would have been a victim.

"You come in here because I keep your son's head looking tight."

"Yeah, but I'm not sure it's worth it if every week you are putting me down or making fun of me."

Karen spoke with her hand on her hip. She had fire in her eyes. She continued to shoot eye daggers at Gucci, speaking with such rage that Darren thought she might actually try and fight the seven-foot-tall man.

"Maybe you should get a new job. I can't make fun of you if you have a real job."

"I have a job and right now that job is what puts food on my table."

"Yeah, but wearing clear heels at night doesn't count as a real job, not a respectable one, anyway. How can you look for any type of respect with an unrespectable job?"

Gucci high-fived one of the other barbers in the shop. He shot eye daggers back at her. Although he sounded as if he were joking, his looks, his facial expressions, and his body language showed a bit of rage of his own. Other people were too busy laughing to notice his body language, but that was part of what Darren did for a living. So, as everyone watched the beautiful, scorned woman, Darren watched Gucci as they exchanged shots.

"And cutting hair is so damn great?" she snapped with her hand on her hip.

"It's better than doing what it is that you do."

"I do what I have to do to take care of my family! That's more than half the men in here can say."

She pointed at a few of the men as she spoke.

The trifling ones were easy to spot. Many of them were getting their own hair cut but their sons' hair was looking a mess. With the trifling men, the only reasons their sons were there was because it was their visitation week with their kids. Also the trifling ones could only afford to either get their own hair cut or their sons' hair cut.

Naturally, being selfish, they opted to get their own hair cut, not thinking that even if they couldn't contribute much, they could at least get their sons' hair cut and save their child's mother that expense. Many of the trifling men spent what little money they did get at the strip club. When the woman pointed at them, Darren noticed many had looks of guilt on their faces.

"Hold up, you're not going to come up here disrespecting my customers. Everyone in here works."

"Yeah and everyone in here has been over to the club too."

"Then that means that everyone in here is helping you to keep food on your table. It's a group effort. The brothers love the kids. They aren't over there for themselves, they come over there for the kids."

Again there were laughs. Karen was angry and sad at the same time. She looked as if she might even be ready to cry. She was way too pretty to cry. At least to Darren she was. He could tell that she was not proud of her occupation but like she said, it kept food on her table during one of the worst economic times on record.

"Are you finished with my son?" Karen asked one of the other barbers who was cutting her son's hair today.

"Almost," the other barber said.

"Gucci, I swear to God I'm never coming back in here again!"

"I'm sorry, Special K. I mean Karen."

More laughs erupted from the patrons.

"Gucci, that's enough" Darren interrupted. "Her shorty's here."

"You're right, D. My bad, Karen. Seriously, I apologize. You know how we get carried away in the shop here sometimes."

"I can't believe you. I can't believe that you just played me like that." She shook her head as if she were hurt, genuinely hurt by the performance that Gucci put on.

Her little boy didn't know what they were talking about. He was a little fella. He was a handsome little man who was getting a fade. He didn't know what anyone was talking about, but he did know that the men in the shop were upsetting his mother. Karen was still scowling. Gucci's words cut deep. The two of them continued to exchange dirty looks.

Darren tried to switch topics.

"So, my name is Darren. And your name is Karen, right? It's nice to meet you."

Karen continued to cut Gucci evil looks. He stopped playing with her. Darren surmised that they had some type of history together. Only a woman with prior history with a man could shut a man down with one fierce look.

"Yes, my name is Karen." She shook Darren's hand.

Darren put his head down so Gucci could finish lining up the back.

"By any chance do you know someone that needs to see a therapist?" Darren asked.

"Yeah, my cousin does. But I don't think she can afford three hundred an hour."

"Does she have insurance?"

"No."

"Medicaid?"

"No. She doesn't have any benefits."

Figures, Darren thought to himself. He let out a sigh before speaking.

"Well, I have to do so many pro bono cases per year. I also do a few on a sliding scale. Here is my card." Darren reached into his pocket to grab a card while Gucci finished lining up the back of his neck.

"What's bono? And what's a sliding scale?"

Gucci was just about to laugh when Karen cut him another look. It was a look that quickly silenced the gentle giant.

"Pro bono means free." Darren said. "Sliding scale means that I charge you according to how much money you make. Tell your cousin to call me and we will work something out. Tell her to make sure she tells me that she is the cousin of the woman I met in Gucci's shop."

Karen seemed relieved and grateful. There was warmth in her eyes that said thank you. When her eyes finished saying thank you, her mouth followed.

"Thank you. Thank you so much."

The one barber working on her son had just finished. Karen paid him in singles, which caused a bit more laughter and whispering among the men. She took her son's hand and led him out of the shop. The little man was frowning because he knew the men inside had upset his mother. After she left, many of the men began gossiping about her They talked about how she moved her ass in the club and they each told lies about the things she would do for money at the club. Gucci faked a smile here and there, but it was obvious to Darren that he actually didn't like hearing any of it. It seemed to be one thing for him to poke fun at her, but he didn't seem to appreciate others doing so.

The men in the shop thought Karen was looking at Darren's car because she was trying to get paid. Darren knew as a therapist that many women measure a man's success by the car that he drives. It wasn't a good measuring tool, but was sometimes how things were looked at in the hood. Since he drove a nice sports car, Karen assumed he was a pretty good therapist. When she heard that he had counseled a pro athlete, she figured that he had to be really good at what he did.

Darren knew that Karen was looking for a therapist, either for her cousin or for herself. It was always amazing to him how many people wanted to talk to you once they found out that you were a therapist. Black people loved to talk to therapists . . . for free. Darren thought to himself that Karen would likely give him a call in the next few days.

"That was nice of you, D. Are you going to see her cousin?" Gucci asked.

"I might."

"How much are you going to charge her?"

"Her sessions will be free if you tell me what the history between you and Karen is."

Darren raised an eyebrow as he turned around and looked up at his longtime barber.

Gucci had a look of shock on his face and shrugged his shoulders as if he didn't know what Darren was talking about.

"What? Man, I don't have any history with that girl."

"Uh-huh, don't forget what I do for a living, playa. What's up with you and Karen?"

Darren looked at Gucci as if to say stop playing.

When it was obvious that there was some history there, and when Gucci confirmed it with a look of guilt written across his face, he became silent. All the barbershop patrons were all ears, waiting on Gucci to respond. It was so quiet in the shop you would've thought the place was closed.

***

"D, really, I hope you can appreciate this . . . I really can't talk about it."

Once again the entire shop erupted in laughter. This time even Darren laughed.

"Okay, I can respect that," Darren said, laughing.

"I thought you might."

"Yeah, confidentiality," Darren said while giving Gucci an understanding look.

"But you can tell me what's going on with my boy."

"No, Gucci. I can't."

"I'll tell you about me and Karen."

"No deal," Darren said, laughing.

Gucci wanted to know why his friend's scoring average dropped so low and the truth of the matter was the ballplayer had a lot on his mind.

It wasn't that Bryce was getting married that was bothering him. What was bothering him was that Bryce's male lover was pissed that he was getting married, and that the wedding was all over the television airways.

Gucci thought it was Maurielle that was blowing up the athlete's cell phone when he was getting his hair cut. It wasn't—it was the man he was cheating on her with.

Bryce wasn't gay. At least that is what he said. He was on the down low. He was bisexual. His secret was driving him crazy and he was very distracted by the possibility of being outed to the world.

In his counseling sessions with Darren he confessed that he loved Maurielle and his male lover as well. His scoring average was dropping because his lover was threatening to out him at his wedding or go to the press.

Bryce couldn't concentrate on basketball. If his secret was put out there he stood to lose both people that he loved and millions of dollars. His lifestyle would be severely compromised.

In therapy, Darren and Bryce discussed issues of sexuality, then infidelity as well as how he came to have an affair with another man to begin with. This was the one point that Darren was definitely confused about.

It seemed that Bryce had been dating Maurielle well over two years. Their relationship had its rocky moments, including a not-so-private moment of domestic violence that played over and over again in the tabloids.

The relationship had its great times too. Bryce loved the singer, who was also pregnant with his child at one point. Maurielle's manager explained that it was not a good time in her career to have a child, so she aborted, a decision that did not sit well with either of them. It was a sore point in their relationship and Darren surmised it was one of the things pulling the couple apart. In an effort to save his relationship with her, Bryce proposed. That didn't save the relationship, but it did seem to mend some of the pain. To Maurielle it was validation. It showed her that Bryce was committed to their relationship.

Darren asked Bryce how he came about the affair he had. Darren wanted to know the name of the man he was cheating on Maurielle with. He was dying to know, but it really wasn't necessary, however, in order to treat Bryce, so Darren asked that he not mention the other man by name. Darren's fear was that he would repeat it to a colleague and then the word would spread quickly.

Bryce said that in a moment of weakness, after playing against a West Coast team, he hung out with one of the guys from the opposing team. It was the same

guy that burned him for twenty-four points, eight re-
bounds, and three steals. Bryce's opponent took him
out to dinner one night as if to say no hard feelings.
They also went to a nightclub and stayed out very late.
They did a lot of drinking and a lot of partying that
night.

As the limo took the guard back to his hotel, the two
men, both in a drunken stupor, laughed and joked
about various things they saw at the club and all the
different women that tried to get them to take them
back to their hotel rooms. They continued to drink in
the limousine. The next thing Bryce knew, the opposing guard smiled at him. It was a smile that Bryce confessed he was unaccustomed to getting from another
man. Bryce said the other man knelt in front of him
and buried his head in his lap.

Initially he protested.

Initially he confessed he was scared.

He then told Darren that the liquor weakened his
inhibitions.

And supposedly it was the liquor that made him have
a same-sex affair.

Bullshit, Darren thought. But he didn't say that.

One thing reportedly led to another, and the men had
been seeing each other ever since. The press thought
they were good friends and competitors because of the
rivalry between their teams. When the two icons went at
one another on the court, they went at each other hard.
The competiveness helped ratings, apparel sales, and
ticket sales. The two men went at each other like they
hated one another on the court, but off the court and in
the press they seemed like the best of friends. They had
each often said in the media that they could be friends as
well as rivals. It turned out they were more than rivals,
they were lovers.

***

Darren believed that Bryce used alcohol as his excuse for his sexual tryst. He used alcohol to take the blame for something he had always been curious about. Darren remembered how he continued to question Bryce about the affair.

"So let me get this straight. He's in the league also?" Darren asked.

"Yes."

"And he is just as famous as you are?"

"Yes."

Darren racked his brain to try and figure out who Bryce's lover was.

"So wouldn't his career take just as much of a hit as yours would if he were to out your affair?"

"It would."

"So what makes you think that he would out you and not look bad himself? He can no more afford the bad press than you can."

"That's what I'm struggling with."

"Your fiancée, does she know?"

"No, of course not."

"Don't you think she has a right to know?"

"Uh . . . no . . ."

"Wouldn't you want to know?"

"I'm not gay."

"I didn't ask you if you were gay."

"I'm just sayin', I'm not gay."

"Are you trying to convince me, or yourself?"

"I'm just curious."

"For more than a year? It sounds to me as if you are a little more than curious."

"Okay then, I'm confused."

"That's why you're here. We need to sort things out."

"Do you think I should call off my wedding?"

"It doesn't matter what I think. What do you think?"

On and on the sessions went. Some were good, some were great. Week after week, however, Bryce became more and more comfortable with who he was. As the wedding date came closer, eventually he made a stand. He broke up with his male lover and decided to go forward with his wedding.

Darren thought Bryce should have canceled his wedding. At the very least, Darren thought he should have postponed it. This was his personal opinion, but his personal opinion had no place in his sessions, so he kept his opinion to himself. All he could think of was the fact that Bryce was putting Maurielle at risk. She would be at risk for STDs, HIV, and celebrity mayhem. This was Darren's life: celebrity chaos.

After Darren got his hair cut he told Gucci he would see him later and told everyone in the barbershop good-bye. He headed to the mall and strangely enough, found himself thinking about his ex when a special slow song played on the radio. As the song played, Darren went over in his mind the first time that he met her, her smile, and the first time that they danced. He also thought about the first time they made love and how magical it was. He then wondered how could he have ever let her go. He thought about all the good times, all the places that they had been, and how they used to confess their dreams to one another.

As the song went off, he tried to shake thoughts of her. Their time together ran its course, or so he thought. He went to the mall to do some heavy shopping. As he was coming out of a men's store with his third bag of items, he saw her. She was looking great, in good shape and, what was worse, she looked happy.

She hadn't seen him. She and her man kept walking hand in hand and occasionally they kissed like teenagers. They were several stores away from him and they looked so happy as they shopped, looking so in love.

Darren found himself following them. His heart skipped a beat with every kiss. Jealousy from nowhere welled up inside of him with every smile that she gave him. They were walking slowly, hand in hand. It was a lover's stroll. Darren was walking fast, faster than he knew to notice. He closed the distance between them and as they reached the food court he felt stupid.

It wasn't her. It was a woman that looked a lot like her. His heartbeat regulated and his jealousy tapered off. He had to have a seat in the food court to get himself together.

What the hell was that about? Why am I buggin' all of a sudden? She must be somewhere, talking about me. Do I still love her? Do I still have feelings for my ex? Nah, it can't be. It was just the song. The song in the car must have triggered something, right? After all, it's been five years since I last spoke to her. There is no way that I'm still holding a torch for my ex-girlfriend. That's crazy, isn't it?

Chapter Four

Korie and Jayna were in the last leg of their two-mile run at Millennium Park, when they noticed two black men jogging in their direction from the opposite side. One man was older and resembled the actor Denzel Washington. He was in great shape for an older man and his hair looked as if it were just beginning to turn gray.

The younger man running with him was about thirty and at a distance he was nice looking, but as he got closer he was fine as hell. He was Hershey chocolate in complexion, had pearly-white teeth, and appeared to be in peak shape.

As the two women passed by the men, Korie noticed that the younger man smiled as they approached, and he turned around to look at their rear ends after they ran by. Korie and Jayna were used to this. The younger man said something to the older gentleman and then turned around to catch up to the two women. The older man shook his head, laughing, and continued with his run. Korie and Jayna ignored both men and continued to run in the opposite direction. A few minutes later, they heard the younger man speaking to them.

"Excuse me, ladies, can I run with you?" The younger man ran up on them, smiling.

Fortunately for both women, they just finished their run. They stopped their full run and slowed down to a jog and then a walk. They kept walking some distance and didn't even acknowledge the young black man. They stopped walking about fifty yards away from where he originally caught up with them.

"I'm sorry to interrupt your run, but I was wondering if I could run with you."

"We're done running," Jayna said.

"Perhaps another time, then?"

"We run alone." Jayna was cold in her response, almost as if to dismiss the man.

Jayna looked at the brother and assumed he was broke and not worth her time. He was very handsome, but nothing on his body was name brand. His shorts, shoes, and shirt had no known logos. Although everything on him was new and clean, he looked as if he bought all of his gear from a wholesale retailer.

"What my friend means to say is we just completed our run," Korie said politely, looking at Jayna as if to say, your mother raised you better than that, at least be polite.

Korie thought the young man was fine. He was definitely in great shape and she did think he was handsome. She didn't mind that he wasn't dressed in name-brand clothing. He had great teeth and a great smile and she thought to herself that she was somewhat taken with him. Jayna was quick to shut the man down, but Korie was admittedly intrigued.

"Well, can I run with you all some other time? Do you ladies run here often?" he asked.

"Is that your best pickup line?"

Jayna placed both hands on her hips as if she were a superhero or something and started laughing at him, laughing at him as if he were nothing.

The young man looked at her as if he was pissed that she was being so cold to him. He gave off the vibe that he was not used to women casually dismissing him.

"Well, yes. That is my best pickup line and I was hoping that you would like it. So since that's not working and I can't obviously coincidentally catch up to you another time in the park, how do I go about getting your number?" he said to Jayna. It was obvious that he didn't give up easily either.

"You don't. You keep running with your daddy's Vietnam buddy that we saw you with."

Jayna was still busy being cold to the young man. Korie was slightly hurt that the man barely noticed her. He smiled at her as he ran by, but he was obviously interested in Jayna. Korie was used to this happening a lot. Next to Jayna, guys seldom noticed her.

Korie was shaping up to be fit and toned but Jayna's body looked as if she were turning into a work of art. Korie hated to admit it, but she was a little jealous. Not enough for it to affect their friendship, but enough for the jealousy to affect her self-esteem.

"That's not my dad's buddy, that's my boss," the man said.

"Even worse," Jayna said, laughing.

"Look, I blew my boss off to come and introduce myself to you. My boss is a pretty influential man in this city, and he's not used to being blown off for women and—"

"Hold on!" Jayna cut him off. "We didn't ask you to come over here. So your ass can just keep on running for all we care. Don't start tripping because you came over here in pursuit of us. Who is your boss anyway?"

"His name is DeVaughn Harris, but that's not the point. The point is I would really like to get to know you a little better and I kind of lost points with my boss for putting off our morning meeting to chase some tail, as he would say."

"Morning meeting?" Jayna asked.

"Yeah. We run every morning, but we also discuss how we expect the day to go and our mutual expectations for business."

Korie was blown away that the man kept trying to get with Jayna even though it was obvious that she wasn't interested. Korie couldn't understand why he kept pursuing Jayna even though she was clowning him. He must have really wanted a serious taste of her honey. Then in an even more bizarre twist, Jayna threw Korie off with her next response.

"So what's your name?" Jayna asked.

"My name is Brandon, Brandon Lloyd."

"Well, Brandon Lloyd, if I were to let you take me out, where would we be going?"

Brandon began to smile wide like a Cheshire cat. He felt good that in spite of playing hard to get, he might conquer the beautiful African queen before him. He ran his fingers across his chin and thought about where he might take her, and then spoke smoothly.

"Sweetheart, we can go wherever you want to go."

"Okay, don't let your mouth write a check that your behind can't cash. I'm not a cheap date." Jayna folded her arms as she spoke.

Korie thought, that's for sure.

"Well, if you will allow me the pleasure of your company this evening, we can go anywhere in the city you want to go, as long as it's after six." Brandon's voice changed and now that he saw he was getting his way, his voice was sounding smooth and confident.

"Okay, well, this evening I would like to go to the Chicago Firehouse."

"Okay, well, if you give me your number, I'll pick you up around eight."

"Here is my card. My mobile number is on it." Jayna retrieved a card from her bag.

"Great. Well, I'll see you this evening. It was nice to meet you, uh . . . Jayna."

He had to look at the card to see her name.

"It was nice to meet you too, Brandon Lloyd."

"And it was great to meet you too. What was your name?" he asked Korie.

"My name is Korie." She gave a half smile, thinking Brandon had been rude to not acknowledge her until the last minute.

"You ladies have a nice day. I need to catch up to my boss."

"That should be easy considering that he's a hundred years old." Jayna said.

"You're something else, you know that?" Brandon spoke from a distance while jogging in place.

"Baby, you have no idea," Jayna said.

"My boss is not as out of shape as you think. He runs seven miles a day and he's only forty-six."

Brandon sprinted across the park to try and catch up to his boss, who was long gone and out of sight.

Jayna smiled to herself as she and Korie began to walk back to Korie's place. Korie was looking at Jayna like she didn't recognize her. Jayna saw the look of confusion on Korie's face and spoke.

"What?" she said, smiling with her hands on her hips.

"I'm shocked, that's all. He's not your normal type. What made you give in to him?"

"He said his boss was DeVaughn Harris."

"So?" Korie said with a puzzled look on her face.

"DeVaughn Harris is a multimillionaire. He purchases companies that other businesses can't successfully buy because they don't have the capital, and he then sells the companies that he buys to other companies that want them for generally twice the asking amount. He has a lot of Fortune 500 companies paying him in installments, through stocks or seats on their boards. The man is brilliant and off the chain when it comes to finances."

"Why haven't I heard of him before?"

"Because that's how he operates. He's quiet and reserved. He's really an amazing man."

"So what does that have to do with Brandon?"

"Girl, if Brandon is working for DeVaughn Harris, he must be paid too. I'm betting he's just not the type of man that flaunts his money."

"So it's about the money?"

"No, he's not bad on the eyes either, but the fact that he is paid helps."

"Jayna, that's scandalous and wrong."

"It may be wrong, but that's the way things are. Look, I've bust my ass at work, gone to school to get my MBA. I come in early to work and I leave late just to get the respect of the men at my firm. My colleagues respect me and my bosses respect me. I'm just saying that I want a man on my level, that's all. Brandon must make more money than I do, and I don't remember the last time that I met a black man that makes more money than I do who isn't married."

"How do you know Brandon isn't married?"

"Aw shoot, you're right. Well, that will be the first question that I ask him when he picks me up tonight."

"How do you know he makes a lot of money for this Mr. Harris? He could be the guy's dry cleaner for all you know."

"That will be my second question," Jayna said, laughing.

The two women walked back to Korie's place and Korie asked Jayna a million more questions that she should have asked Brandon before agreeing to go out with him. As they walked the trail on the way back to Korie's place the two women laughed and joked about the various things going on in their lives. Jayna began to tell Korie about the date she had last night. Korie didn't hear her because she saw a couple walking across the park holding hands. They were about a block away, but the man looked familiar to Korie. He had a small child in one arm and was holding the hand of a beautiful black woman with the other. Korie was speechless. She couldn't take her eyes off the couple. She was so engrossed into watching them that she didn't hear Jayna calling her name.

"Korie? Korie. That's not him?"

"Huh?" Korie finally came out of her trance. "Him who?"

"Girl, stop playin', you know damn well who. That's not him.

"Oh. Well, I, um, thought—"

"You thought it was. It's not. That's the same couple that was getting out of their car when we started running. It looks like him, but it's not him. Besides, chances are, he is with some white woman somewhere."

Jayna's voice was filled with venom, but she tried her best not to judge Korie because she didn't want to be judged herself. The women decided to let the subject go and move onto something else.

"Do you have a lot of clients to see today?" Jayna asked.

"Yeah. Yeah, I do. You going into your office today?"

"Yeah, I'm going to go in for a few hours. I'll walk you back to your place and then catch a cab back to mine. Call me later."

"Okay, I will."

The two women walked in silence for a time. Jayna was worried about her friend and Korie was wondering why she was so preoccupied with her ex. She walked back to her place with him on her mind.

Chapter Five

Darren finished his errands, saw a few clients, and headed to the gym. He ran two miles on the treadmill, hit the weights hard, and then headed home to shower. As he walked into his condo, he played music overhead as he again ran bathwater. "Before He Cheats" by Carrie Underwood was playing overhead. Darren secretly liked this tune and laughed to himself as he thought about what black people would say if they knew he listened to country music from time to time.

Darren loved R&B, rap and a host of black music. He also secretly had a love for tunes by many of today's country artists. To Darren, country music was nothing more than blues set to a different type of music.

Darren saw six clients today. Each one ended up writing him a check for at least 1000 dollars. It was now six o'clock in the evening and he was exhausted. Talking to clients was always draining. The average person had problems such as the economy, behavioral problems with their kids, or relationship issues. Celebrities and the city's elite had deeper issues going on that stemmed all the way from childhood.

One client he saw today had been using steroids since he was fourteen. Now he had the body of a powerhouse linebacker, but a penis the length of a crayon. He had a beautiful wife and kids, but most days his body was incapable of functioning sexually, and as such, he would become frustrated and beat his wife.

Another client that he saw today was yet another pro athlete with a drug issue and out-of-control behavior. This included running from the police, racing his cars on Lake Shore Drive, and also beating on women. He almost always paid the woman off that he beat, but the athlete knew there would be a time that he would go too far and one of his victims wouldn't want money. It would be just a matter of time before someone, or some advocacy group, would want to see him in jail.

Another client had an addiction to high school girls. Yet another client had a problem with gambling, and the last client that he saw today had a more intriguing issue. He was addicted to escorts. His case was the most harmless and the least difficult that he had today. This behavior was obsessive, but not necessarily destructive, because of the money that the client made. It was this case, however, that Darren found to be the most fascinating of the day.

The client in question was almost always seen in Chicago's high-society magazines as a playboy of sorts. The man was in his mid-forties. He was handsome and he drove the finest cars, ate in the finest restaurants, and had the finest women on his arm. It turned out that many of the women on his arm who looked like models,were actually escorts.

Darren was surprised that a man this handsome and with his stature would even use an escort service. The client's rationale was simple: He paid for a service, the woman provided that service, and there were few complications.

According to the client, he could pick the women online, or as a member of the VIP club he could have a private showing in his home, which he had done from time to time. Many of the women made 1000 dollars an hour or 5000 for the entire evening. According to Darren's client, it was worth every penny.

No drama. No courting. No arguing. Simply the company of a beautiful woman, stimulating conversation, and as much sex as a man could stand. Shit, it's like an all-you-can-eat buffet with the perfect foods, Darren thought.

Darren asked the client in the session earlier today what his problem was if he was so happy with the service that was provided. The client explained that between the cost of Viagra and the cost of women every other night, he figured he had a problem. He wasn't going broke, but at five thousand a night, four or five nights a week, by fifty-two weeks in a year, he was spending close to one million dollars a year on just courting women. Darren thought to himself, Are you kidding me?

Of course he couldn't say that out loud. Again, Darren's opinion had no place in therapy. However, he did find this case quite interesting. He and his client worked on his compulsive behavior and discussed his issues with greed and obsession with sex.

As weeks passed, they came up with a plan to wean the man off the escort service. The first step was to cancel his VIP status. The next was to use the less expensive women, and perhaps only see a woman once a week. The third step was to get into other activities or hobbies such as running, tennis, going to the gym or something that he used to do years ago that he didn't do anymore. Darren surmised that the client needed a healthy outlet; something legal that could keep him focused.

Darren then asked the client when was the last time he asked a woman out on a date. A real date. Surprisingly, it had been quite a few years. Darren asked the client if it was because he lacked confidence. The client stated he simply didn't have the time. His company was one of the top in the nation and to keep it on top he had to give the business all his focus.

His board of directors and chief financial advisors told him they thought the escort service was a great idea. The financial department looked for ways to write it off. As far as they were concerned, it might have cost the company a million dollars, but the client was a multimillionaire and the company was making billions. It was an intriguing story, one that stayed on Darren's mind long after the session was over.

Before leaving, Darren took the client's membership card away from him. The goal was to take a step each week away from the escort service, and one step toward finding a real woman to have in his life. The client's goal was to find a real woman; someone that could provide more than a service to him.

A real woman. Ain't that something? Here I am telling someone how to get their love life together, and here I am with no one to call my own, Darren thought to himself.

Darren had money, good looks, a great car and now, a great career. He had women that pursued him doggedly. He had great physical chemistry with some women. He had amazing friendships with others. Getting a woman in his bed was no problem. Giving a woman his heart . . . that was something altogether different.

He acted tough on the exterior, like nothing bothered him. He acted like he was happy. On the outside looking in, he was. He was the type of man who seemed to have it all together. Many men would kill to live his lifestyle. Still, every day for more than a few years now, at least once a day he found himself thinking about her, and what she might be doing.

Darren eased into the tub and reflected on his day. His last client told him he thought it would be a good idea if Darren learned how to play golf. It was one of the things that the man hadn't done in years and it was Darren's suggestion that the client go back to an activity that he used to love doing.

The client was pushing hard for Darren to learn how to play. Apparently, golf was not only a place where high-profile men made business deals. It was also a place where men shared their deepest, darkest secrets. It was kind of like the barbershop.

Darren's last client told him that he could make a killing financially if he secured clients from some of Chicago's more elite golf clubs. The client even offered to buy Darren a membership and introduce him to some of Chicago's upper-echelon businessmen.

Darren asked his client to give him some time to think about it. The prospect of making more money was becoming more and more appealing, and already he was leaning toward giving in and telling his client yes.

Darren made a little over 100,000 dollars a year after taxes. If he met up with friends of his client, that figure could easily jump up to a million in a year or two. He was making money hand over fist and was making more and more contacts each week. At the rate he was going he might be able to one day afford escorts like his client did. Not that he was thinking about doing such a thing, but the concept was interesting. There was just one thing: Black men don't pay for sex, right?

Chapter Six

Korie, pulled up in front of her first client's home—a five-bedroom, five-bathroom, and three-car garage home. She was impressed; it looked magnificent. Korie often got excited when she saw a house that she really wanted to decorate. For her, sometimes seeing a home and all the possibilities that it offered made her as giddy as a schoolgirl.

Her heart sank in her chest when she saw the '88 Chevy Impala out front with the chrome rims on the car. Her heart sank even deeper when she saw the beat-up minivan that was on the side with chrome spinners on its wheels. The rims had to be worth more than the van itself. As she chirped the alarm on her car, she let out a heavy sigh as she thought one thing; Niggas.

This couple was recommended to her by a friend of a friend of Jayna. That was why Korie agreed to see the house. She explained that her fee was 2000 dollars. The couple on the phone stated that money was no object. That being the case, Korie scheduled the appointment for 1:00 P.M.

She hoped in her heart of hearts that her gut feeling was wrong. She hoped that she wouldn't ring the bell and some country or ghetto-ass black person answered the door. She hoped that the car that was in the front belonged to the couple's son and the van perhaps belonged to a friend of the couple's son.

She rang the bell. From the inside she heard, "Shani-qua, get the door!"

Damn, she thought.

Whoever it was that yelled was right there in the living room. Whoever it was obviously decided that it was not his job to get the front door. Seconds later, a heavy-set black woman with bronze-colored skin and blond highlights answered the door—in a house robe.

Yep . . . country or ghetto . . . or both, Korie thought.

"Uh, hi. My name is Korie. Are you Mrs. Underwood?"

"Yes, I am. You must be the interior decorator lady."

"Uh, yes, that would be me," Korie said with a half smile.

"Well, come on in, girl!" Her tone was inviting; loud, but inviting. Quite country, Korie thought.

The woman hugged Korie as if they were age-old friends. Korie reluctantly hugged back. At first she was apprehensive about working with the couple. As she saw the house, she wanted more and more to have the responsibility of decorating it.

On the couch was an overweight black man who re-sembled the eighties rapper Biz Markie. He was play-ing PlayStation 3 on a plasma-screen television in his robe and slippers along with two of his friends. One of them was most likely the owner of one or both of the cars in front.

All three men looked to be in their forties, and all three looked as if they would struggle with completing a job application. Korie tried hard not to be judgmen-tal, but she thought to herself, sometimes you can just look at a man and see that he has little if any potential. None of the three men looked as if they had any poten-tial. They each looked as if they had already peaked in life.

Korie tried to ignore the men as she toured the rest of the house. The men each looked up at her as if she was a piece of meat and they were carnivores. The looks they gave made her feel uncomfortable; as if they each were undressing her with their eyes. Still, she ignored them and followed Mrs. Underwood into the grand home.

The house had a two-story foyer, a two-story family room, and a two-story state-of-the-art kitchen with a hearth room. It had a front and rear staircase, and a stunning master suite with both a huge fireplace and master bathroom inside. There was also a second kitchen in the home, a wet bar, a wine cellar, a theater room, exercise room, and a circular drive.

At first glance the house had to cost at least three million dollars. It was Korie's dream house, and even she couldn't begin to think about buying a house this expensive. It was immediately obvious that the couple was living way beyond their means.

"Wow, you really have a lovely house."

"Thank you."

"So if you don't mind my asking, what does your husband do for a living?"

Korie couldn't help but to ask. Based on what she saw in the living room versus what she was looking at in the home, something in this picture just wasn't clicking.

"You mean where the money came from."

Mrs. Underwood's tone was sharp, but not sharp enough to be rude. It was a tone that suggested she had heard that question before. It was becoming more and more obvious that the Underwoods had no business in this section of town.

The house was grand, but the furniture was cheap. The couch looked as if it came from a storefront on

Chicago's west side. Many of the accessories, towels, and accents of the home reeked of flea market values. There were dishes in the sink, pots and pans with the Teflon scraped off the bottom, and curtains where there should have been drapes. Then there was the distinct smell of hog headcheese on crackers, leftover food that was fried rather than grilled, and cheap accessories that were nailed into the walls. Just looking at the place, it was clear that they needed help decorating. It was also clear that they did not fit the area that they were living in.

Most people from the hood had champagne taste and a malt liquor budget. The Underwoods seemed to have a champagne budget and malt liquor taste.

"Mrs. Underwood, I didn't mean anything by my question—"

"Sure you did."

"Excuse me?"

"Come on, sister, you know what I mean. I bet you are wondering how someone like me and someone like my husband could afford a place like this. Everyone else we've called to help us out pulls up to the house and are all smiles until the moment we open the front door. Everyone wants to know how people like us ended up out here. No offense, but your face gave you away the moment I opened the door. It's obvious that you are wondering how we get to live out here and you probably can't afford to live out here yourself."

She was right. Silence fell between the two women. Korie decided if they were going to work together, she needed to keep things real.

"Well, to be honest with you, the thought did cross my mind."

"Thank you for your honesty."

"So can I ask? How did you all come to live out here?"

"Well, I don't mind telling you, we're lottery winners."

"I see."

Figures, she thought.

"You don't think we belong here, do you?"

She spoke as if she had heard this a million times before.

"Let me ask you this, how much money did you win?" Korie decided to be more direct.

"A million dollars, after taxes."

"And how much did you put down on the house?"

"My husband put down a half-million dollars."

Korie thought to herself, a half-million dollars on a house that cost almost three million? This is a setup. This is one of those deals where some finance company probably raped them on the paperwork.

The taxes alone would have them in bankruptcy court inside of a year. Korie knew they wanted an interior decorator, but they needed a financial advisor. The Underwoods were in over their heads, and had no idea what was in store for them in the immediate future.

Korie didn't know a lot about finances, but she did know that there was no way the Underwoods would be able to maintain a mortgage on a three-million-dollar home. She wondered why no one had talked to them before about the mistake they were making. They shouldn't have even been able to get financing on a home like this.

Korie remembered something that he used to tell her all the time. A million dollars is not a lot of money. A million dollars is nothing if you don't make it work for you. That's what he would say.

"So, will you help us decorate the house?" Mrs. Underwood asked.

"No. No, I'll do something better for you."

"But I—"

"Trust me, sister, the last thing you need right now is an interior decorator."

Korie wanted to call him. She wanted his advice. Truth be told, she just wanted to hear his voice. This situation would be the perfect excuse to call him. After all, he was the educated one, the one that was financialy savvy.

It had been years since they last spoke. She still had his number in her phone and wondered if it had changed. She would never call him. She was too proud for that, but wasn't too proud, however, to make sure that she kept her same number all these years. Korie might have changed cell phone carriers, but she kept her number. She kept her number because deep down inside she longed for him to call.

Once they said good-bye, he never called her again. He was too proud, too arrogant. To call her would be a sign of weakness. She too was a strong and proud black woman. She didn't need a man. She never did. She never would. She may not have had a formal education, but she knew the meaning of hard work. She knew what it meant to struggle and what it meant to go hungry, but one thing she didn't know how to do was give up. She wanted to use this excuse to call him, but instead she called her girlfriend; she called the one person who always had her back.

Korie called Jayna and asked her to meet her at the home of the Underwood family. In the meanwhile, Korie continued to tour the grand home. An hour later, Jayna was at the Underwood home. She had the same first impression that Korie had. Jayna knew immediately why Korie called her. Minutes after getting there, she was explaining to Mr. and Mrs. Underwood why putting a half-million dollars down on a three-million-dollar home was foolish.

Jayna explained that one third of lottery winners who had won a significant amount of money went bankrupt within a few years. She also explained that with a three-million-dollar home, the taxes would eat away at them after the first year alone.

Jayna explained to Shaniqua and her husband, who was hardly listening, that they needed an attorney, a financial consultant, and above all else, they needed to get out of that home as soon as possible, despite having no equity in it. Shaniqua's husband wasn't listening to the advice.

His position was, we asked you here to decorate, not to lecture us.

He spoke as if his pride was hurt. He spoke as if he hated being ignorant about financial matters. Most of all, Korie and Jayna got the impression that Mr. Underwood did not appreciate the counsel of women. He struck them both as the type that was ignorant and sexist; a man who was ignorant of his own ignorance. When his language began to become abusive, Jayna, Korie, and Shaniqua went outside for a sister-to-sister talk.

"Mrs. Underwood, we're just trying to keep it real with you. I don't know what lifestyle you all came from, but whatever style it was, you will be back to living that exact same way if you don't make wiser decisions about your money. You need to get out from under this house immediately and try to live within your means."

This was Jayna's advice and it was sound advice.

Mrs. Underwood understood everything that was being told to her. She understood that the taxes alone would be a problem; it was clear by the look on her face, however she was living before, she didn't want to go back to that lifestyle.

It was also clear by the look on her face that her husband held the purse strings. The look on her face said it all. There was no way in hell that her husband would listen to two women, and let them advise him on how to conduct business. Qualified or not, Mr. Underwood would not heed counsel from two black women. Something about their strength made him feel visibly insecure.

Korie felt sorry for Mrs. Underwood. Jayna, however, had a look on her face as if she were deep in thought. She then had a look on her face as if she had an epiphany.

"Mrs. Underwood, did your husband specifically give you any money?"

"He gave me two hundred and fifty thousand dollars. He kept two fifty and he put the rest on the house, why?"

"I'm going to be your personal financial advisor. In the meanwhile, you need to try and convince your husband to get a smaller home. You can get a nice home for about two hundred thousand once you sell this one."

"Isn't it going to be hard to sell this house?"

"It is. But I have a friend that might be able to help you."

Jayna got on her cell phone and walked toward her car to talk with someone. Mrs. Underwood and Korie walked toward Korie's car. A single tear streamed down Mrs. Underwood's face at the prospect of downsizing. It was written all over her face that this was the house of her dreams; hell, it was the dream house of many women.

"It's a really beautiful home. It's my dream home, Ms. Dillion," she said. Her face was worn and weary at the prospect of losing such a beautiful place.

"It's indeed beautiful. It's very nice. But you'll drown in this house if you stay."

"I know. It's just that no one I have ever known has ever had a home like this. Our friends and family have been out here. They will all look at us funny if we downsize. How can we face them if we give up this house?"

"Pride comes before the fall, Mrs. Underwood. Buying this house was a mistake, nothing more. No one can fault you for wanting to buy this place. It's magnificent. But I'm sure you can find a smaller house that will also capture your heart if you look hard enough."

"I want to thank you for your advice."

"No problem. Sometimes sisters need to look out for one another."

"I also want to apologize for my husband and his attitude."

"That's all right. Men can be like that sometimes. Can I ask another question?"

"Sure."

"How did the two of you end up together?"

It was another one of those situations that to Korie didn't quite compute. Mr. Underwood was a sloppily shaped man with a poor disposition. At first glance he seemed to have few redeeming qualities.

Mrs. Underwood, however, looked like Jill Scott. She had kind eyes, a great smile, and she looked like back in the day she was quite the catch. That is, before life happened. Although her husband seemed like an abrasive man, Mrs. Underwood smiled when she spoke about him. She smiled as she reflected about their life; their love.

She went on to tell Korie how Mr. Underwood was the star running back at Harper High School back in the day, and how she was the head cheerleader. After high school she went to college for maybe a year. Then she became pregnant, and then she lost the baby. Back then they had seen many hard times.

He went on to work at Henderson Steel. He made good money for years, and then the economy began to decline. With that decline came layoffs. Since then, Mr. Underwood had worked temporary jobs, janitorial jobs, and anything that he could do with his hands. He was seldom without work, but it seemed that each time that he got settled somewhere, the company outsourced the labor. Life for the Underwoods always seemed to be uphill.

Mrs. Underwood loved her husband unconditionally. She too had trouble finding permanent work. Since high school she had been temping for the same company. She brought in decent money as an administrative assistant, but like forty-six percent of Americans she had no health insurance and few employment benefits.

For years Mr. and Mrs. Underwood struggled. Neither had ever been out of Chicago in their life. They had never taken a vacation together. Like many other couples they had their problems, but they never took life out on one another. They never went to bed angry, no matter what they were up against. They loved each other and they always had one another's back.

She explained that her husband could be an ass at times. She knew that he wasn't without his faults. She also knew his heart and knew that the love he had for her had no bounds.

When he hit the lottery, the first thing he did was find out how much they were getting after taxes. He then split that fifty-fifty, no questions asked. Mrs. Underwood was more that his wife; she was his partner and without her, Mr. Underwood confessed he was nothing.

Mr. Underwood felt like less than a man all those years that they struggled. He was a man who was tired of just getting by.

Mrs. Underwood explained that the day they won the lottery, it was a great day for her husband. It was if he won more than the money that day. It was as if he won his manhood back. When they were younger, he always promised that he would buy her the biggest house in the world. When he closed on this house, he felt as if he fulfilled that promise; as if he redeemed himself.

"So you see, Ms. Dillon, losing this house is not only a loss because it's so beautiful, but I don't know if my husband's pride can handle a blow like that."

"I hear you, Mrs. Underwood, but—"

"Please, call me Shaniqua."

"Well, Shaniqua, if he loves you, he will get your family out of this house. As long as you stay by his side, I'm sure he'll be okay. He may be hurt, but eventually he'll get over it. You all need to talk. I'm sure Jayna will be able to point you in the right direction."

Just then, Jayna got off the phone, all smiles. She headed toward the two women with a look of determination.

"Mrs. Underwood, I'd like to sit down and have another talk with your husband." Jayna walked pass Mrs. Underwood and headed back in the direction of the house as if she were about to do battle with Mr. Underwood.

"I don't know if he'll listen to you." Mrs. Underwood spoke in Jayna's direction as she headed up the walkway.

"Oh, he'll listen. I think I might have already found a buyer for your home."

Jayna stopped at the entrance to the house. She looked back at Mrs. Underwood and ushered her back toward the house.

Korie looked at her watch and then headed back to her car.

"Korie are you coming?" Jayna yelled.

"I can't. I need to be heading to my next appointment." Korie chirped the alarm on her car. "It was nice meeting you, Mrs. Underwood."

Mrs. Underwood walked back to Korie and gave her a hug.

"Thank you, sister."

Korie was all smiles.

"No problem, sis, we each need to look out for one another from time to time. Listen to my girlfriend. She will take good care of you and get you going in the right direction."

"Thank you again."

"No problem." Korie hurried down the path and opened her car door. "Jayna, I'll call you later."

"Okay," Jayna responded. She and Mrs. Underwood headed back into the house.

Korie jumped in her car and headed east to her next appointment.

She drove on the expressway. While in the car she was listening to old school love songs. As the songs played, Korie thought about the Underwoods. She thought about everything that they went through. She then thought about the fact that no matter what happened they stayed together; to this day they remained in love. She thought that was touching. She thought it was romantic. Then she heard his words in her head.

There is nothing romantic about being broke.

As she drove, she wondered was he right. She wondered what he would say about the Underwoods. She wondered what he was doing right now.

Lord, why can't I get this man out of my head? Why can't I get him out of my heart?

Chapter Seven

Korie's next appointment was forty-five minutes away. She had already driven twenty minutes and her every thought was of him. She turned on the radio and "On Bended Knee" by Boys II Men was playing. Every song after that seemed like it was a wedding song. Korie turned the music up, and before she knew it, tears began to stream down her face.

Apparently the songs touched her and opened up a door that she thought was forever closed. She thought about him. She thought about his touch, his voice, his smile, and his very scent. She could almost smell his chrome cologne. She thought about the last time they made love, the first time they made love, and the first time that they kissed. She knew in her heart of hearts that he was the one. She simply couldn't understand why he didn't see it. She couldn't understand why they weren't together.

They should be on at least their third wedding anniversary by now. She should have had his first child by now. Instead she was working hard on her career and he was God knows where, working on his.

Korie loved him. Jayna hated him. Korie thought he was the greatest man alive and Jayna thought he was the son of the devil himself. Let Jayna tell it, he was one uppity, arrogant sonofabitch.

All Korie knew was she wanted to spend the rest of her life with him from the very first day that they met. She wanted to live with her man. She wanted to be married, and she wanted a bunch of his babies. He didn't want any of that, at least not when she wanted it. The last thing in the world he ever wanted in life was to struggle. He made that perfectly clear.

Korie didn't fear struggle. She didn't mind it at all. Like Mrs. Underwood, as long as she had the love of her man, that was enough for her.

Something he used to say was, "Love isn't enough; it may be poetic, but it's not enough, it's never enough."

"Bullshit!" Korie said aloud as she switched lanes and thought about those words. She was just as upset remembering them as she was when he first spoke them to her.

What was so wrong with struggling? This is what Korie asked herself at least a million times. She struggled, her parents struggled, and their parents struggled. Hell, struggle was part of African American culture as far as she was concerned. Even his parents struggled. So why couldn't they? Why couldn't they be a couple?

In spite of what he said, she thought there was something romantic about the struggle of a young couple. She thought it spoke volumes for a couple to work through something together. She thought it strengthened black love to face adversity together.

Korie didn't care if she had a career or a job. She didn't want a big house; she did want a house. She didn't have to have a fancy car; but she did want a car. As long as the bills were paid and she was in love, as far as she was concerned, life was okay.

When they were together, she would always plan grand vacations for them. He would always cancel. She was the one who was considered the dreamer and he was the one who kept them grounded. When they were together they were getting by okay financially. The only thing was he never wanted to just be getting by.

She would often find new things for them to do.
Many times—not all—the answer was no. She longed
for three-day vacations in Vegas. For a while they went;
they went twice a year. Then the trips stopped. He had
to work. He was always working.

She knew the relationship was in trouble when he
one day paid for her to go to Vegas . . . with Jayna.

He was always too busy. Always working, always
planning, and always chasing that next dollar. Sending
her to Vegas with her best friend was the last straw.

There were times when she thought he was cheating;
times when she was sure there was someone else. From
time to time, like most black women, she started to pay
close attention. She started to check up on him. She
searched hard for evidence of another woman.

There was none.

He was cheating on her; but not with a woman; No,
not with a man; he was cheating on her with the pursuit of his career.

He promised her a big house, just as Mr. Underwood
promised his wife. He promised that they would see
the world one day. That day never came. She tried
telling him over and over again that she didn't share
his fascination with things. She tried to explain to him
countless times that all she ever wanted in life was him.
That simply wasn't what he wanted. He wanted a lifestyle that she thought was unrealistic.

She went to Vegas. She went with Jayna and she had
a good time. But there wasn't a day that she was there
that she didn't want him beside her. When he told her
that he was going to begin interning on top of working
a full-time job, Korie became incensed.

Korie was a patient woman. Some might say that she
was the perfect woman. Her patience, however, was
running out. She loved her man. The good times were

really good. The bad times? The bad times were really bad. Their biggest argument was not over money, not over another woman, and not over anything petty. Their biggest fights were about the use of his time. She said she didn't get enough, and he explained that she monopolized all the free time he had. There just never seemed to be enough hours in the day for her. She never had his full attention.

He told her that she didn't understand things. He explained to her if she were to return to school she might see things his way. He already had his bachelor's degree. She was upset when he pursued a master's.

She only had a year of college under her belt. She discovered quickly that college just wasn't for her. He used to tell her that a degree would open up doors that were forever closed to the average man. She explained to him that hard work and prayer can open any door.

It was a point that they both had to agree to disagree on. His argument was the degree made all the difference in the world. Her point was there were a lot of degreed people out there with book sense and no common sense.

She had since changed her mind.

She had changed her mind now that she ran her own business. There were some things that she saw now that she didn't see then. She understood many of the things that he meant when they would argue about money or time. She understood the drive that came with pursuing one's dreams; she now understood his passion. What she didn't understand is why they couldn't do these things together. She didn't understand why it had to be a five-year-plan as opposed to a ten or twelve-year plan, as long as they were together.

Back then sewing was her side hustle. Sewing was her hobby; that and helping her girlfriends decorate and rearrange their houses. She had a skill for both and made money on the side helping people from the church or friends of friends.

There was a time when she loved prom season because of all the extra money that she would bring in. It was when she was making dresses for young high school girls that he would try to persuade her to go back to school or at the very least take a few business classes so she could hone her skills or perhaps open up her own business, either sewing or decorating.

He saw the talent she had. He saw the potential. The thing was she saw what she did as a hobby or a side hustle. He saw it as an opportunity.

When Korie was younger she had two dreams: Being a seamstress and decorating homes. They were dreams that he always encouraged her to pursue. He even went as far as putting a marketing plan together for her in his spare time.

That upset her as well because that spare time could have been her time.

When they were together they ate at all the finest restaurants in Chicago. They stayed at Chicago's finest hotels for weekend getaways. They had a good time in the Windy City, and as previously mentioned, the good times were really good.

Korie wanted more.
She wanted more of his time.
It was time he refused to give her.

They argued a lot. He would always tell her that he had a five-year plan and she needed to simply be patient. She hated the five-year plan. She hated hearing those words. When their sex life began to decline, she took drastic measures to slow him down. Taking time away from her was one thing. Not making time to make love to her was something altogether different. You make time for that. If nothing else, no man should neglect a woman in the bedroom.

There were times that he would work, go to school, and do the internship. He would come home dead tired . . . exhausted.

Korie thought to herself, not my problem.

She didn't tell him to go back to school.

She didn't tell him to work these insane hours.

They were doing fine. They were getting by. She felt he needed to make her his priority.

He explained that he was exhausted. It was an excuse she heard way too many times. He explained that he was working hard today to make a better tomorrow for them both. She explained that if he didn't make the time, her time would belong to someone else. Tomorrow would come, but the question was always if she would still be there. She didn't care that he was tired. She didn't care how his day went. She wanted quality time with her man. She wanted to be desired. She wanted happily-ever-after, and she didn't want to wait an eternity for happily-ever-after to come. She needed to give him a moment of pause. She needed to shift his focus to more important things, things that couldn't be so casually dismissed.

She became pregnant.

She became pregnant on purpose.

She stopped taking her pills.

He never stopped using condoms.

She sometimes put pin-size holes in the condoms.

Still, she never became pregnant.

Either the condoms held, or he was shooting blanks.

She then lubed herself one day with baby oil before making love to him.

She knew that baby oil practically destroyed condoms.

One day the condom broke.

Six weeks later she was pregnant.

Pregnancy put a smile on her face.

It put a look of despair on his.

Shortly after that the arguments started. The word sabotage was used. It had already been on his mind, but one day he had the audacity to say it. It was one of the most heated arguments they ever had. At the high point of the argument, she confessed her transgression. It was a confession that she now knew should have never left her lips. That was a secret that she should've taken with her to the grave. She would never forget the hurt in his eyes that day.

His five-year plan was in ruins. At the very least, severely delayed; compromised. He confessed his five-year plan was not just for him, but for them. He wanted a baby; but not now; not two years into his five-year plan. He wanted to be a father one day, but not now, not this way, not . . . unmarried. He confessed all this to her. She was unmoved by his words.

"Marry me, then," she said.

"I'm not ready. We're not ready."

"You mean you aren't ready."

"Okay then, I'm not ready, now what?"

"Why not?"

"I want to be in a better position financially if I'm going to be a father. I want my child to have more than what I had as a child. I want money to be no object. I want to be more financially secure."

"It's not like we're struggling now!"

"No, but it's not what I anticipated. It's not something I'm ready for. Korie, you know that I have a plan . . . a five-year plan and—"

"Fuck your five-year plan!" she heard herself say. "You can't plan life!"

"No, but you can obviously plan an unwanted pregnancy!"

"I love you!" she screamed.

"Love doesn't trap people! Love doesn't sabotage; love should be patient."

"Fuck patience! I want us! I want our lifestyle back! I want things back to the way they were when we first began dating! I want you to be with me!"

"What about our future, Korie? What about my career?"

"Being pregnant doesn't mean you can't have those things."

"No, it just means that it will take longer for me to have the things that I want."

On and on into the night they fought. Harsh things were said. By the morning neither was sure they wanted to be with the other. They both began to think that perhaps they weren't soul mates. Weeks after that, two people that were very much in love were strangers to one another living under the same roof.

The tension in the air was as thick as black smoke. The animosity burned the very essence of the air they breathed. They would each come home and simply not speak to one another. He would go in one room and she would go to the other. Both would stay out late some nights, and neither called the other to inquire when the other would be home. They both thought it was the beginning of the end. Neither of them, however, was bold enough to say it.

A few weeks after that, Korie miscarried.

With her first words to him in months, she blamed him.

He blamed her.

She said it was the stress he put her under.

He said perhaps it wasn't meant to be.

She went back to the room she was in.

He went back to his home office, where he slept most days.

They returned to their mutual corners like prizefighters—neither won, both seemed to have lost and lost big.

She cried at night. She didn't let him hear her, but she cried each and every night after losing the baby.

He lay awake at night staring at the ceiling and sighing with a heavy heart. He wondered, Was he wrong to not want to struggle? He wondered, Was he wrong to deny himself happiness? He loved Korie. He wanted to give her the world. He lay in bed at night and wished each night that he could fast-forward time so she could see that he was right. They could have everything their hearts desired if she was patient.

She lay awake at night crying herself to sleep at times. She reminisced about the way things once were, and the way that things could be; struggle or not. She too wished that she could fast-forward time so he could see that struggle wasn't so bad. She wanted him to see that she was right, that they could make it on what they made.

They both wondered what could have been. They wondered how life would be different with a little one. They both wished, they both wondered, but neither said anything to the other. Their love life was in limbo. They seemed no longer like a couple so much as they were two people in the same household who simply . . . coexisted.

One day Korie came home and everything he owned was gone. He left a check on the counter and a letter. She sarcastically wondered how giving her that check would affect his beloved five-year plan. She read the note.

Korie,
We want different things. It's obvious that we are on two different paths. I always hoped that no matter what path I took, you would be there by my side. This isn't good-bye forever, but it is good-bye for now. Sweetheart, I work as hard as I do today to prepare for a better tomorrow. I know you think it's okay to struggle. I don't. There's nothing romantic about struggle. I know our parents struggled and they made it. I don't want the life they had. I want much more. I deserve more. You deserve more. I'm hurt that you decided to become pregnant. Starting a family is something that should be mutually agreed upon. Korie, I'm not ready for all that yet. I need to work on my career. That needs to be my focus right now. I can't be distracted by the drama in our relationship. I shouldn't wonder in the back of my mind if you and I are on the same page, or be anxious when I make love to you and wonder if you are trying to sabotage things. Perhaps we'll find our way back into one another's lives. I do want to spend the rest of my life with you, but only after I'm successful—only AFTER my five-year plan. I'm sorry. The rent is paid for the remainder of the year. The check on the table should be enough for you to make ends meet. My number won't change and you can feel free to call me anytime, day or night.
I love you

He left. He wasn't man enough to say what had to be said to her face. He took the coward's way out. Bastard, she thought. He left. She never saw him again. She never called and neither did he. There was no good-bye, no explanation; she didn't even get to express her side of the story. He left her in the worst way that a man could leave a woman. For that, for a time, she hated him.

She got off of the interstate and headed to Bolingbrook, Illinois. The house that she pulled in front of this time was smaller than the Underwoods' home but was still quite magnificent from the driveway. The home had been sold just a few days ago to a young Hispanic couple. The home was listed at 900,000 dollars. The listing said that it had four bedrooms, three and half bathrooms, and was about five thousand square feet. The home was two stories tall. It had hardwood floors, window treatments, and a huge family room, den, kitchen, and a full basement. The appliances were stainless steel. It had granite countertops and there was a golf course off in the distance to the rear of the home. The best feature of all? It was empty. The couple she was meeting with wanted to start with all new furniture.

Korie got out of her car and was greeted by a beautiful woman named Maria Santiago and her husband, William. The couple was all smiles and quite excited to see her. This was yet another referral that came from Jayna. The Santiagos were customers of Jayna's firm, and they did quite well for themselves by investing.

"Ms. Dillon?" Mrs. Santiago asked.

"Yep, that's me." Korie said, smiling from behind her designer shades.

"I'm so excited to show you my home."

"I'm very excited to see it."

"Please . . . come in."

Mrs. Santiago asked Korie to make her home look like something you would see on MTV's Cribs. Korie stated she would do her best. Mrs. Santiago wanted tips on each room in the house, and Mr. Santiago wanted to know what Korie's fee was. Korie stated her fee was 2000 dollars to decorate their home. Of course, the cost of the furniture and furnishings would be paid for by the Santiagos. When Mr. Santiago didn't question her price, Korie knew that she was in business. One thing that she loved to do these days was spend someone else's money.

Korie and Mrs. Santiago walked through the house and in each room Korie gave her decorating ideas. Mrs. Santiago confessed that as soon as the house was complete she wanted to have a huge dinner party.

With a dinner party in mind, Korie explained that rather than have a huge gathering in one area, perhaps the thing to do was stage the house in small gatherings throughout. She suggested occasional chairs around the house, two sofas facing one another in one room, with a single chair at either end. This way up to four conversations could take place at once.

Korie walked into the living room, which was huge, and explained that formal living rooms tended to be symmetrical. She suggested one large painting to anchor the space. Because the couple was Hispanic, Korie suggested an oil copy of a work by Goya: La Gallina Ciega, an amazing period painting that was two dimensional, but would perfectly accent the Santiagos living-room wall. The painting would match the upholstery of the furniture that Korie planned to buy and would harmonize the setting.

Korie suggested ottomans, footrests, and tables where her guests could put their drinks.

Mrs. Santiago inquired about color schemes and what color to paint the walls. Korie explained the walls should remain neutral, that white or neutral walls, ceilings, curtains, and woodwork made a perfect backdrop for dramatic evenings and comfortable days. She explained that the trick to a successful event was mostly about staging and lighting, whether it was letting in natural light or making use of a fireplace. She explained that accent lighting, dimmers, and even candles strategically placed, could go a long way.

Korie could see that Mr. Santiago was feeling left out so she then looked at the room that would be his office. She explained that her vision for his office was a grand cherrywood desk, with bookcases on the walls to the right and left of the entrance.

She stated rather than have two executive chairs in front of the desk, he could have two very nice recliners. His chair, of course, would be top of the line. For him she suggested a chair that cost 500 dollars. Mr. Santiago expressed he wanted the most expensive and comfortable chair on the market. When Korie explained that chair would be the Aresline Xten, Mr. Santiago said that he wanted one.

When she explained that chair cost one and a half million dollars, Mr. Santiago laughed and said that he would take the 500-dollar chair.

Korie asked how much was the budget that the Santiagos were looking at to decorate their new home. Mr. Santiago said no more than fifty thousand. Korie shook his hand and stated that she and Mrs. Santiago would begin shopping right away. She broke out her laptop and cell phone and as Mrs. Santiago agreed on styles, Korie began making orders.

Korie shopped for Mrs. Santiago online for most of the afternoon. She made all types of phone calls and vendors that she had business relationships with. Each agreed to give her a five percent commission on the money that her clients spent. It was like a double fee for Korie and she loved the money that she made.

Before leaving the Santiago home, Korie spent about 35,000 dollars. Mrs. Santiago told Korie that she was sure she could get another 50,000 out of her husband and to come back next weekend. Mr. Santiago gave Korie her fee up front. On top of that Mrs. Santiago gave her another thousand. Korie was making a name for herself as an interior designer. Although her fee was only 2,000 dollars, her tips were generally anywhere between 2,000 and 5,000 dollars. Korie was beginning to make nice money hand over fist.

By the time she finished shopping she was exhausted. She loved her job. She loved spending someone else's money, but it could prove to be draining. She got back into her car to head home and once again her thoughts were about him. This time she wasn't thinking about what could have been. This time, she was thinking to herself that in a way, he was the reason for her success.

Back when they were dating they used to watch television together. They would watch HGTV, the DIY Network, and anything dealing with home and gardens. They would also watch cooking shows, fashion shows, and any and everything that had something to do with one of her two dreams, sewing or interior design. As they would watch TV he would sometimes comment to her that perhaps she should go back to school for fashion design.

Always back to school. Why does every conversation lead to going back to college? she thought.

If he didn't mention fashion design he would mention business classes. If not business classes, then marketing classes. If Korie didn't blink at any of those ideas, he would offer to buy her tickets to some seminar where some man somewhere who was supposed to be someone's expert, was giving an entrepreneurial class.

He always told her that he was trying to be supportive. She always told him that she thought he was telling her that he felt she wasn't good enough—as is.

She knew that he was trying in some way to get her as engaged and excited about something as he was his precious five-year plan. Korie refused to buy into it. To her, nothing was more important than being together, one day getting married, and starting a family. Looking back, perhaps he was right. Perhaps they were on two different paths.

Still, the plans that he laid out for her on her laptop were great. He advised her on how she should begin to start up her business, what classes to take at Kennedy King College, and also how to go into each project as if she were decorating her own brand-new home.

He had a separate plan for her if she decided she was going to simply be a seamstress. He had a plan where he agreed he would finance the mother of all sewing machines, materials, and even laid out a plan so she could be a limited partnership that had financing options and could accept credit cards.

He laid out a plan where parents of potential promgoers could pay all year round the year before senior prom and finance the dress that they wanted for as little as forty-five dollars a month. When Korie thought about it, he did have her back, and it seemed that he saw the potential she had long before she saw it herself.

When Korie got laid off from her job two years ago, she was at a loss as to what she might do for a living. After all, she was a hard worker and had a reputation for her work ethic, but it seemed that the company didn't care about her hard work after all, even after eight years of service.

They did give her a great severance package, however. Rather than wallow in pity or try to find a job out here during one of the worst economic times on record, she thought long and hard about investing in a product she thought to be priceless . . . herself. Rather than take her hard-work ethic to another employer to make that company rich, she decided to work for the fairest employer she could find. She decided to work for someone who would acknowledge all her hard work. She decided to work for the one person who could pull the very best out of her. Korie went into business for herself.

She started off small. She started off with friends, then church members, and then family, friends of family, and colleagues of Jayna. From there she made a small name for herself and tried her best to be someone other than a local businesswoman. One day while fooling around on her laptop, she came across the plans that he typed up for her more than two years prior to her layoff. She looked at the plans that he laid out and had an aha moment.

She took a business class.

She took a few marketing classes.

She did some research.

She traveled to a number of entrepreneurial workshops, and she even went back to Kennedy King College to get her associate's. She didn't finish because work became more and more demanding as her business began to grow. She was blessed that she was always able to find work; she was blessed that people liked her taste in clothes, furnishings, and accessories. When Korie began to truly market herself and throw herself into her business, she began to thrive.

She purchased a Web site. She took before-and-after photos of the homes that she decorated. She even got business cards, T-shirts, pens, and a million marketing tools to help spread her name around Chicago.

Before she knew it, she was on her way to being one of the hottest names in interior design in some circles of the city. She understood what he meant by pursuing his dream. She still thought there was no reason that they couldn't have done so together.

It dawned on her that had she had a baby, chances were she would not be the professional businesswoman she was now. It also dawned on her that having a baby at that time would have compromised his dreams considerably or at the very least slowed him down.

She wanted to call him and tell him that she now understood what he meant, but her pride wouldn't let her. Her pride still called him a coward because of the way that he left. She felt he wasn't man enough to see things through. As far as Korie was concerned, he still had a special place in her heart, but he jumped ship. For that, she thought to herself, he can burn in hell.

Korie got home, undressed and jumped in the tub. She had a good day, but it was a Calgon day, nonetheless. She made herself a bubble bath, poured a glass of wine, and relaxed in the tub while reading a new novel by Brenda Hampton. She just started the second chapter when her cell phone began ringing.

"Hello?"

"He's not married."

"Oh . . . kay?" Korie looked at the phone. It was Jayna. She must have thought Korie was suddenly interested in her love life.

"And get this, girl, he's Mr. Harris's chief advisor."

"Who are we talking about again?" Jayna was always going on about some man in her life and this evening seemed no different.

"Brandon."

"Who?"

"Brandon Lloyd, from this morning."

Oh yeah, the brother who snubbed me to get to you, Korie thought.

"Oh yeah, the brother from this morning. Okay." Korie feigned ignorance.

"Well he and I are going out next weekend and guess what?"

"What?" Korie asked dryly.

"Mr. Harris wants to go out with you."

"Uh . . . what?" Korie almost spit out her wine.

"You heard me. DeVaughn Harris wants to go out with you."

Silence fell over the phone. Jayna seemed excited but Korie was hardly impressed.

"Korie? Korie, are you there?"

"I'm here." Korie had to put her drink down on the side of the tub.

"So what do you think?"

"I think that one, he's old enough to be my father. Two, uh . . . ewww. And three, he didn't hardly see me, and I couldn't pick him out of a lineup if he was in front of me now. I got a brief glance at him and he had a brief glance at me."

"What did you think when you saw him?" Jayna asked.

"That he was old," Korie said sarcastically.

"Well, he noticed you. According to Brandon, he noticed you right away. He says that he would love for the four of us to go out next weekend and I already kind of said that you would go."

"You did what?"

"Korie, come on. You haven't been out in a long time."

"I've been out plenty of times. I just haven't gotten laid in a long time."

"All the more reason to go out with Mr. Harris."

"Again . . . ewww." Korie looked at the phone as if to say, Are you crazy?

"Korie, come on, it will be fun. Do it for me. Didn't I just help you out earlier today?"

"Uh . . . no."

"With the Underwoods?"

"Again, no. You didn't help me out, you helped them out. I'm sure that chances are you found a buyer for their home, and a commission from both the potential buyer and the commission that you will get from Mrs. Underwood as her investment broker. So don't go acting like you didn't get anything out of the deal. In fact, if anything, you owe me." Korie tooted her lips then let out a small laugh.

"Okay, true and true, but still, you're my best friend. Just have dinner with him, nothing else. What's the worst that can happen?"

"Girl, I never ask that question. You will be surprised at the worst that can happen."

"Okay, then, what is the best thing that can happen?"

"The best thing that can happen is that dinner will be really, really good."

"So you'll go?"

There was a long silence on the phone.

"Korie, please. Will you go?"

Korie let out a sigh.

"Okay. I guess, I'll go," Korie agreed reluctantly. "I'll babysit this old man."

"He's not old. He's forty-six."

"Yeah, Jayna, that's helping. I'll have dinner with him and that's all. Now girl, I have to go. I was enjoying a long, hot bath."

"Alone?"

"Uh, yeah, alone. What's wrong with that?"

"Nothing, I guess."

"I'll talk to you later Jayna."

She said that she would go and then got off the phone with Jayna so she could finish her bath.

The things we do for friends, Korie thought.

Chapter Eight

Darren sat across from a beautiful black woman who had a light brown complexion. She had long, free-flowing legs, smooth skin, and a nice smile. She was obviously biracial and had the best of both worlds from what he could see. He sat across from her listening attentively as she spoke to him about her problem, high risk behavior with men that she has met over the years and her desire to stop.

She confessed that she had no fantasies about men. No fantasies about anything. She was a beautiful woman in her early thirties. Since she was a teenager, she had never had any fantasies or dreams about men or women. Her fear was that she was asexual. However, her behavior spoke the opposite extreme.

This beautiful, educated woman was meeting men in bars, public places, and clubs and having multiple one-night stands with them. She said that she couldn't help herself, that she had tried all her life to fight these urges. She confessed that in grade school, high school, and even in college, she was looked at as a whore.

She talked about all the hearts that she broke, all the marriages that she ruined, and the friendships that she lost. For whatever reason, if she could find an opportunity to sleep with a man, she would. Not just any men either, but bad boys; men that could potentially hurt her.

She confessed that she tried masturbation, as Darren suggested in a previous session. Her body wouldn't respond. She confessed to using visual aids, toys, and even role-playing with her husband, a high-profile minister in the Chicago area with a fast-growing church. Nothing worked. She admitted that she was in constant need of attention sexually and that she couldn't seem to get enough sex. Part of the reason she confessed is because the only time that she felt anything is when she was actually in the middle of the physical act.

She expressed that she hated sex with her husband but loved sex with everyone else. When asked why she stayed with her husband, she admitted that she loved her husband-the man. She also liked the lifestyle that he provided for her. Physically, she confessed that she was simply not attracted to him and never had been.

This has got to be one of the most beautiful women in the city, Darren thought to himself.

He knew immediately that her diagnosis was some type of hyperactive sexual disorder. He thought that the woman's husband was both a lucky and an unlucky man. He was lucky because his wife was stunning and unlucky because she was repulsed by him.

Darren listened empathetically to the woman go into great detail about her exploits with men and her desire to please them and be pleased. He tried his best to be objective, but found himself imagining what it would be like to be with this woman. He listened to her and had to stop himself on more than one occasion from looking at her long, shapely legs, her hips, her pronounced cleavage, and her smile. He imagined in his mind the details that she was giving of her exploits, and found himself quite . . . intrigued.

Because he struggled with keeping his focus, he referred her to another counselor.

At the end of the session Darren felt anxious. He had a lot of pent-up energy that needed to be released. To quell his desires, he hit the gym hard. While in the gym, he watched the bodies of the various women doing Pilates, aerobics, and those working out with personal trainers.

Some women were dressed rather provocatively for the gym. Some wore cat suits, some wore biker shorts, and others wore tight spandex running pants. Curves were exposed, breasts were exposed, and some women, no matter how they tried, could not conceal their perfectly round bottoms.

Next there were the grunts and moans that came from the women on the machines. Many women made facial expressions that were similar to the faces made in the throes of passion. Darren came to the gym to let off some steam and it seemed that all working out did was make him more aware that he was overworked and undersexed.

Darren did curls, hit the bench press, did lateral pulls, and ran an estimated two miles. Still, with the sweat pouring from his body and his endorphins firing, all he succeeded in doing was getting more anxious and horny. Again he thought about her.

He thought about the many bouts of bedroom warfare they would sometimes have. Sometimes he would win, sometimes she would win. In either case, warring with her in bed was fun. He had to leave the gym. Being in the gym was almost like being in a club. He jumped in his car, drove home, jumped in the shower, and took a nap.

While he slept, he thought of her. In his sleep, his hand found its mark and once again he found himself thinking about her, desiring her, and in his dreams making love to her. In actuality, he was touching himself as he slept.

He awoke at 9:00 P.M. It was dark in his condo and the only light in the whole place was the moonlight from the living room window. His breathing was pronounced and his body was glistening with sweat. He was aroused and he wanted the company of a woman. Deep down he wanted her, but his pride wouldn't allow him to call. He was beginning to think that leaving her was a mistake. This woman haunted his dreams, his thoughts, and his most carnal visions.

The silence in his condo was deafening. He could hear the sounds of his own heartbeat and the thunderous sound of him swallowing. His breath was hot, desirous. The scent of his skin was that of pheromones. It was a thick scent, a primal scent. Accompanying that scent was the desire of flesh on his tongue.

The silence was too much for him. He turned on the stereo and every song was about love or making love. He jumped in the shower and lathered up his body. The fragrance of his body wash reminded him of her. The music on the radio reminded him of her. He thought to himself, All these years later, why is it that I can't seem to shake her? She must be talking about me somewhere. She's probably talking about me like a dog. Forget this. I'm out!

He got dressed in black from head to toe and sprayed on his most expensive cologne. Darren planned on going out. He planned on getting laid. He needed the company of a woman and he needed to work out this pent-up energy he had. He tried to leave, but stopped just short of the door.

That's where he saw it.

On the bookcase by the front door was a business card that he took from one of his clients. It was the business card for the escort service. He picked it up and looked at it. He ran his finger across the lettering, holding the card firmly in his hands. He began twirling it with his fingers. He stood there in silence . . . intrigued.

Do I really feel like going to a club? Do I really feel like trying to get to know a woman or possibly bringing one home tonight into my bed? I should have kept in touch with Maria or Trina or one of my ex-girlfriends. Tonight is the perfect night for a booty call. I don't feel like formally getting to know anyone. All I really want right now is someone to hit it and quit it; someone who mutually needs their needs met. Right now I have no one. Right now I don't want anyone. I just want to fuck.

He stared at the black business card with the gold writing. Elite Escorts were the only words on the card. There was the company name and there was a number. He picked the card up and twirled it more in his hand, walked around his condo, then looked at the number and sat by the door in his favorite recliner chair after letting out a heavy sigh. This card was a problem. This card was trouble. This card . . . had him, at the very least, curious. That's when he began talking to himself.

"D, man what are you doing? This isn't you. Brothers don't pay for companionship. Black men . . . real men . . . don't pay for sex. Put that shit down, go to a club, dance, grind on some honey, mention what you do for a living, and bring someone home. Put in the work. Dance, talk, have a few drinks and then fuck . . . it's that simple."

It's that simple.

However, there was also another simple solution in front of him, a solution that could be solved by Visa, a solution with delivery.

Darren was in a losing argument . . . with himself.

He thought about the words spoken by his client in their session earlier in the week.

No arguments, no drama, just the company of a beautiful woman; a woman that provides a service.

Darren tried to talk himself out of the situation. He tried to convince himself that there were other alternatives. This was solicitation, an act of desperation. It just wasn't something that black men did. This was something that wealthy white men did. No matter how you colored it, it still amounted to a form of prostitution; degradation; exploitation of women.

He tried to justify the very notion of making the call.

It's a service that is provided.

What makes me any different from a man picking up a streetwalker on a corner?

One way or the other, you end up paying for it anyway.

What man pays for sex?

Every man pays for sex.

I'm a professional. What do you say about a man who can't get a woman and resorts to something like this? What kind of man pays for the company of a woman like a food delivery from a grocery store? Men with way more money than you do this all the time.

Desperate men . . .

. . . Powerful men, men of all races . . . professional men.

The cost, what about the cost?

What about the cost?

What about the cost? How much money were we talking here? Darren thought to himself. His client spent close to a million dollars a year. He could not afford anything near that. His client told him on average he paid 1,500 dollars a night.

"Fifteen hundred dollars?" he said aloud in the solace of his condo. "I must be trippin'."

Try it at least once. See what all the hype is about. You can afford fifteen hundred. Who are you kidding?

Fifteen hundred dollars is a lot of damned money.

You make a lot of damned money.

I worked hard for that money.

You work for money, to spend money.

I can't pay for sex.

Every man pays for sex. One way or another, every man pays for sex.

Darren picked up the phone. Unconsciously, he found himself dialing the numbers on the card. He tried to stop himself, but he was curious, damned curious.

"Hello?" a soft, sultry voice said on the other end.

"Um . . . hi. Is this, Elite Escorts?"

"It is."

"I . . . um, would like to make an appointment."

"And how were you referred to us?"

"I saw you on the Internet."

"No sir, you did not."

That gave him a moment of pause.

"I'm sorry?"

"We don't advertise on the Internet. We only advertise by personal reference. Can you give me the name of the person that referred you? If not, I'm afraid I will have to disconnect this call."

Damn! Darren thought. What do I do now? I can't exactly leave the name of my client.

"Hello? Sir? The name of your reference, please."

Silence hung on the phone. Fifteen seconds later, the unidentified woman hung up. It was that simple. In just thirty seconds, it was over. Darren stared at his phone. He looked stupid, rejected.

He placed his cell phone on the table, hung up and let out a heavy sigh as he contemplated what just happened. Now he was more curious than ever before. He sat in silence in his condo.

What just happened? he wondered. He began whispering to himself quietly.

"Maybe it's not meant to be. Maybe not getting through is a sign from God. I don't have any business trying to make a phone call to pay for sex."

Every man pays for sex. Whether through marriage, dating, or even a booty call, every man ends up paying for sex in some way.

He let out a heavy sigh as he dialed the number again.

"Hello?" the same voice answered.

Darren held the phone in his hand and took a deep breath. He was nervous, anxious.

"I don't want the person that gave me the card to know that I am requesting the use of the service."

"That's fine, sir. We will respect your privacy. But we will need the name of the reference. I assure you, we will keep the name in strict confidence."

Again Darren was silent on the phone.

"Sir?" the voice asked.

"Okay, Okay. I'll give you the name."

Darren gave the woman the name of his client. His heart pounded in his chest as he did so. He was fearful. Making a mistake here, breaching confidentiality, chancing that his client might find out, put his license in jeopardy.

"Okay, that's fine. That wasn't so hard now, was it? And your name, sir?"

"Darren. Darren Howard."

"Okay, Mr. Howard, now what is it that you are looking for?"

"Uh . . . looking for?"

"What kind of women do you like?"

"Uh . . . pretty ones?"

The women on the other end gave a mild laugh. For such an articulate man, Darren was struggling with his words.

"I meant, sir, what kind of woman do you like? Let's start with ethnicity. White, black, Asian, Indian, Iraqi . . ."

"Whoa, um . . . let's keep it simple. I'd like . . . an African American woman."

"Okay. Do you prefer women heavy, petite, blond or athletic? Do you like an intellectual woman? Any fetishes?"

"No . . . no, hell no. I mean . . . no. No fetishes. I do, however, like fit women."

"How tall, sir?"

"Uh, I don't know."

"How tall are you?"

"Six feet two inches."

"You want a woman your height, shorter or taller?"

"Wow, you have women that are taller than me?"

"We have everything that you desire, sir."

"Everything?"

"Everything."

"Okay. Then I will take a pretty, fit, African American woman, but shorter than me. Maybe five feet four inches tall."

Darren felt insecure. He felt weird, as if he were ordering pizza from a new restaurant in town. He paced back and forth in his condo.

"I need more detail than that, sir."

"I'm sorry?"

"Pretty is too subjective. In order for this to work, Mr. Howard, I'm really going to need you to tell me exactly what it is that you want."

"I'm not sure if I know what I want."

"That's fine. Is this your first time?"

"Can't you tell?"

Darren laughed a bit himself this time. So did the woman on the phone, but she still remained professional.

"Mr. Howard, let's try a new approach. Describe an African American woman who you think is beautiful. You can even give me the name of a celebrity and I can take care of everything from there."

The whole conversation seemed surreal. Darren couldn't believe that he was going through with this. He felt nervous at first, but the more he talked to the sexy voice on the other end of the phone, the calmer he became. After a while he began to feel more confident. He decided to take on the persona of his client, a confident and influential African American man.

"Okay. I think Keyshia Cole is beautiful. I also like Jada Pinkett Smith. There is also Meagan Good—oh, and I also happen to love Serena Williams. I think Serena has an amazing body."

"Slow down, Mr. Howard, I think I have an idea of the scale you are looking for. Let's begin slowly. Would you like someone this evening who looks like Keyshia or Serena or a combination of both?"

"A combination of both? Is that even possible?"

"It is."

"Damn, what are you guys doing over there, building them in a lab?"

"No sir, we are simply . . . elite." The woman spoke in a very sexy tone.

"Well, let's start with a woman who looks like Keyshia."

"Do you want a woman who looks like Keyshia Cole in the 'Shoulda Let You Go' video, or the 'Playa Cardz Right' video?"

"Wow. I think I'll take blond Keyshia."

"Will she be there for a few hours or overnight?"

"Uh . . . How much is each?"

"A few hours, three to be exact, is fifteen hundred. Overnight is four thousand."

Ouch! Darren thought.

There was a brief pause on the phone.

"Mr. Howard, are you still with me?"

"Huh, oh . . . yeah. I'm with you . . . four . . . thousand . . . dollars." Darren couldn't believe it himself.

"I tell you what, Mr. Howard, since this is your first time and you have been referred by an elite VIP, I will charge you two thousand for an overnight. This option is a onetime offer. But you will have to act now. How does that sound?"

"Uh . . . um . . . okay. Two thousand. I'll take the . . . um . . . two-thousand dollar package."

Darren couldn't even believe he was saying this. He couldn't believe he was doing this. Two thousand dollars? That was four car payments, or a round-trip ticket to Vegas. Hell, it was only sixteen hundred dollars for his trip to Brazil last year. This was two thousand dollars for one night. He was beginning to have doubts—serious doubts. He was zoning out until the operator pulled him out of the daze he was in.

"Okay, Mr. Howard and how will you be completing your transaction?"

"Huh?"

"How will you pay for this?"

"Visa."

"And this card number, will this be the card that you plan to use in the future?"

"Uh . . . I don't know that I will be using you again in the future."

"Oh, I think you might," the woman said confidently.

"Really? What makes you so sure?"

"We're Elite . . . remember?"

"Elite . . . yeah . . . got it."

Darren and the phone operator exchanged information. His heart was pounding hard in his chest the whole time.

"Okay, Mr. Howard, you are all set. I just need your address."

"3324 Jefferson"

"House or apartment?"

"Condo. The garden unit."

"Your package will be there in two hours. There are just a few rules; they will be explained to you upon the package's arrival. Thank you for using Elite."

"Thank you."

Darren let out a heavy sigh. He was really going to go through with this. He was already dressed, but became anxious at the prospect of having a call girl come to his home. He looked around his condo, which was always clean, and for whatever reason decided to clean up more.

He waxed the hardwood kitchen floor, wiped down the granite countertops, and sprayed glass cleaner on the cocktail table in the living room. He remade his bed, pulled out a few candles, and strategically placed them all over. He sprayed air freshener and pulled out some custom-made CD's. He pulled fresh fruit from the fridge, and staged his condo as if he were getting ready for a date. Only this date was costing him two large.

He paced back and forth and soon after lost his nerve. He started to call the escort service and ask them for a refund. He was sure there would be a no-refund policy or at the very least a cancellation fee.

He wanted to cancel, but by doing so, his client whom he used as a reference would surely be notified. He had to see this thing through. The problem was he was worrying himself to death. When he looked up, it was 10:59 P.M. At exactly 11:00, his bell rang.

Darren's heart pounded in his chest. His breathing was erratic and he was nervous, more nervous than he had ever been in his life. He was even more nervous now than he was at graduation. He swallowed hard before opening the door. His jaw dropped as he looked at the stunningly beautiful woman who stood on the other side.

"Hello, Mr. Howard." The woman's voice was smooth, sultry, and seductive.

Darren was speechless.

"My name is Keyshia."

He stood there in the doorway in complete awe. There, in front of him, was a woman who looked the spitting image of the celebrity singer. Darren's mouth was wide open and he took a second to gather his composure. The woman was absolutely . . . breathtaking.

"Wow," he said in a voice just above a whisper.

The woman blushed and smiled at the compliment.

"Can I come in?" she asked.

"Please. Please do."

She had a honey-brown complexion, long, dark eye-lashes, and a soft pink lipstick that perfectly comple-mented her bronze complexion. Her hair was a short feather cut and it was blond. She had pearly white teeth with a slight gap in the front two teeth and a smile that spoke volumes of seduction with a hint of shyness.

Her eyebrows were dark brown and she had big, beautiful brown eyes. She was top heavy and her stom-ach was flat, but not ripped. At first glance, she looked and sounded exactly like the R & B singer. She was dressed in a dark green strapless dress with matching heels. She had on gold hoop earrings and her nails were painted the same pink that matched her lipstick. There was no other word to describe her other than breathtaking.

"Please, sit down," Darren said. "Do you want something to eat?"

"No, thank you. I would like a drink, though," she said.

"What would you like?"

"Just water for now."

He went to the kitchen and retrieved a glass of water, handing it to her as she sat on the couch. He sat across from her. Darren was nervous, but he was no longer thinking about the coin that he spent. The escort spoke first.

"So, I hear this is your first time." She looked at him seductively, innocently.

"It is."

"Well, there are a few rules. Do you mind if I go over them?" She placed the glass of water on the table as she spoke to him.

"Uh, no. Please. Please do." He poured himself a drink: rum and Coke in a short glass.

"Well, for starters, there is no kissing on the mouth. If you want to initiate intimacy, you begin by kissing me here, on the neck. I don't play rough, and I don't expect you to. I use protection and I supply the protection. At any point if I feel unsafe or I say stop . . . I expect you to do just that."

Darren felt uneasy at this point; he felt dirty. Suddenly he felt very wrong in doing this. Again, however, he felt he needed to see things through. He started this and like many experiences in life, you can't un-ring a bell.

"I . . . uh . . . I understand," he said.

"You can touch me anywhere. You cannot digitally penetrate my backside, however. Also, just as a disclaimer, the agency knows where I am, and they have all of your information. I provide a service. You pay for the fantasy and are entitled to the fantasy, but in no way, shape or form, are you entitled to the woman. Are we clear on that?"

"Uh . . . crystal clear."

"One more thing. I don't date clients. I don't see anyone outside of the realm of this arena. I do not share personal information. So please don't ask me how or why I'm in this business. Please don't try to save me from this business and should you see me in public with anyone, male or female, please do not approach me. I could be with a customer or I could be with family. In either case, I don't mix my business with my personal life. If it's possible for me to approach you to say hello, I will. If I don't, well, please don't take any offense. I expect you to conduct yourself as a professional. Are there any questions?"

"Uh . . . no."

Darren looked quite disappointed. The look on his face spoke volumes about how ashamed he was to have called a service. He felt dirty, seedy, and desperate. He didn't feel like a professional at all. Nor did he feel like a man who commanded respect. Upon hearing the disclaimer, he immediately felt that this was a mistake. The escort could see the regret on his face. She got up and sat next to him to reassure him.

"I know this all sounds . . . impersonal; maybe even cold. But once we establish the boundaries, I assure you everything else will fall in place. I also promise you that I won't disappoint you."

He could smell her perfume. It was expensive. She smelled amazing. She wore scented body lotion that smelled like fresh fruit. She looked good and smelled good. Good enough to eat. Darren was at a loss as to what to do next, so he asked her.

"So . . . what do you want to do? I mean, how do we do this?" He replaced the glass on the table.

"Everything is up to you. You have me for the entire night."

She took his chin in her hand and kissed him on the cheek.

"You're beautiful, you know that?"

"Thank you."

She smiled a beautiful smile and Darren thought his heart might just stop then and there. He had to keep telling himself this wasn't real. It was a fantasy, a very expensive fantasy. He immediately could see why his client was addicted.

"Do you want to go out and get a bite to eat?" he asked.

"If you're buying, I could eat."

Darren smiled. "Okay, then. Let's go." He took her by the hand and they left.

They went out to the garage that was attached to the condo and headed to Darren's car. They went on Lake Shore Drive and took in the city's beautiful skyline while listening to soft music. They took Lake Shore Drive to Roosevelt Road and then drove from South Michigan Avenue to North Michigan Avenue. From there they drove to Rush Street and had dinner at Gibson's steak house.

They had dinner and they each exchanged not-so-personal stories about themselves. Darren was careful not to ask too many questions, but being a therapist, once he relaxed, it was easy to get information from her. It was especially easy once she found out that he was a therapist.

He didn't have to ask much. Like many people, once she found out that he was a therapist, some things just came out. Before the night was over she confessed that her birth name was Stephanie.

As they ate, people stared at the couple. Many people thought Stephanie was actually the singer. After multiple times of her explaining that she wasn't, Darren and Stephanie decided to head back to his place. The drive back was slow and deliberate.

They took in the sights of the city as they made their way back to his place. He drove and she laid her head on his shoulder as if they had been a couple all of their lives. This was something else that he liked about her. She was smart, charming, and witty. Throughout the night she smiled at him, looked at him adoringly, and laughed at his jokes. She patted his hand attentively and even stroked his hand lovingly throughout their conversation at dinner. She was warm and inviting, more than any other woman who he dated; any other woman except her. He had to keep reminding himself that Stephanie was saying all the right things because that was her job.

They parked and held hands as they made their way back to his place. Darren opened the door and invited Stephanie in. She sat on his couch with familiarity. For whatever reason she put him at ease and before he knew it, he was treating her as if they had been a couple and known each other for three years rather than three hours.

Darren played Joe's song "Majic." While the music played, he fixed her a drink of Sprite and Hypnotic. He turned on the central air and walked over to her on the couch. She smiled at him, he smiled at her, and after they both downed their drinks he softly kissed her on her neck—he initiated intimacy.

His warm breath on her flesh made her swoon. She let out a gentle sigh and a smile as he kissed her neck. He desperately wanted to kiss her on the lips. He wanted to taste her drink, but he tried to be mindful of her rules; rules that were a constant reminder that this was business, not personal. He wanted it to be personal. He wanted to make love to her—all of her. His money only gave him limited access. He wished he had an all-access pass.

Kissing was forbidden. Because it was forbidden he wanted her more. He kissed her neck and she kissed his. His hands found her breasts and her hands found his package. They began kissing and petting like teenagers, only they kissed everywhere but the lips. Her heart was pounding. He could feel it. His heart was pounding, she could feel it. He took a firm grip on her backside and she let out slow, repetitive purrs as they caressed one another.

Minutes passed and the level of passion in the room rose with the temperature, in spite of Darren having turned on the central air. Stephanie continued to kiss his neck; she unbuttoned his shirt and kissed his chest. After that, it only took her a few minutes to undress him. She paused and admired his body. She liked what she saw; she liked his chest, his flat stomach, muscular arms, and even the Calvin Klein briefs he wore. To her, he looked darned good in them. His package . . . his bulge, looked even better.

She reached in her nearby purse. She pulled out two condoms and held them in her hand, smiling as she spoke.

"Black is for sex. Green is flavored," she whispered.

Darren licked his lips in anticipation.

"You do think of everything, don't you?" he said softly.

"Tonight my only goal is to please you." She looked him up and down. Her look was a provocative one. Again she smiled.

She stepped back and slowly peeled off her clothes. Her beautiful body kept him mesmerized. He was living a fantasy. In his mind, he was about to sleep with a celebrity. It might not have been the real thing, but for the next few hours that followed he pretended it was and he had his every way with her. He pretended that for one night he had his way with his celebrity crush. Pretty soon she stood across from him, near naked and flawless. Underneath her dress were matching lace panties and a bra. Her nipples were hard, her breasts were taut, and the place between her legs was meticulously trimmed and wet. He looked at her sweet spot as if it were his last meal. He walked over to her and placed his hand on her ass and again kissed her neck and collarbone. As he kissed her, she placed the flavored condom over him. She then began to please him.

In his mind, he had his way with the stunningly beautiful R&B singer. This night cost him two thousand dollars and by morning he felt it was worth every dime. They made love to his favorite music.

They rested, made love, and rested again. By morning they were both spent. When he awoke after the third orgasm she gave him . . . she was gone. By the nightstand was a kiss print on a napkin and a note.

Thank you for a wonderful night.
—Keyshia (Stephanie)

"Damn, that was incredible," he said when he awoke. He then realized that he might have an addiction. He felt like an addict after his first hit. The high he was on was amazing. The sex was great, the passion was intoxicating, and the thrill and rush of doing something that was considered illegal, immoral, and dirty all at once was appealing to him. The way he felt when he woke up was great. He felt alive. He felt refreshed. He was tired, but it was a good kind of tired. And there was no stress, no drama and, no awkward moment afterward. He was hooked. The question that bothered him, however, was whether or not he had the willpower to stop.

I could go broke easily doing this shit. I see why my client was so addicted. Yeah, I spent a lot of coin on last night, but right now it seems like it's worth every penny. I mean, that's why I work, right? I work to have the ability to provide myself with the things that I want and need. I may not need another night like last night, but I definitely want more nights like that. Besides, I could quit anytime, right?

Chapter Nine

Korie hadn't been out on a date in a long time. It had been six weeks since her last date and almost six months since she had last been intimate with a man. The last man she slept with was a waste of time. He was handsome and he was well endowed, but he had no idea how to work what he had. On top of that, the last man thought he was God's gift to women.

He wasn't. He was more like God's prank.

Korie had no plans on sleeping with DeVaughn Harris, but she did wonder what the day was going to be like. Korie didn't even know why she agreed to go out with this man. She felt like Jayna put her in an awkward position by telling him that she would go out with him.

As far as Korie was concerned, she was simply running interference for her friend—nothing more. She assumed her role would be to keep Mr. Harris occupied while she and Brandon became more acquainted. This was not a date. It was just a favor. This is what she told herself as she got dressed at home. This is what she told herself as she applied her M·A·C makeup, her best dress, and her best heels.

"This is not a date. This is just a few people going out to dinner. It's a free meal."

Her reflection looked back at her and gave her a look as if to say, so why be so nervous, then?

Although it was not a date per se, Korie had never gone out with a man of means before. She also had never gone out with an older man before. She had dated men with good jobs before, but never anyone who owned his own company. She never dated anyone who made more than 5,000 dollars more than she did.

She didn't know how to dress, how to act, or how she should present herself. It wasn't a date, but she didn't want to look like Cinderella before the ball, either.

"He's just a man, an old man at that. Girl, stop trippin'," she told herself.

Korie wondered what kind of man he was. As far as she knew, most wealthy men were arrogant. They felt as if the world owed them something or as if they were better than everyone else. She had to pause for a minute, however, and remember that the only rich men who she knew were the ones on TV and she didn't really know them.

Just because he was rich didn't mean that he was arrogant. Just because he was rich didn't mean she couldn't have a good time with him. Just because he was rich didn't make him better than her.

She continued to get dressed and wondered why this man wanted to go out with her. Why not Jayna? Why not some wealthy woman? At the very least, why not some white woman. After all, isn't that what successful black men did these days?

Over and over and over again, Korie asked herself, why her? It wasn't until she finished dressing, finished applying her makeup, and finished putting on her favorite perfume and checking herself out in the mirror that she finally said, why not her? Korie looked in the mirror one last time and spoke.

"You're a beautiful and strong black woman. That's why he wants to go out with you."

She went to her car in her house slippers and held her heels in her hand. She had agreed to meet Mr. Harris, Brandon, and Jayna at the Grand Lux Restaurant. She decided to take her own car. This way everything would be done on her terms. If Mr. Harris turned out to be an ass, she could politely excuse herself and leave. If Jayna decided to pull a move and leave early, she could go at her own pace and wouldn't be dependent on anyone for a ride. And if everything went well, for whatever reason, if she and Mr. Harris decided to take in a late movie or something, she would be safe in her own car.

Korie started her car and headed to the Grand Lux in downtown Chicago. She chose the Grand Lux because it was her favorite place to eat. It wasn't too expensive and if she needed to leave for any reason, she could pay her portion of the bill, and go shopping downtown and then home.

She listened to love songs on the radio as she drove down Lake Shore Drive. Inside of twenty minutes she was at the parking garage not far from the Grand Lux. She put her heels on, checked herself out in the rearview mirror one last time, and headed to the restaurant. She walked confidently in her heels through downtown Chicago toward the eatery.

Men of all ethnicities looked at her with desire. She loved the attention and finally began to feel good about herself. With all the hard work she and Jayna put into their runs at the park and at the gym she deserved to feel desired. With each step she grew more confident. With each step, she felt more secure.

As usual, the restaurant was crowded. There were couples standing outside waiting, couples inside waiting, and people at the bar waiting to be seated. On any given day you could see Chicago's elite at the Grand Lux. Businessmen ate there as well as many of Chicago's athletes. Because of this, there were many young gold-digging women that frequented the place as well as the wives of many of Chicago's athletes.

Once upon a time, people went to the Grand Lux to get away from a certain element in the city. When that element found out how good the food was as well as the clientele, many people from all walks of life began to dine there; even people who could not afford to. The restaurant wasn't expensive, but it was easy to spend a hundred dollars for two people with drinks.

Korie surveyed the lobby and looked at all the beautiful women and the men who accompanied them. There were women there of all races, women of all shapes and sizes, as well as outfits that would put some models to shame.

Korie had on her best dress. Compared to many of the women who dined there, her dress looked like something off the rack from a thrift store compared to some of the dresses other women had on.

Still, Korie didn't feel too bad as she looked at all the young women with their body parts out. You could tell the pretenders from the wealthy, as well as the poor. Those people that were there simply being themselves were the ones that Korie could best identify with.

Korie made her way to the reservation stand as she called Jayna on her cell phone to find out if she made it there yet.

"Hello?" Jayna answered.

"Where are you?"

"I've been seated already."

"So where are you guys at?"

"Ask for the Harris party. I think you will be pleasantly surprised."

"What do you mean?"

"You'll see."

"Hello? Hello?"

No, this heifer did not just hang up on me, she thought.

Korie walked up to the reservation stand where there was a beautiful Trinidadian girl with her hair pulled tightly back. The young woman looked as if she should be on someone's runway rather than taking reservations. Her skin had a reddish-brown tint and she had high cheekbones. Her smile was welcoming as she spoke.

"Hello, welcome to the Grand Lux. How many in your party?"

"I'm here for the Harris party. I believe they've already been seated."

"Would that be Mr. DeVaughn Harris?"

"Uh . . . yes. Yes, it would." Korie smiled a polite smile, although on the inside she was nervous.

"Right this way, Ms. Dillon."

Korie followed the young, beautiful woman up the escalator and toward the rear dining area. Most days when Korie and Jayna went, they were seated overlooking beautiful Michigan Avenue.

As she was led to the back of the restaurant she noticed an elevator that she'd never seen before. She and the young lady took the elevator further up and the young woman could hardly contain her smile.

"Wow. I have been here quite a few times and I have never seen this elevator before," Korie said.

"Yes, ma'am. Well, it's really easy to miss and we only use this dining area when we are extremely crowded or when we have special guests dining with us."

"Special guests? Like who?"

The young woman told Korie that many pro athletes ate at the restaurant. So did a lot of Chicago's coaches, the mayor; even the president had dined there a time or two. Korie was admittedly impressed that she, her girlfriend, and these two men would be dining in such style. She smiled and said to herself that this evening wasn't going to be so bad after all, although she told herself again that this was not a date.

Korie got off the elevator onto a floor that was completely empty. The floor had one single table and at the table was Mr. Harris, who stood up as he saw Korie being escorted to him.

Korie looked around for Jayna but didn't see her. Brandon was not there, either. Initially she was a bit apprehensive, but she was a grown woman, so she decided to see what was going on. As she got closer and closer to Mr. Harris, she noticed that he was ruggedly handsome. He had a smile that seemed to bring her at ease and Korie thought to herself that he looked damned good in a suit. Still, first things first. She wanted to know where her girl was.

"Where is Jayna?" Korie had a look on her face that had a slight air of attitude.

"Well, good evening to you too, Ms. Dillon," DeVaughn said while smiling.

Korie thought to herself that she had better manners than that.

"I'm sorry, Mr. Harris . . ."

"Please, call me Vaughn."

"Okay, Vaughn. If you don't mind my asking, where are my girlfriend and her date?"

"Jayna and Brandon are down in the dining area. They will be joining us for dessert. I hope you don't mind, but I took the liberty of arranging dinner just for the two of us. You know, so we could perhaps get to know each other better."

"I guess that's fine, but I thought we would all be eating together. That is what we agreed on."

"Ah, I see. So you thought that you would run interference for your girl. This way if she's not into Brandon, you could find an excuse to leave and if you're not into me, you could do the same, right?"

He smiled at her and although he was right, his smile still put her at ease. He reminded her of Denzel Washington. He was cool, calm, collected, and confident.

"You're right on both counts, but also, I would simply feel more comfortable with my girlfriend here."

"Okay, that's fair. Well, dinner should only take an hour and like I said, they'll be joining us for dessert. I was hoping to have you for myself for at least an hour . . . for dinner, I mean."

He smiled at her again and pulled her chair out for her.

Korie sat down. She was put off-balance by how direct he was, but she was also intrigued. Vaughn sat across from her and poured her a glass of wine, pouring himself a glass as well. Before picking up the menu he looked Korie directly in her eyes as he spoke softly.

"You look stunning, by the way. I like your dress."

Korie blushed and smiled. It had been a while since a man gave her a compliment on her attire or her looks, rather than a body part.

"Thank you," she said graciously.

"So, Ms. Dillon, I hear that you are an interior designer. How did you get into that line of work?"

Korie told Vaughn how she struggled to break into the business. She told him about her past relationship with him, and how he saw her dream of being an interior designer long before she saw it for herself. She talked about her education, her goals, her views on love, religion, children, and politics. Vaughn hung on her every word and throughout the evening, he kept telling her how beautiful she was.

He then told her about how he was once married but lost his wife to breast cancer and also how he made his first million dollars. Like a lot of millionaires, he began his career in real estate. He had no formal education other than the adversity that life threw at him. With everything he'd been through he jokingly said that he had a doctorate in reality.

He spent most of his young life working for the dollar and decided at one point that he was going to turn things around and make his dollars work for him. He talked about the differences between building money and building wealth. Wealth, he explained, made money for a lifetime, whereas being rich often simply meant having more debt than the average person.

They discussed the presidential election, the war overseas, the economy, and they both discussed ways that they would expand their businesses. Korie talked about her fitness goals and talked at length about the lack of responsibility in the black community. Vaughn discussed more of the same, as well as his efforts to clean up communities and the various scholarships that his company offered. The next thing that they both knew, dinner was over and Brandon and Jayna were being escorted upstairs to them.

Korie hadn't noticed that all the music playing overhead were custom slow songs—all of her favorite songs. She also hadn't noticed the dozen roses that were sitting on the chair next to Vaughn, until he presented them to her.

"Your girlfriend says that you like pink roses." He smiled as he gave them to her.

"I do." She smiled as she accepted them.

"Now that's what I have been waiting for all night . . . a full smile from you."

Korie blushed again. She had to admit to herself, she was having a wonderful time with DeVaughn Harris.

She was almost upset when Brandon and Jayna joined them.

"So, is everyone behaving over here?" Brandon said jokingly.

"Yes, we're fine," Vaughn said, while never taking his eyes off of Korie. His eyes said that he was very satisfied with what he saw and the company that she kept.

"So, are you ladies ready for dessert?" Brandon said.

"I've got room for dessert," Jayna said.

"I guess I do too," Korie agreed. "Where is the restroom?" she asked Vaughn.

"Right there in the back," he said as he finished his wine.

"Please excuse me, I'll be right back."

"I'll go with you," Jayna said.

"Please excuse us, then," Korie said.

Korie went to the bathroom, used it, and then adjusted her makeup in the mirror. As she checked herself out, Jayna was looking at her like a Cheshire cat, giddy like a schoolgirl, all smiles and bug-eyed, waiting anxiously for Korie to say something. When Korie said nothing and continued to do her makeup, Jayna couldn't contain herself any longer.

"So . . ." Jayna asked.

"So, what?" Korie said. She looked at Jayna as if she had no idea what she meant.

"Bitch, stop playing. Are you feeling him or what?"

Korie laughed.

"Vaughn is a nice man. I have to admit, I am enjoying dinner."

"And?"

"No and." She continued to reapply her makeup "He's a nice man."

"So this will be the first of many dates?"

"I don't think so. Don't get me wrong, he's a real sweetheart, but he is a lot older than I am."

"So?"

"So . . . I don't know. I don't think so, but anything's possible. So how are things with you and Brandon?"

"Great. I think there is really some potential there. I'm more curious about you."

"Don't be. Like I said, I enjoyed myself, but I don't see things going much farther than they have today."

"Why?"

"Because he's so much older. And he's not the type of man that I'm used to."

"You mean, handsome, respectful, unmarried, no issues, and rich?"

"I don't know that he doesn't have any issues."

"As wealthy as he is, any issues he might have can be easily taken care of."

"Money can't take care of everything, Jayna."

"No, but it can make almost anything more comfortable."

"I need more than that. He's financially stable, that's obvious. But I want more for my life. I want someone I can spend the rest of my life with."

"Why can't he be that man?"

"Because of our age difference. I would like to spend the rest of my life with my man. Not the rest of his life. Plus, this was just one date. How do I know that he even wants to see me anymore? Like I said, he's a nice man, but I don't see things going any farther than they have."

"Girl, you must be out of your damned mind. You must be out of your body. That man is wealthy beyond your wildest dreams, and of all the women in Chicago he asked to go out with you. "

"That's another thing, Jayna, why me? He could probably go out with anyone, so why me?"

"Korie, why not you? You're a beautiful woman. Instead of constantly asking why you, maybe you should be asking why not you. And rather than ask me, why not ask him? Ask that man why he wanted to take you out."

"I think I will."

"Good, because . . ." Jayna started to say something but let her voice trail off.

"Because what?"

"Nothing."

"Don't do that, Jay—say what's on your mind."

"I'm just wondering, Korie. You haven't been serious with anyone in a while. I'm just wondering, is it because you just haven't found the right person, or if you're still waiting on someone else to come around? I know you'll always have a special place in your heart for your ex, but sister, isn't it time to move on? Isn't it time that you moved forward?"

"I'm over him, Jay."

"Are you? I mean, really. This could turn out to be something with Mr. Harris. It could be something, or it could be nothing . . . in either case, I think you should give him a chance."

"Because he's rich?"

"No, because from what I am hearing from Brandon, he's a damned good man."

"And the age difference?"

"The age difference is healthy. If he turns out to be a good man who's good to you, what difference does that make?"

"I hear you."

"I'm just saying, give him a chance. At the very least, see this evening through before you pass judgment."

"That I can do. Let me ask you something, Jayna; are you saying all this because you want to see me happy, or because you hate him so much?"

"I want to see you happy."

Jayna hugged her.

"And I can't stand his ass."

Both women shared a small laugh.

"Do you think rather than have dessert, you and Brandon could maybe make yourselves scarce?"

"If you're serious, we will."

"Yeah, I think I am. Let's see where this path leads with Mr. Harris. Maybe you're right. Maybe it's time that I moved forward."

"That's my girl."

The two women returned to dinner. Before they could order dessert, Jayna spoke to Brandon and Mr. Harris.

"Mr. Harris, I know that you were expecting to have dessert with Brandon and me, but we have to leave unexpectedly. I got a call from my mother and I have to leave."

"I see."

"So, Korie, I will give you a call later?"

"That's fine."

Mr. Harris looked as if he expected Korie to find an excuse to leave. Instead, she picked up the dessert menu.

"So for dessert, what do you recommend?"

Mr. Harris was surprised. He was pleasantly surprised. He smiled as he picked up the menu.

"I thought this was your favorite place. What do you recommend for dessert?"

"I have never stayed for dessert before. I'm usually full when I leave here."

"And you're not full today?"

"No, I am. But I'm not in a rush. So I figured we could take some time and talk a bit more while I decide on dessert."

Mr. Harris smiled at Korie. He smiled at her and this time he more than put her at ease. His smile said that he loved being there with her. His smile said he was having fun and happy that she decided to stay.

"Okay, then. I like that. Take all the time that you need."

"I plan to."

"So, would you like something else to drink?"

"I would . . . as long as you have no ulterior motives."

Mr. Harris smiled again. He leaned in to whisper to Korie. He motioned for her to lean in as well. She did.

"Ms. Dillon, I assure you, I have no ulterior motives—tonight. Right now, I'm only interested in getting to know you better, that's all. But I will say this. I'm quite happy you decided to spend more time with me."

He placed his hand on hers. His thumb rubbed her fingers. His touch was light and affectionate. He sat back in his chair and reviewed the dessert menu.

"So, I have a question," Korie began to say.

"Go ahead, shoot."

"Why did you want to take me out? I'm sure a man of means like you could go out with anyone."

He licked his lips before speaking. Korie thought he looked incredibly sexy each time that he licked his lips. He looked at her confidently and spoke.

"I probably could have gone out with just anybody. But what if I wanted more than that?"

"What do you mean?"

"I wanted to go out with you because I thought you were beautiful. Also, because I wanted to go out with someone who was real."

Korie blushed. She smiled a wide smile before catching herself.

"Okay, wait a minute. I looked a hot, sweaty mess when you first saw me. I didn't even have any makeup on."

"My point exactly. When I first saw you, I thought to myself, Wow she is really beautiful; naturally beautiful."

"And the sweat?" Korie said.

"Oh, I didn't mind that," he said, laughing. His laugh reminded her of how Denzel Washington sometimes laughed in his movies. "I didn't mind that at all. Besides, I didn't think you were sweating so much as you were glistening."

"And the difference between the two?"

"Sweating is kind of . . . well, primitive, carnal . . . maybe even nasty."

"And I wasn't any of those things?" Korie's eyebrow went up.

"No, you were none of those things. Like I said, you were glistening. Your skin, it had this . . . copper shine to it. It was kind of a glow."

"A glow?" Korie said sarcastically.

"Yes . . . a glow. It wasn't nasty at all. It was rather . . . exotic."

Korie blushed. As she blushed, Vaughn smiled. Then the two shared a laugh.

"Better Days" by Joe was playing overhead.

Korie asked Vaughn a million questions. He gave her a million answers. They all seemed correct. The next thing that she knew, it was almost eleven o' clock. They talked most of the night over wine and dessert. With all the love songs that played, it was like she was in her own world with the only man in the city who mattered. She enjoyed his smile, his rugged good looks, and his conversation. Before long, they spoke to each other with an ageless familiarity. They talked like old lovers or old souls.

Initially, Korie was apprehensive about coming out this evening on this non-date. As the night went on, all she could think was how much she would have missed out on had she not gone. At 11:15, Korie decided it was time to say good night. She gave Mr. Harris her card and a smile.

"I enjoyed myself this evening, Vaughn."

"I enjoyed myself as well."

"I think I'll be saying good night now."

"I'll walk you to your car."

They both got up from the table and Korie noticed that he didn't pay a bill and one was not brought out to him. Then it dawned on her that he paid for this evening in advance. When they left the Grand Lux, the dining area where they had eaten was then opened up to the public. People looked at them as they exited the dining area. Some looked as if to say, Who are you? Others looked at the couple as if they were royalty or celebrities. Some of the looks made Korie uncomfortable. Vaughn, however, walked with confidence as if he were used to these looks. It didn't faze him in the slightest way.

When they reached street level, Vaughn offered Korie his arm. They walked together slowly and deliberately as they laughed and continued to talk. It was obvious that neither wanted the night to end. Korie started to ask Vaughn to come back to her place, but her manners told her that would be unladylike. Jayna was probably in bed with Brandon right now, but Korie wasn't like that. She was selective with whom she gave her body to. Rich or not, Mr. Vaughn Harris would have to wait for her goodies, if and when she decided to give them to him.

He walked her to her car, arm in arm. She chirped the alarm and unlocked her doors. He opened the door for her and leaned in and casually kissed her on the cheek. She was both surprised and impressed that he didn't try for a kiss on the lips.

"Good night, Ms. Dillion."

"Good night, Mr. Harris," Korie said, smiling.

"Here's my card. Please call or text me to let me know that you're home safe."

"Call or text? I'm surprised you're text savvy."

He laughed. "Because I'm older than you? Or because you think I'm old?"

Korie's expression changed. It didn't dawn on her that her comment might seem offensive.

"Because you don't seem like the type to text anyone."

"Okay . . . well, you have a good evening. Call or text to let me know you got home safely."

Korie started up her car. More slow songs were playing on the radio. Korie watched Vaughn walk away all smiles. She had to smile to herself as well because she had such a wonderful time with him. After he got on the parking garage elevator, she sat in her car and listened to the music for a while. She wondered if anything could happen between them. She wondered how much potential they had as an item. She wondered how much potential they had as a couple. Just as quickly as she thought of it, she dismissed it. She knew in her heart that statistically if they were to even attempt to get into a relationship, it would be doomed to fail.

Because she always had her guard up, Korie wondered if this was just a thing or a phase for Vaughn. She wondered was he just a rich man looking for a booty call from an average woman. She thought to herself that some men liked women with big butts. Some liked women who were top heavy. She wondered if in some sick way, DeVaughn Harris was a man who got off on sleeping with middle-income women.

Girl, you're trippin'. This could be a black version of Cinderella or Pretty Woman, she thought.

Then reality hit Korie quite hard as she continued to think about what could develop between the two of them.

Or, it could be another heartbreak, she thought to herself.

She sat in her car and simply exhaled. She made up her mind that as far as she was concerned, the ball was in DeVaughn's court. If he chose not to call then it would be his loss. She did, however, make up her mind that she would be fair with him.

She drove through the parking garage and down eight floors where she paid for her parking. The bill was twenty-two dollars. She was miffed at the expensive cost of parking downtown. Still, she had a great night. As she pulled out of the garage, "the Daddy Thing" by Jaheim was playing. She looked at her backseat and put Darrin Lowery's book The Daddy Thing in her purse so she would remember to read it.

As she pulled out of the garage, she headed east to State Street. She then headed south on State Street, where she saw a familiar figure walking and looking at the storefront windows. She drove slowly beside the tall figure and rolled down her window.

Vaughn was taking a late-night stroll down State Street.

"What are you doing?" she asked.

He looked up at her and smiled. He was not expecting to see her.

"Just taking in the sights, and thinking about you."

"What about me?" Korie said, smiling.

Vaughn walked over to her car and knelt before the driver-side door. Korie cut off the engine.

"I was just thinking how nice it was to have dinner with you. I was just thinking that I seldom take time out for the important things in life."

"Things like what?"

"Things like family, marriage . . . love."

Korie was stunned. She was apprehensive and anxious all at once.

"Love?"

"Relax, Ms. Dillon. I'm not saying that I love you."

"Whew, I'm glad to hear that because I was just starting to like you," she said, smiling.

"Oh, so you like me," he said, smiling.

She thought to herself, He has such a wonderful smile.

"You're okay, I guess." They both laughed.

"So what I was saying is tonight got me to thinking; thinking about the important things in life: family, people and love. Not that I'm in love, but for a long time I haven't been open to the idea of love. "

"So what have you been doing all these years since your wife passed?"

"Making money." He stood up and put his hands in his pockets, staring off in the distance as if he were disappointed in himself. "Making lots and lots of money. I think that's my only skill."

"That's not a bad skill to have."

"Perhaps not, but it's a lonely business."

"I'm sure. I'm also sure that you have other skills. Outside of business, when was the last time that you went out to enjoy yourself?"

"I have dinner at different places all the time. In fact, I went to Vegas just last week."

"When was the last time you went skating?"

"Skating?"

"Yeah, skating," Korie said, smiling.

"Shoot, I don't think I've been skating since high school. Hell, that might have been before you were born."

He laughed.

She didn't.

She briefly thought about the age difference. Just as quickly as she thought about it, however, she dismissed it.

"And what was the last book you read for recreation that wasn't about finance?"

"Uh, that would have been quite some time ago,, and it was The Coldest Winter Ever."

"Great book. It's one of my favorites. What was the last movie that you saw?"

"At the theater?"

"At the theater."

"Well, not to brag, but I have a theater at home."

"I'm sure you do, but that doesn't answer my question. What was the last movie that you saw at the theater among other people?"

He had to think about it. He was almost ashamed to say.

"I believe the last movie I saw at the theater was The Five Heartbeats."

"Oh my god."

"But I've seen all the current movies. I just haven't seen them at the show."

"We'll have to do something about that."

"Oh really?" he said, smiling a full smile.

"Really. The next date is on me. I'm going to take you out and we are going to have some fun."

"I like the sound of that."

"What's your schedule like over the next few weeks?"

"I have a lot of things scheduled for this week, but you know what? I'll make the time . . . for you."

"I like the sound of that."

They both stared at each other like two teenagers. They looked at each other lovingly. And for the first time, Korie didn't see him as the older man. She just saw him as a man.

"Okay, well, I have to go home," Korie said.

"Well, good night again, Ms. Dillon." He leaned in a second time and kissed her on the cheek.

He smiled.

She smiled.

She then pulled off, turning the car stereo up and heading back to her place. Thoughts of this evening played over and over again in her head. Korie didn't remember the last time that she felt so good.

Then it dawned on her. The last time she felt this good about a man it was him. She turned the stereo down and drove in silence on the way back home. She thought about the gamble she was taking. She thought about the last time that she was hurt and she weighed her options again for the hundredth time.

That man is not this man. We need to give this man a chance. We need to give him the benefit of the doubt. Let's just see where this thing goes. These are the things she told herself.

Korie went inside her place and the first thing she did was get undressed and jump in bed. She lay down and stared at the ceiling, smiling to herself at how the evening went.

Not only was Vaughn handsome and financially stable, he was a gentleman the entire night. He made no effort whatsoever to come home into her bed, or to get her into his.

Korie admired that. She sent him a text that said she was home. His return text thanked her for a great evening. Just as she was ready to turn over and go to sleep her house phone rang.

"Hello?"

"Are you just getting home?"

It was Jayna. She was looking for dirt, no doubt. Korie smiled to herself again when she thought about how wonderful tonight was.

"Yes, Mama, I'm just getting home."

"And how did the evening go?"

"You know what? It was great. I'm glad you set it up."

"See, I told you he was the guy for you! Are you going out with him again?"

"Yep."

"Where is he taking you?"

"I'm taking him. I think I'm going to take him to a Bulls game."

"A Bulls game? Hold up, Did you say you were taking him?"

"Yes and yes. What's wrong with that?"

"You shouldn't be taking him out. Hell, if anything he should be taking you out. You should be going with him to Paris or something."

"Girl, stop. I'm taking him out because he seems a little removed from the black community and he can't remember the last time that he just kicked it and went out."

"Uh, okay Korie. As far as being removed from the black community, that's called progress. And as far as kicking it, a man of his stature needs to focus on one thing: Making millions for himself and billions for his company."

"Well, if we are going to see each other, I'd like him to focus on other things."

"Like what?"

"Like me."

"So you're telling me that you're really feeling him, huh?"

"I am . . . a little."

"Good. So . . ."

"So, what?"

"What happened? Spill it."

"We talked. We laughed and then he kissed me on the cheek."

"That's it?" Jayna sounded disappointed.

"That's it. How did things go with Brandon?"

"They went fine; he's here with me now. He's 'sleep."

"You ho!" Korie said playfully.

"It's not like that. I think he could be the one."

"After one night, Jayna?" Korie was concerned about her girlfriend's judgment.

"I don't know what to say, we just clicked."

Korie thought to herself, How many other men have you clicked with? The two women talked for about a half hour about their expectations. Minutes after that, they hung up. Throughout the conversation there were plenty of times that Korie had to hold her tongue. But again, she kept telling herself, sometimes being friends means not being judgmental. Besides, who was she to judge? Just days ago she was still thinking about her ex and now she was thinking about dating a man old enough to be her father.

Chapter Ten

Darren thought to himself, I'm finally rid of her. For the first time in a very long time, he hadn't thought about her anymore. He saw his clients, he went out on dates, and he occasionally paid for the company of Stephanie.

They'd gone out for the past six weeks and each time had been more amazing than the last. Darren tried to tell himself that there was nothing wrong with what he was doing. He tried to tell himself, like his client said, that he was simply in need of a service, and Stephanie provided that service. He knew that he sounded like one of his clients. He also knew that he was hooked like an addict.

It was costing him a pretty penny at 6,000 dollars a month, but he felt it was worth every dime. He simply saw more clients to offset the expense. It didn't dawn on him that in a year's time he would have spent 72,000 dollars.

He stepped his game up. He saw more elite clients. He took his last client's offer of learning how to play golf. As he learned to play golf, his client introduced him to more and more affluent men. Men whose issues ran deep, but whose pockets ran deeper. Darren began seeing many of the men at the club and started making more money inside of a few months than he had ever imagined.

His client, DeVaughn, had shown a great deal of progress. He confessed that he met someone and stopped spending money on the escort service altogether.

Darren thought, Tell me the secret so I can wean myself off.

His client stated that he met a woman; a remarkable woman who made him feel young again. His client thanked Darren for helping him with his addiction. He also thanked him for saving his company millions and millions of dollars.

"Mr. Howard, I really want to thank you for all your hard work. Initially I thought therapy was just some BS, but thanks to you, I am happier than I have ever been in my life."

"I'm glad I could be of help. If you think you're ready, perhaps we should end our sessions together then."

"Doc, are you breaking up with me?" he said, laughing.

"No. No, I'm not. But I do think you're ready." The two men sat and shared a drink on the ninth hole.

"So why do you think I did it all these years? What made me turn to escorts? Any idea?"

"What do you think?" Darren asked.

"I'm asking you what you think."

"It doesn't matter what I think."

"Forever the therapist, huh? Do you ever answer a question directly?"

"I do. But not during a session. Listen, therapy isn't about voodoo or curing people with some magic pill or anything. It's like two people walking on the same journey, and on that journey, I'm not the guide: You are. I'm simply the companion. My job isn't to answer questions. My job is to ask you difficult questions that you may be afraid to ask yourself."

"I thought we just agreed to terminate our sessions," the client said.

"We did," Darren said, laughing.

"Then answer my goddamned question," the client said jokingly.

"Okay. Okay, I will. Just this once. I think you had a need that needed to be met. I think you needed affection and you needed some stress relief. A man in your position needs some sort of healthy outlet to relieve all the pressure in his life. At the same time, you didn't want to betray your wife's memory. So you used a service. You used the service because it met your needs without becoming personal, without crossing boundaries. It allowed you to be a man, but also allowed you to be a faithful husband. Faithful to the memory of your deceased wife."

Darren took a drink of his beer.

His client shook his head in agreement, and then came the tears; tears he held back as he swung at the golf ball.

"You know. Mr. Howard, you're pretty good at what you do."

"Please, call me Darren, and thank you. I should be good at what I do, for what you're paying me."

His client smiled and laughed. "Just one more question."

"Okay, go ahead."

"How do I continue to go out with this new woman without disgracing my wife's memory?"

"Your wife will always have a special place in your heart. If you truly want to honor your wife, then honor this new woman. Take care of the living, but never forget the honored dead. It's time for you to begin healing. It's time for you to begin living again. Don't you think your wife who loved you would want that?"

"I'm sure she would. But it's hard."

"No one ever said it would be easy. If it ever gets to the point where it's too hard, and you need someone to talk to, you have my number."

The two men shook hands on the ninth hole. Just as they were ready to call it a day, it began to rain. They both headed back to the clubhouse. They changed clothes in the locker room and said their good-byes.

"Darren, before you go, I'd like to give you something."

"That's really not necessary."

The client reached into his jacket pocket and handed Darren a small envelope.

"You saved my company and me millions of dollars. On behalf of my company and me, we'd like to give you a token of our appreciation. Consider it a commission on the money that you saved us."

"Thank you, Mr. Harris."

"Please, call me Vaughn."

DeVaughn Harris put his hand on Darren's shoulder and the two men shook hands again before Mr. Harris left.

Darren sat on the bench in the locker room and opened up the envelope.

It was a check for 100,000 dollars.

"Damn!" Darren said. "I guess I've finally made it."

He considered calling her. After all, it was she who he wanted to be with when he was successful. That's why he left her to begin with. He left to lay a foundation for the rest of their lives. He left to get himself together. He left so they could have a happy ending.

I should call her. Shouldn't I? Maybe it's too late. Maybe it's been too long. After all, I have Stephanie now, right?

Chapter Eleven

Korie and Vaughn went skating. Other activities included the zoo and the Field Museum. They saw all that Chicago had to offer.

She took him to a few Bulls games. He insisted on floor seats and she insisted that they sit among everyday people. She took him places he hadn't been in years, such as J&J Fish, Leon's Barbeque, and places in the hood to get a good hoagie. Of course, Vaughn never had more than a bite or two, considering his health and age, but he enjoyed that bite or two of food immensely.

They went to the movies—at the theater. They went to plays, they went to after-five events, and they also did simple things like picnic and go for long walks. The courtship lasted ten weeks off and on. It was off and on because Vaughn was forever traveling. He was always busy making millions for his company.

He traveled the world. No matter where he was, he always made time to call. He always sent her flowers, and no matter what he was doing night or day, if she wanted him she could call him. She could reach him. There were even times where he might be in the middle of a board meeting, unknown to her, and he would politely excuse himself just to talk to her for a few minutes about nothing.

He was attentive, affectionate, and loving. He was all these things and they still hadn't even slept together yet. For him, she was the perfect woman and to her, he was becoming the perfect man.

Initially, she thought the age difference would get in the way. She thought that eventually she might one day become bored with him. Nothing could be further from the truth.

Each day, Vaughn found a way to reinvent himself. Korie made him smile. Korie made him feel loved. Korie made him feel young.

When Vaughn was in town, he went running many mornings with Korie. Korie seldom ran with Jayna anymore. Jayna had her hands full at work and with her courtship with Brandon. Korie would wake up in the morning and Vaughn's driver would be out front waiting for her to take them both to the park where they would run. It was a pleasant difference between her runs with Jayna. In the limo, coffee would be waiting and Vaughn with one of his million-dollar smiles. It felt weird getting out of a limousine at the park to go jogging, but riding in a limo was definitely something that Korie could get used to.

Like Vaughn, Brandon was always busy. Because he wasn't the boss, he couldn't simply move his schedule around as Mr. Harris could. Still, he spent every moment he could with Jayna. He also made more money than Jayna did—a lot more money. For Brandon, although he didn't command the money that Mr. Harris did, money was no object. There was nothing that a man could get Jayna that she couldn't get for herself. There were, however, things that Brandon could get Jayna that no other man could: Weekends in Vermont on short notice, for example.

It was little things like this that made Jayna swoon. Although it was true that the trips cost money, and on the outside looking in it might appear that Jayna was indeed a gold digger, she wasn't. She simply wanted a man who could be romantic on a whim and do romantic things for his woman without being preoccupied with cost.

Jayna also spent her money on Brandon and she bought him things that few women could afford to buy for men. Just as Brandon paid for lavish trips, it was not uncommon for Jayna to spend her hard-earned money on him as well. She bought him ties, suits, and the occasional watch.

For the first time in a long time, Korie and Jayna were happy with their love lives. For the first time in what seemed like forever, Korie thought she might be open to falling in love again.

At private events, Vaughn introduced Korie as his lady friend. It was an old term that meant girlfriend, and Korie didn't mind it at all. It was a moniker that she would proudly wear. Vaughn was attentive to her and, in spite of all the incredible responsibility that he had within his company, he made time for her.

Work was secondary, or at least he made her feel that it was. Korie's thoughts of him were growing less and less each day. Rather than think of the past, Korie was beginning to look toward the future. She was finally beginning to see past the hurt. She introduced Vaughn to her world and he introduced her to his.

She took him go-kart racing.

He took her for a ride on his Hinckley T38R convertible speedboat.

She took him to see the new Tyler Perry play.

He took her to see the New York Metropolitan Opera . . . in New York.

Some nights were spent in one another's arms in the apartment she once shared with him.

Then there were the nights that she spent in his mansion in Wilmette.

She introduced him to Aéropostale, Tommy Hilfiger, and Nike.

He introduced her to Vera Wang, Donna Karan, and Paris Hilton—literally.

She took dancing lessons; salsa, mambo, and merengue.

He took flying lessons. When he felt confident enough, he bought a plane.

As a man, he grew into this loving, caring person he never knew he could be again.

As a woman, she grew as a professional and as a companion.

Vaughn was becoming Korie's Adam. Korie was beginning to become Vaughn's Eve. They held hands, told secrets, and talked about ambition.

And then there was the first time that they made love.

He was attentive. He was tender and he made her feel like a woman. Korie hadn't felt like a woman in a long time. Once they began making love, Korie remembered what it was like to be with a man again; a man who cared. They didn't make love often. Vaughn would often blame it on his business, but Korie knew it was because he couldn't always hang with her in the bedroom. For her that was fine. There was more to life than sex. There was more to a relationship than sex. There was also love. Although Korie wasn't in love with Vaughn yet, she was more open to being in love with him one day. And so, they made love as often as they could. After all, Korie hadn't been sexually active at all. She eventually came to feel that occasional sex was better than no sex at all. She soon after discovered that she missed sex. It was like not having chocolate for a long time and then being given some as an afterthought. It was after she became active again that she remembered how great it was to feel the embrace of a man, his scent, and his strength.

It was a warm day in May and Vaughn had to meet with Japanese buyers. He met with them in his downtown Chicago office, and for the first time in a long time, he had trouble doing business; he had trouble closing a deal. This hadn't happened since his wife died. Brandon and the board of directives figured something—or someone—was distracting him.

Rather than say anything, they left their CEO alone with his thoughts. Was he distracted? Was he suddenly losing it? Vaughn knew what his employees were thinking. In the back of his mind he wondered if they were right. Lately he had been acting giddy; like a teenage boy. People seldom said no to DeVaughn Harris, and with the non-closing of this deal, he felt something that he hadn't felt in years: fallible.

He didn't express his concerns to Korie. He liked where he thought their relationship was headed. He did, however, need to speak with someone. He picked up his cell phone and dialed a number.

"I need to see you as soon as possible," he said.

"Okay, Mr. Harris, when?"

"How about now?"

"Now is fine . . . my office?"

"No. My home in Wilmette. I'll send my driver."

Vaughn left his company early that day. He had his driver take him home and then sent his driver to pick up his therapist, Darren Howard.

Chapter Twelve

"Don't ask me to do this."

"I'm asking you to at least think about it."

"I told you in the beginning to never ask me to do this."

"All I'm saying is I think we can have more than this."

"What if I don't want more than this?"

"That's crazy, why not?"

"Because I like the way that things are! I like the arrangement that we have."

"I'm trying to tell you that I care about you. I'm trying to tell you that I am willing to offer you the world."

"There is nothing that you can do for me that I can't do for myself."

"By whoring yourself?"

"Was it whoring when you picked up the phone and made the call?"

"Tell me that you're not feeling me. Tell me that you don't think we would make a dynamic couple."

"I can't tell you that because we might. What I will tell you is that I've made my decision and the answer is no. You've crossed a line here."

"Maybe, but you crossed the line yourself last week. You broke your own rules, not me."

"You're confused."

"You're damned right I'm confused, especially after last weekend!"

"Last weekend was a mistake."

"You can't mean that. Look me in my eyes and say it again."

"Last week was a mistake. I made an error in judgment. It was nothing. It was my fault."

"Because you were feeling me?"

"Because I can't give up the lifestyle that I've grown accustomed to."

"What makes you think I can't offer you that same lifestyle?"

"Unless you're sitting on millions, you can't."

"So this is about money?"

"It's always about money."

"What about love?"

"Shit, what about love? Fuck love. Besides, you can't love me."

"How do you know?"

"You don't even know me!"

They had been arguing well over an hour. It had been four months of weekends and Darren had spent close to 24,000 dollars on Stephanie. And that was just her fee. Each weekend was more lavish than the last one.

This weekend, he purchased dozens of roses, had all of her favorite foods and fruits around his place, and he had her favorite music playing and her bath drawn. This weekend, like every other weekend, he treated her like his woman. He was falling in love with her; better yet, he was falling in love with the fantasy that she provided.

He was addicted to her. She was his drug. She said all the right things, did all the right things, and made love to him as no other woman had. No other woman since her. She fed his ego, she rocked his body, and she made him shake with waves of orgasm and most of all, she made him smile.

She was the perfect woman.

The point he was missing was that she was the perfect woman—for a fee.

His objectivity had been blurred. So had her professionalism, her rules. She loved the way that he treated her. She loved how attentive he had been. She also made the mistake of breaking her own rules. She gave him personal information, she kissed him more than once on the lips, and once, just once, she made love to him and talked to him. Not like she would talk to a customer, but how she would talk to a man—her man. She told him of her dreams, her aspirations, and places she wanted to travel and the way she wanted to live her life.

She told him how she wanted a grand house, in the south, with a white picket fence, two kids, and a dog. She wanted two boys. Their names would be Jeremy and Allen. She told him how she wanted happily-ever-after. How she wanted to see the world. Paris. Rome. Italy. She talked about how one day she wanted to be nothing more than a mother and a wife.

He listened to her.

He genuinely listened to her.

And this week, there were flowers, music, a drawn bath, and a card that read Be my lady. Let me take care of you. Let's take this to the next level.

The lines that were once drawn in the sand were now blurred.

He wanted more.

Secretly, she wanted more.

But then, there was this line that had once been drawn.

She thought he was handsome. Rugged. The type of man that a girl wouldn't mind bringing home. He was educated. Refined. He was like no other man she brought home before, when she lived with her adoptive parents. He was a good lover, a smart man. She knew he cared for her and she cared for him. She looked forward to his phone calls. She looked forward to seeing him.

But then there was this line that had been drawn.

She knew weeks ago that she had feelings for him. She knew weeks ago that he was someone special. Initially she chalked it up to an orgasm and nothing more. Orgasms made women weak. It made them blind to certain truths about men. Damn him. Why did he make her come? Better yet, why did he make her come so hard? It was more than an orgasm. It was a connection.

He made her come the first night they laid down together. That first night was special. That first night he was shy. She thought being shy was cute. Then there was the way that he looked at her, the way he touched her. There was also the fact that he had this amazing body, muscles upon muscles, and his man muscle was, in a word, nothing short of amazing.

Generally men like him feel entitled. They felt that they were kings and women were concubines. They may not have said it, but their actions spoke volumes. Customers were generally selfish lovers. They were there to be pleased, to be waited on, and to have their egos stroked. They paid for a service and a service was provided.

Stephanie had provided plenty of services. She sold fantasies like the late Billy Mays sold products. Like Arabs sold oil. She owned the fantasy she sold, and she played her part well and for that, she was paid well. She was paid handsomely. She thanked God for Keyshia Cole and their strong resemblance.

She studied Keyshia, emulated Keyshia and coming up, pretended to be her. When Keyshia changed hairstyles, Stephanie changed hairstyles. When Keyshia dressed a certain way, Stephanie did. One day a man approached her about the proposition of being an escort and the rest, as they say, was history. Stephanie stayed in shape, she studied videos, and she even had a gap placed between her two front teeth to sell the fantasy.

That was a few years ago. That was one hundred men ago. That was when she was young and still wet behind the ears. Not the savvy businesswoman that she had become.

He wanted her. From the first moment he saw her, it was clear that he wanted her. He desired her. It was a look she had seen a hundred times before—literally. It was a look of lust in his eyes that she saw. But behind those eyes she also saw kindness. Behind those eyes she didn't just see desire, but potential, tenderness, and a world of possibilities. It was his first time, so they told her at the agency to sell it hard. When she saw him, she knew she was in trouble. She had a weakness for him. He was her type. He was what she was looking for in a man. Before the first nervous word, he already had her wet.

She assumed he would be primal. She assumed he would fumble and be nervous. Rather than jump into things, he took her out. He broke the ice. He made her feel . . . real. He got to know her, as much as she would let him. He pulled her chair out for her. He smiled at her. He wasn't just a customer. Again, there was a connection.

Then there was the lovemaking. It was gentle, passionate, and deliberate—the first time. And he made her come. The second time, that same night, he was deliberate and forceful in his lovemaking; still passionate, and yet he took his time. Again, he made her come. The third time, that same night, he fucked her. He fucked her like he was trying to chase away demons.

He fucked her like he was trying to force memories of another woman or another love clear out of his head. He fucked her well. He became primal in his lovemaking and again he made her come.

The fourth time, she awoke to his warm, wet kisses all over her body. He was tender and sweet and he whispered sweet nothings to her, telling her how beautiful she was, how stunning she was. By the fourth time, her womanhood was sore, her vaginal lips swollen with heat and passion. He kissed her everywhere but there, and again blood flowed to her vagina, life flowed to her vagina and dare she say it, love flowed to her vagina.

As he made love to her that final time, he touched her. He caressed her. He looked deep into her warm, brown eyes as he made love to her. He kissed her neck, her collarbone, her breasts, and her arms. His strokes were long, slow, deep, and deliberate, but yielding . . . feeling . . . pulsating. He fought back the urge to come himself. That was the patience he showed with her, the passion he showed with her. He savored her sex. He savored her touch, and just as he held back the urge to come, she held back the urge to kiss him.

He made her feel like no other man had.

He made love to her like that each and every time.

It didn't help that he also took her out on dates.

It didn't help that some days they didn't even make love right away. Some days, he simply massaged her back, or rubbed her feet, or took her into his arms upon arrival and slow danced.

She was selling a fantasy.

But he was selling one as well.

And then there was this line that was drawn.

And then there was last weekend.

Last weekend he took her to the movies. They held hands and went for a long walk afterward. He took her to the park, where she sat on a swing. They went out for ice cream later, then dinner, then dancing, where they had a few drinks and then they went back to his place.

They went back to his place where they made love. She went to sleep, and when she awoke, he was sitting there, watching her. He watched her as she slept. When she awoke, he was caressing her face and smiling.

Again, her bathwater was drawn. He then did something no other man had ever done. He picked her up, carried her to the tub, and gently laid her in. He then lit a few candles, turned on some soft music, and began to wash her back.

He bathed her.

He bathed her like she was his woman.

He touched her as he bathed her.

He touched her, bathed her, planted kisses all over her neck and shoulders and again, told her how beautiful she was; how stunning she was.

He washed every inch of her.

He then dried her off.

He carried her back to the bed, where he slowly and methodically made love to her. He was deep inside of her when she kissed him. He was deeper than any man before him had ever gone. He touched places no other man could reach.

By that, he touched her heart.

She kissed him.

He reciprocated.

That night, they made love over . . . and over . . . and over again.

All week long she thought about the fact that she kissed him. All week long she thought about that passionate love that they made. All week long, she was conflicted about him.

This week she tried to go back to the way things were. This week she tried to go back to business as usual. This week she tried to put her emotional walls up that came tumbling down after months and months of orgasms.

It was sex. That's all it was, sex. Sex accompanied by orgasm; strong, long-lasting waves of orgasm. It was physical, nothing else. This was the lie she tried to tell herself. Then there was the line that had been drawn.

It was a very blurry line at this point.

She tried to go back to the way things were before the kissing. Darren wasn't having it. Apparently, he thought a lot about last week as well. What she felt, he felt. What she wanted secretly, he wanted openly. He hadn't felt this way about anyone in a long time. Not since her. Not since Korie. He was finally at a point in his life where he was comfortable calling her by name. Before the kiss with Stephanie, Korie was just her.

He wanted to move forward. She wanted to move backward. Backward was safe. Two weeks ago was safe. Someone had to draw a line in the sand and Stephanie figured it had to be her. Darren was a customer. He was a john. He was nobody. That's what Elite Escorts would say. Stephanie's heart and vagina would argue that he was something more, he was something special.

But the line had been crossed, and with that passage there were words, emotions, and ties that bind people together. Their arrangement had evolved from something more than a consumer and a provider of goods.

The fact that they were arguing confirmed that it was much more.

"So you're telling me that you feel absolutely nothing for me?" he asked.

"I'm telling you that you are a customer and as I told you initially, there can never be anything between us."

"And the kiss?"

"The kiss was a mistake."

"And for you, it's only about the money. All I am to you is a means to make money?"

His question hurt. His words hurt. Pain was clearly written across his face. There was both pain and confusion. Confusion that she placed there, when she placed her lips on his.

"It's more than the money. This is unrealistic."

"Why?"

"Because it is. Because of how we met. If we met under different circumstances, then maybe—but we didn't! We can't even think about being together because it's wrong."

"Because you're an escort?"

"Because I'm a whore!"

She said it. He thought it, but he wouldn't dare say it, not again. The elephant in the room was now visible. Clinically, he opened a door that he chose before now not to see. Clinically, he opened up more than her heart. The words that would follow would make their arrangement either evolve further, or fall completely apart.

Silence overtook the room.

Tears streamed down Stephanie's face.

Desperation was on his.

One of them needed to break the silence. Because he had the degree and the credentials, and because he wanted to make an argument to be with her, he broke the silence first.

"You're not a whore."

He walked in her direction. He tried to hug her, but she kept him at arm's length.

"I made three hundred and sixteen thousand dollars last year."

She spoke with tears in her eyes and she took a step back from him.

"I made three hundred and sixteen thousand dollars last year sleeping with men. And that's after taxes. Do you know how many men that is? Do you know what I had to do to make that kind of money?"

Her eyes were bloodshot. She stepped away from him and sat in the chair.

"Stephanie. We can do this. I'm serious. We can make this work."

"And then what?" Her voice was filled with anger.

"What do you mean?" He had a look of confusion on his face.

"I mean and then what? Say we became a couple. What do we tell people? How do we say that we met? What would we tell our kids? Daddy got horny one night and called an escort agency and the rest is history?"

"Don't do this."

"Don't do what? Tell the truth? Don't you think this is a bit crazy? The truth of the matter is you're a customer that pays for pussy. The truth is that I'm a woman who provides pussy for a fee. Darren, you are not the first man to fall for an escort. Thus, the rules I told you about when you first called me. Men fall in love with strippers, escorts, and whores all the time."

He walked over to her and caressed her back.

"I care about you," he said.

"You care about the fantasy. You don't know me."

"I know that you want a picket fence. I know that you want two kids and a dog. I know that you want to see the world. I know that you want to see Paris, Rome, and Italy. I also know that I want to do those things with you."

Stephanie stood up and walked across the room. She didn't want to be touched and it was clear she had a lot of her mind.

"And what would we do for money? Here's a better question: What would I do for money? You certainly aren't going to pay me three hundred thousand plus a year."

Darren let out a sigh. "No, no, I'm not. I guess we'll cross that bridge when we get to it."

"No. No, we won't. Do you know how many men I've been with?"

Silence.

"Do you know how many trips I've been on? How many men I've gone out with? Hell, I'd have to leave Chicago alone just so I wouldn't be recognized. And by the way, how would that make you feel? How would you feel if everywhere we went there were men who walked up to me and spoke while I was with you? Men who have been intimate with your woman?"

"I can handle that."

"Can you?" She placed her hand on her hip.

Reality was starting to set in. Her words were harsh, but they were real.

"No. No, I guess not. I guess . . . I just got caught up in all of this. I guess when you kissed me—never mind."

He looked dejected. He looked hurt. She felt hurt as well. She walked over to him and kissed him on the cheek. She placed both hands over his face before speaking.

"You're sweet. But you can't turn a ho into a house-wife."

He placed his hands in hers.

"You're not a ho."

"No. I'm an escort, and you . . . you are a customer. That's all that can ever be between us."

Her words were confident, definitive. He was just about to speak when his cell phone rang.

"Hello?"

"I need to see you."

"Who is this?"

"DeVaughn Harris."

He said to Stephanie, "Give me just a minute. I need to take this call."

He took the call in the next room.

When he came out, Stephanie was gone.

An hour later, a limousine was out front waiting to take Darren to Wilmette.

Chapter Thirteen

Darren stepped into the limo and let out a deep sigh. He would have loved to have driven his new Mercedes Benz CL-Class sports car, but he had too much on his mind. It was good that Mr. Harris sent his driver. Darren was too preoccupied with his situation with Stephanie to drive, let alone drive in rush-hour traffic. He used the check for a hundred grand that Mr. Harris gave him to buy a top-of-the-line Mercedes. He traded in his sports car and hadn't looked back since.

He loved his new car. He loved his new lifestyle. The only thing that could make things better would be to have Stephanie on his arm. He couldn't help feeling as if they just broke up, although they were never really a couple.

She was right, though. Escort was just another way of saying high-priced whore. Darren wondered to himself where he went wrong. He wondered to himself when things got so out of control. He thought, this must be what it's like when an addict realizes that they have a problem. This must be what Mr. Harris was going through.

It was then that Darren decided that he needed to follow his own advice. It was then that he decided that he needed a woman in his life, a real woman. As the limo drove him to Wilmette, he pulled out his phone and sent a text. He sent a text to a number he wasn't even sure existed anymore.

IS THIS STILL YOUR NUMBER?
-DARREN

He let out a heavy sigh and his heart skipped a beat when he hit SEND on his cell phone. He closed the cell phone and tried to get his head back in the game. Mr. Harris was one of his best clients. And, considering the last time that Darren helped him, he got a 100K tip, he needed to bring his "A" game with his client.

I hope things are still okay with him and his new woman. The last thing in the world I need to be doing right now is giving anyone relationship advice. I need to get my own shit together. Maybe Korie and I can pick up where we left off. Nah, who am I kidding? She's probably sitting up somewhere fat as hell and has probably had at least two kids by now. There is no way in hell she still has the same number.

Darren dismissed the idea of getting back with Korie as quickly as he thought about it. There was probably no hope for him and Korie, but he knew what he wanted in life. Now he finally knew. Being with Stephanie these past few months gave him some insight into what he wanted. He couldn't but help feeling that he had it all before when he was last with Korie. He had all that and more. Still, Korie was his past and he needed to look forward to the future. He was sure that she had long since moved on, so perhaps he should too.

Darren resigned himself to think that the next woman he fell in love with needed to provide the same love and support and passion that he once shared with Korie. He wanted her to be as down to earth as Stephanie. He wanted a woman like Stephanie in the bedroom, and a woman like Korie everywhere else.

Darren made up in his mind that he and Stephanie would go back to simply being customer and service provider. That was the smartest thing that either of them could do. They would keep things strictly physical. Emotions had no place in their arrangement.

It was 6:00 P.M. when Darren arrived at the Harris estate. The driver pulled up to the front door and Darren was met with a smile from Mr. Harris, who met him halfway after opening the door. The two men shook hands.

"Wow, this is an amazing house," Darren said.

"Why, thank you. Please come in. I hope I didn't put you out by calling you here on such short notice?"

"No, no, you didn't. How can I be of help to you, Mr. Harris?"

"Let's go in my study where we can have some privacy."

"Okay, sure. Any chance I can get a tour of the place?"

"Sure. I'm sorry, where are my manners? Please, let me show you my house."

Mr. Harris's home reminded Darren of the rapper 50 Cent's home on MTV Cribs. It had vaulted ceilings, marble fireplaces, limestone moldings, a library, skylights, balconies, and a wet bar. He had a number of custom hot-tubs, a sauna, steam room, home theater, and a basketball and tennis court in the back. His kitchen boasted marble countertops, stainless steel appliances, art deco furniture, and a grand pool out back. Darren thought to himself, This is how I want to live one day.

When the tour was over, Darren and Mr. Harris retired to the study. Mr. Harris poured himself and Darren a glass of bourbon and offered Darren a Cuban cigar. The two men sat across from one another. Before speaking, Mr. Harris grabbed a small black remote. He pressed the sensor twice and the fireplace in the den lit up.

That's some player-ass shit right there, Darren
thought.

"So, Mr. Harris. What's going on? You're not having
problems with the new woman in your life, are you?"

"No, no, no. Nothing like that. In fact, things with
her couldn't be better." Mr. Harris smiled.

"Then how can I help you?"

"Well, now, here's the thing. For starters, I think I
might be—not sure—but I might be in love."

"Okay," Darren said, laughing. "That's a good thing,
right?" He lit his cigar.

"Yes, yes it is. But here is the problem. I'm worried
that I might be in love and, by being in love, losing my
edge in business."

"Why is that?"

Mr. Harris went on to tell Darren about his deal with
the Japanese. There was a company called the Aichi
Corporation, that was trying to move in and merge with
a larger company, but couldn't raise the capital they
needed. Mr. Aichi, the CEO, was looking for a partner,
one with majority shares but minor input. Mr. Harris
was going to back the Aichi Corporation and play as if he
had little interest in the company's long-term holdings.
Then, just as they began to grow, he planned on taking
over the company entirely and expanding in the Asian
markets.

"Okay," Darren said. "So what happened?"

"That's just the thing. I don't know. One minute everything was cool, and the next, they backed out of the
deal."

"So . . . what makes you think that you're losing your
edge?"

"I don't know. Everything was just so unexpected.
I mean, they need the money. Not working with me,
means this deal doesn't get done. It also means that

Mr. Aichi's dream is done before it even gets off the ground. They need me. I can't figure out for the life of me what went wrong."

"Did you ask them?"

"They haven't returned my calls. They simply sent a letter saying that they can no longer move forward with our business venture. Ain't that a bitch?"

"Sounds rude."

"It's damned rude."

"Let me ask you a question. What was the last thing that happened before the deal was severed?" Darren's clinical skills told him to trace Mr. Harris's steps.

"We were in the middle of talks. I had my people on one side of the table, and he had his people on his side. I received a phone call and I asked him politely if we could caucus. You know, have a short recess."

"And did he cancel the deal after your phone call?"

"No."

"Did he seem offended by the call? Not to be racist, but it's my understanding that the Japanese are very particular about business."

"They're damned particular, but he was fine after my call. In fact, negotiations were in full swing."

"Then what happened?"

"The deal was moving forward; we shook hands. We were scheduled to celebrate that evening, and about forty minutes after our meeting concluded, I got a phone call and then a letter."

"Sounds to me like you need to find out what happened between the time that the deal was closed and the forty minutes that they cancelled the deal. It also sounds like you are due an explanation . . . face-to-face, if you can manage it."

"Face-to-face, huh. Not on a conference call?"

"If it were me, I'd do it face-to-face. You can hide emotion on a conference call. Body language in person is something altogether different."

"Hmm. I like the way you think." Mr. Harris took a sip of his drink. "Those little motherfuckers do kind of owe me an explanation."

"If you don't mind my asking, why did you think you were losing your edge?" Darren sipped his drink and took a puff of his stogie.

"Well, Mr. Howard—"

"I thought we agreed you could call me Darren."

"We did. I also thought we agreed you would call me Vaughn."

"You're right, I did. So, Vaughn, what happened?"

"Well, Darren, I have to admit . . . the phone call that I took, it was from her. It was from the new lady in my life. I put off a multimillion-dollar deal to talk to my woman on the phone. I've never done anything like that before. I never even did anything like that when I was married."

Mr. Harris finished his drink and got up to pour another.

"Sounds serious." Darren got up and had a second drink himself.

"That's just the thing . . . it is. I love her. It hasn't been a long time and I already know that I love her."

"Well, time has nothing to do with it. You can't put a timetable on these things. If you feel it, you feel it, you know?"

"Yeah, but . . ."

"But what?"

"I can't help thinking that it's hurting my business. When I took her call, my chief advisor and my board of directors, my lawyers—hell, everybody—gave me these . . . these looks." Mr. Harris took a long sip of bourbon.

"And what did you see in their faces as you looked at them?" Darren asked.

"Fear. Lack of confidence. And on some faces, jealousy."

"Hmm."

"Yeah. I've never seen those looks before from my people." Mr. Harris downed another drink.

"Let me ask you a question, Vaughn. If you didn't get this deal done, would your company go under?"

"No."

"Is there any danger of your company going under any time soon? I mean, is your company in any trouble?"

"No."

"How are your stocks?"

"Stronger than ever in a failing economy."

"So let me ask you another question."

"Shoot."

"How did not making this deal happen affect them?"

"They would have seen nice commissions across the board by the beginning of next quarter."

"So this deal would have fattened their pockets then, huh?"

"Yes. Yes, it would have."

"And on their faces, what was it that you said you saw again?"

"Fear, lack of confidence, and jealousy."

"Because you acted improper?"

"Because I acted irregular. Because my actions that day were . . . uncharacteristic."

"Hmm. One last question."

"Okay."

"You're still the boss, right?"

"Yes, I am."

"Fuck 'em."

Mr. Harris laughed. Darren laughed as well. The two men sat back across from one another and talked. Darren began first.

"Vaughn, you're in love. There's nothing to apologize for. Now let me ask you something. Could that phone call have waited? What would have happened if you let your phone go to voice mail?"

"She would have left me a message and I could have called her back later."

"So why did you answer the phone?"

Mr. Harris took another drink and another puff on his Cuban.

"Man, look. I just . . ." Mr. Harris started to say something and then he stopped.

"You just what?" Darren said, smiling.

"I don't know how to say this. I just wanted to hear her voice."

Darren laughed a little.

"Man, you got it bad."

Mr. Harris laughed.

"Yeah, yeah, I do. Putting off multimillion-dollar deals to talk to my woman? Yeah, I do."

The two men continued to share a laugh.

"So what did she want?"

"That's just the thing . . . she didn't really want anything. She just wanted to hear my voice and you know what?"

"What?"

"I don't mind.

"Well, Vaughn, it sounds to me like you have something really special there."

"I do. I do. She keeps me grounded, she makes me humble, and when I'm with her, I just want to be a better man. I can't wait to see her, I hate it when she leaves, and not a moment goes by that I don't think about her. I fact, she's on her way here now and I can't wait till she gets here. Darren, man, what should I do?"

"Hold on to her, Vaughn. Hold on to her and never let her go."

"That's your clinical advice?"

"Yeah. That, and next time let the phone go to voice mail." The two men laughed again. "Listen, your subordinates were probably worried about you. Actually, they were probably worried about them and how your being in love may affect them. You're in love. Never apologize for that, but take care of your business. This is just new territory for you, that's all. It doesn't sound to me like you're losing your edge. It sounds to me like you are gaining a new perspective."

"Once again, I like the way you think. So what do you think I should do about the Japanese?"

"Go see them."

"In person?"

"In person, And you know what? Take the little lady with you,"

"You think so?"

" I think it will be a trip of a lifetime."

"My man," Vaughn said, smiling. "I like the way you think. Any other advice?"

"Find out why they changed their mind and if it was something that you did wrong, learn from your mistake."

The two men finished their cigars.

They finished their drinks and Mr. Harris gave Darren a blank check. He looked at it with confusion.

"What do I do with this?"

"Right now, nothing. I plan to pay you for coming out here today. But I have a personal ritual that I do with people close to me; people I trust. I only trust six people in this world and each one has one of these from me. It's a show of faith. It's a show of trust. It's simply a blank check."

"Wow. I don't know what to say."

"There's nothing to say. It's a token. It just means that I trust you, that's all. If you ever need to use it, feel free. Chances are I'll get you another one."

"These other people that have these checks, have they ever cashed them before?"

"One person has. It was my minister. He needed to give fifty grand to build a homeless shelter."

"And you didn't trip?"

"No, I didn't trip."

"What if I wrote a check for a million dollars to myself?" Darren was joking when he said it.

"Well, if the bank cashes it, I guess you would have a million dollars. Chances are, however, that one of my accountants would catch it first."

"I would never do anything like that. If anything, I might frame it."

"I know you wouldn't. I just wanted you to know that I trust you and hey man, I'm grateful for your help."

"That's what I'm here for."

The two men shook hands again and Vaughn's driver took Darren home. He went home and took his clothes off and got ready for bed. Before going to bed, he pulled his cell phone out to place it on the charger. When he looked at his phone, he had a text message. It simply had one word.

YES.

Chapter Fourteen

Earlier that day, Korie was out on the east side of town meeting with the Chicago rapper Goldie. He was purchasing a loft apartment and wanted help decorating it. Korie had been recommended by a friend of the rapper, so Goldie decided to give her a shot.

Korie had been on a roll with business and was seeing more and more clients each day. She finally had to consider getting an assistant because business was so good, and she was also looking at getting commercial office space rather than working out of her home.

These were suggestions by Vaughn and they were suggestions that she didn't take lightly, considering how business-savvy he was. Vaughn had friends who began throwing work Korie's way, and they had friends as well. Korie moved from helping people decorating their homes, to also decorating businesses, nightclubs, and even churches. Business was booming and not just because of whom she was now dating, but because Korie had a true talent that was beginning to shine.

She traded in her economy car for a BMW. Although she didn't accept favors from Vaughn, she did allow him to call a friend of his to work out the financing on her BMW. Because she was self-employed, some dealerships were "skeptical" about selling her a car. Her credit was not great, but it wasn't bad either. The fact that she had been out of work and self-employed for so long, made it "challenging" to get the car she wanted and the financing she wanted, even though it was obvious that she could make the payments.

Because she was working with a more elite clientele, Korie needed to step up her game. This too was at the suggestion of Vaughn. He explained to her that she couldn't sway the minds of customers who had personal tailors, while she was still shopping off the rack at department stores. Korie resisted this notion initially, stating that she wasn't trying to be something she wasn't, but she understood Vaughn's point. She understood that sometimes you have to fake it till you make it.

For Korie, this meant buying items one piece at a time and one outfit at a time. Vaughn, of course, offered to buy Korie whatever she wanted, but she refused. She didn't want to give up her independence. She also wanted to remain grounded while she dated him.

She did, however, take the occasional gift, jewelry or a memento that he would give her, but she explained that anything outside of their courtship was unacceptable. Instead, she bought her own items that she thought would help her image, one outfit at a time. Sometimes this meant that she would have to wear the same outfit to see twelve different clients, but she wore the hell out of those outfits and she wore them well. With the clothes and the car came a new air of confidence.

She felt more confidence getting out of a BMW to see a client than she did her economy car. Her clients began to give her looks of confidence as she stepped out of her car to meet them. Her clients seemed to look at her with admiration as they saw her in outfits by Gucci, Prada, Fendi, Chanel, and Valentino.

Many of the clients recommended by Vaughn were impressed with her personal style from the moment they saw her. This gave her professional suggestions more credibility when she suggested ideas that were simple or not the norm.

The more clients Korie saw, the greater her reputation. Her portfolio was growing and growing fast. Korie marveled at the turn her life was taking. Five years ago she would have never imagined that she would be where she was today. She would have never dreamed that she would be working for herself and rubbing elbows with the city's elite. She never knew that life could be lived like this. Once upon a time she simply wanted a simple life. She was beginning to think that years ago she was simpleminded. Then she thought of him.

I wish he could see me now, she thought.

Korie pulled up in front of a set of loft condos in the south loop of Chicago. Where these lofts stood, once were projects, the fabled Cotton Club of Chicago, and one of the worst neighborhoods in the city. Now with gentrification, south Michigan Avenue boasted shops, salons, grand churches, businesses, and multimillion-dollar lofts.

Korie pulled up and looked at the building where she was scheduled to meet her client and thought to herself, I wish I had the foresight to buy property down here when it was still the projects. She got out of her car and headed to the doorbell panel. She rang it and a voice on the other end answered.

"Who's this?"

"Uh. It's Korie Dillon, I'm here to meet with Goldie."

"Okay, come on up."

The loft the rapper was buying was one of the smaller lofts for sale. He was buying it as his second home and somewhere to relax while in downtown Chicago.

He explained that he wanted it to be a home away from home. Korie took one look at the place and explained to him that it could be so much more.

The loft was 2,800 square feet. It had three bedrooms, two bathrooms, and a world of possibility. Rather than look at it as a home for the rapper to sleep, she thought it would be the perfect place to entertain guests, shoot music videos, and meet and greet with clients.

Korie pulled out her laptop and showed the rapper other condos, lofts, and homes that she helped to decorate. She told Goldie that her vision for his place was a combination of all the places she ever decorated.

She told him that she wanted all the hardwood floors resurfaced and waxed. She explained that the living room area should have a bar and the atmosphere of a small nightclub. This way, he could have small, private parties; if he was ever out and a place was closing, he could take the after-party to his house.

She also explained that he could always shoot video scenes here, and what better place to have models audition for his videos than his place? What better place for video footage, than a live video from his home? Goldie was feeling her every suggestion. He sat and listened to her attentively like she was one of his managers. By the time Korie finished with her presentation, Goldie asked her would she ever consider decorating movie sets or music video sets. Korie explained that she had never done anything like that before, but she would indeed consider it.

Blessings and opportunities continued to come Korie's way and with each opportunity, came a windfall of money. Korie was realizing her dreams. Dreams that once upon a time, she didn't imagine could be a reality.

She walked up and down the loft and continued to make suggestions. As she and the rapper and his managers were deciding on what to do with his outdoor deck, her phone vibrated in her purse. She smiled to herself because she knew it was Vaughn. Her breath was almost taken away when she saw the text message.

IS THIS STILL YOUR NUMBER?
-DARREN

Are you fucking kidding me? This is what Korie thought as she looked at the screen. She looked at it a few times, to make sure she wasn't dreaming any of this.

"Ms. Dillon? Ms. Dillon, are you okay?" Goldie asked.

"Yes, yes, I'm fine. I just got news about my next appointment, that's all. It's a cancellation."

"Oh. Well, good, I guess that means you can give me more of your time."

"I'm all yours for at least another hour. Let me text my client and inform him that I got his message."

"Okay."

Korie wasn't sure how to answer Darren's text. She wasn't sure what to say. She wasn't even sure that she wanted to respond. Here she was just getting him out of her system and like a typical man, he came back and infected her with his presence the second she thought she was immune. She wasn't sure how to respond, but she knew she had a client waiting. Figuring the best thing to do was keep it simple, she wrote a small answer and hit SEND.

YES.

She then went back to her client.

Chapter Fifteen

The next weekend came and Darren dialed Elite Escorts. He was looking forward to seeing Stephanie and explaining to her that he was okay with things going back the way that they were. He knew that things had gotten way out of hand and he needed to keep things simple. He needed to look at things as his client looked at things: He paid for a service and the woman provided that service.

Darren realized that he had a problem, but was not a willing participant to simply give it up. Like an addict he still wanted the drug, and just like an addict, he decided that he needed to wean himself off, or to simply cut back. There were two modes of thought here. One, he would slowly wean himself off of Stephanie and the escort service entirely and two, he would consider pursuing Korie, his ex. She invaded his thoughts a lot these days and he couldn't help himself. Since she was the only thing on his mind, he assumed she was meant to be with him.

He liked the idea of still seeing Stephanie. He liked the way things went with her. Sex, the activity, and everything was at his will; his choice. The fact that Stephanie had such a great personality was just a bonus. He decided he would have the best of both worlds. He had Korie's number. If she wasn't fat, married or had a bunch of kids, he could court her again and start over; start fresh. Their relationship could pick up where it

left off and they could go where their relationship originally was destined to go. Hell, with the money Darren
was making, he figured they could even start thinking
about a family.

He would have his cake and eat it too. He would sex
two beautiful women; one whom he still obviously loved
anyway, and the other whom he had no obligation to.
A woman he could leave any minute without reason or
argument. It was the perfect situation.

Now all he needed to do was get in touch with Korie.
He sent her a text.

I'D LIKE TO SEE YOU.

He wasn't sure how she would respond, but being a
therapist, he knew that it would simply take some time.
She would need time to adjust, time to figure out what
it was that she wanted to do.

He was sure she wouldn't be single. He was sure that
she would want to see him again. Even if she had another man, because of the bond that they once shared,
she would be conflicted; she would meet with him, she
would have to. Part of this was his arrogance speaking.
The other part was his experience. No man could know
Korie like he knew her. No other man could offer her
what he could.

Darren thought that he was fit, educated, nice looking, and now paid. He made three times as much as
the average African American man. Korie would think
about all that he had to offer and she would call him.
She had to. This is what he told himself. He closed his
cell phone after sending Korie a text and got himself
ready to go to work. He was seeing five clients today,
one of which was pro bono.

After getting dressed he made a second phone call. He called the agency. He wanted to see Stephanie this weekend. He wanted to make the appointment now. He dialed the number that before needed the assistance of a business card. Now the number was burned into his head, alongside childhood memories, fantasies, and important things. He knew the number by heart.

If his phone were checked, it would show that he dialed double E more than he dialed family members. A smooth female voice answered on the other end.

"Hello?"

"Hello, this is Mr. Howard. I'd like to make my weekend appointment. Same girl, same service."

He talked to the operator like he was ordering takeout. The woman on the other end was the same woman he talked to that first night. The same woman who heard him trip over his words before. Things had changed. He was no longer nervous, no longer fumbling. Spending over 24,000 dollars did that to a man. It made him more confident. It had to. In a few months time, he spent enough money to outright buy a car. He spent that much money for the company of a woman.

There was a pause at the other end of the phone.

There had never been a pause before.

He thought to himself that perhaps there was a problem with the payment, but there couldn't be. There was plenty of money in his account.

The pause brought back his nervousness, anxiety. His mouth became dry and his breathing rapid.

"Is—there a problem?"

He heard typing on the other end, and he heard the operating breathing. He knew she was there, but she didn't readily answer.

"Hold on, sir."

It was another pause.

A pregnant pause.

It was the pause you hear when bill collectors call. The pause when bill collectors put you on hold so they can look at your account; more importantly so they can look at documentation on the account. He heard typing. He heard breathing, but that was all.

"Uh, hello?"

"I'm here, sir. One moment."

The voice was no longer smooth. The voice was now impatient. The voice now had a certain tone to it. The operator let out a small sigh. And then she spoke.

"Sir, that package is unavailable. Would you like another?"

The voice was smooth again, but not as it has been before. Not as if she was selling a fantasy. This time the smooth voice was fake. It was clearly fake. It was as if she were trying to feign professionalism. It was if she were not trying to lose his account, his money. It was clear there was some notation on the file.

"What do you mean, unavailable?" He looked at the phone with frustration.

He tried to keep his voice calm, without cracking; with no anxiety. He was standing up when he made the call, but now he had to sit down. He had to calm himself. He felt a rush and then warmth. It was like a dealer telling an addict that he was out of product.

"That package Mr. Howard . . . is unavailable. Would you like another?"

Her voice was patient again, but unwavering. It was a tone that he had heard before. He knew one wrong word, or one word out of anger, she would disconnect the call.

He surmised the woman on the other end was African American. All this time, he couldn't tell what nationality she was over the phone. Prior to today, her voice was always at the same pitch. Her voice was usually smooth. Perhaps it was from previous years of practice or just a marketing technique, but over the phone initially you could not tell anything about the operator over the phone other than the fact that she had a calming demeanor.

Today he was sure of it. Today he was sure that she was an African American woman. Her voice rang of impatience. She read something in his file that put her in sister-girl mode. She was professional, but she had that tone that black women sometimes have that says, I'm barely putting up with your ass and my patience is running out.

"Sir, that package is unavailable." This time she was cold. Flat.

"Until when?" Darren asked.

"Indefinitely. Would you like another package?"

He could tell this was the last time the operator would ask.

"Um . . . no, thank—"

"Thank you for your business, Mr. Howard."

The call was disconnected. Before he could say thank you, the call was disconnected. He felt ashamed. He felt embarrassed. He wanted to know what was in the file, but the truth was, he would never know.

What have I done? he thought to himself.

He took a few more minutes to get himself together and then he went to work. His stomach was knotted up and it felt as if it were burning with acid. This thing with Stephanie felt like a breakup and it hurt. He let out a sigh. He then stood up to leave when his cell phone buzzed in his pocket. He read the text on the other end.

NO.

It was from Korie. His stomach knotted even more.
She just needs time, he thought.
Only now, he wasn't as confident.

Darren went to work. He saw his first few clients. Two
were depressed. It was hard to listen to them because
clearly he was depressed as well. He did a good job of
pretending he wasn't. He listened and he listened attentively, but in the back of his mind his thoughts were
about two things: Stephanie and Korie. Both women
were now a part of his past and at one point, he thought
both might be a part of his future. He counseled his clients and took breaks between sessions. He needed time
to get himself together and was surprised at how things
were affecting him.

He needed time to regroup. He needed to get his life
back to normal, whatever that was. He decided to leave
work early and not see his last client. How could he advise others when his own shit wasn't together?

He walked out to the parking lot to his new car. It
was his new toy. It was what he used the check for that
Mr. Harris gave him. He needed to let the top down,
to drive around town. He needed to be seen. His ego
had already taken two major blows today from the
two women who he wanted most. He needed to patch
up his ego. He needed women to look at him like the
hardworking professional black man that he was. He
needed idol worship. Envy. Jealousy. He thought that
the best way to get a woman off your mind is to get another in your bed. This time, he thought, it won't be a
woman who requires a credit card.

He just chirped the alarm on his new car when he
heard his name called.

"Excuse me. Excuse me, uh, Darren?"

Shit, he thought. He just knew it was another client. He was pleasantly surprised when he turned around and saw Karen; Special K, the dancer he met at the barbershop.

"Oh. Hello, how are you?"

A few weeks prior, she called him. She inquired about services and he referred her to another colleague. He would have taken the case himself except for two things: He no longer accepted the lower-income clients, and then there was the fact that she had such an incredible body.

He had forgotten about her. He had forgotten about the day at the barbershop. She remained true to her word and had not been back since to get her son's hair cut. Darren got his hair cut there every week. From time to time, Big Gucci would inquire about her. He'd ask if she called, but she hadn't. Darren chalked it up to perhaps her losing his card, or not being serious to begin with. He forgot about her entirely until a few weeks back.

He was sitting in his office just getting ready to leave when his Administrative Assistant called him to the front lobby. There she was with her son. She wasn't dressed up provocatively. She wore a sundress, glasses, and sandals. She was dressed common, respectable. Her breasts weren't as exposed as they were in the shop. She no longer looked like an exotic dancer who had just gotten off work. She looked like an everyday woman. She looked like a mom.

She showed up unannounced, a definite no-no. Darren hated unannounced visits. He hated surprises. But there she was one day with her son in tow. She was there and she needed help.

Darren interviewed her. She explained, just as he thought, that it wasn't her cousin who needed services.

It was her. She explained that her son had been abused by a man who she thought she could trust. She went to the club one day to dance and left him home with her then boyfriend. Unknown to Karen, the man in question would sometimes slap the boy. One day while she was gone he beat the boy mercilessly. She came home and her boyfriend was gone, but her son was battered and bruised. He obviously left when he realized the damage that he had done. Her heart was broken and so was her faith in men.

She never called the police. That was something that she felt guilty about also. She never called the police because she was afraid that children's services would be called. She was afraid that she would lose her son, the only light in her life. She had the locks changed on her apartment, she stopped dancing for close to a month, and she nursed her son back to health. She rocked him, nurtured him, and gave him children's Tylenol until his wounds were healed. A year later, when she needed to enroll him in kindergarten, it was discovered that her son, Jacob. had a significant hearing loss in his right ear. It was a loss obviously due to the beating at the hands of the boyfriend.

It was a secret that she held for years. It was a guilt that ate away at her each day; guilt for not pressing charges against the man that abused her child. It was guilt over her negligence as a parent. Her son didn't talk much. He wasn't cognitively delayed, but he was withdrawn, as children whom have been traumatized often are. With every day that he was withdrawn, the guilt ate away at Karen. She needed help. They needed help.

A colleague owed Darren a favor. Darren's payment was that he be the one to treat Karen and bill her sessions pro bono. His colleague didn't want to treat her for the same reasons Darren didn't want to treat her. Once you saw a woman in the capacity of counselor, she was off limits to date. Both men wanted her. Karen was a little rough around the edges, but she was attractive. Darren's colleague had been seeing both Karen and her son in individual counseling sessions and saw them together as a family. Her progress had been great, from what Darren had been hearing, and for that he was pleased.

Now she was flagging him down in the parking lot. She approached with a warm smile, an inviting smile. Then her eyes went to the car. He saw the way she looked at his last sports car. Now he had something new for her to see.

Her eyes were practically glued to the new luxury automobile. It was what the white boys called a pussy magnet. Black men called them groupie cars, or a flossin'-ass whip. To Darren, it was a look-at-me car. It was the car's job to attract a woman's attention. It was Darren's job to keep the attention there. He leaned back on the car as Karen walked up to him.

"You got another car?"

"Yeah, I got another car. It was time. I work pretty hard. I had to do something nice for myself."

"This is nice."

"Thank you. How have you been?"

"You know, I've been great. I just came over here because I wanted to thank you for everything that you've done for me and my son. You wouldn't believe how hard it is to get a child seen by a therapist."

"Actually, I would. I always wondered what took you so long to call."

"Ego. Embarrassment. I told the other women at the club that I was thinking about bringing Jacob to a therapist and they all said the same thing."

"Let me guess, black people don't go to counselors. They either go to church or women call their girlfriends. That's what they said, right?"

"You know it."

"Well, I'm glad you stopped listening to them. I'm glad that you got your son the services that he needed. How is he, by the way?"

"He's great."

"And you?"

"I'm great."

"Yeah, well. You seem like it. I'm happy for you."

The chemistry was in the air. Her vibe, however, was admiration whereas his was lust. He looked at her. His eyes traveled her body, caressed her curves. His mind's eye was already playing an adult film in his psyche. She smiled at him, he smiled at her, his slacks began to stiffen, and he controlled his breathing so she would be unaware, but they both were giving off pheromones. They both were undeniably interested. The question was who would address the obvious.

She was thinking to herself that he had a world of potential. He was thinking that she had an incredible rack. Her breasts, which looked like they were ready to pop when he first saw her, were now subdued in the jeans and T-shirt that she was wearing. She wore a cardigan over the T-shirt and her breasts didn't look fake the way she had them dressed up. She looked as if she had nice, natural breasts and a really nice shape for a woman her age. She spoke first.

"Listen, can I get you a cup of coffee or something? I really owe you."

"I tell you what, let me buy you a cup of coffee sometime."

"Okay, when?"

"Where is your son?"

"Today he's with my mother."

"Then today."

She smiled. It was a wonderful smile and a smile a man could get used to.

"Today, when?"

"Right now."

He chirped the car to unlock it and held the door open for her. She smiled again as she stepped in the luxury automobile. Soft music began to play when Darren started his car.

"So where is the best place to get coffee?" she asked.

"Oh, I have a few ideas," Darren said smiling at her. He needed to get Stephanie and Korie off his mind and Karen would prove to be the perfect distraction.

Chapter Sixteen

Korie was blown away as the limo took her and Vaughn to the airport. She had never been out of the country before. She never dreamed she would ever leave the country and here she was heading to Tokyo. The limo headed to O'Hare International Airport, and the whole time she was nervous. Vaughn held her hand and smiled at her reassuringly as they pulled up to the airline gate.

"This is pretty big. I mean, us taking a trip out of the country." She could hardly contain her smile.

"It's just the first of many things to come, sweetheart. I wish I could say that this trip was completely about us, but I have to remind you. I'll be here on business, at least the first day. After that, however, it's you and me and I can't wait to show you everything." He leaned in and kissed her.

"Everything? You mean all of Tokyo?"

"No, sweetheart. I mean the world. I want to show you the world. Given the chance, I think I'd like to give you the world as well."

Vaughn held her hand like he had been her boyfriend for a lifetime. Korie held his hand back and smiled at him. She was still an independent woman, but the way Vaughn treated her, she thought I could really get used to this. Korie blushed. Vaughn smiled. He kissed her again before they exited the limo.

"Okay, so let's do this."

They got out of the car and headed into the airport. No luggage, no checking in. They went straight to the gate and straight to boarding.

It must be nice to be wealthy, Korie thought. Had this been her on a simple trip to Vegas, she would have been lugging around multiple bags. There would have also been an extremely long line for checking in and the hassle of all the checkpoints.

As VIPs, she and Vaughn had two checkpoints: The first gate with the metal detectors and a final one at boarding. It was an incredibly long flight, but flying first class had its privileges, such as full meals rather than the peanuts Korie was used to when she traveled, and movies that were still at the theater. She experienced a level of comfort she didn't think was possible on an airplane. This was especially important since it was a twelve-hour flight.

Upon their arrival to Narita Airport in Tokyo, the first thing that Vaughn did was phone the Japanese to let them know that he had landed. In doing business with the Japanese, it was customary to confirm meetings two hours prior to a meeting.

Upon landing, Vaughn had an estimated two hours before their scheduled meeting. After confirmation, Vaughn and Korie were met by a driver who took them back to the hotel in a Rolls-Royce. Korie had never seen a Rolls-Royce in person, let alone ride in one. She was impressed with the vehicle, although she tried hard not to show it.

It was hard to contain her awe. For Vaughn this was business as usual and he smiled as he looked at Korie. He had to keep reminding himself this was all new to her. He liked watching her look at things in wonderment. It was like watching a child's first Christmas or a child's first major trip. There were many sights and sounds to see and although Korie didn't want to ignore Vaughn, she was practically glued to the window while looking at the sights and sounds of Tokyo.

For Vaughn, he simply seemed to be in a rush to get to the meeting. He periodically checked his watch. He didn't want to offend his clients any further, especially considering he had no explanation as to why they backed out of the deal to begin with. If anything, their backing out pissed him off, but he had to contain his emotions just as Korie tried to contain her excitement.

The Rolls-Royce pulled up to the Tokyo Peninsula, one of the most elegant and impressive hotels in the country. The hotel had an international design, but was in every way Japanese in its conception. The hotel was across the street from the Imperial Palace and just a few short blocks from the shopping capital, the Ginza. Korie was in awe as she stepped out of the Rolls-Royce like an American princess. She stopped and placed her hand to her mouth in awe as she looked up and around 180 degrees. Vaughn looked at her and simply smiled. Again, it was like a kid at Christmas.

"My God, it's beautiful here."

"Yes, it is. It is impressive. But not half as beautiful as you. Come on, let's go."

Korie walked over to Vaughn and took his arm. She was still looking everywhere as they walked toward the hotel entrance. It was like being on a new planet—a beautiful new planet.

"Hold on, Vaughn, can't I just take all this in for a minute?" She stepped back to look at the hotel again from the outside. It was magnificent.

Vaughn laughed and smiled at her before kissing her on the cheek.

"Sweetheart, we can take it all in. As soon as I'm done with my meeting, I plan to show you everything. I promise."

The front lawn of the hotel on the outside looked like aged, flat bedrock with cracks in the cement. From those cracks rose fountains of water. Lighting accented the water that spewed from the ground the same way the light reflected the water at the Bellagio in Las Vegas.

Two Japanese lions guarded the front of the hotel along with two doormen. The doormen were dressed in all white and had warm, welcoming smiles. They both welcomed their guests and they both bowed as Korie and Vaughn entered.

"Welcome back, Mr. Harris," one doorman said. His English was impeccable.

"Thank you."

"Will you need anything while you are here?"

"Uh, no . . . I won't be in need of anything this trip."

"Are you here on business or pleasure?"

Vaughn looked at Korie and smiled.

"Both."

"Very well, if you need me, please do not hesitate to call."

"Thank you, but I'll be fine."

They walked into the foyer and the hotel was adorned with hues of brown and tan as well as Japanese artistry. The chandelier was adorned with what looked like real diamonds, and the lighting from the chandelier was brilliant and breathtaking.

Again Korie was amazed and again Vaughn looked unfazed by the place. He adjusted his tie and nodded to the concierge as they were escorted to their room. Vaughn and Korie were escorted to their elevator where they seemed to ride forever to the top.

The room that they had was absolutely magnificent: glass all the way around, and the king-sized bed in the bedroom area overlooked Tokyo. At first glance, Korie's equilibrium was off, because of the breathtaking view. The bedroom was bigger than Korie's apartment.

While Korie looked in wonderment around the hotel room, Vaughn ordered a tie from room service. When the attendant arrived, Vaughn told the attendant to treat Korie as he would treat him. A few more words were exchanged in whispers and then Vaughn bowed to the man before heading to the door.

"Sweetheart, I have to go. I know this is short notice, but I have a surprise for you in a few minutes. By the time you're done, I should be back."

"Done? Done with what?"

Vaughn stopped short of the door and turned back to Korie and smiled.

"Done with your spa treatments."

"Really?"

"Really." He winked at her. "See you later."

With that, Vaughn was out the door and on his way to meet with the Japanese delegation. He had his game face on and although he was here for both business and pleasure, Korie could tell by the look on his face that business was about to be his primary focus. As he walked out of the door, it seemed that Vaughn was psyching himself up as athletes must do before big games.

Korie walked around the vast room and smiled. This was all so surreal. She thought briefly about what Darren would think if he could see her now. She pulled her camera out of her bag and began to take pictures of everything. She took pictures of the room, the view, and even the Jacuzzi in the bathroom. She had come a long way since being an AA. She had even come a long way in creating her own business. She was just starting to come into her own as a businesswoman and now, not even a year later she was halfway across the globe.

She thought to herself that chances were she would never leave the country again and she wanted pictures of everything. So she continued to snap photos with her camera. A few minutes later, there was a knock at the door.

"Uh, who is it?"

"Room service."

"I didn't order anything."

"Mr. Vaughn did," an Asian voice said.

Korie thought, Wouldn't the spa treatments be downstairs?

She opened the door and there was a team of Asian women and men there to take care of her. Some had towels, others had lotions and oils, and some had manicure and pedicure kits.

"Wow!" Korie said. "So I guess you guys want to come in?"

"No, ma'am. We are here to escort you to your treatment suite."

"My treatment suite?"

"Yes, ma'am."

"What does a treatment suite look like?"

"It has all the same amenities as your room and a few more," one Asian woman said, smiling.

"Well, uh, let's not waste any time. Let's go."

Korie's only regret was that Jayna couldn't see her right now.

This shit is like a fairytale come true. Vaughn keeps this up, I might have to marry him.

She was joking, of course.

Wasn't she?

Chapter Seventeen

Brandon awoke in the middle of the night. He was clearly upset. It was storming outside. Lightning stretched across the Chicago sky. Thunder rolled across the heavens and the winds blew hard outside. Chicago thunderstorms were serious. The television and radio warned that the storm was dangerous and that Chicagoans shouldn't travel unless they absolutely had to.

It was 3:00 A.M. and as the war of the heavens and elements raged outside, Brandon stayed by the window looking out into the storm from his penthouse condo. He was clearly upset about something. The storm seemed to reflect his mood.

In his bed Jayna slept. She looked like a work of art. The cover was off of her and her back was to him. Any other man would be watching her as she slept. Any other man would be running his hands along her curves and kissing her sides. She was a vision of African American beauty. She had amazing curves. In bed her silhouette looked as if he had Beyoncé in his bed.

Her legs were shapely, her hips curvaceous, and her ass ample. Any other man would be in bed with her right now. Any other man would be kissing her hips, her thighs, and her now ripped stomach. Any other man would practically worship this African American beauty.

Any other man. Not Brandon Lloyd.

Brandon had other things on his mind.

***

Jayna slept peacefully. She slept especially peacefully after the passionate lovemaking session that she and
Brandon had. With having stepped up the intensity of
her workouts, she had been warring with Brandon in
the bedroom. Sometimes he would win, sometimes she
would win. Being more fit now than she had ever been
in her life certainly had its advantages.

Since Korie was no longer available, Jayna worked
out with Brandon. He pushed her, he challenged her,
and she met that challenge every step of the way. She
ran with him, competed against him, and even talked
finances with him. In every way she was his equal. In
every way she was his competitor.

Jayna was impressed with Brandon every step of
the way. She was impressed that such a nice-looking
and well-sculpted man like him had the business mind
that he had. It was like he was a man capable of doing
anything he set his mind to. Jayna thought that she was
lucky to have him.

She still couldn't believe that all these months later,
she almost passed up on him because she thought he
was average. He turned out to be so much more than
that. From time to time she wondered what other men
that she thought to be average, had a world of potential. It didn't take long for Jayna to fall in love with
Brandon. He practically captured her heart from the
very beginning.

Brandon enjoyed Jayna's company. He enjoyed her
every conversation and he especially enjoyed her sex.
To him, she had the body of Beyoncé, but in bed she
was a magnificent lover. In bed she reminded him of
the Colombian-born singer Shakira. She was a sensual

lover, a patient lover, and a woman willing to give her all to a man in bed.

Because she slept with him the very first night, Brandon always wondered whom else she gave her secrets to. How many other men had she pleased along the way of finding him? He didn't look for these answers that were burning in his mind, but it seemed that even when you didn't want it to, the truth would find you. He didn't ask the questions, but the answers . . . the answers found him. Because of this, he was upset. It was just one of many things on his mind.

Fidelity and promiscuity, these were the other things that were bothering him as she slept. As one storm waged outside, another war waged in Brandon's heart. In truth, Brandon loved Jayna. She was everything that he was looking for in a woman. She was smart, business savvy, she made her own money, so she wasn't after his, and she challenged him. She challenged him in the bedroom, in the gym, and in business. He had never met a woman capable of being his equal and here she was lying in her bed looking . . . simply . . . perfect.

He turned to face her. He looked at her amazing body, her chocolate-covered skin, and her ample behind. He looked at her long, flowing locks and her shapely legs. He thought, she is so incredibly beautiful. But then there were the things that he found out. They were the things that kept him from giving her his heart. They were things that kept him up this early in the morning and made him mad at the world. He turned his back to her and continued to look out into the storm.

His primary reason for being up was his boss. His thoughts were of his boss and what he might be doing right now. Brandon was concerned about his situation with Jayna, but business was first. Business was always first. Money before the honey, as Vaughn would say.

Each time in the past, if Vaughn took a trip out of the country, that meant Brandon had to leave the country as well. Instead, Vaughn took her. Korie went from being this wonderful woman who captured his mentor's heart, to simply her.

She had become a sore point of conversation. She had become the thing no one in the boardroom wanted to hear about. She had become a distraction that Brandon and the others thought was costing them millions of dollars.

Costing their futures millions of dollars.

Interfering with the college tuitions of grandchildren not even born yet.

She—was a problem.

She had to go.

The board of directors even went as far as to have a meeting without Vaughn about a hostile competitor: Korie Ann Dillon. As far as the board, the shareholders, and high-level executives were concerned, she was a liability.

The company's stock hadn't dropped in ten years, even with the economy. Since the death of his wife, no one ever had to question where Vaughn was. After his wife's death, he threw himself into his work. Over time, he was either in the company of a paid escort or he was at work. Most times, he was at work. He was killing himself at work, pushing himself harder than he ever had when his wife was alive. It was like he was trying to kill himself or trying to join her.

His hard work, his diligence, his obsession with making the company grow, made men rich. It made generations to come wealthy. His drive took the company head and shoulders beyond their competitors. His edge, took the company places that analysts never dreamed the company could go. In ten years, no matter what was going on in the global market, the company's business grew.

Then it happened.

The stock dropped a few points.

Four lousy points.

That four points translated into millions of dollars.

Dollars that could have lined the board's pockets.

Or gone to their wives.

Or their mistresses' rent.

Or their mistresses' implants.

Or their cocaine habits.

Again . . . she was a problem.

Brandon looked on as the storm continued to rage. He watched the winds blow the waves on Lake Michigan, and watched the storm topple some small boats that were anchored below.

Brandon wondered how the meeting was going with the Japanese. He wondered how things were going without him. Not out of insecurity, but concern for his financial portfolio as well. He wondered how much of a distraction she would prove to be on this trip.

He thought about flying out to Tokyo, just showing up. This was not something that you did with DeVaughn Harris. Mr. Harris would see it as an insult. He would see it as a lack of confidence. A lack of confidence was not something he should see from his second in command, his right-hand man. Brandon hated it, but he could do nothing. He waited patiently by the window. He had to let his boss do his thing—alone. Brandon hated that.

He went to a drawer near the window and pulled out a large envelope, looking at the contents. He shook his head in disbelief and replaced the envelope in the drawer. He continued to look outside with his hands in his silk pajama bottoms. Suddenly there was a loud, rolling boom outside.

Thunder had announced its presence to the entire city of Chicago. It was a noise that shook the windows and made car alarms go off with its vibration. It was if God cleared his throat. The noise stirred Jayna from her sleep. She looked to the window where she saw her man standing there with his back to her. She wondered why he wasn't next to her in bed, resting peacefully. She looked on and wondered why Brandon was standing at the window looking out into the tempest.

She looked at his muscular frame. Even with his back to her, he looked magnificent, sculpted. His muscles were prominent in his back and neck. His arms were taut and powerful. He also had a nice ass, which made Jayna smile to herself. She loved this man. She loved the way that he made her feel. Not just in the bedroom, but wherever they were. She enjoyed waking up to him. Sometimes she would wake up and watch him sleep. He was ruggedly handsome and she loved the way he looked when he slept; especially the way he looked when he slept after making love to her.

It had been a long time since she met a man who treated her the way that Brandon did. They walked everywhere hand in hand. He kissed her often and without reason. He held her, hugged her and told her how beautiful she was every day that he was with her. He was her man and she was his woman.

Jayna bedded many men, but few left the impression on her that Brandon had. Few were as patient and as loving as he. No man was his equal in bed. No man, at least, who she had ever experienced. He could make love all night and was endowed well enough to reach places no other man before him had. He touched her as they made love. He held her hands as they made love, and he looked into her eyes when they made love not just with passion and lust, but with admiration. He made her a better woman. She would like to think that she made him a better man.

No man captured her thoughts as he had. No man invaded her dreams or her fantasies as he had. When she was not with him, she thought of him. Nights that he couldn't be with her in her bed when she slept, she often thought of him.

Nights that she spent alone, she thought of him and him alone as she touched herself. She loved his smile, his frame, and his very scent. She sat up and watched him as he looked outside and thought to herself, I want to have this man's babies. Jayna was definitely sprung. She was definitely in love.

"Are you okay?" she asked.

He said nothing. For a full minute he said nothing. She assumed he didn't hear her. She assumed it was the noise of the storm that drowned out her voice, or the storm itself which had his focus. She spoke again.

"Are you okay?"

"I'm fine."

His response was flat, without feeling. He hadn't even turned around to acknowledge her.

"Is something on your mind?"

"I have a lot on my mind, but nothing you need to worry about. Go to sleep, Jayna."

Jayna? He never simply calls me by my name. Usually it's babe or sweetheart. Something's wrong. Something is definitely wrong, she thought.

"Are you sure everything is okay?"

"If it's not okay, it will be."

"Is it something at work?"

Jayna kept probing. She wanted to know what upset the man who brought her such pleasure. Little did she know he was about to bring her equally as much pain.

"Work is only part of the problem."

Again, his response was flat.

"Anything else?"

Silence. At least on their side of the window, things were silent.

"Brandon?"

"Yeah, there's something else, your girlfriend. I think she's too much of a distraction. I think her relationship with DeVaughn is compromising our business."

That made Jayna sit up completely. She didn't like the fact that her man was upset, but she didn't want him blaming her best friend, either.

"A distraction? You mean by being in love?"

"He doesn't love her."

"Oh, I think he does."

Jayna got up and went to the bathroom to pee.

"Then things are worse than I thought."

Jayna didn't like this line of discussion. She didn't like where this conversation was headed.

"Brandon, I don't understand. What's the problem?"

"Jayna, go back to bed."

His voice was flat but stern. It was as if he were trying to warn her to back off without being too harsh with her. On most other women this might have worked. For the average woman who would be glad to have a man such as Brandon, his tone would have definitely silenced them.

Not Jayna.

No man, not even her father, told Jayna what to do. No man would challenge her in any capacity, and she not meet that challenge. His tone put her on the defensive. His tone had her instinctively put her hand on her hip and look at him in a different light.

"Go to bed? What, am I, five years old now?"

Her tone was equal to his. Her tone reminded him that they were equal. Separate, but equal.

"I don't think tonight is the night to discuss your friend."

His voice was just a bit higher than a whisper.

"Okay, then let's not discuss her."

Now Jayna placed both hands on her hips. Her silhouette looked more like Serena Williams before a match than it did Beyoncé.

"Fine."

"But let's do discuss the way you just addressed me," she said with her finger pointing at him.

From where she stood, she could hear the sigh that he let out. She could also see the muscles in his neck and back stiffen. Something was bothering him, something besides his boss's relationship with Korie.

It had been a long time since Jayna found a man who she really cared about. It had been a long time since that care, love, and admiration were reciprocated. She walked over to him, stopping just a few feet before him. He hadn't turned around or acknowledged her. Lightning flashed in the windows and the wind howled outside and still his gaze seemed transfixed on the storm outside and the weather below. She wanted to hold him. She wanted to touch him. She wanted to tell him that whatever made him upset, she could make it right.

That's what she wanted to do.

What she had to do was stand her ground.

What she had to do was make it abundantly clear that he could not simply address her, or talk to her any kind of way. Boundaries needed to be set.

This looked as if they were about to have their first argument. Although she didn't know what they were about to argue about, she knew she needed to make him understand some things. She didn't want to make the mistake that a lot of black women make and let him talk to her any kind of way. That would establish a precedent and a pattern of disrespect. Once a woman started down that path, there was generally no turning back. Jayna loved Brandon, but she would not be disrespected by any man. Not even her man.

"I don't want to talk right now."

He continued to face the storm, but he turned his head to the side as if to acknowledge her. His statement wasn't a request or a plea. It was more of an instruction. It was as if to say, I don't want to talk right now, go away until I do. His tone was dismissive. Again, most women might have waited. Most women might have chosen to fight this battle another day. Jayna thought to herself there was no time better than the present.

"So when do you want to talk about it? Should I schedule an appointment? Or should I simply start in with this first thing in the morning?" She was cynical.

He turned to face her. She was still looking breathtaking. She stood there naked as the day she was born, and she looked flawless. Naked or not, the look on her face said that she was not to be trifled with.

Most men looking at her would have given a moment of pause.

Most men would have taken Jayna back to bed.

Not Brandon. He wanted to. But a man's pride can be a powerful thing.

She would not back down, and neither would he.

"What don't you understand about my not wanting to talk right now?"

"What I don't understand is the way that you just addressed me."

"I don't know what you're talking about."

"Don't you? Your tone, it was dismissive. I'm not your damned concubine or an AA or some groupie. I just want to make sure we're clear on that."

"I never called you any of those things. You're reading too much into this."

"Am I?"

"You are."

"Then tell me what is bothering you."

"Didn't I just say I didn't want to talk about it?"

"That's what your mouth says, but your body is saying something altogether different."

"Oh, you're a damned therapist now?"

"I'm a woman; it's pretty much the same thing."

"No, it's not. Jayna, I have a lot on my mind right now, that's all."

"Then say that. Don't disrespect me."

"Disrespect you? Who the hell is disrespecting you? I have a lot on my mind and I don't want to talk about it right now. I told you that."

"Again, it's not what you said, but how you said it."

"Jayna, I hope this isn't what I have to look forward to each time we have a disagreement."

"It's not, if you come at me the right way."

"Hold up! Come at you the right way, just who the hell do you think you are that I'm supposed to walk on eggshells around you?"

"You don't have to walk on eggshells, Brandon, but like I said, you aren't going to just talk to me any kind of way, either!"

"Look, woman!" He took a step in her direction.

"Look what?" She took a step forward in his direction.

They were just a foot away from one another. Again, he was taken by her. She challenged him. In every way,

she challenged him. In every way, she was his equal.
Even now, with being upset with her, he loved her. The
things he hated most about her, he loved about her as
well. He stood there with fire in his eyes. She stood
there with fire in hers. Brandon was well built and was
a man who could instill fear in other men with just a
glance. With Jayna, she just looked at him as if he were
another mountain to climb, another obstacle in her
way.

She took in his Issey Miyake cologne. He took in her
Delicious by Donna Karan. He looked at her flawless
body, her well-sculpted abs, and her ample hips. She
looked into his dark brown eyes, his smooth skin, and
his ripped midsection. For seconds they stood silent,
watching one another. The storm continued to rage
outside, and there was one brewing in his bedroom.

He wanted her.

She wanted him.

He wanted her more than he had ever wanted anyone.

At that moment, she wanted him more than she had
ever wanted any other man.

"Do we have to do this now?" he asked.

He wasn't rude. He asked. His reasons for asking were
obvious.

"No. We don't have to do this now."

Her tone was almost forgiving.

He walked over to her. He invaded her space. He
looked down and she looked up. They both were poised
like two prizefighters.

"But we will finish this conversation."

"Oh, you can count on it. We will finish this conversation."

"But not now."

"No, baby, not now."

He pulled the drawstring on his silk pajama bottoms. As he did, they dropped to the floor. He stepped out of them and took yet another half step forward. This time he more than invaded her space. They were pelvis to pelvis. His hands explored her backside and her arms reached up and around his neck.

They kissed.

A storm waged outside the bedroom and another waged on the inside.

He picked her up and carried her to the bed. He turned on his iPod and soft music began playing. He laid her down on the bed and began kissing her ever so slowly on her soft lips. Their naked bodies touched. Pelvis to pelvis they felt one another's heat. It took virtually no time for his manhood to ease inside her. Her vaginal opening welcomed him freely. When he entered her, they both let out a sigh. They both exhaled and felt relieved. They both felt each other's passion.

He began with slow, deliberate strokes. She ran her hands alongside his muscles and across his face. She looked deep into his eyes as he glided in and out of her. Her mouth was open as he gently and deliberately hit her spot. She closed her eyes and enjoyed the feel of him. She enjoyed his length, his girth, and the deliberate taps to her cervix.

Muscles flexed throughout her body. Her legs pulled him in further and her vaginal muscles gripped his penis like a farmer grabbing a cow's utters. Her vaginal muscles flexed. Her Kegel exercises came in handy during love play. She held him. She held him with her love, her passion, and her pussy. Her breasts were swollen with passion and her nipples were erect. She enjoyed him. She enjoyed every inch of him.

Their tongues danced with one another. He reached beneath her and grabbed her ass as he forced himself deeper inside of her. She let out a guttural groan and he let out a primitive growl. He went deeper inside of her, deeper than even he had ever gone before. He began fucking her. He fucked her like he was trying to release all his demons in his seed. He fucked her as if he were making a point. He fucked her like he was trying to leave his mark on her forever in the bedroom. Together they rocked and bucked and began to sweat. She matched his intensity blow for blow. Together, as they made love, they looked like a muscular sculpture of two people in a passionate embrace.

The bed rocked. It was a 4,000 dollar bed that had never moved before since Brandon owned it. Tonight it was rocking. Tonight it was being tested. Brandon said things he never said before in bed. He called Jayna's name and said vulgar things in her ear as he penetrated her, things that could only be said in the throes of passion. She said a few things back and together they talked so dirty and so foul that Larry Flynt would have been proud. Two hours later they came. They came and they both collapsed.

Morning came. With the morning came the aftereffects of the storm. Irreparable damage had been done. The storm left its mark on the city and both Brandon and Jayna left their mark on one another. Each had the other's scent on their body. Each was sticky from their night of passion and each seemed to have enjoyed their primitive moment. Still, Jayna couldn't help wondering what had Brandon so distracted.

Brandon got up from their bed of sin and went to the shower. He had a lot on his mind. Part of what was on his mind was contained in the envelope in the drawer of his nightstand. The other issue was about Jayna. He loved her. There was no doubting that. The question was, Could he love a woman like Jayna? He let the warm water cascade over his body. Slowly her scent left his body and went down the drain. All his muscles tensed as he thought about the conversation they would soon have. He knew Jayna. Last night she wanted him just as much as he wanted her. Now that their lust had been quelled, it would just be a matter of time before they began again. It would be just a matter of time before she came and approached him about what was really bothering him last night. He lathered up his body in an effort to wash away his thoughts, his issues. While he stood in silence with water running over him, he exhaled. He knew their next conversation would not be a kind one.

While he contemplated things on the outside, Jayna was in bed thinking about things as well. She loved Brandon, that much was obvious, but what was last night about? She understood finances. She also understood that the company's stock had taken a dip in recent months. It was a decline that coincided with Korie and Vaughn's relationship. The company was still doing well, but to a stockholder any decline in funds would be closely monitored. Jayna wondered if Korie could be distracting Vaughn. If so, those distractions could indeed be costing the company tens of millions of dollars.

Jayna thought to herself that even if that were the case, what went on between Korie and Vaughn needed to stay between Korie and Vaughn. As far as Jayna was concerned, it wasn't her business. It wasn't Brandon's business, either. She understood his concern from a financial standpoint. Personally, however, she didn't see where it was anyone's place to butt in. Besides, what did her friend's relationship have to do with her? Jayna decided that she would not challenge Brandon about her girl. That wasn't her fight. All Jayna needed to know was that everything was okay between her and her man. That was what she decided, and that was what she was going to tell him.

She got out of bed, his scent on her flesh. She made up the bed, got a bottle of water, and then walked to the bathroom. She knocked and then slowly walked in.

She stepped into the shower with him, kissing his back and shoulders and hugging him from behind. Again his muscles flexed. He closed his eyes and took in the scent of last night's session. He turned to her and hugged her, then stepped out of the shower and began to dry off as she began to wash.

She lathered with her favorite scent from Bath & Body Works. She had clothing at his place, toiletries and even a few pair of shoes. She lathered her body up and washed last night's scent off of her. Silence overtook them both. Jayna spoke first.

"So . . . do you want to tell me what was really bothering you last night?"

Brandon closed his eyes as he let out a small sigh and continued to dry off.

"Do I have a choice?" he said almost jokingly.

"We can ignore the elephant in the room or we can tackle it head-on, sweetheart."

Brandon nodded his head in agreement. He put on his boxers and Jayna began to rinse off.

"Okay. Okay. Part of the problem that I have is that your girlfriend has my boss kind of sprung. Under normal circumstances I wouldn't say anything but—"

"But that distraction is costing the company a considerable amount of money."

"Yes."

"Babe, I understand your concern, and I mean no disrespect, but is that really your business?"

Silence overtook the room again. Brandon began to moisturize his body and Jayna turned the water off.

"As one of his chief advisors, yes. Yes, it is. In fact, the board of directors is monitoring my response to the situation."

"I wasn't aware that you had responded to the situation."

Jayna moved the shower curtain back and retrieved a towel to dry off.

"That's just the thing. I haven't. Vaughn is more than my boss and more than my mentor. He's also my friend. He is also not the type of man who you tell what to do or the type of man who you readily challenge. Our friendship, our business relationship is now somehow . . . complicated."

"It's never been complicated before?"

"Not until Korie."

"So no other woman has ever captured his heart like Korie?"

"No woman since his wife."

"Well, as his friend, is that a bad thing?"

"As his friend, no. As his chief advisor it's a problem. A huge problem."

"So what can you do?"

"As his friend, I can just leave him alone and hope for the best, which is what I have been doing. As his advisor, there are provisions where I can ask him to step down from his duties. His contract is very specific in these areas. There are checks and balances. If the company stock reaches a certain point, or if he is somehow deemed negligent in his duties, then he can be asked to step down."

"Step down? For how long?"

"Temporarily . . . indefinitely. It depends on the situation."

"And who would be his successor?"

Again silence took the reigns. It was clear to Jayna whom his successor would be.

"Oh. Wow. That's a lot of pressure, isn't it? It would be you. And you aren't ready to take the helm of the company yet, are you?"

"Oh, I'm ready. I've been ready for some time. Vaughn has been grooming me to be his successor for years now. The thing is, neither of us saw that happening for at least another four of five years."

"Are things really that bad?"

"No, they aren't as bad as the board of directors thinks. But things have changed. The thing that bothers me most about the situation with Vaughn is that he has excluded me from the process. Generally I'm there to provide him with counsel. Whenever he leaves the country, generally I leave the country. When the Japanese backed out of this last deal, Vaughn lost face with the board. When he left to pursue the Japanese, that didn't look good either. Vaughn never chases anybody. He lost additional points with the board when he decided to fly after them rather than have them return to us. When he left without me, the board became concerned. When word got out that he was taking his girlfriend with him on a business trip that could make us millions, he lost the board's respect completely."

"Has he called you?"

"No. And here's the thing. He needs to close this deal. Otherwise the board may just go ahead and appoint me to take over. I want the big chair; I want to run the company, but not this way."

Jayna understood why he was so conflicted and distracted. What she didn't understand was why he couldn't tell her; why he hadn't confided in her.

"You could have told me all this last night."

"I could have. But that was only part of what was on my mind last night."

"There's more? What else is bothering you?"

"Us."

"Us? What about us?"

"I think I love you."

"Okay . . . I know that I love you. Is that a bad thing?"

"You tell me."

"What is that supposed to mean?"

Jayna was completely dry and began to get dressed into her warm-up gear. She assumed she and Brandon were going running this morning. Instead, Brandon sat on the toilet with a towel wrapped around him and his head in his hands.

"Brandon? What's wrong?"

"Did you ever date or sleep with Harold Thomas at the Gideon Group?"

That stunned Jayna into silence. Her heart skipped a beat as the words left Brandon's mouth.

"Uh, I did date him. But—that was before you—and—"

"Did you sleep with Mike Johnson over at P and G?"

Each name hurt Jayna like a dagger. She tried to get angry, but her voice was almost taken away.

"Uh . . . Brandon . . ."

"Cyril Harris at Chase"

"Brandon . . ."

"Charles Gandy at MGM? Fred Michaels at First Chicago, Torrence Koonce at Cardinal, Rodney Harris over at Lasalle Corporation, the DA, an ADA—, hell I think there are another ten or twelve names of affluent Chicagoans that I can go ahead and name. Jayna, did you bed all these men?"

She was speechless. Stunned. She was hurt beyond words and in that moment she felt a lifetime of regret. In that moment only one word could describe her as she had an epiphany. One word summed up her multiple trysts: Whore. Her bottom lip began to quiver.

"Where are you getting this?" she said with tears in her eyes.

"Is it true?"

"Where are you getting this?"

"Is it true!" he snapped.

He stood over her and she slumped to the bathroom floor. Tears streamed from her face.

"Yes," she said in a whisper while her bottom lip continued to tremble. "Yes, it's true."

Tears filled Brandon's eyes. He stormed out of the bathroom and headed to the bedroom. He heard the words that he already knew to be true. He began to get dressed, cursing the whole time.

"Brandon." Jayna's voice was filled with hurt and anguish. "Brandon." The second time that she called him, her voice was almost pleading.

"What?"

"It was before you . . . all of them were before you."

"All of them. Do you hear yourself? All of them? You have slept with just about all of Chicago's most prominent businessmen. What was I, Jayna? The crown jewel?"

"It's not like that. It's really not like that."

"You know what's messed up? You're business-savvy and you're smart, intelligent, and you know your stuff, but this laundry list of men that you have slept with kills your credibility. People that know you know that you made it to where you are on your own merit. Everyone else thinks you whored your way to the top. A lot of people have been making fun of me at my expense for being with you. This is the other thing that was on my mind last night. The board of directors isn't exactly thrilled with me, either. As far as they are concerned, Vaughn has lost his sense of judgment by being with your girlfriend and I look equally as stupid for being with her friend, the whore!"

"Don't talk to me like that! You hear me? Don't you dare talk to me like that!"

"Why not, Jayna? How else should I see you right now? The board of directors thinks that my boss and I have lowered our standards to whore chasing."

"Korie is not a whore. That's my best friend and I would appreciate it if you didn't disrespect her like that. I would appreciate it if you didn't disrespect me like that."

Brandon sat down with his head in his hands again. He was angry. He was furious. He wanted to stop, but he had been holding this information for well over a week now. As much as he wanted to stop, the words continued to flow from him.

"People think that you are loose—a whore—that makes your girlfriend carry the same title by association. Do you have any idea how bad things look?"

"They can't look too bad. It didn't stop you from taking me to bed last night!"

"That's just the thing. That's the one thing that you just don't get."

"What?"

"It looks like my girlfriend is a whore. And what's worse is that I love you. How can I continue to love you? I don't want to. God knows, I want to hate you right now, but I don't. I love everything about you . . . everything but this. Jayna, how could you?"

Tears streamed down Brandon's face.

Tears streamed down Jayna's as well.

"Brandon, baby, we can get through this. I love you. I have never wanted anyone as much as I want you. I want to be with you. I want to have your babies. Brandon, I love you."

She ran to him. She hugged him, she kissed him, and he hugged and kissed her back. Together they embraced for what seemed like an eternity. Then he said something that turned her universe upside down.

"Jayna . . . it's over."

Chapter Eighteen

One hundred business cards.

That is what was expected on each and every trip to Japan. That was the number of cards that Vaughn was always advised to bring with him to Japan. He had been to Japan at least twenty times before. Each time he brought at least one hundred business cards. This was a common courtesy in Japan. Aside from having enough, it was also customary to present each card with two hands. The card had to also be face-side up, with the wording written in Japanese.

I hate these damn rituals, Vaughn thought. How am I supposed to present a card to another man that I can't read myself? Vaughn knew how to present the cards, however. His company logo was on the card, so he knew how to present the card not only face-side up, but right-side up.

Miserable little men. If they paid more attention to their business practices rather than ancient customs, perhaps they wouldn't need my help. Vaughn simmered on the inside. On the outside, however, he smiled, bowed, and he made his way into the Aichi Corporation's boardroom. He was offered tea and other beverages as well as water. Minutes later a team of men came in; all Japanese, all well dressed. Vaughn stood to meet them and bowed to each of them, which was customary in these types of meetings. Mr. Aichi sat across from Vaughn with a pleasant smile on his face.

"You are here alone on this trip?" Mr. Aichi asked.

"I came here alone, yes." Vaughn knew how they felt about women. He knew that saying he was here with his girlfriend would be poor business. Instead of explaining himself, he simply answered Mr. Aichi's question.

"Where is your advisor, if I may ask?"

He meant Brandon. Vaughn went few places without Brandon. It was obvious to the Japanese delegation that Vaughn was like a wise old lion, whereas Brandon was the young lion; the one not afraid to sometimes show his teeth. Vaughn smiled to himself regarding the suggestion. On the inside, he missed Brandon's presence. On the inside, he regretted not bringing his protégé. But what was done was done and the old lion needed to stand alone.

"Regrettably, Mr. Lloyd took ill. He was not able to make this trip. He sends his best regards. He loves Japan and everything that it has to offer."

"I understand. So, Mr. Harris, why have you chosen to come all the way to Japan after it was made clear that we would not be doing business together?"

Straight and to the point. Vaughn liked that. It was how things were done in America and how he preferred things. So he decided to be straightforward as well. Vaughn smiled a pleasant smile, adjusted his tie, and sat forward in his chair to speak with Mr. Aichi and his delegation.

"Mr. Aichi, let me ask you a question."

"By all means, please."

"Have I disrespected your customs?" Vaughn presented his hands in an open fashion. "Have I disrespected you or your culture in any way?"

"No. No, Mr. Harris you have not. Not in any way."

Vaughn shook his head in agreement. He rubbed his hands together and again straightened his tie.

"That's good. That's good. I just wanted to make sure, because I feel like I have been disrespected, and in my culture when black people are disrespected we respond. Respect is an important factor in the African American community and an even bigger factor in business."

Vaughn smiled and then sat back in his chair.

"Respect is a huge component in the Japanese culture as well. I am not sure that I follow you. Where have we been disrespectful?"

Vaughn leaned in again and smiled just a bit. It was a smile meant to put Mr. Aichi at ease, but it was a smile that also hid Vaughn's disdain.

"Well, in my country, if someone decides that they don't want to do business with you, they at least give an explanation as to why."

"As we told you before leaving, we did not think it was in our best interest."

"Yes, yes, that's what you told me. But that is not an explanation. That's what we call in the States PR or BS."

"And you flew all this way for an explanation?" Mr. Aichi's expression was one of concern.

"Yes. That is one of the reasons that I came here. I flew all this way because I think that I am due an explanation."

"And the other reason?"

"The other reason is to prevent you from making a grave mistake that not only will affect your company, but will be a reflection on your culture."

"How do you mean?"

"Well, first things first. I'd like to know why you decided not to do business with me. It's clear that you need my financial backing and it's also clear that other companies have no interest in helping you, but acquiring you. So I'd like to know why you backed out of a deal that would save your company and future generations of your family. I'd like to also remind you that you all sought me out, not the other way around."

"Well, in case you haven't heard, we have found financial backing from the McCullen Group."

"I know about the McCullen Group. I also know that the McCullen Group is having financial problems as well. I also know that working with you is a huge financial risk for both companies."

"Yes. Well, Mr. McCullen has assured me that he can make this deal happen. He has confidence in his ability and that of his subordinates."

"Okay. Okay, that's fine. But that still doesn't explain why you backed out of the deal with me. Shoot straight with me, Mr. Aichi. Why did you back out of the deal?"

When it was obvious that Vaughn had no intention on letting the matter go, Mr. Aichi decided to be honest.

"Fine. Well, we were looking forward to working with you. That is, until your phone call. You stated you needed to take the call. We found out that was not the case. We found out that you put us off for a woman."

"And that is not a good practice."

"No, that is not a good practice."

"I see."

"We have also made note of your recent drop in stock prices and holdings. It was mentioned that this drop, this distraction, coincides with your relationship with the woman that you interrupted our meeting for."

"Is that right?"

"Yes. That's right."

"I see. And because I let a mere woman interfere with my business, you think—"

"We think your judgment at this time is clouded. Had the situation been reversed, the phone call would have waited, even if it was news of a death in the family. The news would have waited."

"So you would rather do business with McCullen."

"We would rather do business with McCullen. He has no distractions."

"I think what you mean to say is that he has no woman."

"Excuse me?"

"What you mean to say is that McCullen has no woman. He does, however, have a man."

"A . . . man?"

"Yes. Oh, you didn't know? He's openly gay. In fact, he is sleeping with his chief financial advisor."

"His chief financial advisor is a man."

"I know. That's what gay means. Same-sex relationships."

Vaughn got up and straightened his tie as he walked to the window of the conference room to overlook the view of Tokyo.

"You know, I have no problem with same-sex relationships. I don't care if a man is straight, gay, or what his religion or color is. I do have a problem with someone thinking that my judgment is off. I also have a problem with having my character questioned."

"Your stocks are down and—"

"My stocks are down as is the Dow; as are the stocks of many other corporations."

"So you are saying that drop along with the timing of your new relationship—"

"Is A, a coincidence and B, not your concern."

" I see. You stated that I was making a grave mistake . . . culturally. If you don't mind, could you please explain that?"

"I can do that. Mr. Aichi, I want to help you. I want to make this deal happen. I am looking forward to helping your business grow and looking to network with you in the future one way or the other."

Vaughn took a seat and faced Mr. Aichi as he spoke. His game face was on and it was clear that he was about to play his hand.

"If you want me to help you, I will. I will loan you the capital that you need to expand your business. We will continue with our deal as outlined in Chicago and we can move forward as equal partners in this new venture."

Vaughn smiled.

"And if I decline?" Mr. Aichi sat with his hands folded.

Vaughn stopped smiling.

"If you decline. That's fine. Aichi? That's a common Japanese name, is it not?"

"It is. It is like the name Johnson in America."

"Hmm. Well, Mr. Aichi, If you decide to go with Mc-Cullen I have a sneaking suspicion that McCullen will go out of business a few weeks afterward, and your stock and theirs will plummet as I acquire you both. And then it won't be an equal partnership. It will be a dictatorship. And unlike most other companies, I won't change the name of the company. It will remain Aichi. Not only will it remain Aichi, but there won't be a Japanese employee left. In fact . . ." Vaughn got up to look out the window again, turning his back to the Japanese.

"In fact, every employee will be a person of color. Your dream of a Japanese business will end up looking like the Harlem Renaissance. In addition, I will buy the biggest sign that money can buy that says Aichi Corporation. The sign will be so big it will outdo the Great

Wall of China. Not only that, but when I say that every employee will be black, I mean there will be sharp-dressed black folk running a Japanese business during the day, and the crew that cleans the place at night will look like clones of Fifty Cent and Snoop Dawg. You do know who Snoop Dawg is, don't you?"

Mr. Aichi nodded with disapproval. It seemed that he was discovering the hard way that the old lion still had some teeth. Mr. Vaughn played his hand and played it well. Mr. Aichi learned the hard way how business was done in Chicago. DeVaughn Harris brought Chicago all the way across the globe to Tokyo, Japan.

"You would do all this . . . just to make a point?"

"Could you excuse everyone for a moment so we can talk one-on-one?"

Mr. Aichi nodded to his staff and ushered them to leave. There was some dialogue back and forth in Japanese with his chief advisor, but then Mr. Aichi ushered him out with a harsh Japanese tone. Whatever he said was enough to silence his advisor, who simply bowed and excused himself. The two men sat down across from one another. They were about to talk man-to-man. Vaughn spoke first.

"I would do all this because you disrespected me. You disrespected me in front of my colleagues, my staff, and most importantly you disrespected my woman. In the African American community there are three things that you don't mess with when it comes to black men: Their money, their car, and their woman. Now, I can get another car. Hell, I can buy a fleet of them. But pulling out of this deal messed with my money. As far as these concerns with my woman go, a good woman is hard to find. I found one. In fact, I love her. In fact, she is, if anything, my partner, so disrespecting her means that you're disrespecting me. Now you have two choices: We go with the deal we had on the table in Chicago, or I put a whole new deal on the table and put all my resources behind taking over your meager company."

"You would embarrass me like that?"

"I'll open a chicken-and-fish joint right next to this mothafucka. The first International Chicken Shack will be right next door to Aichi headquarters. I'll have this whole area smelling like hair-care products and fried foods."

The silence and tension between the two men was incredible. Vaughn showed Mr. Aichi why he was the king of the jungle, so to speak.

"How do I know that you will not try to acquire my company at a later date?"

"Because of the contract that we drew up. I brought a copy with me. You can have your lawyers proof it and we can sign it in the next hour. Do we have a deal?"

"This seems so . . . wrong. So coerced."

"This is how things are done in America all the time. This is how things are done in Chicago. It's not personal. It's business."

"I will have my people look at the contract. You will have your answer in the next hour."

"Thank you." Vaughn stood up and bowed. Mr. Aichi had an unpleasant look on his face. But he bowed as well. He called his advisors and proceeded to leave the room.

"Mr Aichi? One last question."

"Yes?"

"Who told you about my relationship with the woman? How did you know that that was my girlfriend on the phone that day?"

"American women. They gossip. After our deal was done and when we were waiting for you outside the conference room, we overheard the women talking about it. They assumed we didn't speak English. They said many things about you. The chief thing that they said was that you were—how do you say? Sprung. They said something about you having your nose open, not acting your age, and the last term had something to do with disrupting a cradle."

"I'm sure the term is robbing the cradle. Well, I apologize. And I thank you."

Mr. Aichi bowed and then left to take the contract to his advisors. Vaughn glanced out of the huge window and looked out on Japan.

Then he called Brandon.

"Hey man, what's going on? Yeah. I know it's late. Listen, the Aichi deal is done. We're signing the papers now. I want to meet with the board when I return. When? I'm thinking a week from today. That's fine. I should have brought you here with me. The next time that I try to leave the country I need you to insist on going. Yeah, I know. I know I can be stubborn at times, but that's why I need you. You're my right-hand and I appreciate your counsel. Okay, man . . . cool. Well, listen, I gotta go. I will see you in a week. Hold things down for me till I get back." Vaughn laughed. "All right, then. Oh, one more thing, fire Carmen and Loretta. I'll explain when I get back."

When Vaughn returned to the hotel, Korie had been pampered like she had never been before in her life. She had a manicure, pedicure, and a massage. She ordered room service, purchased a dress from one of the hotel galleries, and even picked out food for Vaughn. By the time he returned, she was dressed in silk pj's and sleeping like a baby on the bed. The flight had been long and she had jet lag. She left him a note saying to wake her when he returned. Instead, he smiled at the vision of loveliness that she was. Vaughn crawled into bed with her and turned off his cell phone before going to sleep. It was one of the best sleeps either of them had in weeks.

Over the next week, Korie saw all there was to see of Tokyo. Vaughn had been there many times but saw little of the magnificent place, short of its business district and its escorts. When Vaughn usually saw Tokyo it was a combination of business and pleasure, but neither was ever very far from the hotel where he stayed. While he had Korie with him, he decided to see all there was to see of the magnificent city.

Korie was like Alice in Wonderland or Dorothy in Oz. She was in constant amazement at how beautiful and magnificent Tokyo was. It had the bright lights of New York. It was a city rich in culture and also rich in tradition.

One afternoon they saw a baseball game and a sumo-wrestling match, all in the same day. They walked hand in hand in the downtown area while eating, shopping, and seeing all the sights there were to see. They saw an ancient Bunraku puppet theater, and also saw an anime film that same night. They frequented karaoke bars, shopping districts of which there were many, and they even went on a romantic walk on the secluded northern island of Hokkaido. It was a beautiful island paradise reminiscent of Oahu, of the Hawaiian Islands.

Each day was a new adventure. Each day brought a promising new thing that few people even dreamed about, let alone dared to do. Vaughn promised to show Korie the world and he started with Japan.

Their week in Japan turned into eleven days. There was just so much to see that they couldn't leave. They saw the sights by day, made love well into the night, and got to know one another on a whole new level. They saw Tokyo's Imperial Palace, with its grand walls, moats, and most of the imperial grounds that were open to the public and even a few that were not.

They saw Kokyo Garden, Mount Fuji, Hakone National Park, and the Sumo tournament known as Hatsu Basho. They watched fire-walking at the foot of Mount Takao and they even watched a 1400-year-old ritual of Yamabushi monks meditating in the mountain region. With everything that they did, Korie took pictures.

They went to the village theater in Kyoto, and they had a somber visit to Genbaku Dome, the only surviving structure from the bombing at Hiroshima. All these years later, you could see images of people that died and the exact place where they died as the world's first atomic bomb was launched. All these years later, there were still outlines of the dead. Being there was reminiscent of being at Ground Zero in New York after 9/11.

Their last days there were also full of adventure. They visited Hokkaido one last time because it was so beautiful, so serene and so secluded from the rest of the world. It had a dense forest and an unspoiled wilderness at its national park, also known as Daisetsuzan. Korie commented that the place was so beautiful that she wouldn't mind one day returning there to be married. On their last day in Japan they went to a Kodo drum festival and went bike riding in the Tono Valley.

That last evening in Tokyo they had dinner at Aragawa, the most expensive restaurant in Tokyo. The eatery was in the basement of a business building in the Shinbashi business district. It was a small and humble place, but it was also elegant, romantic, and truly a spot for only the country's elite. They specialized in Kobe beef, which Korie never had before. They also had an amazing wine list.

Korie and Vaughn had an elegant dinner and as they waited for dessert, she excused herself and went to the restroom. She relieved herself and was re-applying her makeup when a beautiful Japanese woman walked into the restroom. She looked like the Japanese model Miri Hanai.

She had a small frame, was top heavy, and her make-up was flawless. She wore a nice black formal, Manolo Blahniks, and flawless diamond earrings. She looked like a supermodel or a real-life model for an anime production. She stood next to Korie in the restroom and retouched her makeup.

Korie had seen the woman in the dining area. She was with an older Japanese gentleman in the rear of the restaurant. She was very pretty and Korie wondered if the man she was with was her father or grandfather. She smiled at Korie before speaking. Her English was okay, but very heavy with a Japanese accent.

"You are very pretty."

"Thank you. You look amazing yourself. I love your earrings."

"Thank you. Which a-gen-see are you with?"

"Agency? I'm sorry, what do you mean?"

"You are with Dee-Vawn-Har-iss, right?"

"Oh, DeVaughn . . . yes. Yes, I'm with him. But I'm not with an agency."

"Not with an a-gen-see?"

"No. No, I'm not one of his clients. I'm his girlfriend."

The Japanese woman's expression changed.

"Girlfriend?"

"Yes. He's my boyfriend."

A few seconds later, a few more women came in. Two were Asian and the other was white. They were all equally beautiful. Their makeup was flawless and they each had on formals or form-fitting dresses and heels.

The white woman went to the bathroom. The two Asian women engaged the first Asian woman in conversation. One of the two new women asked Korie the same question. This one spoke better English.

"You are not with an agency."

"Uh . . . no."

"And Mr. Harris is your boyfriend?"

"Yeah, is there a problem?" Korie assumed they had a problem with her and Vaughn's obvious age difference.

"*Okinoduku*," one woman said. [too bad]

"*Kurombo*" another said. [negroid]

"*Baka-mitau!*"[that's stupid]

"*Kyapi kyapi gyaru.*" [bimbo]

"*Busu!*" [ugly]

" *Gaijin Kono ama!*"[foreign bitch]

On and on they went. Between speaking they laughed as they applied their makeup. Korie assumed the women thought her relationship with Vaughn was disgusting, but then it dawned on her that the first woman was with a man who was at least Vaughn's age. She definitely thought he must have been related to her. Korie knew what ridicule sounded like, but did her best to ignore it. She pretended she was back home in the States; she pretended these Asian women were no different than Hispanic women who start a conversation in English and then switch to Spanish.

Just because they were speaking in Japanese didn't mean they were talking about her, but the looks they were giving showed that they were. Korie didn't know that many of them had been to bed with Vaughn before. She didn't know that they were employees of the Elite Escorts Japanese office. She had no idea that once upon a time, Vaughn bedded women all around the world.

Just as Korie started to confront the Asian women, the toilet flushed and the white woman surfaced. She began washing her hands and in the middle of the Asian women bantering, the white woman scolded them.

"*Yamete yo! Dame yo! Nande sonna koto shita no? Hottoke yo! Muko ni itte yo. Bako amas!*" [Stop it! You shouldn't do that! Why would you say such things, leave her alone. Get out of here, you stupid bitches.]

The Asian women stopped their tirade. They each looked at the white woman, who was short and curvy. The white woman was built like a black woman. She had legs like Serena Williams and a butt that reminded Korie of Jayna's backside. She also had implants. She was thick in all the right places and ripped in all the right places as well.

The white woman gave the Asian women a look as if she were from the hood, and that was enough to make them stand down. Korie was impressed with how the white woman was built and equally impressed with the fact that she spoke Japanese. Korie didn't know what was being said, but she knew at that point the Asian women were clearly jealous of her and clearly talking about her. Korie was ready to fight if she had to, but the Asian women made a hasty retreat. The white woman then started doing her makeup.

"They were talking about me, weren't they?" Korie asked.

"Yes, they were."

"What were they saying?"

"Among other things, they were saying that you are a foreigner."

"Okay. But I'm guessing that's not the worst thing that they said."

"No, no it's not."

"Do you mind sharing?"

"Sorry sister girl, it's not my place to say."

"Then why come to my defense?"

"The shit they were saying was out of order. And you're American."

"Well, thank you. My name is Korie."

"Korie, my name is Tenae." She pronounced it Ten-ay.

"Nice to meet you."

"Same here. Are you really Vaughn's girlfriend?"

"What is so hard to believe about that? Do I look that bad?"

"No, no you don't. No offense, you're a pretty woman, but Vaughn—I mean, Mr. Harris—travels the world with women who are taller, slimmer, and who have quite a few more artificial parts. He's sort of a playboy and again, no offense, but you seem . . . well, average, pretty, but average."

"What's that supposed to mean?"

"Just that you're not a model or a celebrity. In fact, I'm betting you have a job, don't you?"

"Of course I do."

"Amazing. Well, like I said, no offense, but usually Vaughn—I mean, Mr. Harris—dates women who are looking to be kept. You look like an independent woman."

"I am."

"Well, good for you. I love it."

Tenae laughed a bit and then headed toward the door. Korie was lost, confused, and obviously felt out of her league. Her self-esteem had taken a major blow and she was not feeling very good about herself. Before Tenae left, Korie asked her a question.

"Tenae?"

"Yes?"

"What did they mean by asking me if I were with an agency?"

"Not my place to say, Korie. Not my place to say."

Korie exhaled as she tried to take in all that just happened. When she surfaced from the bathroom, the Asian women had rejoined the men they were with, and none of them made eye contact with her. Tenae walked by Vaughn and to the man she was with, a professional basketball player who was in Tokyo for a preseason game. Korie sat down, still confused about everything that just happened.

"You ready for dessert?" Vaughn asked.

"Actually, I'm ready to go home."

"Okay, sweetheart, then let's go." Vaughn smiled at Korie and kissed her reassuringly as they left. That put Korie at ease—some.

But now her radar was up.

Her women's intuition was telling her something was wrong.

Her spirit told her that there was more to the bathroom incident.

Her heart told her to let it go.

By the time Korie left, she knew more about the history of Japan than she did Chicago. When she returned the first thing that she wanted to do was tell Jayna everything. Vaughn gave her a trip with memories that would last a lifetime. There was much more to see, but Korie saw all that she could see in the time that she was there. Vaughn needed to get back to work. He needed to make some things clear to his board of directors. He needed to show everyone that he wasn't losing his edge. His priorities had changed. He wasn't losing his competitive nature, he was simply in love. Before meeting with his board of directors, however, he wanted to meet again with his therapist. He sent a text message to Darren the minute he touched down in Chicago asking to meet with him that following weekend on the golf course. He also thought that his therapist should meet the new lady in his life.

Chapter Nineteen

Darren awoke with Karen beside him. She was nicknamed properly with the moniker Special K. She definitely had skills. Her breasts, though fake, were flawless. Her ass was flawless. Her weave was impeccable. To top all that off, she had amazing skills in bed. She knew how to move her body. She knew how to give herself to a man.

She was almost as good as Stephanie, almost as good as Korie. She had a few major flaws, however, none of them aesthetic. She was uneducated and she needed to step her vocabulary up immensely. She also had a tendency to swear a lot. Darren talked to her about the way she spoke, the ways she presented herself. She tried to curb her language. But just like a person with Tourette's, sometimes things just blurted out.

"That shit was fucking amazing," she said as she climbed on top of him.

Case in point.

"You know, it was amazing. I don't know if you have to say fucking amazing, but it was good. You were incredible."

"Oh, that's right, you don't like it when I swear."

"No, I don't, but do you, sweetheart."

"Hmm. Maybe I will just do you."

She went down on him. He let out a sigh of pleasure as she began pleasing him yet again. She had an amazing appetite for sex and she also had amazing skills. As she pleased him, he grabbed a fistful of her hair to assist her. His breathing became rapid and his eyes closed. As his eyes closed he imagined that it was Korie pleasing him. The more he thought about Korie the more aroused he became. The more he thought about her smile, her body, and her personality, the more he missed her, even now. Even with another woman between his legs, he thought about Korie. He thought about the first time that they made love and every single time after that. He thought about the times that he "won" in the bedroom, the times she "won," and times that they went at it like two porn stars.

He thought about his ex. It angered him, but he thought about her still. Minutes later he was coming. As he came, Karen, aka Special K, continued doing her special thing.

"Wow, I bet you didn't know a sistah had skills like that, huh?"

"Again, you were amazing," Darren responded.

You didn't do anything. It was my ex. It was all my ex, all these years later, he thought.

"So I guess we're done, huh?" Karen said with a devilish grin.

"Uh . . . no. We're far from done," Darren said, smiling.

He climbed on top of her and began planting kisses all over her body. He then reached for a condom and made his way inside of her. She let out a gasp as did he, as he slowly began to go in and out of her.

She thought he was amazing. Intelligent, fit, attractive and paid.

He thought she was a beautiful woman with good bedroom skills.

She looked at him with lust and wanting. As they made love, she wondered if he could be a male figure for her son. She wondered how far things could go. She wondered if they would have a long-term relationship, great sex like they were having now, and perhaps one day, babies.

His eyes were closed and he was enjoying the sex, his mind somewhere else. His mind with someone else. With each stroke, he thought of Korie. He occasionally looked at Karen and her beautiful body. That helped him maintain his erection, but as he thought of her, as he thought of Korie, he took his lovemaking to a new level.

He turned Karen over and took her from the back, gently caressing her back while he was inside her and occasionally grabbing a fistful of her 2,000-dollar weave. He slapped her ass from behind. He kissed her neck. He fondled her breasts and he took methodic slow strokes when he felt himself on the brink. They switched positions at least four more times before they both came simultaneously. They laid in the bed in each other's arms. Her back was to him and she smiled to herself as he caressed her side. It had been a long time since a man made her feel as Darren had. It had been a long time since she felt pleased mentally as well as physically.

"What am I going to do with you?" she said, smiling "You make me feel so good."

Darren said nothing, but continued to caress her. He then looked up at the ceiling and wondered, What am I going to do with you? That is the real question. She was beautiful, but she wasn't Korie. She had a great body, but she wasn't Korie. He thought to himself that he could grow to love her . . . maybe. But he knew Korie still had his heart. He grabbed his cell phone and went to the bathroom as if he were cleaning himself up. He sent a text message.

I REALLY WANT TO SEE YOU.

-D

He cleaned himself up some. He brushed his teeth and ran a quick shower. He locked the bathroom door so Karen couldn't just readily walk in, looking for yet another bout of sex. A few minutes later, he received a text.

I SAID . . . NO.

-K

What the hell is up with her? he thought. He lathered himself up and quickly rinsed off. He then dried off, left the water running, and sat on the toilet seat to think.

He felt rejected yet again. He wanted to see Korie. He needed to see Korie. If nothing else, he needed to get closure or to get her out of his system so he could move forward. Was she married? Was she seeing someone? Had she gotten fat and had a bunch of babies? He needed to know. He thought about simply showing up to the apartment they once shared, but did she still even live there?

A million thoughts ran through his head about her, mistakes he made, and where he might have gone wrong. Korie had him sprung, and they hadn't seen each other in close to five years. Just as Darren thought about calling her directly, there was a knock at the bathroom door.

"I have to piss," Karen said.

Crass . . . this broad is so crass, he thought.

"You mean you have to pee?" Darren shouted.

"Um, yeah."

He grabbed his phone and put it on silent. He then turned on the security code and turned his cell off and placed it on the bathroom shelf. He opened the door and stepped back into the shower. Karen came in, looking good. That gave him a moment of pause. She looked so good that he felt his manhood pulse just a bit. She looked down and saw that he was almost ready to go again and smiled.

"Dang, does it ever stop?" She put the toilet seat down, sat down and went to the bathroom.

Crass, he thought. She's already comfortable enough to pee around me.

"You do that to me. He likes you," Darren said, referring to his penis. He closed the shower and simply let the water rinse him off again. He could hear the trickle of Karen peeing.

"So what was up between you and Gucci, really?"

"You sure you want to talk about that?"

"Uh, yeah. Why not?"

"Because of us."

Us? What us? We just had sex. That's all. Why must women assume things? he thought.

"I want to know," he said.

"Well, I knew Gucci when he was still playing basketball. I used to go to the games all the time and one day I saw him while I was with my girls and he asked me out."

"Okay, and?"

"And we went out a few times. I slept with him a few times, but nothing more ever happened. The only time he called me was when he wanted some ass. Well, I wasn't about to just be his ho and I told him that. Then we went out a few more times and our relationship was nice, really nice. Back then he was caring. He started calling more and he used to send me nice gifts and stuff."

"So what happened? Why do the two of you argue like Ike and Tina?"

"You mean Bobby and Whitney." They both laughed. "Well, Gucci never asked me what I did for a living. I never told him, either. We were kicking it this one night, I will never forget; it was a Thursday. Well, he said he was flying back to Philly, so we said our good-byes and I thought he went to the airport. I went to work."

"And what happened next?"

"He saw me on stage at the club. He saw me getting my paper and I guess his heart was broken after that."

"He didn't know at all? I mean, he had no clue?"

"None. His boys brought him there before they went back to Philly. His boys knew, I guess. They clowned him because he had real feelings for me. You know how you men get about your pride and shit. He started cursing at me and calling me everything but a child of God. He threw money in my face and walked out. We talked a few times on the phone after that. But each time ended up with him calling me a ho. I don't play that shit."

"So you all broke up?"

"Yeah, we broke up. A few years after that, he blew out his knee. To support him, I started bringing my son to the shop."

Darren cut off the water and dried off.

"Can you start the water again for me?"

Darren started the shower again as Karen brushed her teeth.

"Let me ask you something. If he asked you to leave that life, would you?"

"If he made enough to support me. I have a mouth to feed at home."

"But if he did, you would have left the life?"

"Yeah. I don't do this shit because I want to. I do it because I have to."

"Okay, then, what's the plan?"

"Plan, what plan?"

"You can't do this forever. You have a nice body and the implants are amazing, but you can't do this forever. What is your plan, long-term?"

"Are you asking me to leave the life?"

Darren laughed. "Uh, no. I'm asking you what are your plans for your future and your son's future."

"I've saved away a little money."

"And what was the plan? Real estate? Are you going back to school? Seriously, what do you plan to do with the money? How much do you have saved?"

"I don't know you well enough to tell you all that."

Are you fucking kidding me? You slept with me on the first date, and you just pissed in front of me! Darren thought.

"I was just asking," he said.

"I have about fourteen thousand saved."

"Not bad. So what was the plan?"

"I never really had a plan other than saving money."

"Really?"

Karen's voice trailed off as she stepped into the shower.

"I always thought some man would take care of me."

At least she's honest, Darren thought.

"Because you're pretty?"

"Because I'm pretty and I have these implants. Hell, I'm a nice woman, I know I am."

"I'm not disputing that."

"Then why do you sound so disappointed?"

"I don't know that I'm disappointed, so much as I'm surprised. I mean, you're pretty. You have a nice body. But that doesn't guarantee anything."

"Yeah, I'm starting to see that."

Karen continued to shower. Darren admired her from the shower. He wasn't thrilled that she and Gucci had slept together, but that was a discussion for another day. His thoughts were about Korie and then about Stephanie. To hell with them both, he thought. Stephanie was a ho hands down, and Korie? Korie probably was sitting somewhere fat as hell with a bunch of babies. Karen? Well, Karen was here. She was real. She was a bit rough around the edges, but he began to see her in a different light. He thought to himself that maybe they should try and see where things might go. That didn't mean marriage or that he would be her steady boyfriend or anything. He did think, let's see where this might go.

He turned his cell phone back on and headed to the master bedroom to lay out his clothes. As he turned his cell phone back on, he had a message. It was from Vaughn, inviting him to the black creativity ball. Vaughn was sponsoring it this year and it was being held at the Field Museum of Natural History in six weeks. It was a fund-raiser where a lot of Chicago's African American elite hung out each year. Deals and connections were made, and it was a great place for Darren to expand his practice. He called Vaughn immediately.

"Hello?" Vaughn answered.

"Vaughn, it's Darren, I got your message. I'll be there."

"Good. Good. I have a lot of people that I think you should meet."

"Great! Great. How was Tokyo?"

"It was amazing. I closed the deal. I'm heading to a meeting now with my board of directors. Sorry I had to cancel our meeting. I initially wanted to meet with you the minute that I touched down, but I had to bring my chief advisor up to speed on everything. Anyway, I'm headed to the office. I plan to fire a few people on my board of directors and remind the remainder who the boss of the company is."

"Are you firing them because they are incompetent or firing them because you are pissed off?" Darren went right into clinical mode.

"Probably the latter. But I can do that."

"But is it the right thing to do?"

"Sometimes in business, Darren, there is no right or wrong. It's just business."

"This sounds personal, though."

"Yeah, well, sometimes contrary to popular belief, business can become personal. At least on my level it can."

"Okay, well, if you are sure about this."

"Yeah, I'm sure. Besides, I didn't become me by second-guessing myself. I called you to invite you to the party and maybe a game of golf, not an impromptu session."

Both men laughed.

"Okay, then. I guess I will see you there."

"Looking forward to it."

"Okay, thanks, man."

Business, it seemed, was looking up. Darren smiled to himself at the endless possibilities. Just then Karen stepped out into the bedroom naked. She smiled at him and he smiled at her.

"So what's next?" she asked.

"I was thinking we should hit the gym."

"The gym? Okay."

"Or . . ."

"Or what?"

"Come here."

They kissed. He grabbed her ample behind and they kissed for minutes on end. He went to retrieve a condom and smiled to himself while looking at the vision of loveliness in front of him. He decided to pause and ask her a question.

"If I wanted to take you somewhere where you had to dress up, would you let me buy the dress?"

"Hell, yeah!"

"And could you refrain from swearing the whole night?"

"Um, yes. I think I could do that."

"Then I think we should go shopping later . . . after."

"After what?"

"Come here and find out."

They didn't make it to the gym or the mall that day. They had six weeks until the ball, so they had time.

Chapter Twenty

Over the next four weeks Karen curbed her swearing and Darren took her to places she had never been before. Karen had breast implants that cost several thousand dollars, a 2,000-dollar weave, and she still shopped at cheap bargain stores. Her idea of fine dining was the neighborhood chain restaurant.

Over the next four weeks, Darren showed her a whole new world. They ate at the finer restaurants, they went to Six Flags Great America, and to all the Chicago museums. They hit a few plays, concerts, and movies. She was still a bit rough around the edges, but she was real.

He never asked her to stop working at the club. He wasn't feeling her like that yet. But the more they went out, the fewer days she worked. It got to a point where her self-esteem elevated to a point that she didn't want that life anymore. She applied for regular jobs, but no one was calling. The places that did call weren't offering enough money. The fact that she even considered leaving the club, however, spoke volumes about her character. It spoke volumes of the woman she was now aspiring to be.

Darren offered her money from time to time, but she declined. Karen didn't want to be dependent upon him. She made her paper, but she also looked into bettering herself. When it was obvious that she couldn't get the job she wanted, she looked at possibly going to City College during the day. She decided that she would major in business.

More and more Karen began to look like a celebrity. Dating Darren elevated her from makeup at drugstores to M·A·C makeup. She went from beauty salons in the hood or someone's basement, to beauty salons downtown. She even got her son's hair cut at the same places that she went.

Darren took her to see a licensed cosmetologist who gave her tips on hair care, makeup, and skin care. Shortly after that, Karen saw a dietician, a personal trainer, and she began jogging. They each took better care of themselves and for Karen, many of the things that she did were lifestyle changes. They were changes for the better. Just as he did with Korie, Darren tried to show Karen that there was more to the world than the simple things that they knew.

Over the next few weeks Karen became Darren's new project. Initially, he thought she would just be something to do, but the more he became involved, the more he liked her. Again, she was rough around the edges, but she was real. What he thought they were beginning to have was real.

They were a couple. Darren came to like Karen a lot, and she quickly fell in love with him. Darren had to admit they looked good together. After a few shopping sprees, personal training sessions, and a makeover, Karen went from being this cute woman who looked like a stripper or porn star, to a woman who could model for a magazine.

With each change that Karen made, people around her began to see her not for who she was, but who she had the potential to be. Men hit on her before, but now that she was turning her life around, more professional men took notice of her. Even at the club she began to see bigger tips, just by waiting on men and giving them a few minutes of conversation. The tips were still nothing compared to the money she would have made doing lap dances, but the money was enough for her to get by. At this point she was just waitressing.

Karen began using better skin care products. She began using skin care renewal and new moisturizers. She learned to take a soft toothbrush and brush her lips, to exfoliate them to make them softer. She learned other beauty tips such as using concealer for the not so obvious blemishes in her skin. She even decided to lose the weave and work on her own natural hair and take better care of it so it would grow. To help it grow, she had her natural hair braided.

Friends of Darren suggested that she see a dermatologist. Many of these women were the wives of prominent Chicago businessmen, and they too once walked the path that Karen walked. They too were at one point at a crossroads where they wanted to look their absolute best, only for them money was no object because of the men they dated. Karen listened to their advice and took everything to heart to look better for Darren.

She was told that a dermatologist could look at her scalp and help with treatment and advice on hair-care growth. Karen learned that fungus on the scalp is a common problem with women of color, which can cause dryness, flaking, and shedding. She learned that this is a common reason that some black women with long hair can cut it, and the hair seems to never grow back. She began taking better care of her hair and scalp and also bought high-end conditioners and shampoos. It became obvious to her that men love a woman with a long mane and Darren was no exception.

Karen took exceptional care of herself and Darren took her to places she had never been before. They saw The Color Purple starring Fantasia, they saw Lyfe Jennings and Common in concert, and they even went to the gospel fest in downtown Chicago. Karen began reading more; she became more and more interested in world events as she progressed in school, and although the topic never came up, she wondered what it would be like to be married to a man like Darren. She knew that she shouldn't even consider such a thing because it had only been a short time since she began seeing him, but she wondered exactly how far things could go. She also wondered what kind of father or father figure he would be. Shortly after that, she stopped taking her birth control.

Chapter Twenty-one

Darren and Karen quickly became an item. What was supposed to just be a physical affair turned into much more than either anticipated. Darren figured that he was rebounding whereas Karen felt she found the real deal. They had pretty good physical chemistry, they looked good together, and more than anything else Darren wanted to expose Karen to new things and she wanted to experience them. The longer they dated, the better she became as a woman. She went from dancing at the club to serving drinks and although it didn't pay as much money, she was happy. For the first time in a long time, she was happy.

Karen reconnected with her mother. When her mother found out that she was going back to school and doing her best to leave the club entirely, she was more than willing to offer her help. She was more than willing to babysit Jacob, her grandson, more often. Generally when asked to babysit there was always some feedback. Now that her mother saw she was trying to change her life, she didn't hesitate to help.

Darren wasn't sure if he was ready to be a father or a father figure, but he did know that Jacob needed support, and he did his best to shape Karen into the woman that she needed to be to support her son.

Darren explained to Karen that it was not wise for him to meet her son. Karen explained that she and Jacob were a package deal. Darren explained that was fine, but also explained that a woman should not have any and everyone around her child unless she was sure the relationship was serious. After a few weeks, Darren and Karen had yet to define exactly what it was that they were doing. They had dinner, dates, a host of fun and a lot of sex, but nothing was definitive yet.

Upon returning to the United States, one of the first things that Vaughn did was phone Darren and tell him how well things went in Japan. Securing the deal with the Japanese eased the anxiety of his shareholders, and Vaughn felt like he was back on top of the world. He asked Darren to meet him at the golf club so they could hang out. Darren assumed it was an impromptu session where Vaughn was perhaps seeking validation. It seems that Darren's office had been replaced with the golf course or Vaughn's home.

Vaughn and Darren met on the golf course. Vaughn was a powerful man with great responsibilities. By the same token, he was enjoying himself. He was enjoying being in love; although he wondered at what cost. The two men met on the course and discussed the millionaires' life over drinks.

"So how have things been?" Darren asked.

"Good. Good." Vaughn nodded with approval as he drove his first ball.

"Hmn. Well, they can't be too good."

"Why do you say that?"

"Because we're out here. What's on your mind, Vaughn?"

"Love. Love is what's on my mind."

Laughing, Darren asked, "What's wrong with love?"

Darren hit the ball and drove it quite a few yards.

"There's nothing wrong with it. At least, not on my end."

"But you're worried about your shareholders and board of directors."

"Yeah, I am. I mean, I love my woman. She is . . . what can I say? She's amazing. She makes me smile and she makes me feel alive again."

"Then again, my question is still the same. What's wrong with that?"

"My subordinates. They make me feel guilty."

"Guilty, why?"

"Money. It all revolves around money. I can admit that I'm distracted. I'm on top of my game, however. I mean, the company makes money hand over fist."

"Then, what's the problem?"

"I could be making much more than I'm making now. I know this, and my board of directors knows this. So do my shareholders. I closed a deal the other day for a hundred million dollars for the company. I could have closed it for a hundred and ten million."

"I'm not sure that I understand. I mean, what's ten million dollars to a billion-dollar corporation?"

"That's just the thing, Darren. Rich people are like drug dealers."

Vaughn hit his ball and drove it just as far as Darren drove his.

"How so?"

The two men walked to the next hole with two caddies in tow. They stopped where their balls landed and Vaughn began to explain.

"A major drug dealer in the hood will kill you over twenty dollars. In the end, twenty dollars means nothing to the dealer financially, but it's the principle of the thing. Wealthy men became wealthy by watching every dime, by watching every nickel. The difference to some of the men on my board is no different than that of a drug dealer on any corner in the ghetto. Closing that deal for a hundred million when it could have been a hundred and ten million means the same to my board of directors as if I could have given them each ten million dollars, as if I had taken ten million dollars from them. What if I were to write you two checks right now, one for a hundred thousand and one for ten million. I mean, really. If you had a choice right now for me to write you a check for a hundred grand or ten million right now, right here on this golf course, which one would you take?"

"The ten million, of course."

"Why?"

"Because of what I could do with ten million dollars. Ten million dollars could significantly shape my future. For these men, I'm sure ten million is nothing."

"On the books it's nothing. In reality, to them, it's everything. To them, not closing at a hundred and ten million means that I've lost my edge."

"Okay. That's what they think. What do you think?"

Vaughn kept his eye on the ball and drove in the next putt. It was good on his next attempt.

"I don't know, man. I mean, sometimes I wonder how much money is enough. I mean really. How much money do these men need? That's what I keep asking myself. I'm in love. For the first time in a long time, I'm in love and I feel good about myself."

"Then why the conflict?"

"The old Vaughn would have closed for a hundred and ten million. The old Vaughn would never have settled for just a hundred million. The old me would have closed that deal and went on to the next one. Instead, I closed the deal and took my woman out to dinner to celebrate."

"And that's a bad thing?"

"I closed one deal this week, one. The old me would have closed three. Being in love is costing the company millions and some rather influential people aren't happy about it."

"But you're happy."

"You know what?" he said. looking up, "I am."

Darren took his shot and missed. He had a look of frustration on his face, but then had a drink of beer.

"Then again, Vaughn, why are we out here?"

"I don't know if I have the right to be happy, for one. And also, I'm feeling guilty."

"Because of the shareholders?"

"And because of my wife. I mean, I know she died. Since she died, I have had this hole in my heart. This void. And . . ."

"And the new woman is beginning to fill that void, and for that, you feel like you are betraying your wife's memory."

"Yes. Exactly."

"Okay. I can see that."

"So what do I do?"

"What do you want to do?"

"I'm thinking about stepping down from my position."

"Really?"

"Really."

"Wouldn't that affect the company even more adversely?"

"That depends."

"On what?"

"On whether or not my protégé is ready to take over."

"Is he?"

"He's close. But if I had to guess, I would say not yet. I think he will be ready in the next three to five years, but not yet."

"Then why do it? I mean, is it fair to put all that pressure on him?"

"He's under some pressure now."

"How so?"

"I'm sure the board has been pressuring him about every decision that I have made thus far."

"How does he feel about your being in love?"

"He has the same fears that everyone else has. He even suggested that I go back to seeing escorts." Vaughn laughed as he watched Darren make two more attempts to sink his ball.

"Hmm. And what did you think about that idea?"

"For a while, I thought it was a good idea. I mean, I do miss it . . . a little, I mean. And it would be the perfect solution to our problem."

"How so?"

"I would get my edge back in business. Brandon wouldn't have to take over until he is ready. I wouldn't disgrace my wife's memory, and everything would be back to normal."

"So is that what you want to do?"

"What do you think I should do?"

"You tell me."

"I can't do it."

"Because you are in love."

"Because I'm in love."

"Good for you."

"So, I still have a problem, though."

"Which is?"

"The millions that the company is losing."

"The company isn't losing money. From what you're telling me, they're just not squeezing blood from a rock like they normally do. And like you said, how much money is enough? Next issue."

"My second in command isn't ready yet."

"But in a few years he will be. And from what I hear from you, you aren't ready to step down anyway. That's not a problem. Next."

"The shareholders."

"Fuck 'em. Next."

"My wife. I feel as if I am betraying the memory of my wife."

Darren stopped trying to hit the golf ball, and stopped to address Vaughn's most pressing issue.

"Two questions: Do you believe in God, and do you think she wouldn't want you to move on?" Darren rested on his golf club as if it were a cane.

"I do believe in God. For a long time I didn't. Especially after my wife's death. But I do. And with regard to moving on, my wife would want me to move on. It's just . . . it's just that I feel so guilty."

Vaughn hit Darren's ball for him and it went right in.

"And why do you feel so guilty? What's the source of your conviction?"

"I love my girlfriend. I love her. I love her a lot."

"Then continue to love her."

Darren replaced his club and reached for a new one.

"And my wife?"

Vaughn stood over the ball and hit it a hundred yards and onto the green of the next hole. Even Darren was amazed at how easy this game came to Vaughn.

"Well, you said that you believe in God. That stands to reason that you also believe in heaven. It sounds to me like you and your wife were blessed to find one another. It sounds to be like you both had a chance to experience a strong bond and true love. And now, your wife is in heaven. If you believe in God, and if you believe in heaven, I would think that you also have to believe that heaven is paradise. I think the love, the bond, and the friendship that you share with your wife is a bond that can never be broken. In the same token, I think your wife is smiling down on you from heaven because you found love again. And I think she is okay in heaven because God has something for her that is greater than love; something where she doesn't have to worry about you and you don't have to worry about her. How do you know that God didn't send this new woman in your life in lieu of your wife? How do you know that your relationship for your wife wasn't just preparation for you to fall in love with this woman now? How do you know, Vaughn, that everything going on with you right now doesn't have some greater purpose?"

Darren's words sunk in. They hit home. Vaughn had his doubts about his relationship with Korie. But those doubts were put to rest that day on the golf course. He decided that nothing would stop the progress of his relationship. He decided that nothing would get in the way of his happiness. That day on the golf course, he decided not only he did want to be in love, he decided that he deserved to be in love. He handed Darren a check and the two men finished their game of golf.

"You know, I'm going to enjoy having you on retainer for a long time. You always know what to say."

Vaughn smiled at Darren.

"Well, that's my job. But here's a secret about therapy . . ."

"I'm listening."

"The client has all the answers."

"Kind of like, the customer is always right?"

"Exactly."

"Then why am I paying you all this money?" Vaughn began to laugh.

"Because you're a generous man, Vaughn."

"Very generous, apparently. Open up that envelope and look at that check."

Darren opened the envelope and even he was surprised at the amount.

"Very generous," Darren said, smiling.

"Welcome to the big leagues, Darren. That check is a monthly check. You will get that amount each month, whether I see you or not. The thing is, when I need you, I need you. I'm not asking you to not see other clients. But when I call, I'd like to be able to know that you're on your way."

"Well, if you call, I'll be there. But I don't think you need to see a therapist any longer. I think you just need some reassurance from time to time, some validation."

"Well, will that amount get me my reassurance?"

"Yes it will."

"Then we have a deal."

The two men continued their golf game.

The following week, Darren and Karen went to the Bulls game. The Bulls were playing the Lakers and Darren bought tickets for seats three rows away from the floor. Darren had on his custom Lakers jersey and Karen had on a custom Bulls jersey as well. They both had on team hats. Darren loved everything about Chicago and cheered for the Bears, Sox, Cubs, Hawks, and Bulls in almost every game. In basketball, however, he loved the Lakers. He had been a Lakers fan since Magic Johnson's showtime Lakers of the eighties.

Darren and Karen cheered, laughed, and occasionally kissed as they watched the Bulls and Lakers battle it out on the hardwood. It had been a long time since Darren had this much fun at a Bulls game. Going was something that he used to do all the time with her. Every year, Darren and Korie went to the Bulls – Lakers game. Darren never stopped going to the annual game. He never took anyone else, however, before now.

At halftime, Darren went to get more beer and snacks. He walked up to the concession stand. While there, he figured he needed to go to the bathroom first rather than make two trips after getting the snacks. He moved ever so slowly through the thick crowd of hundreds of people trying to do the same thing as him, which was to pee and get snacks before halftime was over.

While maneuvering through the crowd, he saw her. Is that? Is that—it can't be.

He saw her. Korie's back was to him and her hair was in a ponytail. He hadn't seen her in years, but he knew it was her. It had to be. He moved closer and closer, working his way through the crowd and bumping people in an effort to get to her. She was in line to go to the ladies' room. He got right behind her, much to the dismay of the other women in line. He knew it was her. He just knew it. He tapped the woman on the shoulder and she turned around. She looked amazing.

"Hey," he said.

She turned around and didn't look pleased to see him. She wasn't mad, but she wasn't happy either. Her affect was flat.

"Hey." She tried to force herself to smile.

The hallway was noisy. It was incredibly loud, but the silence between them was louder than the hundreds of people around them.

"You look great."

"Great" was an understatement. She looked stunning. She looked fit, she looked beautiful, and more than anything else, she looked happy. The three things no man wants to see from a woman after a breakup, after she has moved on.

"You look good yourself."

She too was blown away. The years had been kind to Darren. He was more fit than she remembered, taller than she remembered, and his smile, even after all this time, still made her weak; surprisingly weak. He looked good. He looked as if he had been taking care of himself. More than that, he looked as if his five-year plan had been all that he wanted and then some. He looked successful. Even in his sports gear, he looked confident. More than that, she was afraid of what she saw in his eyes. In his eyes she saw regret. She saw love. More than that, she saw that same love, that same regret mirroring her own face within his eyes.

"I've been trying to call you."

"Yeah, yeah . . . I know."

"I'd like to see you."

He was abrupt. Everything else in his world stopped. In this one moment he forgot he was here with someone. In this one moment, all that seemed to matter was her.

"I can't. I'm here with someone."

"It doesn't have to be today. I mean, I can call you later and—"

"I'm seeing someone."

She blurted it out. She had to. She felt herself being drawn to him. She wanted him. She wanted to talk with him. She wanted to know how he was doing, how he had been, and she wanted to know had he thought about her. So many thoughts ran through her mind. There were so many memories, so many emotions. She wanted to sit down with him and talk; at least her heart did. Her head, however, had different plans. Her head informed him that there was another rooster in the henhouse. Perhaps even that love didn't live there anymore. Her head put up a defensive wall, to protect her. She had never loved anyone like she loved Darren. In the same token, no man had hurt her as Darren had.

"You're seeing someone. Oh."

Her words hit him like two heavy, closed fists. They hit him in his chest and they hit him hard. He didn't know what else to expect. He didn't know why he hadn't expected her to be seeing someone; she looked incredible. There is no way she could have waited all this time for him. There is no way a woman this beautiful would be single. There was no way that another man hadn't staked a claim to her and couldn't be calling her his own. He scanned her hand for a wedding ring. There wasn't one. That gave him hope.

"I'm sorry," she said.

"Is it serious?" he asked quickly, almost out of desperation.

He tried to compose himself. He tried to act as if he didn't care. He asked again almost matter-of-factly.

"This person you're seeing, is it serious?"

"I don't know yet. I mean, we've been together for a while."

She faked a smile. She wondered what was going on in his head. She wanted to run away, but she seemed glued to where she was. They both moved in line and waited as the line to the women's restroom became shorter.

"Is there any way that we can talk? I mean, the next time I call, will you pick up?"

"I can't."

She didn't want to hurt Vaughn. She was, in fact, falling in love with him. Out of respect for Vaughn, she declined. Her heart wanted him to call, but right now her heart wasn't in control. Her head was.

"You can't answer, or you won't answer?"

He was confused. Hurt. He knew. Seeing her, he knew leaving her was a mistake.

"I won't answer. I'm sorry, Darren. You will always have a special place in my heart, but that time is gone. Besides, my new man doesn't put me off for his business plans."

There it was. She said it. She was clearly still upset about the five-year-plan; even all these years later. That upset Darren. But clinically, it still meant that she cared. He wanted her back. He wanted her in his life, in his bed, and in his heart. But he also wanted her to know that the plan had its merit. His plan was the reason he was the success he was today.

"He may not put you off for his plans, but I bet he's nowhere as busy as I am, either."

Darren sounded confident, arrogant. He was still the man who she remembered. His arrogance was one of the things that she loved about him. It was also one of the things that she hated about him as well.

"Oh Darren, I bet he is."

She tried her best to hide a frown. She tried her best not to show her contempt for his arrogance.

"I'm a therapist now. I work for a thriving practice. I see some of Chicago's most elite citizens."

He spoke with that same tempered arrogance he had five years ago. He said it in hopes that she would understand how hard he worked. How much he sacrificed. Although it was clear he sacrificed way too much. He said it, but she didn't seem impressed.

"Good for you, Darren. Good for you."

"Korie, look, I—"

"I have to go to the bathroom."

"Can I wait here for you?"

"I would rather you didn't."

"But—"

"Good-bye, Darren."

She went in the bathroom and stayed there for what seemed like an eternity. Darren tried to wait. He didn't know that she went to the bathroom to relieve herself and then to cry. He waited for her. He waited and pretty soon, Mother Nature called on him as well. He went to the bathroom and when he came out, she was nowhere to be found. He looked everywhere for her and didn't see her.

Then he remembered Karen.

He wasn't here alone.

He went to the concession stand and got snacks and beer. He made his way back to his seat where the game had well been underway. The entire time he looked for a glimpse of Korie throughout the stadium. He looked for her but couldn't find her anywhere. He handed the snacks and beer to Karen, who had a puzzled look on her face.

"Wow, it took you a long time."

"Oh. Yeah, well, the line was ridiculous."

"It must have been. The Lakers are winning so far, sixty to fifty-eight."

"Huh? Oh."

"Are you okay?"

"I'm fine."

Darren looked above and into the crowd. He tried to scan the entire stadium for Korie. He had to see her again. He looked at the cheap seats. He scanned all the bargain seats and all the places that he and she used to sit when they were together; when they were poor. He looked, but he couldn't find her.

He looked for her in the cheap seats.

He never thought to look for her in the floor seats, next to the players.

He didn't think to look in front of him.

She was, in fact, on the floor, right in front of him.

He was behind her.

Compared to where she and Vaughn were sitting, he was in the cheap seats.

He never saw her. She saw him. She saw him look for her.

At the end of the game, Darren took Karen's hand and left.

Vaughn took Korie's hand and left as well.

Vaughn had no idea that his therapist was his girl-friend's ex.

Chapter Twenty-two

Bitch.

This is what Darren thought to himself as he headed home. Karen went on about how great the game was and Darren's thoughts trailed off to her. How could she not want to see him? He was even more fit now than he was when they were together. He was doing better now than he had ever been financially in his life. His five-year-plan paid off. Perhaps Korie needed to see that.

Perhaps she needed to see the hundred-thousand dollar car that he was driving. Perhaps she needed to see the new condo that he lived in. Perhaps she needed to see that he was fast becoming one of the city's elite, with invitations to the mayor's ball, Bears games, and glamorous city functions. Whomever she was seeing couldn't be half the man that he was. Whomever she was seeing couldn't offer Korie the things that he could. The only thing that he could think about was how good she looked. She was looking good, damned good.

As Karen talked, all Darren could think about was Korie's full, kissable lips, her incredible figure and how good she smelled. He took Karen home and bedded her. She thought he was being extra-passionate, where he was really trying to take his frustration out on her in bed.

As they made love, he thought about Korie. He imagined himself with her. Having seen her gave him a clear mental picture. She still wore the same perfume, she still looked incredible, and she was still the one thing in this life that he had a weakness for.

He kissed Karen but he thought of Korie. As the two embraced during the most intimate of sessions, "Walk Away" by Christina Aguilera began to play. The lyrics burned in his head as he made love to Karen. He always thought that he would be the one thing that Korie would never walk away from. The fact of the matter was, she moved on.

His pride was wounded.

His arrogance was tempered.

His heart was broken.

His arrogance would be his undoing. When he left her all those years ago, in the back of his mind, he knew he would be with her again. He knew in his heart that she could never completely walk away from him; or so he thought. He figured that day that he left that at any time, he could come back, as long as he came back successful.

That's what he thought.

Apparently, Korie didn't get the memo.

He was passionate with Karen. Passionate. Primitive. Carnal.

He and Karen went at it like Ali vs. Frazier, Kobe vs. Shaq or Obama vs. Hillary.

Like Hillary, Karen lost. Her breath was taken away. Her body glistened with sweat. Initially, she lay in bed with him with a smile on her face. Then that smile changed into a frown.

"So, who is she?"

Darren had a look on confusion on his face. Confusion as well as a look of riddled guilt.

"She, who? What?" He tried to feign ignorance.

"I'm not stupid, Darren. Your body is here, but your mind is somewhere else."

"What? No. No, you're mistaken."

"We never went at it like that before. You're . . . different. Today you went at it like never before."

"Maybe that's the effect you have on me."

"Maybe. Or maybe there is someone else on your mind."

"You're mistaken."

"Okay. I'll take your word on that—for now."

Damned women's intuition. It's scary how accurate that shit is, he thought.

"So are you telling me I need to hold back with you from now on?" Darren tried to throw Karen off.

"Hold back?"

"Yeah. How do you know that I haven't been holding back my feelings for you all this time and tonight I just decided to let go?"

"Is that the case?"

"It is."

Darren held Karen in his arms and soon after she fell asleep.

He lied. Like any other man, he lied.

She was on his mind.

As Karen lay in his arms, he stared at the ceiling and a million thoughts ran through his head. He thought back to how they met. He thought of their first kiss. He also thought about their first date and the first time that they made love. He thought about how nervous they were with one another. He also thought about how quickly they became familiar and comfortable with one another.

He thought about the days when they were poor; the days that they struggled. He thought about the times that they lay in each other's arms and talked about their dreams. He thought about their courtship; back when he had no car; back when they were both on the bus. He thought about the days that they went to Dairy Queen because he didn't have money for much else. He thought about days that they stayed home and watched videos because they couldn't afford to go to the movies. There was a time that they struggled, but everything was okay as long as they were together.

It was poetic; the way that things used to be. All these years later, he finally understood what it was that she meant. He finally got what it was that she had been trying to tell him. Struggling, in fact, was romantic. They had a few hard times, but all that mattered to Korie back then was that they endured them together.

Darren got it.

The thing is, he got it too late.

Five years too late.

Chapter Twenty-three

Bastard.

Why did he have to look so good? I mean, really, why did he have to look so damned good?

This is what Korie thought to herself as she rode back to Vaughn's place in a chauffeured Phantom Rolls-Royce. She and Vaughn watched highlights of the game on TV in the car as they were driven.

Vaughn poured himself a drink of bourbon from the car's minibar and Korie had a diet soda. She and Vaughn enjoyed the first half of the game. By the time the second half began, all Korie could think about was him. Her head was on the defense. Her head said things to Darren that her heart didn't want her to, but now as she rode home with Vaughn, all she could think about was him.

She took a few sips of soda and leaned on Vaughn's shoulder as if she were going to sleep. He enjoyed her embrace and smiled at her. He enjoyed their urban outings. He enjoyed it when they went among average people, and did average things like attend sporting events, go to the movies, or even roller-skating.

Both Korie and Vaughn relaxed in the car in each other's arms. Vaughn thought to that he was lucky to have her. Korie thought that she was lucky to be with a man like Vaughn. Still, her thoughts were of him. She tried her best not to compare the two men. She tried her best not to think of Darren and cherish the times that she shared with Vaughn. Still, she couldn't help wondering what could have been. She couldn't stop thinking about where they might be now, had they stayed together. She asked herself if she would still be as successful as she is now. Would he? Would they have children by now and be struggling, or would they still have made it to where they were now?

She certainly would never have seen Tokyo had she stayed with Darren. Chances are she might never have pursued her dreams had she not been laid off. Chances were if she would have been laid off, Darren would have picked up the majority of the bills, and she might have just ended up being a housewife or a stay-at-home-mom had they stayed together. She thought about what if. She also thought that he hadn't changed much.

He still wore Aqua Di Gio by Armani. He still wore his head in a bald fade. He still had an amazing smile, and he was everything that she remembered—tall, dark, and handsome.

He was also arrogant. He was also presumptuous. He looked good. But his attitude seemed ugly. The years had not humbled him much. In fact, he might have become the man that she was worried he would become when they were struggling.

I bet he's not half as busy as I am.

That's what he said. That's what he let walk out of his mouth.

Korie thought about it. He might have been right. Vaughn was a remarkable man. Had she been dating anyone else, chances are they would not have been half as busy as Darren was.

If she were dating any other man.

But she wasn't.

She was dating DeVaughn Harris. She dated him because she chose to; because he was interested in her, and because of the woman that she was. Korie wondered why Darren seemed to expect so little of her. Then she thought back to the woman who she was five years ago.

The woman who she was five years ago would not have landed DeVaughn Harris.

The woman she was five years ago could barely hold on to Darren Howard.

Darren pushed her in the right direction. He saw the potential that she had, even when she didn't see it for herself. In part, she was who she was today because of him. He was the one who suggested that she open her own business. He was the one who suggested that she go back to school. He was the one who created her business plan on her laptop years before she seriously considered opening her own business.

He had two business plans on her laptop. One was for sewing and the other was for interior decorating. She used every idea and every spreadsheet. Korie thought that everything that he created was well researched and done exactly the way she would have done things. He did a good job. He created the business plans for her as he would have done for himself; with great care and detail. He really wanted to see her succeed.

All she ever wanted was him, struggle or not.

All he ever wanted was for her to be patient. In truth, he wanted the very best for her, whether he supplied it, or she supplied it for herself, he wanted nothing but the best for her.

He was right.

She was also right.

And they both were wrong.

She lay in Vaughn's arms and wondered if she had been too hard on him. She wondered if she should have taken his phone calls or at least listened to him.

She wanted to be fair. She wanted to especially be fair with Vaughn and see where their relationship might be going. She weighed her options. She thought briefly about both men and decided in her head that she was done with Darren. She thought about how he left, without warning and without discussion.

She thought about the check that he left.

A check that she never cashed.

She didn't need his damned handout.

She didn't need anything from him.

She never asked for anything . . . but his love.

No. She would stay with Vaughn. She decided that she would move forward. It made no sense to move backward. She had a man. She had a man who was loving, caring, and attentive.

She had a man who had the ability to give her the world. A man who wanted to give her the world; a man who would never put her off for a five-year-plan, even if that plan had the best-laid intentions.

Darren was not that man.

That's what her head said.

Her heart; her heart was not so sure.

"So, what do we do next?" she asked Vaughn.

"Well, I need to put in more hours at the office. I have a number of loose ends to tie up this week and this weekend"—he gave her a kiss—"you and I are going to the black creativity ball."

"A formal outing?"

"A formal outing."

"Good. I'd like to take my hair down and dress up. It'll be a great change of pace."

"What? You didn't like the Bulls game? It was your idea."

"I loved the game. I love hanging out and doing things like this. I love the fact that you're open to trying things in my world. Now, I think I'm ready to enjoy some of the things in your world, on two conditions."

"And those conditions are?"

"One, no work at the event. And two, you dance at least three times with me."

Vaughn laughed."Okay. Okay, I can definitely keep my end with the dancing part, but I'll have to do some business while I'm there. It won't be much more than shaking a few hands and letting a few people know that I have my eye on their companies, but after that, I'm yours. So I tell you what, let me handle my business first, and after that, I'm yours for the night to do whatever you want."

"Whatever I want?"

"Girl, you know I could never deny you anything."

"Then what I want is in a few weeks, we go out for a three-day weekend, my treat."

"Where do you want to go?"

"Hawaii."

"Hawaii? Why Hawaii?"

"Because I've never been and after I finish decorating the district attorney's house next week, I should have enough money to take us both."

"Girl, you know money is no object."

"It is when I'm spending it."

They both laughed.

Korie lay back in his arms as they headed back to Vaughn's place.

After arriving at Vaughn's place, he went to his den to get some work done and Korie went to the master bedroom and changed into her silk pj's. Since dating Vaughn she had a full closet full of clothes at his place.

The closet in Vaughn's master bedroom was about as big as Korie's apartment. Their relationship moved at a very fast pace. Korie spent at least three days a week

at Vaughn's home. Sometimes he wasn't home. Sometimes he was working, but there were days that he got
off and she would be waiting for him. For Vaughn it
was always a pleasant surprise. Very often these days
he asked her to move in with him. Korie declined. She
told him it was too soon and she also wanted to maintain her independence. Vaughn understood.

Korie wondered what it would be like to be married
to Vaughn, to manage his grand home, to decorate his
home and to be a woman of means like the Real House-
wives of Atlanta, only not so dramatic and narcissistic.

She wondered what it would be like to live with him.
She hadn't lived with a man since Darren. She didn't
want to make the same mistake twice. Before moving
in or even taking their relationship to the next level,
Korie had to know exactly where the relationship with
Vaughn was going.

She decided the next time he was available, she wanted to redefine their relationship, to talk, to find out what
exactly it is that they were doing and what exactly were
Vaughn's intentions.

Their relationship was far from strictly one of a sexual nature. In truth, they only had sex maybe once or
twice a week. Their relationship was more about their
friendship; their bond. When other needs had to be
satisfied, Vaughn broke out the Viagra and met Korie's
physical needs. She wished they had sex more. Vaughn
was a patient and attentive lover, but he was also in his
late forties.

Because he was in such great shape, Korie was often
surprised that he needed Viagra. Vaughn blamed his
inability to perform at times on his job and his levels
of stress. The truth was sometimes he was bored with
Korie sexually. Considering all the models and escorts
that he dated, when it came to beauty, the bar had been

raised too high. It was like a man who masturbated frequently to porn, and couldn't perform with his wife.

He often needed Viagra with the escorts as well. Being with exotic women had become all too boring to Vaughn. When he was seeing the escorts sometimes it was to get his physical needs met. Sometimes it was strictly for image purposes in high-society magazines. Other times it was out of routine.

Dating Korie was a novelty to him because she was real and because she had flaws. He liked her personality, her natural breasts, and the fact that she was real. His past sometimes crept into his relationship with Korie, however. One time specifically was when he offered to pay for implants for her. This sparked their first argument because Korie thought Vaughn was trying to change her. He was. But his excuse was it was only a gift and meant as a kind gesture. At the time he made the offer, he was in fact thinking about an escort that he once saw who reminded him of Korie.

That was the only time that he offered to augment her body.

It was not the last time, however, that he thought about it.

Chapter Twenty-four

Korie hadn't heard from Jayna in a while and didn't want to be like some women who get a man and don't keep in touch with their girlfriends. Korie had been sending Jayna text messages and e-mails, but they hadn't seen each other in close to a month. Since she had free time on her hands, Korie decided to call her friend.

"Hello?" a groggy voice said.

"Jayna, it's me."

"Hey girl." She sounded flat, exhausted, depressed.

"You okay?"

"I'm fine. How are things with you?"

"Things are great. Vaughn keeps asking me to move in with him, but I'm not sure yet. Jay, I am so happy that you convinced me to go out with him."

"That's great, sis. How was Tokyo?"

Korie went on to tell Jayna how Tokyo was, and all of the wonderful places that she and Vaughn went. She talked about the sights, the food, and the madness that happened in the bathroom on the final day. She told Jayna how Vaughn wanted them to move in together and how they were going to the black creativity ball that weekend.

"That's great, Korie."

Jayna still sounded a bit flat, but she was engaged in the conversation.

"Jayna, is everything okay? How are things with you and Brandon?"

There was silence on the other end of the phone.

"Jayna?" Korie called out.

"We broke up." Jayna sounded depressed and broken.

"When? Why?"

"While you were in Tokyo. We broke up because I'm a ho."

"What? I don't understand."

Jayna recounted how everything went down between her and Brandon. She went on to tell Korie how her past had finally caught up with her. Jayna was broken. She was hurt beyond words. Korie asked Jayna if she was okay and Jayna said that she wasn't but she would be.

Jayna started going back to church, she got back in therapy, and she continued on her grind at work. It was hard getting through the days. She took each day one at a time. It was especially hard to get through her days without Korie's support. But like a true friend, Jayna didn't want to burden Korie with her problems. Especially considering how happy Korie was.

It had been a long time since Korie had been so happy. Jayna finally figured out that she needed to work on herself. She needed to change the woman she was on the inside if she were to ever find love again. She loved Brandon. She missed Brandon. She wanted him back in her life. He hadn't called and she respected his wishes and didn't call him back after their last night together. Jayna was miserable without him. She prayed each night to God that one day Brandon would return to her.

Korie was mad that Brandon would leave Jayna over her past. What was in her past, was her past and none of his business, she thought. When she got off the phone it was almost an hour later. She then went down to the den to speak with Vaughn, who was working at his desktop computer. She walked in upset, although her issue was not with him.

"Did you know that Brandon broke up with Jayna?"

Vaughn didn't even look up from his computer. He adjusted his glasses and continued typing.

"Yes, I did." His response was flat, matter-of-factly.

"Do you know why?"

He continued typing. "Yes. I believe it had something to do with her being promiscuous."

"And you think he was right?"

Korie placed her hand on her hip. She was upset, but again, Vaughn was not the source of her ire. Brandon was.

"It doesn't matter what I think. It's none of my business."

"But you know what happened."

"Of course I do. Brandon is like a son to me."

"Were you going to tell me?"

"No. Actually, I wasn't."

Vaughn continued to type.

"Why not?"

He stopped typing. He took his glasses off and placed them on the desk, then leaned back in his chair and rubbed his eyes and yawned before speaking. He was still in the same clothes he wore to the game.

"Well, I assumed your girlfriend would tell you. In fact, that was a while ago that they broke up. I assumed that she told you."

"And you didn't bring it up at all this whole time since you've known?"

"Why would I? Again, it's not my business. Actually, it's not your business either."

"That's my best friend."

"Then be there for your friend. Support her. Her thing . . . their thing . . . has nothing to do with us."

Korie fell silent.

"You're right," she said.

"I know."

He continued typing. He hadn't even looked up from the computer. That response took her by surprise. It reminded her of Darren. That was not a good thing.

"You know?"

Now both hands were on Korie's hips.

Vaughn laughed.

"What's funny?"

"You are. Look, did you just really want to fight and that's why you came down here? Or are you upset about what happened with your girlfriend and you need to vent? If so, I have a really good therapist on retainer you can talk to." Vaughn put his glasses on and went back to working.

"I don't believe you think this is funny."

"Look, sweetheart, it's not funny, but your superhero pose right now is. Babe, I have a lot of work to do. I'm sorry about your friend's situation with Brandon, I truly am. But sweetheart, I'm not your enemy. And I'm not going to argue with you about Brandon and Jayna. In fact, I don't plan to discuss it at all."

"And if I do plan on discussing it?"

"Then, sweetheart, that is one conversation you will be having by yourself."

"Do you think Brandon was right?"

"Korie . . ."

"Just answer that for me. Do you think he was right in leaving her?"

"I do."

"Why, if all that was in her past?"

Vaughn took his glasses back off. He got up and went to the bar in his den and poured himself some bourbon. It was clear that Korie was not going to simply let this go. He stretched before speaking.

"Okay, look, you really want my opinion?"

"I do."

"You and Jayna, you all are in a different league now with a different set of rules. You all are society women now. Not that you weren't before, but the social circles you are in now are quite different from the social circles you all are used to. This is a close-knit group. Now how would it look for Brandon to go to, say, this event this weekend, for example and Jayna has slept with twelve of the thirty most prominent men who will be there. She'll look like a ho. Right or wrong?"

Korie shrugged.

"Now here Brandon is walking around town, claiming your girlfriend, telling people how much he loves her, and taking pictures for the press, when he hears from his staff members—his subordinates, mind you—that she has been around. Our lawyers, our public relations people, and many of our consultants, one of which who has slept with Jayna, tell Brandon that she's bad business or that she's damaged goods. Mind you, they told him months after he's been seeing her. It's pretty hard to bounce back from that when it's common knowledge that the woman you are telling everyone you love is a whore."

"Whore is a bit extreme and if she were a man—"

"But she's not. That excuse is not a valid excuse and it has never been. I know what you were going to say. Had she been a man, she would be considered a hero or player, whereas when a woman does the same things as a man she is considered a ho. Well, Korie, I have a few things to say about that. One, she's not a man, so stop with that. Two, sleeping with a bunch of men makes a woman a ho. Is it right? No. But that's simply the way things are."

"But if men and women are equal—"

"They're not, period. There are exceptions to the rule. There are things that some woman can do that men can't do but if you want the truth, men and women are not equal. You all have your roles and we have ours. In the absence of one, the other sex must fulfill certain duties. But men and women, sweetheart, are by no means equal. We're stronger, and we have our dominate traits whereas women have their dominate traits. We're the hunters and you all are the nurturers."

Korie was becoming incensed as the argument went forward. She kept telling herself that she opened this door, but she also needed to close it. But she did want to know more about Vaughn, more about who he was, and where their relationship was going, so she left the door open.

"What type of antiquated bullshit theory is that? Next you are going to tell me that I should be in the kitchen in some damn heels and an apron!"

"Why do things have to be that extreme? Seriously, why? In fact, why are we arguing about this? We were having no problems until your girlfriend—the ho— called."

"The ho?" Korie raised her voice even more.

"I'm sorry. The whore. Let's keep it real. That's what you young people say now, right? I'm quite sure that you were privy to your girlfriend's sexual escapades. I'm also quite sure that you don't approve."

"I don't approve, but it's not my place to judge her. Only God can judge her. Neither you or Brandon have the right to judge her."

"You know what? You're right. I don't have the right to judge her. She's not my woman and I'm not sleeping with her, but Brandon has the right to decide not to continue seeing her."

"Because of her past?"

"Because of how her past may affect his future. Their future."

"And if I slept with a bunch of men would you feel the same about me? Or would it be okay as long as I stayed in my place as a woman?"

"Okay, back to that. Maybe I should not have said that men and women are not equal."

"You think? So you see that you're wrong, then. right?"

"No, I see that's one opinion I should've kept to myself to keep the peace."

"So you really feel that way?"

"I do. But listen; to clarify what I mean, I will say this. Men should respect women. Women should respect themselves. It's obvious to me that in the case of Jayna, she didn't respect herself or her body. She put herself at risk. Now, without saying a whole lot, one of the men she slept with has syphilis. It's in its advanced stages, and he's had it for years. He had to step down from his post as a CEO at forty-five years of age because the STD damaged his brain. Now, does that mean your girlfriend has syphilis? No. But she put herself at risk. What if it had been AIDS? Your friend, Brandon's girlfriend, put herself at risk. In turn she could have put him at risk, period. Now back to what I was saying: A man should respect a woman. A man should respect his wife. If that man does not do his part, then the woman should step up and fulfill that role."

"And aside from that, you're saying that a woman shouldn't do what a man does?"

"No, what I'm saying is that a woman should fulfill her role, whatever that is. Men and women should have the same goals, not the same roles. In that, I mean that although we may have common goals, we will most likely take different paths. Men and women are different physically, mentally, and spiritually. We are. We're more aggressive, you all are more subtle. There is strength in both, but we have, in my opinion, two totally different core strengths. We are givers, you are receivers; we're hunters, you are nurturers; we're stronger and you all are weaker . . . physically. We should be taking care of you—in our way. You should be taking care of us—in your way. Then together, we should be moving toward that common goal."

"Vaughn, there are a lot of weak-ass men out there and there are women who will work circles around some men and Jayna is a prime example of that."

"Okay, that's fair. In the workplace there are some formidable women out there. I will give you that."

"Then that point I just made shoots your argument all to hell."

"Maybe, maybe not. Listen. Once upon a time, giraffes had smaller necks. But over time, when food was scarce, their bodies adapted so they could get to the foliage above them. Over time, they did what they had to do to survive and save the species. It's the same thing with men and women. There are a lot of weak-ass men out there and in order to save the species, women had to step up and fill that void."

"And you're trying to take us back to caveman times?"

"No, I'm trying to take you back to the way things should be. Korie, if we are a couple and you work, you should work because you want to work, not because you have to work. Korie, you should be taken care of."

"Vaughn that's fine and all, but it sounds like you want me in the kitchen and in the bedroom."

"Again sweetheart, I think you're taking this to the extreme. And by the way, if you were my wife I would want you in the kitchen, and in the bedroom, and raising my kids and working . . . if you want. But don't get it twisted. I want you in the bedroom because you're beautiful. I want you in the kitchen because you're a great cook. I want you raising the babies because if we marry, I want you to raise our children with the best qualities of both of us. I want you teaching them, nurturing them, and you're the only person aside from me that I want influencing them. By the way, we are not equal. In some ways you are stronger and in some ways I am stronger. That's what I mean by not equal."

"Then that is what you should've said in the first place."

Korie kissed Vaughn and headed toward the door.

"You have work to do."

Vaughn laughed.

"Shit, I said that twenty minutes ago."

"My bad." Korie walked away.

"Korie . . ."

"Yes?"

"If you had been with as many men as she had, I would have stopped seeing you too."

She let out a sigh.

"I just don't think that's fair."

"Life's not fair."

"Okay, then for now, can we agree to disagree?"

"I can do that. But just one more thing."

"What?" Korie thought Vaughn was about to say something insensitive.

"He was going to marry her. At this event this weekend, he was going to propose. He bought a ring a few months ago. I told him it was premature then, but he was going to ask her to be his wife."

Korie stopped and leaned in the doorway.

"You told him it was premature?"

"I did."

"I thought it was none of your business."

"It's not. But he's like a son to me. And I want what's best for him, just like you want the best for your girl-friend."

"What if what is best for them is each other? In spite of her past and in spite of his ego, what if she's what's best for him?"

"She's not. At least, I don't believe that she is."

"What if you're wrong?"

"I'm seldom wrong."

There was that arrogance again. Korie hated it. What softened her stance was the fact that he even said the word marriage. Although they were arguing, she was under the impression Vaughn did see her as a wife. She also kept telling herself that she started this argument and she needed to finish it. Initially, she felt like she won, but she also couldn't help thinking that she lost. She decided in her head to call it a draw and simply go to bed.

"Okay, Vaughn. I'll let you get back to work. I'm go-ing to go lie down."

"Are we cool?"

"We're cool."

"Can a brother get a kiss?"

Korie walked over to Vaughn and kissed him. She then retired to bed where all she could think about was Jayna's loss and Vaughn's antiquated views. He made some valid points, but she was still not comfortable with the views. She then thought long and hard about their age difference and weighed the pros and cons of their relationship. The good still outweighed the bad, but Korie couldn't help thinking that the scales might be tipping just a little. More and more she began to see him as a potential husband. She also thought about cutting her losses and breaking up with him before her feelings became even stronger. He was set in his ways and at times he was opinionated, but he was also caring, challenging, and he had a way about him that she was drawn to.

I need to move in with this man, marry him, or leave him alone altogether. I need to make my mind up and it needs to be soon.

Chapter Twenty-five

The Friday before the event, Darren went to the barbershop to get his hair cut. He hadn't been to the shop in a while since he began dating Karen. He had been going to the same salon that he sent Karen and Jacob to. For this event, he wanted to have his signature look. That meant a bald fade that looked so good; it looked as if it were airbrushed on his head. He also wanted to be edged up with a straight razor. His goatee had to be tight, and he had to look his absolute best for this event. He even went as far as to buy a one-karat diamond earring for the event and a new Movado watch. Darren picked up his purchases before walking into the shop.

"Whaddup, D?"

"Hey Gucci, what's up."

"I got you next."

As usual there were a lot of women in the shop getting haircuts for their sons. In addition, there were bus drivers, police officers, and a few thugs, all sitting or playing games, waiting on Gucci or one of his barbers to cut their hair. Gucci cut Darren's hair next.

"Bald fade, right, D?"

"Yeah, but this time I need to be edged up with a straight razor and I want my fade to look the same way that Nas's fade looked in Belly."

"I got you."

"And edge up my beard too, please."

"Man, you must be about to do it big tonight, huh?"

"Yeah, I got huge plans. I have an event to go to this evening."

"Cool. Cool. So where have you been? It's been a minute since I last cut your hair."

"Oh, well, I've been around, but you know I moved. I live downtown now, so it's hard to drive all the way out to the south side."

"Oh, okay. I see you've been going to one of those salons too, by the way your hair looks."

"Yeah, well. Sometimes I just have to go anywhere that's close. You know some days I get really busy and have to just find the first thing available."

Gucci was concerned. A lot of brothers in the hood were no longer going to see the local barber anymore. More and more brothers were going to the beauty salons or getting their hair cut by the Arabs, who had also recently broken into the barber game. Many of the Arab barbers washed and conditioned your hair before cutting it. They also used special oils and massaged the scalp as well as gave you a fade. Many of them made sure that no hair got in the man's face, and they often used a blow-dryer on a cool setting to make sure that no hair was left on the customer. They did all this and usually for as little as 15 dollars. They also didn't expect tips. Many were just happy for the business and their customer-service skills were impeccable. Darren had been going to one of these shops on the days that he didn't go with Karen to the salon.

"Hey, D. Look, um, have you seen Karen?"

That made Darren's heart skip a beat. He didn't want to mention to Gucci that he had been dating her. Not after all he now knew.

"Karen? Karen who?" Darren feigned ignorance.

Gucci whispered in his ear.

"Special K. She was supposed to be one of your patients, remember?"

"Oh, you mean the sister you were making fun of that day?"

"Yeah."

Gucci sounded as if he were ashamed of his behavior. "Isn't she your client?"

"Oh, no. I referred her to someone else."

"So, have you seen her? I mean at your office—have you seen her?"

"I think I have seen her once or twice, Gooch, Why?"

"Just wondering."

"Hmm, why?"

"She stopped coming here. I think we crossed the line and went too far the last time she was here and she stopped coming. She doesn't bring her son anymore."

"Wow. Sorry to hear that. Is business bad?"

"Nah, business is cool. It's just that—nothing. Never mind."

"O . . . kay. Never mind."

Gucci continued to cut Darren's hair and edged him up properly. As usual guys joked, looked at women's butts as they left, and they signified and talked about one another like they were out on the streets. Floetry was playing overhead. The song "Getting Late" was blaring over the speakers and as Gucci cut Darren's hair, it was obvious that there was something pressing on his mind.

"Gucci, what's wrong?" Darren whispered.

As Gucci finished up, he asked Darren to step out in front of the shop.

"What's up, Gucci?"

"I miss her, D."

"You miss who?"

"Karen."

Oh shit, Darren thought.

"What do you mean?"

"Man, we used to go out. That's why I clowned her so bad last time she was here. I clowned her because I was ashamed."

"Ashamed of what?"

Darren knew the story, but couldn't let on to Gucci that he did. He also couldn't let him know he was sleeping with her, either. It would be like Kobe telling Shaq that he bedded his woman.

"Look, I used to see her, right? This was back when I was playing ball. She's an incredible woman and all. I mean, she's sensitive, she's smart, she's hood . . ."

That's for sure, Darren thought.

". . . and we had a good thing, you know."

"So what happened?"

"I didn't know she danced. I caught feelings for her and I saw her one night dancing up at the strip club, shaking her ass for all those niggas up in there. Man, I just got pissed. My boys were clowning me and shit so I snapped."

"What did you do?"

"I snatched her off the stage."

She didn't tell me all that, Darren thought.

"I snatched her off stage and called her all types of hoes and shit. Then security tried to get at me and we all got into this huge brawl. I even tried to hit her."

"Gucci, you didn't."

"Nah, but I wanted to. I wanted to kill her ass that night, but my boys stopped me."

"You wanted to kill her because you had feelings for her?"

"Because I loved her. I really loved her. Because she danced, I couldn't bring myself to get over it, or to continue dating her. I wanted her to give that life up, but when I was on top, I treated her like a piece of ass and—"

"And what?"

"And now, since she's gone, I miss her. Stripper or not, she was a good woman. She had my back, ya know?"

"Okay. I feel you."

"She was also incredible in bed."

"Hmn. Okay." Darren tried to maintain his composure.

"Anyway, niggas is telling me she ain't at the club no more. One of the guys in the shop says that he's seen her recently downtown at a City College. He said she was looking good. Not just good, but better than she has ever looked. He said she looked like she was getting herself together. He also said that she looked—"

"She looked, what? Finish your sentence."

"He said she looked happy."

"And that's a bad thing?"

"Nah, but it's eating away at me. If she's happy, it should be because of me, not some other cat, ya know?"

"Hey You" by Floetry was blaring over the speakers. The more they sang, the sadder Gucci seemed to become.

"D, you ever fuck up with a woman only to realize that she might have been the one?"

Silence fell between the two men.

"Yeah, I have."

"So what did you do?"

"I'm trying to get her back now."

"So that's what I should do?"

"If that's what your heart is telling you. Then go after her."

Darren couldn't believe he was saying these things. But he knew how he still felt about Korie. Gucci should pursue Karen if he thought she was the one for him. So should any man if his heart told him to. The thing was, Darren was feeling Karen. He was really feeling her and if Korie wouldn't let him back in, chances were he could see himself being with Karen. It was wrong, because he and Gucci were cool, but he figured Gucci messed up. He had his chance. Just then, Darren thought to himself that might be what Korie was thinking: That he messed up and he had his chance. Fuck that. I have to get her back, he thought.

He decided that this would be the last time he got his hair cut at the shop. Darren reached into his wallet to give Gucci money for the cut, but he declined.

"No charge, D. Thanks for listening, man. If you see her, will you tell her I need to holler at her?"

"I'll tell her, Gucci."

"Thanks."

Darren felt like shit. He left the shop and headed back home. He carefully laid out his clothes for Saturday. Friday night Karen came over to spend the night. Darren felt guilty as he made love to Karen that night. The guilt didn't start, however, until after his orgasm.

Chapter Twenty-six

The next day, Darren and Karen were dressed to the nines. Darren was dressed sharply in a black Sean John Tuxedo with matching alligator shoes. Karen wore a black formal goddess-style dress by Badgley Mischka. It had half-length sleeves and was draped and split at the top. It had a deep V-neck, an empire waist, and it was floor-length. It was 100 percent silk and it draped across her body beautifully. She accented the dress with half-karat diamond earrings and a pair of black Manolo Blahniks that could only be seen if she were to dance or take longer strides as she walked.

All week she practiced moving in the heels and dress. Darren purchased both on his AMEX card. This was Karen's first pair of Manolos, so she practiced to make sure she didn't damage them or break the heel. As a dancer, she was already pretty adept at moving in heels, but because she never had a pair of the expensive shoes before, she practiced moving in them to make sure that they would last.

They arrived to the event in Darren's car. As they pulled up to the museum, lights flashed as they both exited the car. All types of media were there covering the event.

Darren walked around the car, took Karen's arm and they smiled as they walked the red carpet to the event. Both were nervous. Darren acted as if he were used to coming to events like this all the time. The truth was, this was his first. He brought plenty of business cards and prepared himself for what could be the greatest marketing night of his career.

They walked up the stairs of the museum where they were greeted by security. Darren gave his name and the couple was allowed entry. They walked into the museum where the vast foyer had been converted into a ballroom dance floor, with tables that surrounded the stage. Each table had a number, and each table had someone of importance in each seat. Tickets to the event were 3,000 dollars each. It was money that went to charity, but money Darren would not have spent normally. To be invited by Vaughn meant that Vaughn paid for his attendance.

This is it! Darren thought. He was here with Chicago's elite, the super-wealthy. There were politicians here, pro-athletic coaches, pro athletes, CEOs, and a host of women whom were obviously "special guests" of these powerful men. It was like the VIP section of a club, only everyone here was a VIP.

The 3,000-dollar price tag was a way of weaning out common folk. Darren didn't mind. He was ready to no longer be among common folk. He was ready to take his career to the next level. He felt if he took his career there, if he stepped up his game just a bit more, there was no way that Korie would say no to him again.

Even now he thought of her. Karen was looking stunning in her own right. She was easily one of the most beautiful women present. She was simply rough around the edges, a woman with her own swagger who Darren had come to love. Still, all he could think about was how bad Gucci wanted her back and how bad he wanted Korie.

The couple sat down at their assigned table, table number twelve. It was right across from the stage and

directly in front. The card at the table said Mr. Darren
Howard and guest. Across from them was a card that
said Mr. DeVaughn Harris and guest. Only Vaughn
hadn't made it yet. Darren and Karen looked around
the room at the vast decorations, the many people who
were there, and the amazing table setting in front of
them. The music was blaring overhead: "Find Your
Way Back In My Life" by Kem. It was a smooth song
that played while the museum workers sat people at
their respective tables.

Already there was some drama going on as various
women seemed incensed at the presence of others. Un-
doubtedly, some of the women were mistresses of the
men who were present; mistresses who were told to lay
low and enjoy the event; mistresses who were disobe-
dient and did not do as they were told. They didn't lay
low, however, and many of them dressed in a manner
where they could not help being noticed.

It was easy to see who belonged and didn't belong
with regard to proximity of seating and assignment of
seating. Many of the mistresses and escorts who were
not with a man at a table were seated in tables at the
back of the room.

Most tables, beginning with the ones on the front
row, had the wealthiest people seated in the front, and
toward the back were the less affluent people. Mistresses, escorts, hookers, and the like were seated in
the back, not directly in anyone's line of sight. This too
was done by design, because some women wore common retail-store dresses to a 3000-dollar event. It was
clear by their attire that they didn't belong, but it was
also clear by the show of security at the front that they
were invited by someone.

The event was just ready to begin when Darren received a tap on his shoulder and a familiar voice spoke.

"Hey man, good to see you. Glad you made it!"

Vaughn was all smiles. Darren stood up to give him a handshake. Vaughn was sporting a tuxedo by Brioni. Brioni was the same designer that did the tuxedos for men who played James Bond on the big screen. Vaughn's tuxedo was black and tailored to him perfectly.

"DeVaughn Harris, I would like you to meet my girlfriend, Karen."

"It's a pleasure to meet you." Vaughn smiled "My, you have a lovely smile."

"Thank you." Karen began to blush.

"Darren, I have someone I would like you to meet as well. This is my girlfriend, Korie."

"Wh—what?"

Darren had a hard time composing himself. His heart skipped a beat.

Korie had a hard time keeping her composure as well.

He was light-headed. His breath had literally been taken away.

This couldn't be the woman who Vaughn had been talking about in therapy. This couldn't be the woman who I convinced Vaughn to doggedly pursue. This couldn't be the woman who Vaughn was so madly in love with. Not this woman, any woman but this woman. Are you fucking kidding me?

These were Darren's thoughts as his chest burned with jealousy and betrayal.

"It's—it's nice to meet you."

He shook her hand. His handshake was firm. He gripped Korie's hand almost as if to send her a message.

"It's—nice to meet you too."

Korie was just as confused and taken by surprise as Darren was.

"She's beautiful," Darren said to Vaughn.

"Thank you," Vaughn said, smiling.

The women introduced themselves to each other.

"Hello, I'm Karen."

"I'm Korie."

Vaughn turned to Korie and spoke.

"I wasn't going to say anything, but Darren is my counselor; my therapist. I used to have a problem with people knowing that I've seen a counselor, but I imagine if anyone should know it's you, and I'm not ashamed to have someone to talk to when the stress of work gets to me."

"No dear, you shouldn't. You have more stress than the average man." Korie looked at Darren as she spoke. "You're busier than the average man, and even busier than those men who aren't so average." She stroked Vaughn's arm as she said so and gave Darren a curious but casual glance.

Ouch, Darren thought.

"Everyone needs someone to talk to from time to time," Darren said.

"I couldn't agree more," Vaughn replied. "Shall we be seated?"

The table was round; Korie and Vaughn sat with their backs to the stage, but directly across from Darren and Karen. Darren tried to make eye contact with Korie, but she wouldn't make eye contact back. Instead, she spoke to Karen and others at the table.

"So, Karen, what do you do for a living?"

"I'm a student at Harold Washington College and I now work at a coffee shop."

Darren was almost ashamed of his date, almost. She was a grown woman attending City College who now worked at a coffee shop. And here she was among the city's elite. Darren would have been ashamed of Karen had it not been for how far she'd come. A few months ago her reply would have been, I dance at a strip club out on Route 57.

"So, Korie, what do you do?" Karen asked.

"I'm an interior designer. I design houses and sets for music videos."

"Wow!" Karen replied.

Wow, indeed. I've been trying for years to get her to follow her dreams, Darren thought.

"Hmm, that sounds like interesting work. How did you break into that business?" Darren asked. He was anxious to hear her reply.

"Well, I had a pretty bad breakup. No offense, honey," she said to Vaughn.

"None taken. That's the past, sweetheart, and I'm only concerned about our future."

Vaughn smiled and caressed Korie's hand. That caress, that simple gesture, had Darren burning on the inside.

Korie continued her story.

"Anyway, I was dating this guy. I thought we were in love and all he ever seemed to think about was work. So, anyway, all he ever wanted to do was make money and all I ever wanted in the world, at that time in my life, was him. We argued about how busy he was, and how little time he invested in our relationship. Well, one day I came home and he was gone. He left a note and a check for the rent, but he left me. He didn't even have the courage to face me and tell me he was leaving."

***

"Coward," Karen said.

Darren had a sip of water. He was pissed; more than that, he was enraged. Korie went on with her story.

"So a few months later, I was laid off. I was heartbroken and all alone. I decided that I was going to work for myself. I decided to invest in myself and I've had a love for interior design and sewing, so I decided to pursue my dreams. Once I decided to invest in myself I never looked back."

"That's amazing," Karen said. "What a jerk, your ex. At least he left you a check. A lot of other men would have just left."

"Yes. At least he left you a check. Sounds like he wasn't that bad of a man" Darren said, "Vaughn, what do you think?"

"I think leaving a check was a noble gesture. By the same token, I can't see why any man would leave a woman like this."

Vaughn took Korie's hand again. Again he caressed it. He held it like a man in love. She reciprocated. Then they kissed. Darren thought he was going to lose his mind. On the inside he was dying a slow death. On the inside, he was heartbroken.

Dinner was served, then dessert. Afterward, there was a series of speeches, a series of requests for additional donations, and a short film on helping the homeless. From there people were given a chance to mix and mingle.

"You should walk with me and meet a few people," Vaughn said to Darren.

"You're right. I should. Let's go. Ladies, please excuse us."

Karen and Korie got to know one another. While they did, Darren tried to get himself together.

Darren and Vaughn walked around the ballroom. Darren saw many of his clients at the event who introduced him to more potential clients. Darren smiled and laughed with various people and acted as if Korie was not on his mind.

She was.

He passed out at least one hundred business cards and when he felt as if he had had his fill, he stopped marketing himself. He continued to walk around with Vaughn, who introduced him to CEOs of huge corporations—corporations Vaughn planned to take over. The two men worked the room in dynamic fashion. When they both were done, they returned to the business of entertaining their ladies. On their way back to the table, Vaughn spoke.

"She's beautiful, isn't she?"

"Yes, she is. So, that's the woman that you're catching all the hell over?"

"That's her. I'm a lucky man. Like you said, how do I know that she isn't meant for me?"

Because she's meant for me, Darren thought.

"Yes. Well, you're a lucky man. We only get a few chances at love," Darren said, trying to remain objective.

"And I have you to thank for that," Vaughn said.

"Me?"

"Yes. I was going to break things off with her. I was even tempted to go back to seeing escorts, and you convinced me to give love a chance. I want to thank you for that."

Great, Darren thought.

The two men shook hands. They returned to their dates. Slow music began to play. Darren took Karen's hand, and Vaughn took Korie's hand. The couples headed to the dance floor and began to dance. Darren held Karen tight. Korie held Vaughn tight.

Darren thought of Korie.

Korie thought of Darren.

They both smiled. They both put up a good act as if the other was not on their mind.

But they both knew.

Korie looked up from Vaughn's shoulder and her eyes finally met with Darren's.

His eyes said he was hurting.

Her eyes said that she was sorry for hurting him.

They might not have still been in love, but they knew this chapter hadn't ended yet. There was more to their story.

They both struggled to get through the end of the night.

The music switched from slow to fast and the second that the fast music came on, the mistresses, escorts, and groupies took the floor. Women dropped it like it was hot. They danced erotically. The women danced with each other, gyrated their bodies, and did their best to entice the most powerful men in the city. This did not go over well with the wives.

Not to be outdone, Karen took off her expensive heels and went to the dance floor. The crass side, it seemed, could no longer be subdued. Karen saw the various women dancing as a challenge, an opportunity. She too went out and danced among the women. She too let her hair down and worked her magic on the floor. Men were mesmerized by her.

Darren was embarrassed. You can take the girl out of the hood, but it seems you can't take the hood out of the girl.

"I apologize," Darren said to Vaughn. Vaughn laughed.

"That's okay. I understand. You better get her, though. Men here will be offering her thousands of dollars to leave you."

Darren laughed. "I guess you're right."

The second he was able to make eye contact with her, Karen stopped. Like a scolded child, she gathered herself together and headed back to his side. He smiled at her for appearance's sake. He leaned in to speak to her as he took her hand.

"What the fuck was that?" Darren whispered.

"I was just dancing. The other ladies were doing it."

"The other ladies didn't come here with anyone. Those are the mistresses and groupies."

"Oh."

"If you want to dance like that then wait until we get back to my place."

"You want your own private show?"

"I do," Darren said, smiling.

Darren had to admit that he liked the way that Karen danced. He loved the way that she moved. This event, however, was not the right place for that. They shared a laugh or two before going back to their table.

"Wow. That was quite a display," Korie said, referencing Karen's dancing but looking at Darren the whole time.

"I'm going to go get a drink. Do you want anything?" Darren asked Karen while returning Korie's stare.

"Seven and seven," she responded.

"Okay. Korie . . . raspberry vodka?"

Korie gave Darren a stunned look. Then Darren thought about it and had an equally stunned look on his face. He couldn't believe how easily it slipped out.

First mistake.

Darren knew that was Korie's favorite drink and he simply blurted it out. Luckily Vaughn was talking with another CEO.

"Uh, sure. How did you know?" Korie tried to play things off. She looked at him as if to say, get yourself together.

"Lucky guess. I'll be right back. Well, not right back. I plan to have a few."

Darren went to the bar and had three consecutive rum and Cokes. As Darren spoke with the bartender, with his back to the event, he experienced an array of emotions. This night was becoming more increasingly difficult, too difficult. He just wanted to go home and crawl in bed so he could awaken from this nightmare.

"Woman problems?" a familiar voice said.

Darren turned around, hoping that it was Korie. He was equally surprised to see Stephanie. He looked at her, frowned, and turned his back. She was looking good, damned good. But she spurned him. He wanted nothing to do with her. Besides, he figured she was here working and on the arm of some mogul at the event.

"Bartender, I'll have another," he said, ignoring her.

"How have you been?" she asked.

"I thought I wasn't supposed to talk to you when you were working."

"I'm talking to you."

"So you are working."

"Yes, I am."

"So . . . who?"

"Does it matter?"

"Nope." He tossed back another drink.

"Are you that mad with me?"

"I am."

"Why?"

Darren was furious with her. Stephanie was the first woman in a long time who took his mind off Korie. In fact, she was the only woman that could truly take his mind off her. Like his feelings for Korie, Darren would have given her the world. It seems that women these days weren't interested in the world. They weren't interested in what a man could do for them. Korie wasn't interested because all she ever wanted was Darren. Stephanie wasn't interested because there was nothing that he could offer her that she couldn't get herself.

"Tell me you didn't think we made a connection," Darren said to Stephanie.

"I can't say that."

"Then tell me that you couldn't see a long life with me."

"I can't say that, either."

"Then tell me what the fuck was the problem."

"It had been a long time since I felt the way that I felt for you. The last time that I felt that way a man broke my heart. Plus, I like my lifestyle. I like the way that I live. I love this life. I had feelings for you too, but in this business there is no room for feelings."

"I would have given you the world."

"The truth is, Darren, there is nothing that you could have given me that I couldn't get myself."

"What about love?"

That shut Stephanie up.

"Two screwdrivers please," she said to the bartender.

She stood next to Darren in silence.

"Once, Twice, Three Times" by Howard Hewett began to play. The fast music stopped and again the mistresses and groupies left the floor. Some danced with the men who invited them, others retreated to their seats.

"The girl you're with, she's very pretty. Can I ask what agency she's with?"

Darren looked at her as if to imply he was insulted.

"She's not with an agency. She's just with me."

"Oh."

"I never used an agency before you and I had no plans to do so afterward."

"I'm sorry, I didn't mean to—"

"Don't worry about it." He tossed back another rum and Coke. He was really buzzed, almost drunk.

"Is she your girlfriend?"

"She's my date. I mean, we're dating. We have been for a while now."

"It didn't take you long to move on."

"Let you tell it, we didn't have anything to begin with. It was just . . . business."

"Darren I'm sorry, I—"

"I need to get back to my date, where I'm appreciated."

Darren took Karen her drink. He was feeling no pain at this point and he asked Karen to dance. She gulped down her drink and the two of then hit the dance floor. "I Can't Stop Loving You" by Kem was playing. Darren held Karen tight and they danced. Next a song by Jay-Z began to play and Darren and Karen danced sexually. They danced until they worked up a sweat and then they took each other's hands and told their good-byes to Vaughn and Korie. They left. It was obvious they were going back to his place. It was obvious that the liquor had Darren in the mood, and the atmosphere had Karen in the mood. Darren took Karen home in hopes of getting Korie off his mind. He began to wonder if that was even possible.

Even now I want her more than I have ever wanted anything or anyone in my life, he thought.

Chapter Twenty-seven

"Like You'll Never See Me Again" by Alicia Keys was playing over Darren's speaker system in the car. He drove down beautiful Lake Shore Drive to his condo. Each cord that Alicia sang resonated with him. With each verse there was a memory of him and Korie.

Karen had a few drinks before leaving and she too was feeling no pain. She held Darren's hand as he drove down Lake Shore Drive.

Like you'll never see me again, is what Darren thought as he drove. He wished he kissed Korie and made love to her that last time like he would never see her again. He had no idea that the last time he made love to Korie would be the last time that he would ever make love to her again.

He thought again about how they met. He thought about every argument and every passionate embrace. He thought about the fact that she was seeing one of the wealthiest men in the world, and that there was no way he could get her back. He felt defeated. There was no way that he could compete with Vaughn's millions. She was the love of his life. And she was the love that he lost.

They walked into Darren's condo. More love songs were turned on. They kissed. Darren's hands explored Karen's backside and he slowly pulled up her silk dress to expose her thick bottom. He gave her ass a squeeze as their tongues danced with one another. She undid her dress and let it slip to the floor.

No panties. No bra. Just stockings, a garter, and 1,500-dollar heels.

Crass. Very crass.

He kissed her again. He bit her ear and sucked her earlobe as he grabbed one of her breasts.

"You don't have on any panties," he whispered softly in her ear.

"With an ass like mine and tits like these I don't need them." She sucked his bottom lip as they continued to kiss.

Crass. Very crass. But very sexy, he thought.

Darren peeled off his jacket and unbuttoned his shirt. His ripped abs were exposed. Karen kissed his chest, neck, and stomach. She then went back to kissing him on the mouth. He walked her over to the wall and spread her hands and legs against the wall as if to arrest her. He took off his pants, shoes, and socks and stood behind her naked as the day he was born.

He kissed her back. He moved her hair aside to kiss her neck, her shoulders, and her arms and licked ever so gently down her back. Karen let out a gentle sigh as she felt his tongue caress her backside. He knelt behind her and kissed the cheeks of her ample behind and also kissed her thighs and calves. Karen shuddered with anticipation. He then turned her around and devoured her. He tasted her sex and she purred like a kitten as he pleased her.

He devoured her.

He had his way with her.

He pretended that she was her.

He made love to her.

He made love to her like he was never going to see her again.

He made love to her. He fucked her. And he made love to her again.

By morning he was spent. He fucked her and he fucked her with all that he had. He fucked her as if he were trying to fuck away all his final memories of Korie. He fucked her as if to try and forget her. He fucked her so hard that he thought all traces of her and all memories of her would be lost in his seed, lost in his orgasm.

He tried to fuck Korie out of his mind and his heart.

He tried to fuck Korie out of existence.

He fucked so hard that he wanted to forget that he ever knew the name Korie Ann Dillon.

He failed.

He failed miserably.

Long after he came, he was looking at the ceiling, thinking about her, as Karen slept.

Chapter Twenty-eight

Korie and Vaughn said their good-byes about midnight. The event didn't end until 3:00 in the morning, but by midnight Vaughn had spoken to everyone he was going to speak to. He wore himself out with all the talking and dancing, but he handled himself well. Tonight he drove. He drove his Porsche. "Beautiful" by Musiq Soulchild was playing on the radio as they headed north on Lake Shore Drive back to his place. He took Korie's hand in his as he drove home.

"Did you enjoy this evening?"
"I did."
"You seem a bit distracted."
"I have a long day tomorrow."
"Oh. Okay. Do you want me to take you home?"
"No. My place is too far. Let's just head back to your house."
"Do you want me to have the driver take you home after?" Vaughn smiled at her.
"That will be fine." Korie smiled back.
After. That meant that Vaughn planned on taking Korie to bed. That meant that once they got back, the first thing they would do would be to take baths in one of the many bathrooms in the house.
The first thing that Vaughn would do would be to take a little blue pill hidden in his den, and then head

to the shower on the first floor. Korie would go to the master bedroom on the second floor and pull out something sexy. She would wait in the tub until the pill took effect. Sometimes it only took fifteen minutes for the blood to rush to certain body parts. Other times it took longer, much longer. In either case, Korie would relax in the tub until he was ready. When he would come looking for her, she would quickly come out of the water, dress in lingerie, and come to him in his bed. It was an all-too-familiar routine. There was little spontaneity these days, little variety.

For what Vaughn lacked in creativity, he made up for in bed. Once he got going, he was a dynamo. He had length, girth, and he knew how to work his manhood. He was a fantastic lover. He was patient, tender, and methodical. He never made his way inside of Korie without kissing every inch of her body. She loved that. She took a hot bath and waited for him.

When he called for her, she went to him in black-lace boy shorts, a garter, and a sexy black bra. She moisturized her body in strawberry-scented lotion prior to coming out of the bathroom and stepped out looking good enough to eat.

She picked up the remote on the dresser in the bathroom and began playing soft music.She walked over to Vaughn and kissed him. He was wearing black silk pajama pants and an open silk pajama top. He slowly kissed her neck, her collarbone, and back up to her eyelids as he cupped her round, firm bottom.

As his hand explored her backside, she grabbed his package. She massaged it ever so slowly as she offered him her tongue. She kissed his neck, his chest, and she ran her hands alongside his thighs. He smiled at her, she smiled back, and she playfully pushed him to the bed.

She turned her back to him and did a sexy dance. He had a front-seat view of her sexy bottom and her long legs. She moved back and forth, dancing slowly, erotically. She teased him with her slow, sexual movements. She looked back at him and was happy to see that he was mesmerized. She smiled to herself as she continued to dance.

"You like that?"

"I love that."

"You want a closer view?"

"I do."

She simulated masturbation as she danced. This was something that he liked. She touched herself, she pleased herself. She became moist and offered him a finger with a taste of her flavor. She then turned her back to him again and slowly peeled off her boy shorts. She left the bra on. She knew how much he loved lace. She then lay him down on the bed and got on top of him to kiss him.

They kissed and touched one another until the song switched. His manhood was so hard he was longing for her, aching for her. New music came on. As the slow song began to play, Korie turned her back to Vaughn again. She mounted him. She then leaned forward and gave him a better view of her backside as he went in and out of her. His manhood was glistening with her flow.

She leaned forward and began to slowly rock back and forth. His well-built chest heaved up and down as his breathing became more pronounced. He tried to control her, tried to guide her. He tried to take things at his pace, but Korie took over. Vaughn didn't know it, but only her body was there with him. Her mind was with him.

Korie let her mind wander to the many times and places that she made love with Darren. She thought of him. She thought about his length, his girth, and the way that he used to make her feel. She longed to feel like that again. She wanted to feel like that tonight. It didn't help matters that she had seen him. Memories that she thought were long gone, were back in full swing.

When they were together, sometimes she and Darren would make love. Other times they would fuck. They would fuck like two prizefighters. They would fuck like two people who loved each other and also hated each other. They would fuck one another for dominance, for bragging rights. They would fuck with the goal in mind to make the other beg for mercy.

Vaughn always made love to her.

Tonight, after seeing him, after the music, after the liquor . . .

Tonight, she really wanted to be fucked.

Her back was to Vaughn. Her mind was with Darren. Her body had plans of its own.

She rode Vaughn.

She rode him hard. Her clitoris rubbed against his package. Her vaginal muscles flexed. She became excited, primitive. She had a heightened sense of awareness. Her nipples became sensitive and every nerve ending was firing, waiting to be touched, longing to be triggered. Her true sex drive had been awakened and she soon after had a feral passion within her that had escaped its confinement.

She had her way with him.

Vaughn tried to control her. He tried to please her, but he wanted her to slow down. Between her pace and the Viagra, it felt as if he were running a marathon.

A marathon he was losing badly.

She rode him. She fucked him. She moaned, she flexed, and released her vaginal muscles as she bounced up and down on top of him. Once she threw her hips into the battle, things went to a whole new level. It was like a high-end sports car racing an economy car. In Vaughn's case it was like a sports car racing a horse and buggy.

She didn't hear the guttural sounds that she made. She didn't hear the primitive grunts. She wasn't aware of his heavy breathing or hers. She wasn't aware of how her breasts swelled with passion, or how her hair began to sweat. She was only aware that there was a penis inside of her that she intended to work like a plow on open country ground. It was a penis she intended to use for its designed purpose; to please her, to fuck her, to take her to the brink of orgasm and beyond.

She rode him until she came. She thought of him, and she came—hard.

Fortunately for Vaughn, he came as well. It wasn't until she got her breathing under control that she remembered him, remembered what his name was. It was then that she remembered that Vaughn was her boyfriend and not Darren. She looked back at him. In that moment he looked old, worn. He looked like a beaten man, a happy man, but a beaten man.

She came, but she wanted to come again. She wanted to do it again. He looked as if he wanted to collapse into unconsciousness. Vaughn was one and done. Korie thought back to her many bedroom bouts with Darren and remembered how some days he would only pause after sex long enough to grab some orange juice to refuel.

"That was incredible. I thought I was going to die for a minute there, but it was great," Vaughn said.

You have no idea, Korie thought.

His voice rang with finality. They would not have sex again this evening. They wouldn't do it again in the morning. They probably wouldn't do it again for a few days. She came. But she wanted more. Her endorphins were firing. Her cycle was due to start soon and although she was satiated, she was not satisfied, not yet. She wanted to be fucked. She wanted Vaughn to fuck her, to spank her, to pull her hair. She wanted him to put her to sleep. She wanted to feel him between her legs long after he pulled out. She wanted more.

He couldn't give her more. He gave her what he could.

Minutes later he was asleep.

She wasn't dissatisfied with him. She enjoyed his performance even though she did all the work. She was content. This evening's sex would get her through the next day. It was enough for her to know that he cared for her. It was enough for her to know that he desired her. But was it enough? Was this the best that he could do? She dismissed those thoughts. She felt guilty having thought about another man while sleeping with her man. Still, her thoughts of she and Darren helped get her there. Those carnal thoughts brought her quickly to orgasm. The sex was the best they ever had. Unfortunately, it was thoughts about her ex that made her come so hard. Korie felt guilty. She felt ashamed.

She got dressed. Vaughn continued to sleep.

Minutes later, Korie was driven back to her place by his driver.

She came, but she wasn't completely satisfied.

How important is sex? she thought as she was driven home.

Until now, sex between her and Vaughn was fine, until now things were good; they were routine.

Until now.

Until she remembered how things used to be, or how they could be.

Sex isn't everything, she thought.

Right?

Chapter Twenty-nine

The next day Korie awoke to a thunderous knocking at her door. She looked at the clock and it said 6:00 A.M. She and Jayna weren't scheduled to run until 8:00. Having only gotten home at 3:00, she was exhausted. She tried to cover her head with the covers and pillow.

The knocking continued. Korie became upset, but then gave it some thought. Jayna recently lost her man. She probably wanted to get an early start to the day. She probably needed consoling and support. Jayna had been there for Korie when she went through her drama with Darren. She was there when Darren broke her heart and was there to pick the pieces up for her. Early or not, friendship had no bounds. Friendship had no time constraints. That being the case, Korie got up from her bed and headed to the door as the knocking started again. Once again she tied her robe over her teddy and headed to the door.

"I'm coming, just a minute."

Korie spoke in the most pleasant voice she could after only having three hours of sleep. She stopped in the kitchen and hit the automatic-brew button on her coffee machine. She would certainly need a cup of java to get through the day. Korie opened the door and was surprised to see Darren. She did a double take. She couldn't believe that he was there.

"What—what are you doing here?"

"I had to see you."

"What? Darren no—I mean, what are you doing here? Vaughn could have been here."

"Is he?"

"No but . . ."

Darren stepped into the apartment without warning. "I need to see you."

"What is it? I mean, what do you want?"

"You, I want you. I miss you. I need to talk to you."

Korie's mouth was open and she was speechless. Darren was dressed in dark blue jeans, white-on-white gym shoes, and a T-shirt. He smelled good, he looked good, and he had a look of hurt and wanting in his eyes. He sat on the couch that was in the same place that it was years ago when he left. On the table were photos of the two of them. It was obvious to him that she too had been reminiscing. She must have just pulled the photos out. He picked one of them up. It was a picture of them when they were their happiest. Seeing the photos sprawled out on the table gave him hope. It told him that there was still a chance. Clearly she had been thinking about him also.

"Darren, what are you doing here?"

"Baby, I miss you."

"I have a boyfriend."

"DeVaughn Harris? He's old enough to be your father."

"Don't go there. He's a good man."

"That I don't doubt. But he's not the man for you."

"Oh really? Let me guess, you are?"

"I am."

"You were."

"You can't mean that. From the looks of these pictures on the table here, you can't mean that." He pointed at the photos.

"I was getting ready to throw them away."

"Bullshit. Korie, I'm sorry. I messed up. When I called you a few weeks back, it was because you were on my mind. It was because you're still in my heart. All these years later I still think about you. Baby, I sometimes dream about you."

He went to hug her. She shrugged him off and walked away.

"I dream about you too. I dream that you and I are together in love, and although things aren't perfect, we're working toward the same goal. Then, in the midst of the dream, you up and leave me. Oh wait, that wasn't a dream. That shit really happened!" She turned around and pointed at him.

"That's not fair."

"Isn't it, though?" Korie put her hand on her hip as she spoke.

"Don't act like I am the only one that caused our break-up. I'm not the only one at fault!"

"No, but you are the only one that bailed out on the relationship! You're the one that jumped ship!"

"That was after you sabotaged our relationship and got pregnant!"

It was a low blow. When they fought, both of them fought to win. Darren regretted saying it the second it walked out of his mouth.

"I didn't mean that," he said apologetically.

"Of course you did. And I admit getting pregnant on purpose wasn't the answer, but I did it to save our relationship."

"You did it to sabotage my plan."

"Oh, here we go with your precious plan again."

"Korie, the plan had merit. There was a means to the end. All you had to do was stay the course and see things through."

"And where would that have led us, Darren? I didn't want to wait for you to be successful. I wanted to be there with you every step of the way as you moved up in your career."

"And had you waited, we would be living nice right now."

"I'm not living bad now. In fact, I have my own business."

"A business that I planned for you. A dream that you had for yourself that I saw for you before you saw it for yourself. Had you just listened to me instead of being so damned stubborn, we could be together doing great things!"

"I do great things on my own, without you!"

"With what? DeVaughn Harris? An old man who is trying to recapture his youth? What's so damned special about him?"

"He took me to Tokyo a few weeks back! Can you top that?"

That shut Darren up. What was worse was the trip to Tokyo was his idea. Talk about bad karma. He paced back and forth as he tried to think of ways to win Korie back.

"Look, I didn't come here to argue."

"What did you come here for?"

"I came back for you. Baby, I need you. I'm sorry."

"Darren, do you remember how you left me? You left with no damned warning and you left a check on the counter over there like I was nothing to you. Like I was a damned whore being paid for her time."

That hit home. She was right. If there was one thing that Darren would have taken back, it was the way that he left her. It was the mother of all mistakes.

"I'm sorry."

"You're damned right, you're sorry."

"Baby . . . look."

"Don't baby me. You lost that privilege."

"Korie, look. Everything that I did then, everything that I do now, is to lay the foundation for us to be together. Back then we needed a break and—"

"If you needed a break then you should have said that you needed a break. Leaving a note like you did . . ."

". . . was the biggest mistake of my life. Leaving you was the biggest mistake of my life. Baby—Korie—I'm sorry. I'm asking you to forgive me."

"Why now, Darren? Why now? Is it because I'm with Vaughn?"

"No. No. I didn't know you were with Vaughn until yesterday. I've been trying to get with you for months now. You've been on my mind everyday since I left."

"I can't tell! I haven't heard from you in years. Years!" she shouted. Korie walked to the kitchen to retrieve a cup of coffee.

Silence over took the apartment. Darren walked around the living room. The place hadn't changed much. There were a few new pieces of furniture, but nothing had really changed. He sat on the couch and thumbed through all the pictures of them. If she was going through the photos, she was reminiscing. She had thought of him. She had been asking herself what-if. It was on him to answer those questions. Korie walked back in the living room and sat across from him. She looked upset with him, disappointed.

"What do you want?"

"I want a second chance."

"I'm seeing someone. In fact, I'm seeing your client. Isn't there some ethics violation there?"

"There may be, but I don't care. I want you back. I want us back."

"What about your girlfriend?"

"Who?"

"Karen, the thirtysomething student who just went back to community college."

Darren let out a sigh.

"It's not a serious relationship."

"She seems to think it is."

"What?"

Darren was confused. He didn't remember seeing them talk at length where they could get to know one another. With the way Korie responded, it must have been written all across his face.

"Darren, I know you. Right now you're trying to figure out when we got so acquainted that I could know this. Well, I got to know Ms. Karen very well at the party."

Darren was still trying to figure out when. Then, as if to read his mind, Korie responded.

"While you were at the bar, throwing back those rum and Cokes when that woman who looked like Keyshia Cole was talking to you."

Darren was thinking, you saw that? Of course he didn't say so, but that too had to be written across his head because again, Korie responded.

"Yeah, I saw that."

He had a look of surprise on his face. She knew him. All these years later and she still knew him—well.

"It doesn't take a long time for women to get to know one another. We know exactly what to ask each other and how to mark our territory. She thinks you're a good man and the real deal. She thinks you're feeling her just as much as she's feeling you. Now if she's mistaken, that means that you've misled her in some way. And if that's the case, that means that you haven't changed one bit. What do you plan on doing with her, leave her a note too?"

It was a low blow. But like Darren, Korie fought to win.

"It's not serious."

"Then what is it?"

"I don't know. It's not us. She's not you."

"Does she know that you feel that way?"

"What? No."

"Then you're not being fair with her. And if you can't be fair with her, how can you be fair with me?"

Darren let out another sigh.

"Korie, this doesn't have to be this hard."

"Oh, but it does."

"Can't we just start again?"

"Are you kidding me? You date me, leave me, don't call for years, and think you can just waltz your happy ass back into my life, is that how this works?"

"No. I will have dated you, left you, which we both know was a mistake, and come back to you after learning from my mistake, and you'll give me a second chance and we'll live happily ever after like we were meant to do in the first place."

"And it's just that simple."

"Well, maybe not that simple. But that's the plan."

"And we both know that you are the master of planning."

"I planned your business pretty good, didn't I?"

"What makes you think so?"

"I looked you up on the Net. I saw your Web site. Every idea that I left on your laptop you used. You even went back to school when neither of us ever thought you would. After all my lecture and insistence, you went and you did well. Just as I knew you would have all those years ago."

"Do you hear yourself? You just said, all those years ago. Darren, it's been five years. We could have been married by now. We could have had at least two babies by now."

"It wasn't our time then. Our time is now. Back then I couldn't give you the lifestyle that I wanted to give you. Back then I couldn't give you the storybook wedding that you wanted. Now I can. I can give you all that and more."

"I never wanted that. I never wanted any of that. That's just the thing. All I ever wanted was you."

"Baby, I'm here."

"Five years later. Five years too late."

"So I guess you get your way and my plan failed."

"Your plan failed when you walked out that door."

They sat in silence. Darren put his head in his hands and Korie crossed her legs and looked away. Both were hurting. Both opened up old wounds and both still cared. Everything that came out of Korie's mouth was from her head. Her head still had her defenses up. Her head considered how Vaughn would feel in the midst of all this. Her heart . . . her heart wanted Darren back. Her heart longed to know how he was. Her heart wanted to hear more about how he missed her. Her heart wanted to open the door again to love.

But it was her head that was in charge.

From her mouth shot venom about sins past. Anguish and hurt that she'd felt over the past five years. She had dated off and on since him. She dated. But nothing ever developed because she always longed to be with him. It was his babies that she wanted, and no man who she dated was ever his match. That is, until Vaughn.

Vaughn was the best person to come along and distract her, but that was because he was charming as well as a man with means. Part of her told her that Vaughn was just a rebound. After all, he was the first real relationship that she had had since Darren. Maybe Darren was right. Maybe Vaughn was too old for her. Maybe their relationship was doomed to fail. In many ways, Vaughn simply reminded Korie of an older version of Darren.

Korie sipped her coffee. She thought about what could have been. She thought about how much she longed for him over these past few years and here he was in her living room. He was right there, but he seemed thousands of miles away.

"The place hasn't changed much."

That snapped Korie out of her trance.

"What?"

"The apartment. It hasn't changed much."

"There wasn't a lot around here that needed to be changed." She cut her eyes at him.

Her tongue was still sharp. She was still mad. But Darren decided if he had to crawl over hot broken glass to get her back, that's what he would do.

"I miss you."

"You said that."

"Yeah, and if I have to, I'll say it a million times more."

Korie let out a sigh.

"Did you buy Karen's implants?"

"What? No." Darren said, laughing.

"How did you meet her?"

"I, um . . . met her at the barbershop. Her son was referred to the agency I work for."

"There's no ethical breach there."

"No. I don't see her like that. She's not my client."

"Hmm."

"How did you meet Vaughn?"

"Jogging. Jayna and I were jogging and he saw me and asked me out."

"Ah, yes . . . Jayna."

Darren never liked her. She was a venomous, hateful, and spiteful woman in his eyes. Jayna was promiscuous, she could never keep a man, and Darren always felt that she monopolized too much of Korie's time. She was a beautiful woman, but she was needy as hell in Darren's eyes.

"Don't start. She was there to pick up the pieces when you left."

"Hmm."

Darren hated Jayna. She was a nice-looking woman with an incredible body but in Darren's mind she was trouble. She always came to Korie crying about some man. She always wondered what it was that she did wrong and why no man would ever fall in love with her.

It was because of how quickly she gave away her goods. She had a problem, a serious mental problem, as far as Darren was concerned. Always she cried to Korie about men and always it was because they slept with her and then dumped her. To be such a smart and business-savvy woman, Darren had no respect for her. He also knew she was trouble because of how provocatively she dressed.

Back when Darren and Korie were together, Jayna would dress in jeans, skirts or shorts that were always too tight. Her cleavage was always too revealing. She wore white pants on the weekends with red thongs or low riding pants with her behind out. She was a very attractive woman. She was dangerous and a temptation for him. That was part of the reason that he didn't like her. Korie never said anything to Jayna about the way she dressed around her man. She never said anything and she never thought twice about leaving Jayna around Darren.

Of course, she should have been able to leave the two of them alone. Jayna was her best friend and Darren was her man. The two people that she trusted most in the world should be able to keep their hands to themselves. Shouldn't they?

Although Darren found Jayna to be attractive, his love for Korie was stronger than his lust. Jayna and Korie were like night and day and for Darren, there was a time that he could have had the best of both worlds. Jayna dressed provocatively and had a reputation for her skills in the bedroom. Everything she wore was revealing, everything about her reeked sexuality.

Korie was just the opposite. She had a nice body, but she remained clothed. Korie always dressed so you would have to imagine what she looked like. She was the type of woman who dressed conservatively on the surface but would have on something naughty and sexy underneath. Darren used to remark how at the end of the day when he would undress her, it was like unwrapping a Christmas present. It was always a surprise. With Jayna, what you see was what you could get.

Darren had his opportunity to get it.

Because he loved Korie, he declined.

It was a hot summer night six years ago that Darren's love for Korie was truly tested. He had the day off and Korie and Jayna were scheduled to go out. Jayna had just broken up with some married executive, and she and Korie were going out for drinks at a nightclub in Dolton, Illinois.

Korie got tied up at work. She couldn't get home until 10:00. She called Jayna and told her. Jayna said she was running late as well. She said she would meet Korie at her place at 10:00. It wasn't uncommon for Jayna to get dressed at Darren and Korie's place. There were many times that Jayna would come over and Darren would go out into the living room, or leave altogether as the two women went out for girls' night. They used to dress up at their place and then go pick up their girl-friend Eula. The three women would often stay out un-til 2:00 A.M. If they were too tipsy, Korie would let them both sleep over and take them home in the morning.

This particular evening, Jayna got to their place at 8:00. Two hours too early. Two hours way too early. Darren heard a knock at the door. He opened it, think-ing it might have been one of his boys, but it was Jayna. Back then, they were cool. The hate hadn't started yet. The hate wasn't warranted yet. Darren opened the door with a confused look.

"Hey Jayna, what are you doing here?"

"I thought I was going to be late, but I got out of work early."

"Oh, well, Korie won't get home until ten."

"Should I leave?"

"Uh, you don't have to. I guess you can just chill here until she gets off."

First mistake.

"Okay, Cool. Can I put my clothes and things in the bathroom?"

"Sure."

She walked by him and headed to the bathroom. She smiled at him. It was a smile that almost made him feel uncomfortable. He could smell her perfume as she walked by. She fumbled around in the bathroom and then called out to him.

"I just bought a new outfit that I'm not so sure about. Do you mind if I try it on?"

"Uh, that's cool, I guess."

Mistake number two.

Darren went back to playing his video game. He was throwing back a few rum and Cokes and playing video games. Jayna went into the bathroom and was back there for a while. Darren kept throwing back rum and Cokes and kept playing the game. Minutes later the phone rang. It was Korie.

"Hey babe, what's up?"

"Jayna will be over close to ten o'clock. I'm going to try and get over there before her. If you're home, will you let her in?"

Darren was on the cordless phone. He got up to walk to the kitchen when Jayna walked from the bathroom across the hall to the bedroom where she laid out her clothes. Darren saw her in the hallway. She walked across the hall to the bedroom with her dress in her hand.

She had on nothing but blue-lace boy shorts, heels, and a matching bra. The side view that Darren saw was perfect. Her stomach wasn't ripped, but it was flat. And that ass, her ass was just . . . perfect. He saw Jayna's perfectly sculpted frame. His mouth dropped as she stepped into the hallway. Her long, flowing black hair was down and full of body. As he saw her, he was simply speechless.

This was trouble, major trouble. She stopped in the hallway and saw that he saw her. She turned as she saw him and put her dress in front of her, but not quickly. Not like a woman who was ashamed to be seen, not like a woman who was in front of her best friend's man.

"Oops. My bad," she whispered.

She smiled a little.

Just a little.

She then kept the dress in front of her but turned to the side where Darren could see the shape and curve of

her perfect and voluptuous backside again. She whispered to him.

"I'll just change in the bedroom."

She pointed toward the bedroom and slowly walked
in. Her ass bounced as she walked. She sashayed as she
walked. Darren was in a trance. He almost forgot Korie
was on the phone.

"Let Jayna in? Right, sure. I'll let her in when she gets
here."

He didn't mention that she was there. He didn't mention that she was there and practically nude in front of
him. Darren took in a gulp of air as he tried to compose
what he just saw.

"Thanks, babe. I'll try and get there before ten."

"Okay. Cool."

"Are you okay?"

"Yeah, yeah I'm cool. I'm just playing video games
and tossing back these rum and Cokes."

"Well, don't toss back too many."

"Oh, I won't. I think I'm done."

"Okay, see you later. Love you."

"Love you too."

Jayna came back out. This time she had the dress on.
She modeled it for Darren.

"So, what do you think?"

"I, um, think it's a bit tight, and a bit too revealing."

"Oh. Okay. Well, I respect your opinion. I'll go and
take it off. By the way, can you fix me one of those?"

"Fix you what?"

"A drink."

"Uh, yeah. Sure."

Darren fixed her a drink. He placed it on the counter in the kitchen. He sat back down to play his video

game. Jayna surfaced again. This time in boots, low rider jeans, and a short top.

"How about this?"

The jeans fit her like a second skin and admittedly looked good on her.

"Better," he said.

"How about that drink?"

"It's on the counter."

She turned to the kitchen and the low rider jeans were low, very low. You could see Jayna's crack and the tops of her butt cheeks. Darren let out a sigh.

Trouble. This is serious trouble, he thought.

He continued to play the game.

"So, this is cool for the club tonight? Do you think this will help me catch a man?"

Or make some nigga catch a case, he thought.

"I think that you will catch a man with that outfit on, yes," he responded.

"Here's a question. How do I catch a man like you? You and my girl seem really happy."

"We are happy." Darren stated it with confidence, as if reminding himself.

"I'll go back and change into my original clothes."

"Okay."

At that point Darren was sweating bullets.

The next time that Jayna came out she didn't have on her original outfit. She came out in a form-fitting black dress with nothing on underneath. The dress wasn't as tight as the first one she put on and was most appropriate for the club. She sat across from Darren bare-legged with her legs apart just enough for him to see her goods.

She was testing him.

Or teasing him.

He didn't approach or proposition her.

He didn't tell her to close her legs, either. He simply enjoyed the view. She knew what she was doing and he knew that she knew. He also knew that his silence said that he was indeed tempted. She knew he wanted her. She knew he thought about it by the bulge in his pants. In her mind she decided she wouldn't cross the line, but she would walk to the line. All he simply needed to do was take one step to the line and he could have her, all of her.

He enjoyed the view.

But he didn't walk to the line.

He stayed where he was.

He felt guilty, however, for not telling her to close her legs.

They talked the next few hours. They talked about relationships, what men liked in bed, her skills in bed, and she later asked him why men only wanted to sleep with her and none of them wanted to make her their woman.

They talked. That was it. Nothing more.

They talked until Korie got home. Korie came home and asked Jayna how long she had been there. Jayna said that she had only been there several minutes. She had been there two full hours. She lied. Because Darren said nothing, he might as well have lied.

Nothing happened. But Darren felt damned guilty. Korie went to get dressed and Jayna went to help her.

"We should have long talks like these more often," Jayna said before going to help her friend.

"Yeah, maybe," Darren said.

"Maybe next time we won't have to do so much talking," Jayna said.

Darren didn't respond.

He didn't say no, either. For Jayna, that was enough. That was confirmation that she could have him if she wanted.

Later that night, Korie was the one who had too much to drink. Jayna drove Eula home and then drove Korie home. Jayna insisted that night that Korie drink, knowing she was a lightweight when it came to liquor. Korie came home and collapsed on the couch. Darren carried her to bed. He offered to drive Jayna home. She declined. She said she didn't want to put him out. Darren was upset that Korie allowed herself to get that intoxicated, that out of control. He thanked Jayna for her help and said that he would see her in the morning.

He closed their bedroom door. His thoughts were consumed with Jayna's earlier behavior.

About 4:00 in the morning, just as the sun began to rise, Darren heard noise from the living room. It was a slight whimpering noise. He got up and looked in on Jayna, who was playing with herself on their living room couch and letting out soft moans as she did. He watched her. Even though her eyes were closed, she had to know he was there. She had to. For quite some time he watched. Eventually she looked up. She didn't stop. She smiled seductively at him.

She asked him to join her.

He told her to get dressed.

It wasn't a request.

It was a demand.

He wouldn't betray his woman any more than he had. He decided this madness needed to stop. He started to awaken Korie but thought better of it. He was a man and as a man, he needed to do the right thing.

He took her home. It was a long and silent ride, but he took her home. They didn't speak the entire time. He took her home and as he pulled up in front of her place, she apologized. Darren said nothing. She explained that she just wanted what Korie had. She explained that it was a mistake and tried to blame it on the liquor. Still,

Darren said nothing. He wanted to, but he knew that he was just as guilty as she was. Jayna cried. She was ashamed and embarrassed.

"Are you going to tell Korie?" She had a look of guilt across her face.

Darren said nothing.

"I need to know if you're going to tell Korie."

Again, they sat in silence. He gave her a fierce look.

"I made a mistake. She's my best friend and I can't afford to lose her."

"She's your only friend." His voice was stern.

"You're right. Okay, you're right. If you tell her you'll be taking away a friendship of more than twenty years."

"I won't be taking away anything. If your friendship is damaged, that will be on you."

He was cold in his response.

"And how do you think she'll see you?"

"I don't know."

"You're just as guilty as I am. It's clear that you were tempted to cross the line."

"True, but as her best friend, there should have been no offer and no line for me to cross."

"Are you going to tell her? Please don't. But I need to know, are you going to tell her?"

"No. I should, but I'm not. Now get out."

She was relieved that she wasn't about to lose her best friend, but in the same token she was jealous, mad, and bitter all at once. Part of her wanted him to tell her. At least, then Korie wouldn't be so happy.

In Jayna's mind, things came too easily to Korie. Jayna had the better body. Jayna was the more attractive of the two, but there was something about Korie that made good men look at her. Jayna might get the more attractive men, but over the years it seemed that Korie always made the better choices. Even now, with her having thrown herself at Korie's man, Korie still had a good man. Darren could've slept with her. Jayna would have quickly given herself to him in Korie's house had he pursued it. But he didn't. He turned her down. He turned her away. This upset her.

After being spurned and rejected, Jayna began to resent Darren. Darren was glad to have her out of the house. He was admittedly tempted. He always wanted to sleep with Jayna. He had always lusted for a taste of her honey just once. His love for Korie, however, was greater than his lust for Jayna. It was a secret that he kept for years. It was a secret that ate away at him over the years. When he left Korie, Jayna was happy. She was happy to know that Darren was like any other man—trifling. She never knew Korie's side of things or her transgressions. All she knew was that Darren hurt her girl and that was enough for her. Jayna didn't know it, but Darren was back. He came back to claim his woman as a good man should.

"Why do you hate Jayna so much?" Korie asked.

Korie's question brought Darren back to the present.

"I have my reasons. But never mind her. What about us?"

"Darren, there is no us. I need you to leave."

Korie got up and headed to the door. She opened it and had a look of regret as she ushered him to go. He stood up and headed to the door.

"Close the door for a minute."

"Darren, I—"

"Just close the door for a minute." His voice was smooth and seductive. "Korie, please."

She closed the door.

He took off his shirt.

"What are you—?"

"Just check me out for a minute."

Next he took off his shoes and pants. He stood there sporting a twelve-pack midsection in nothing more than his Calvin Klein boxers. His bulge was pointing north at her. He looked like a male model in a magazine. The sight of his body took her breath away.

"Korie . . . tell me you don't miss this."

He moved his pecs up and down and flexed every ripple in his stomach. He ran his fingers down his ripped midsection and looked at her seductively. He smiled at her confidently. He reeked of Aqua Di Gio cologne by Armani, her favorite scent.

Every muscle in his body looked as if it were sculpted from granite. His Hershey-colored skin was smooth and flawless. He looked more than good. He looked fine. Fine enough to eat and fine enough for her to have her every way with him. And he didn't need the assistance of little blue pills. All he needed was a glance at her. She was his Viagra. She was his motivation. Her heart rate increased, her mind wandered, and she wasn't even aware that she had a lustful look on her face as she looked at him.

Not to be outdone, Korie, though speechless, was equally confident. She had been working out for the last year and had been working out hard. In a bold move, she took off her robe, revealing her teddy and her shapely legs. Darren was stunned at how good she looked. She looked like something out of his dreams.

She took in a nervous breath as she took the spaghetti straps off of her teddy and tried to let it fall to the floor. The only problem was the delicate material was stopped on its way down by her curvaceous bottom. Her butt was too big for the teddy to hit the floor.

"Oops" she said.

She wiggled her hips from side to side to get the teddy to fall the rest of the way to the floor, but her bottom was too big. She then pulled the material up again and over her head. She tossed it to the floor and looked at him as if to say, now what?

She looked at him confidently and pointed to her own incredible body with her index fingers.

"Tell me you don't miss this!" She nodded her head as if to say, you better recognize.

Darren looked at her well-toned abs, her dynamic legs, and her baby-making hips. He looked at her taut chest and the V where her legs met. She looked absolutely breathtaking. He was confident, arrogant. That is, until he saw what Korie was working with. The years had been kind to her. She looked good, she smelled good, and he was quite sure she tasted good. To be sure, he wanted to see. He wanted to taste her, to devour her.

"Damn!" He licked his lips as he looked at her.

He thought he said damn in his head. He said it out loud. He grabbed her and kissed her; slowly, passionately. He kissed her like he was never going to see her again. He walked over to the stereo and turned on the radio. He picked her up in his arms and kissed her as he carried her to the counter in the kitchen. He placed her on the counter and kissed her eyelids, her earlobes, her lips, and her neck.

His hands found her breasts. They were full. They were plump. His mouth took her chocolate-colored nipples and kissed them, sucked them, and played with them. Korie let out soft sighs of pleasure as he kissed the entire front of her body. He grabbed a fistful of her hair and kissed her neck as his fingers found her wet sex. In and out he pleased her as he whispered to her how beautiful she was; how much he missed her.

Soft music was playing as he picked her up again. His muscular arms picked her up and both hands cupped her bottom as he lifted her up and lowered her onto his sex while still standing up. She wrapped her hands around him as he slowly went inside her. Her mouth opened and her jaw extended as she caught her breath with his penetration.

He was thick like she remembered.

Long like she remembered.

He hit her spot.

It had been a long time since someone hit her spot.

It had been way too long.

His manhood went there. His manhood remembered. It was a perfect fit, like it belonged there. It was as if there was a certain combination inside of her that only he had the combination to.

He stroked her slowly, methodically and gently. The first strokes were gentle. Those that followed were not. Her juices flowed. Her juices flowed as if he had tapped a well. Her juices flowed to express her pleasure and to accommodate him.

He started off slowly, passionately, as he made love to her. He kissed her, ran his hands alongside her body, and he touched her everywhere.

He kissed her everywhere.

He made love to her.

Then he fucked her.

Three more songs had played. By that time, they moved to the bedroom. She was on top of him. Her back was to him. He had the perfect view of her ample ass, her music-video ass, his ass.

He watched as she rocked back and forth, watched her juices lubricate his thickness. When she threw her hips into the mix, he smacked her hard on the ass. Darren placed his hands on her waist and began to move to her rhythm. He wasn't panting, wasn't out of breath, and he wasn't trying to slow her down. His passion matched her ferocity. He forced himself deeper inside of her. She fucked him. He fucked back. She bounced up and down on his sex and he watched. He watched it and he loved it.

Another song began to play when she turned to face him. She continued to ride him. His hands found her ass and helped her move on top of him. Again, they kissed. Again, their tongues met. They kissed, they talked, they whispered, and they moaned.

"I missed you. Everyday I missed you. Baby, I'm sorry. I love you. I love you. I love you."

Over and over and over again he told her how much he missed her, how much he loved her and what a fool he was, and how he was nothing without her.

Tears streamed down her face.

He kissed her tears.

She kissed his.

They continued to make love.

They made love and they fucked.

She came. She came vaginally on top of him. She gasped for air and her nipples hardened as she screamed his name and dug her nails into his flesh.

"I missed you too. Damn you . . . I missed you too," she whispered.

She fell forward on him. She kissed his neck and his chest. He stayed inside her while kissing her, caressing her. His hands ran alongside her body, across her back, and found her ass again.

He gave her time to recuperate. He held her.

When the next song began playing, he was grinding ever so slowly inside of her while she was on top of him. His penis never lost its girth, it never went limp. It was as if his manhood was home. When he began to grind again, blood flowed to her vagina. Life flowed to her vagina. Renewed pleasure flowed to her vagina. They made love on the couch with her on top.

Minutes later she came again. Shortly after that, they went at it again.

It was doggie-style behind the recliner chair.

Woman superior again on the couch.

Side to side on the floor.

And missionary anywhere that could support her weight.

Finally he came. He collapsed in the chair. She knelt before him. She took him into her mouth, bringing his flaccid penis back to life. She resuscitated it. She brought it back to full power. Again she rode him. Again she came. She slept on the carpeted floor and he slept beside her. They had a nap.

It was a power nap.

It was twenty minutes before Korie awoke again.

This time he was between her legs, tasting her, devouring her.

He pleased her like he might never see her again.

When "Pretty Wings" by Maxwell began, she was coming again. She came so hard her stomach muscles hurt.

She needed a break.

She needed sleep.

He picked her up again and took her to bed. He held her as she slept.

An hour later, they were both asleep in the bed where they once slept. She was in his arms, knocked out. It was a good sleep. It was the perfect thing to follow the three hours of sleep that she had the night before. It was the perfect complement to her exhausted body and it was something that she needed. It was everything that she remembered and more.

Sometime later there was a knock at the door. It was 8:55. Darren got up stark naked and walked to the door. For a second he forgot that this was no longer his home. He cracked opened the door. On the other side was Jayna. It could have been Vaughn, he thought, but it was Jayna.

"What—what are you doing here?" Jayna had a look of shock on her face.

"I'm back."

Darren opened the door and walked back inside.

Chapter Thirty

"What do you mean, you're back?"

Jayna walked in looking at Darren like she had seen a ghost.

"What didn't you understand?"

He turned his back on her and walked away.

Darren walked toward the interior of the home. He left the door open and headed to the bedroom. Jayna never saw his front, but she did see his-well sculpted backside. Darren walked in the bedroom where Korie was still sleeping. He put his underwear back on and his jeans. He then came out to the living area and went to the refrigerator to see what Korie had in the fridge. He wanted to continue to sleep. He wanted to continue making love to her. Clearly, that wasn't about to happen, so he decided to get his energy levels back up and prepare breakfast.

Jayna was still standing there with her mouth open. She couldn't believe that Darren was back in Korie's life. More than that, she couldn't believe that Korie would cheat on a man like DeVaughn Harris or that she would take Darren back. She was miffed. She was miffed the way that women often are when their girlfriends take ex-boyfriends back. She looked at him as if she was dreaming and he just happened to be in her dream. She couldn't believe that he was there.

"It's been a few years," Jayna said to Darren.

"It's been five years."

Darren went back to looking for something to eat. He pulled out turkey bacon, eggs, toast, potatoes, and a number of spices.

"What are you doing?"

Jayna sounded as if she were questioning why he was there more than what he was doing with the food.

"Making breakfast. You want some?"

Darren continued, oblivious to Jayna's shock. In truth, he didn't care what she thought. Jayna put her bag down and paced a bit before she spoke.

"You do know that she's seeing someone, right?" Jayna said.

Darren smiled a bit before speaking. His every muscle tensed up in his body. His bare chest and arms flexed a bit as he tried to contain his frustration with her.

"You do know that none of this is really your business, right?"

He began cutting up an onion and pulling out more spices from the cabinet.

Jayna walked closer to the counter to speak with Darren. She walked over as if she were sneaking to say what needed to be said. As if she was feeling guilty. She kept her voice to just a whisper.

"That's my best friend in there," she said while pointing to the bedroom.

"Right. And we know how loyal you are to your friends."

Darren found a carton of orange juice and took a sip directly from the carton, a habit that Jayna hated and one that she knew Korie hated when she and Darren lived together. It was one of those things that Korie used to always complain about. Silence fell between the two of them. Jayna knew exactly what it was that he was implying.

"That was a long time ago. I'm a changed woman."

"Then prove it. Mind your business."

He scraped the onion in a skillet and added diced potatoes, olive oil, salt, pepper, and garlic. He leaned in to smell the mixture as it cooked.

Jayna still was thrown off. She didn't expect to see Darren there. The years had been good to him. He was fit—very fit. He was ruggedly handsome, and he obviously still knew how to make Korie smile. He walked around the kitchen with familiarity. He walked like he owned the place or as if he lived there. It was like he just walked in and picked up where he left off years ago.

He cooked. He cooked the food that was in the fridge and just like years ago, Darren knew his way around a kitchen. He brewed more coffee, made breakfast, and even cut up some fruit. Jayna said nothing initially. She just watched him. He ignored her and turned the radio on in the kitchen while he cooked. He ignored her but that didn't mean he hadn't noticed her. She looked good, damned good. But she wasn't his Korie. And she still had a problem minding her own business. As far as Darren was concerned, she was another obstacle in the way.

Because of her inability to mind her own business, he ignored her. He promised himself he would be cordial, but nothing more. He hated that she was here, but it was obvious that Korie was expecting her. Jayna was in running gear and Darren remembered tossing Korie's running gear aside as they made love in the bedroom.

"I just have one more thing to say, "Jayna said.

"Of course you do," Darren said flatly.

"All I ever wanted for my girl was for her to be happy. If that means that she's with you and you're in it for the long haul, then fine. But she has a good man now. She has a man of means. If he can make her happier, you should consider walking away. He can offer her more than you can. I know that you might find that hard to believe if you're still half the arrogant SOB that you were years ago. The man she is dating is—"

"DeVaughn Harris. I know. And how do you know I can't offer her what he can?"

"Because he flew her to Tokyo recently."

Back to this Tokyo trip again, Darren thought.

"And is that all that is important, what he can do financially? I'm no slouch myself."

"Maybe not, but you're not in the same league financially that he is."

"You're right. I'm not. But there are other things besides finances."

"Like what?"

"Like love. That's what Korie was trying to explain to me years ago."

"Wow, and it only took you five years to figure that out," she said sarcastically.

Darren cut Jayna a look and she cut him one back. Both were trying to be cordial. Both were trying to keep the kid gloves on for Korie's sake.

Darren pointed at Jayna and started to say something mean. Instead, he started cleaning up the counter and putting the spices back.

"Okay, now here you go," he said with his back to her.

"She never told me why you left. Only that you left"

"Then I guess it's not for you to know why. Just know this: I'm back."

"Yeah . . . back. But for how long?"

"Forever."

"You said that the last time."

"And I meant it the last time."

"But you left."

"Jayna, there are two sides to every story."

"And I don't know either side."

"Hmm, I wonder why that is?"

He didn't say anything else to her. He took the bacon and placed it in a skillet as well as the potatoes. He added the spices, surveyed the fridge to see what else was there, and went to work in the kitchen. He had the meal prepared in almost no time. He didn't speak to Jayna again. He couldn't. He knew if the two of them kept at it there would be a fight, a huge one that would end up in screaming and swearing. He didn't need that. His fledgling relationship with Korie didn't need that.

He drained the bacon on paper towels, scrambled the eggs, and made the toast. The potatoes were seasoned to perfection and tossed in the oven on warm. He sliced fruit on a plate and set it out to be eaten. He then went to the linen closet to gather a towel and toiletries. Everything was exactly where it was when he left.

"Excuse me. I need to get in the shower."

He grabbed what he could find and jumped in the shower. Seconds later water was running, the music was playing in the kitchen, and the sun was up and flexing its morning muscle. Jayna was two and a half hours late for their run, but Korie hadn't called, so she assumed Korie was still asleep as she always was when it came time for their run. Jayna figured it didn't matter what time she arrived, and decided to let Korie sleep a little later today since she was at an event last night. Apparently, she had an event this morning as well.

Minutes later, Korie surfaced. Her hair was all over her head and she came out in just a pajama top. She didn't even bother to fasten the top. The smells from the kitchen woke her from her slumber. She was yawning and scratching her head as she exited the bedroom.

She was practically in the kitchen before she bumped into Jayna.

"Oh shit, girl, you scared me!" She fastened her top.

"I don't know why. You obviously have protection sleeping over."

"What?"

Korie then recognized that her shower was on and that someone obviously had to have let Jayna in. She had a look of confusion and guilt on her face and then she just kind of shrugged her shoulders as if to say, I don't know what to tell you.

"Oh yeah, about that . . ."

"Korie. What's going on?"

"I . . . dunno."

"Korie, you're naked."

"Okay, there is a good explanation for that," she said jokingly with one finger up as if she were trying to excuse herself in church.

"Korie, what's Darren doing here?"

"He just showed up."

Again she shrugged her shoulders. The pajama top was his. It was one of the things of his that she slept in from time to time since he'd been gone. Clearly she found it. As she shrugged her shoulders, the oversized sleeves and top practically swallowed her.

"After five years? He just popped up out of the blue?"

"Well, no. He's been trying to contact me for a few months now. I told him no and—"

"And your body obviously told him yes. Let me guess, you accidentally fucked him last night?"

"It wasn't last night. Actually, it's been for the last three hours. And by the way, you're late."

Korie poured herself a cup of coffee.

"You don't look like you're ready to run, anyway. Shit, you look like you just stepped out of a washing machine after the damned spin cycle. Are you seriously telling me that you let him walk back into your life after all he's done?"

"Jayna, it's complicated."

"You're damned right it's complicated. What about Vaughn?"

"I don't know."

"What do you mean, you don't know?"

"I mean, I don't know. I like Vaughn a lot. But I never stopped loving Darren. I'd be lying if I said that I did. I always had a soft spot for Darren. Even after all this time. A lot of women would make up some silly excuse for doing what he and I just did. A lot of women would blame it on weakness, or the man being manipulative, or just being horny. I miss him. I love him. And I know it's not right and he and I have a lot of problems and things to sort out. Maybe I'm being stupid. Maybe sleeping with him was a mistake, but at least I'm woman enough to admit it. And hell, I enjoyed it."

"Girl, did you offer any resistance?"

"Oh yeah. I let him have it verbally. I took my shots. I let him know how angry I was. In fact, I was in the middle of kicking him out before we slept together."

"And then what?"

"And then . . . he took off his shirt."

Korie shook her head in amazement as she remembered what happened. She was forced to smile just a little bit. The whole thing was actually kind of funny.

"His shirt?"

"His shirt."

"And then what?"

"And then his pants."

"For what?"

"He said to show me what I was missing."

"And what did you do?"

"I—uh—I—took off my clothes too." Korie had a sinful look on her face.

"You did what?"

"Shit, I decided to show him what he was missing!"

Korie put her hands on both hips as she made her point.

"You are both a hot mess. What did he say when you disrobed?"

"He said . . . damn!"

Both women laughed, then high-fived each other. Jayna shook her head in disbelief as she took a seat in the living room recliner.

"Oh, I wouldn't sit there until I've had a chance to use some upholstery cleaner."

"What? Ewww!"

Jayna moved to the couch.

"Uh . . . the same with the couch."

"Again, ewww."

"In fact, don't lean on the countertop, watch the floor, let me move this chair—oh, and the cocktail table, as you can see, is broken."

Korie rushed around to tidy up a bit.

"Korie, the cocktail table? Are you kidding me? You didn't lose that much weight."

"We had to try it out."

"Did you now?"

"It was one of those things that just kind of happened."

"You're lucky you didn't cut your ass in half."

"I know, right?"

"So I guess the two of you made up for lost time."

"Girl, yes. I'm surprised I can walk this morning."

"Shit, you're barely walking. You have a noticeable limp."

"Shit, it's a good limp. It feels like swagger."

Jayna pointed her finger at Korie. "Girl, you are nasty. Was it worth it?"

"You know what? It was. It really was. I needed that. I really needed that."

"Isn't Vaughn taking care of—you know—business?"

"Not like Darren took care of business."

"Really?"

"Really. Vaughn visits the tree for honey once or twice a week and he uses Smurfs for support, if you know what I mean."

"Okay, I do. And how many times did Darren visit for honey?"

"Shit, I didn't think Darren was ever going to leave the tree! He commanded my body in ways I forgot were possible. Shit, girl, I think I might have pulled a damned muscle. He made me remember why I was in love with him."

"And did you forget why you fell out of love with him?"

Jayna walked by Korie and went to the first drawer in the kitchen. In that drawer was a check, the same check that Darren wrote Korie five years ago. She never cashed it. She obviously told Jayna about the infamous check more than once. Jayna put the check on the counter. It was a brutal reminder. Jayna knew that she really had no business interfering in their relationship, or booty call or whatever it was that Darren and Korie were doing. She wanted her friend to see things clearly. She wanted her to see things as they were and not as she wanted them to be.

Korie didn't want to think about the check right now. She didn't want to feel that way right now. She wanted to revel in what happened early this morning. She wanted to enjoy memories of his embrace and his scent. She wanted to rest. She could still feel him there, between her legs. That was the feeling that she wanted last night with Vaughn. It was a feeling, however, she wasn't sure he could provide.

"Jayna . . ." Korie's tone was one that politely told her friend to stop.

"Korie. All I'm saying is that there is a lot at stake here and you need to make sure that he isn't playing you for a fool. You need to make sure that he really wants this and that you really want this before you walk away from a man like DeVaughn Harris. Does Darren have any idea what you would be giving up to be with him?"

"I really wouldn't be giving up anything."

"Korie, you can't mean that."

"I do. I mean, granted, Vaughn is a man of means, but he does nothing for me that I can't do for myself."

"Except take you to Tokyo."

"Okay, except take me to Tokyo. But other than that, there is nothing that he does for me that I can't do for myself. Now, I may not be able to dine at all the places he dines, or go to all the places he goes, but I can do just about anything I want to do for a professional black woman on my level. Again, I like Vaughn, but I love Darren."

"Okay, but is love enough?"

"Why wouldn't it be?"

"Weren't you in love before with Darren? It wasn't enough then, what makes it enough now?"

"I don't know. Like I said, things are complicated."

"You just complicated them more by sleeping with him. Sex clouds a woman's judgment."

"That may be, but my plumbing needed a fix and even though I might not be thinking clearly, I feel better than I've felt in a while. I'm just tired as hell."

"So you are just going to up and leave Vaughn?"

"No. But I'm curious as to what both men are putting on the table."

"Well, from where I'm sitting, the only thing Darren has offered thus far is sex."

"He says he wants more."

"Like R. Kelly says, don't talk about it, be about it. You need to see what he's bringing to the table. Vaughn actually probably owns the damned table. So maybe you should ask Darren what it is that he owns or at the very least what are his plans. Let you tell it, he's known for his damned planning, right?"

"Jayna . . ."

"Okay, okay. I'll stop. So I guess we aren't going on our run, huh?"

"Can I take a rain check? I obviously have some things to sort out here."

"Yeah, I guess. Handle your business, girl."

The two women hugged.

"Okay. Have you heard from Brandon?"

Just saying his name made Jayna's heart throb with ache.

"No."

"Call him."

"I can't."

"You can. Girl, he was going to marry you. That's why he was so upset."

"Where did you hear that?"

"Vaughn. He loves you. I know he loves you. Maybe you need to go to him. Maybe you need to get closure with him. In either case, you need to see what's up with him just as I need to see what's up with Darren."

"I'll think about it."

"Jayna, pray about it."

"I will."

The two women hugged again and Jayna left. Minutes later, Darren walked out of the shower. He was fully dressed in the clothes he came in. He came out and walked into the kitchen. He began making two plates for them to eat, first kissing her on the cheek.

"Good morning."

"Good morning."

"That bitch gone?"

"Darren . . ."

"I'm sorry. That was wrong and I apologize. Is Jayna gone?"

"Yes, she's gone." Korie sat in the recliner.

"Ready to eat?"

"Eat and talk."

"Talk? Okay."

"You didn't just think you were going to walk in here, have your way with me, and I take you right back, did you?"

"Nope. That would be too much like right."

"You know, you are one arrogant son of a—"

"You have known that for years and that's what you love about me."

"It's also what I hate about you."

"Okay. That's fair."

"Darren, what are your intentions?"

"What do you mean?"

"How serious are you about all this?"

"Very serious."

"How serious?"

"Marry me."

That took Korie completely by surprise. She wasn't expecting to hear that. Vaughn hinted around about marriage, but Darren said it. He said it crystal clear and sounded like he meant it.

"I'm sorry, what did you say?"

"I said, marry me."

"Do you have a ring?"

"Is that a yes?"

"No, it's a question. Do you have a ring?"

"Maybe, maybe not. If not, or if it's not the ring you want, the jewelry stores open in a half hour."

"Are you serious?"

"As serious as cancer."

"That serious, huh?"

"Yep. So is that a yes?"

"I don't know. I have to think about all of this."

"What is there to think about?"

"I don't know. What about your five-year plan?"

"Done."

"What about living arrangements?"

"You move in with me. I have a beautiful condo that overlooks Lake Michigan."

"What about babies?"

"Let's have a hundred of 'em."

"I'm serious."

"So am I. Look, what's there to think about? This is what you've always wanted, right?"

"It's been five years."

"And my feelings for you haven't changed."

"But mine might have."

Where did that come from? Korie thought.

"Where did that come from?" Darren asked.

"I don't know. This is all so sudden, so fast. I need to think. What about Vaughn?"

"What about Vaughn?"

"What am I supposed to do? Am I supposed to just go tell him that my ex, the man who I told him left me like a piece of used furniture, has returned and I have to go?"

"I would choose different words, but yes."

"He's a good man."

"I know he is. But is he everything that you are look-ing for in a man?"

"I don't know."

"Korie, I can be that man."

"You should have been that man five years ago."

"I know, sweetheart. I know."

"So what do we do now?"

"We eat. While we eat, you think."

"I don't know if I am ready to eat just yet."

"You wanna go back to bed?" Darren looked at her seductively. Like two teenagers, the air was filled with hormones and pheromones.

"You know what? I do."

"Then let's go." Darren smiled at her and pointed toward the bedroom.

"Okay." Korie got up smiling. She wanted to finish talking, but she wanted her physical needs met again and again and again if possible. She got up and headed toward the bedroom. Darren wrapped the food in foil so it would keep.

"But we will finish this conversation," Korie said.

"You can count on it."

Darren walked to the stereo and turned on V103. "Thinkin' Back" by Color Me Badd was playing. Korie waited in the bedroom doorway for him. He pulled off his pants and shirt again and she pulled off the pajama top. He walked up to her and she jumped in his arms. They made up for lost time and stayed in bed until late afternoon. Darren cleared most of his schedule and Korie cancelled all of her appointments.

Chapter Thirty-one

When Korie awoke, there was a single rose beside her bed. When she awoke again it was 6:00 P.M. She had slept all day. Her and Darren's lovemaking session was intense the first time around, but that was nothing compared to the second time. She awoke to a single rose and a box with a ring in it. It was a two-karat solitaire, a ring that they had been looking at years ago. Attached was a note.

I HAVE BEEN WAITING SIX YEARS TO GIVE YOU THIS

-D

She took the ring out of the box and placed it on her finger. It was beautiful. She held it up and it gleamed with light.

This is all happening too fast. Way too fast. Korie couldn't figure out why she was apprehensive. This was what she wanted, wasn't it? She turned on her iPod. "Walk Away" by Christina Aguilera was playing.

How appropriate, she thought.

Korie got up from bed and searched everywhere for her cell phone. She eventually found it in a pile in the corner with her running gear. She looked at the screen and she missed about eight calls.

Six were clients.

One was from Darren.

The last one was from Vaughn.

She hadn't been up ten minutes before her phone rang again. Again it was Vaughn. This was the first time that she was unavailable since they began dating. This was the first time that she missed a call and took longer then fifteen minutes to call back.

"Hello?"

"Hey sweetheart, it's me."

"Hey babe." She felt weird even calling him babe after this morning.

"You just getting home?"

"Yeah. I was just about to jump in the shower."

"Did you get my message earlier?"

"No. I've been busy all day. I was just about to check them now."

"Well, no need. Listen, can I send the driver to come get you? I'd like to do dinner at the Chicago Firehouse this evening."

"Oh, yeah. Sure. What time did you want to eat?"

"Well, I wanted to eat now. But I'm just now getting in touch with you. How about eight?"

"That'll be fine."

"Okay. The driver will be there in forty-five minutes. I can't wait to see you. Did you enjoy yourself last night?"

"At the party? I loved it."

"And afterward?"

He was looking for validation. He needed a verbal pat on the back. Korie decided to reassure him.

"Afterward was even better." She stroked his ego. That's what a good woman does, she thought.

"Okay, well, I'll see you in a few hours."

"Okay."

***

Darren spent the last few hours of the day screening clients. He began seeing the clients that he met the night before at the party. Many were impressed by his résumé and equally impressed that Vaughn Harris recommended him so highly. He did initial interviews with new clients, wealthy clients. He interviewed them and filled his schedule book for the remainder of the month.

Some men were battling drug addiction. Others were workaholics. Others still were emotionally unavailable to their wives, mistresses, and girlfriends. They all needed help. They all had a world of things that they needed to get off their chests and they all tipped well.

Darren screened his clients and made his money. The time went by super-fast because his mind was somewhere else. His mind was on Korie and the wonderful morning that they had. He was just wrapping up with his last client when his cell phone buzzed. He looked at the message.

SEE YOU TONIGHT FOR DINNER

-K

"Dinner?" he said aloud.

Shit. I forgot about dinner with Karen tonight. Tonight he was supposed to meet her son. Tonight the three of them were going to have dinner. Karen wanted to begin incorporating Darren into the life of her child. It was a huge step and one that he reluctantly agreed to. He let out a heavy sigh as he looked at the phone screen.

Shit, he thought again. He left the practice that he worked at and headed toward Karen's place.

An hour later he was at her place. He walked to the door and rang the bell. Karen opened it and on the

other side was Jacob. The same boy he saw at the barbershop. Darren looked at the young man and shook
his hand. The little man frowned a bit when he opened
the door. It was clear he was not fond of his mother
having company. Darren handed the little guy a gift. It
was a basketball. His frown immediately turned into a
smile. The second the boy smiled, Darren saw something familiar in his face.

Darren had a look of confusion on his face as he walked
in. Karen's son ran and showed the ball to his mother.
She smiled at him and told him to place the ball in his
room.

"Thank you for the ball, but you shouldn't have. You
didn't need to bring him a gift."

"Hey, I'm not too familiar with children outside of
counseling them."

"Oh, so you decided to bribe him?" Karen said, smiling.

"I did."

Darren laughed a bit. But there was something about
her son that was familiar to him now that he saw him
up close. He watched the boy and looked at his facial
features. It took a few minutes for things to click, but
when they did, Darren had another question.

"Karen?"

"Yes?"

"Is Gucci his father?"

The question hit Karen like a ton of bricks.

"How did you know?"

"I didn't. Not until I saw him smile. Not until I saw
him with the basketball."

"Oh. Well, yes. Gucci is his father."

Great, Darren thought. He really began to feel like
shit.

"Does he know?"

"No. He doesn't know."

"Do you plan on telling him?"

"I thought tonight was about us?"

"It is. But perhaps that's something that we should talk about."

"Tonight?"

"Well, maybe not right now, but maybe a bit later."

There it is. I have my out, Darren thought. He figured they would talk about Gucci and his feelings for Karen and that would be his out in order to pursue Korie. In the meantime, they were about to have dinner.

"So, what did you cook?" Darren asked.

"Burgers and fries. That's my son's favorite."

"Cool. That just happens to be my favorite too."

They sat down, they ate. They played video games and by the end of the night, Jacob was open to Darren coming around. The thing was, Darren had no plans on coming back. He came over to break things off with Karen.

By 9:00, Karen put her son to bed. In her mind the evening was a success. She tucked her son in and Darren relaxed on the couch. After Jacob went to bed, an hour later she resurfaced in a baby doll teddy. She walked in the living room with heels on and took Darren's hand. She led him to the bedroom where he had been many times before. Only now, her son was home.

"Karen, wait. I thought we were going to talk."

"Can we talk after?"

"I'd rather talk now."

"I'd rather talk later."

She closed the bedroom door. In the bedroom were candles everywhere, "Hypothetically" by Lyfe Jennings was playing. Karen knelt before Darren, unzipped his pants, and looked up at him and smiled.

He tried to stop her.

He protested.

"Karen. I really want to talk to you about your son and about you and Gucci. I really want to—"

He wanted to tell her good-bye. He wanted to break things off. He wanted to tell her that she should be with the father of her son. He wanted to tell her that Gucci missed her.

Then he felt the warmth of her mouth.

It was sweet warmth.

It was warmth that made a man forget his words.

Their discussion would have to wait until morning.

He could give Karen one more night. They would talk in the morning. Right now, he couldn't think. The only thing on his mind was the mind-numbing head that she was giving him.

She had great skills.

Why let them go to waste?

Chapter Thirty-two

"I have to leave town for a few weeks."

This is what Vaughn told Korie in the middle of dinner.

"What? Why?"

"I have a business deal that I'm trying to close in Germany."

"Germany? What the hell is in Germany?"

"Just another merger that I'm working on."

"Exactly what kind of merger? I mean, what the hell is in Germany?" Korie asked.

"Beer."

"Beer?"

Korie was confused. She placed her hands on her hip. She came to see Vaughn to talk to him. She went there to possibly break up with him. Or to solidify what they were doing. She didn't know exactly what she was doing. She got dressed and went outside where his driver was waiting to pick her up. Her plan was to talk to him at dinner. Her plan was to weigh the cons of being with him versus being with Darren. When they sat down to eat he kissed her and the first thing that came out of his mouth was that he had to leave the country and go to Germany.

"So how long will you be over there?" she asked.

"A week. Maybe two."

He seemed both depressed and frustrated at the same time. He was so visibly upset that she decided to put off talking to him about their relationship, at least right now. Right now he needed her to be understanding. Right now he needed her to be patient.

"Is there anything else wrong?" She placed her hand over his to comfort him.

"Well, yes and no. The therapist that I introduced you to at the fund-raiser thinks that he no longer needs to see me. He says that I'm fine and the stress that I've been dealing with is normal for a man in my position."

"That's a good thing, right?" Korie was relieved to know that Darren would no longer be seeing Vaughn as his client.

"It is. But the brother is good. I mean, talking to him put me at peace. Talking to him sometimes helped me to keep things in perspective."

"Are you worried about making a mistake?"

"No, no, nothing like that. It's just that having him on my payroll gave me a sense of security."

"Did he say why he made that decision now?"

"Yes. He said that I didn't need to second -guess myself anymore. He said that it was time. I know that this is going to sound crazy, but I feel . . . depressed a little that I won't be meeting with him." Vaughn laughed and smiled. "It's almost like breaking up with someone. That's what it feels like. Isn't that crazy?"

Korie's heart skipped a beat as he made the comment. Strangely enough, she knew exactly what it was like to break up with Darren. She knew exactly what it was that Vaughn was feeling. Darren had that effect on people. There was no way she could bring up her relationship with Vaughn now. If she did, it would be like two people breaking up with him in the same day; two people who shared the same bed and the same embrace just hours ago.

Korie could still feel him inside of her. She could still smell his scent. Vivid memories of her and Darren in a passionate embrace burned in her head. She enjoyed their passion this morning; she even enjoyed him biting her. She allowed her thoughts to distract her. She was in a slight daze as she remembered this morning. She let out a soft sigh. As she thought about this morning she could tell that she was moist.

"Honey? Honey, are you okay?"

Snapping out of her trance, Korie tried to pay attention to Vaughn, her boyfriend. Her ex had to wait. She tried desperately to push thoughts of both Darren and this morning out of her head.

"Huh? Oh, yeah. Yeah, I'm fine. So, two weeks, huh?"

"Yeah. Do you want to go with me?"

"Uh, no. I can't. I have a ton of work to do. I have a host of new clients that I need to see and I am working on quite a few projects over the next two weeks. You should go alone. We could use the break."

"What's that supposed to mean?"

That came out wrong. All wrong, she thought.

"I mean, if you go . . . you'll miss me more and things will be just that much better when you get back. Besides, when couples spend too much time together, that's when things get boring or routine." She thought quickly on her feet.

"I could never tire of you." He placed his hands on hers lovingly and smiled at her.

This was why she liked him. This is why she might even love him. He constantly complimented her. He constantly validated her. He never shied away from telling her how he felt. He never took her for granted. He never let her down.

Things were still new, however. They had only been dating a number of months. It'd been great, but Korie began to wonder if she could she truly love a man she had only known a short time. She then wondered if it were possible to love two men.

"So what are you going to do again? I mean, what's with the beer?"

Vaughn began cutting up his steak. He smiled when she asked. He loved it that she was so inquisitive. Had she been anyone else he would be wondering about insider secrets or a competitor trying to pump information from him. Vaughn never told anyone outside of Brandon what he was thinking. It was one of the things that kept him on top. He knew that Korie asked because she cared.

"Well, Germany actually makes about five thousand brands of beer."

"Wow"

"Yeah, and I'm thinking about buying a number of companies."

"And bringing their brands to America?"

"No. Actually, I just want to own the companies."

"Why?"

"To monopolize a part of the beer market. I would allow them to continue to be competitive against one another, but the few I would buy would all be under the same umbrella."

"Again, why?" Korie was trying to understand Vaughn's rationale.

"Just to make more money. It would be like buying both Coke and Pepsi here in the U.S."

"Instead of having a Coke customer or a Pepsi customer, you would have both."

"Exactly."

"Hmm. Sounds easy enough." Korie began eating her food.

"Not exactly. The Germans are not exactly fond of Americans taking over their companies and they are less likely to like the fact that a black man will be the sole proprietor."

"So how do you handle that?"

"No one knows me in Germany. No one knows that DeVaughn Harris is black. So, I'm going over there with Brandon and we're going to take one of our staff over to pitch the proposal."

"Let me guess. That person will be white?"

"And German."

"Isn't that dishonest?"

"It's business." Vaughn smiled at Korie.

"So when do you leave?" she asked.

"Tonight."

"Tonight?" Korie was surprised and upset at the same time. This was very little notice.

"Yeah. I have to strike while the iron is hot."

"So when will you be leaving?"

Vaughn gave her a look as if he didn't want to answer. He gave her a half smile.

"Vaughn?"

"Uh . . . I'll be going as soon as we're done with dinner."

For such a powerful man, Vaughn seemed nervous to tell her. As usual, Korie understood. She was more understanding than she had ever been with Darren when he had business to take care of. She didn't see, however, that the two men were very much alike when it came to business. She didn't see how their lives paralleled one another.

"Okay. Will you call me?"

Vaughn smiled. He smiled and was happy that he found a woman who was secure in her relationship, a woman who was understanding and supportive when it came to his business.

"I'll call you every day."

"Okay."

The two finished their meal and talked until it was time to go. Vaughn had his driver take Korie back home. Vaughn had a second driver take him to the airport.

Korie came home. She was deep in thought as she walked down the hallway to her apartment. She was upset that Vaughn just sprang his leaving on her with very little notice. By the same token she was happy that he would be gone. It would give her time to think. Vaughn could offer her the world. What woman wouldn't want that? She would be a fool to walk away from Vaughn and all his millions.

Still, she could live the simple life with Darren. They would work for everything they wanted, but they wouldn't have to work hard, and they would be in love. They could pick up right where they left off. The first thing that Korie wanted to do when she walked in was to sit down in a hot bath and think for a while. All she wanted to do was have a glass of wine, maybe a hit or two from a joint, and sit in silence in the living room and think about the dilemma she was in. It was a good problem to have; two successful black men who both wanted to give her the world. Most women would be jealous that she had one successful black man. She had two. She fumbled for her keys in her purse as she reached her door.

I care deeply for both men. I want both men, but I can only have one. Vaughn is the logical choice, but Darren is not making this easy. Why did he have to show up at my place this morning looking all good? Why did he have to do that? Twenty-four hours ago I was sure what it is that I wanted. Now I don't have a clue. Darren is not making this easy . . . not at all.

Korie opened her door and was immediately hit with the scent of fresh flowers and vanilla.

"What the—?"

She opened the door and the apartment was dark. Candles were lit everywhere. Each one had the scent of vanilla.

A Y-shaped path of roses was on her carpeted floor. One path led to the bathroom and the other to her bedroom. Music began to play softly.

Korie could smell him.

She could smell his Chrome cologne. The music began to play louder. There was fresh fruit on the dining room table and a bouquet of orange roses on the cocktail table. Orange roses symbolized passion. Back in the day, if she came home to orange roses, it meant that she and Darren were going to go at it—hard.

She shook her head. She was smiling, but she shook her head.

He had some nerve.

He always did.

She took off her shoes as she always did and noticed that his were next to where she just dropped hers. She followed the path slowly and noticed that his jeans were on the couch. His shirt was on the floor by the bathroom. She looked in the bathroom first. There he had her bath drawn. In it were bubbles and more rose petals. Candles were all over the bathroom. By the tub was an ashtray with a neatly rolled joint in it.

She looked in the bedroom and he was on top of the bed. He had on black silk boxers and white socks. He was looking just as good now as he was this morning when he came unannounced.

What is it with brothers and socks in bed? she thought while smiling.

Other than that, he wasn't sporting anything else but his twelve-pack and a smile. His hands were behind his head and he was lying there as if he were king.

"Hey babe," he said. He was all smiles, all teeth.

"Hey babe, my ass. How did you get in my house?" she said playfully.

"You never changed the locks."

He held up his keys. They were the same keys from when they lived together more than five years ago.

"Hmm. Something told me to have the locks changed." She held back a smile.

"You can't mean that," he said smoothly.

He got up from the bed and walked slowly to her, holding her shoulders and kissing her deeply on the mouth. He kissed her passionately while running his fingers through her hair. His hands found her backside and she felt his passion against her. He felt her warmth as well. He undressed her as they kissed. He took each item and tossed them into the bedroom. As she stood there naked, he kissed her shoulders, her neck, and down her midsection. He then took her hand and guided her to the bath.

The water was just right.

The candles gave her a peaceful glow.

The herb was Jamaican. It was top shelf.

The white wine was her favorite brand.

She relaxed in the tub. When she was done relaxing, he bathed her. He gave her a sponge bath.

The warm water was relaxing and it caressed her body. He washed every inch of her. He was sure to give special attention to her special places. He held her hand and guided her out of the tub. He kissed her everywhere as he dried her off. Each place the towel touched, he kissed.

He guided her to the bedroom, but not before finding a bottle of body lotion to give her a massage. He laid her on her stomach on the bed, then placed the warm lotion in his hands and slowly and vigorously gave her a full body massage. The scent was country apple. As the music played, Korie found herself resting more peacefully than she had in years. She was caught between a pleasant rest and an intoxicating high. She didn't know if it was his touch, the wine, the herb or certainly all three. She did know this; she didn't want it to end.

He massaged her neck, back, shoulders, buttocks, and thighs. He rubbed her calves and even her feet. Before, when they were dating years ago, he never did her feet. Now it was part of his repertoire. He even had his technique down and didn't tickle her any as he touched her. His touch was electric. It was desired. He rubbed her entire backside with the lotion from head to toe and back again.

Then she felt the warmth of his mouth.

He is not making this easy. Not easy at all, she thought.

She clenched the pillows.

Well into the night she smiled.

Until all the candles burned out.

Chapter Thirty-three

Jayna had been going to church since her breakup with Brandon. Her heart was broken and she asked God to make her whole again. She dressed more conservatively and she changed herself completely on the inside. She had a good time at church and headed home. After church there were a lot of men there who tried to get at her to ask her out, but she declined them all. She wasn't there for that. Naturally, many men began telling her what they could offer her. She explained to each of them politely that there was nothing any of them could offer that she couldn't get herself. She explained that she was in church to work on her, not to hook up with anyone.

A lot of the more beautiful women that were in the church were there for the wrong reasons. Many decided that it was time to leave the bad boys alone and get a Christian man. Others had sinned so bad or come so close to a near-death experience that they were scared into giving God a try. Other women were like Jayna. They were not quite sure what it was they were looking for, but they knew whatever it was, was at church.

Jayna drove home. She played some gospel music on CD. The CD seemed to bring her peace. She came home, undressed, and booted up her laptop. She had a world of things to do, business-wise. She poured herself a single glass of wine and looked at spreadsheets for a presentation she was giving tomorrow. Then she thought of Brandon. As much as she tried to get him out of her head, she couldn't. She held back tears and simply said a single prayer. It was the same prayer that she said each time her thoughts were of him.

God, please. I know anything is possible through you. I know that I have no right, but I want him back. If it's your will for us to be apart, I accept that, but I am asking that you send him back to me when I'm ready. I'm working on me. God, please work on him. Soften his heart. Please help him to see the potential that we have together. Please help him to see how much I love him.

She said her prayer and left it at that. Weeks ago she sent him an e-mail explaining her faults. It explained that she was sorry and it also explained that she was in therapy for her issues. The e-mail explained that she was going to church and that she loved him; that she wanted to be with him. She explained that if he would have her back in his life she would never betray his trust and that she would be a dutiful wife.

She used the word wife.

She felt it was appropriate.

In her mind, it was what God told her to do.

She thought to herself that perhaps it was true that you couldn't change a ho into a housewife. Men said that all the time and Jayna could think of no word that better described her than whore. Still, she had changed. She had begun changing on the inside, and she was better for it.

This must be how Mary Magdalene felt.

Jayna thought about every man that she bedded. She thought about her own self-esteem and self-worth. The more she thought about things, the more she beat herself up for being so loose, so open. She then thought about how Brandon must have felt upon finding out that many men who he knew and had done business with had been with his woman in the biblical sense.

She brought shame to their relationship. Worse yet, she brought shame to herself. For a while, she thought she was just exercising her independence. For a while, she considered herself just a strong black woman doing what men do all the time. Had she been a man, she would have been considered a player. Had she been a man, she would have gotten kudos for all the people she slept with. Had she been a man, society would be more accepting of her promiscuity. As a man, she wouldn't have to deal with such a double standard.

But she wasn't a man.

She was a woman.

And right or wrong, there were two standards. A man who bedded a lot of women was a player. A woman who bedded a lot of men was generally labeled whore. It didn't matter how independent she was, how much money she made, or how many degrees she had. Sleeping around defined her as a whore. Just because she was good in business just made her a business-minded whore or a whore with a good head on her shoulders and a lot of promise between her legs.

All afternoon, Jayna beat herself up. All afternoon, she thought about the things that happened and all that her relationship with Brandon had the potential to be. Still, she could not change the past. What was done was done. She thought to herself that perhaps she was wrong in asking God for Brandon back. Perhaps it was time for her to move on.

Chapter Thirty-four

Brandon and Vaughn boarded their flight for Germany. The two men had wine and chicken as they rode in first class together. They went over the business plan and talked with their associate, Jerry Howard, who would be the front man for their takeover. Jerry was an entry-level man with a lot of drive. He wanted to impress Mr. Harris and Mr. Lloyd and saw this as the perfect opportunity. After reviewing the plan for the sixth time, Vaughn and Brandon dismissed Jerry back to coach. The two men then discussed their personal matters.

"So, how are things going with you and Korie?" Brandon asked.

"They're great. They've never been better."

"Great."

"Have you heard from Jayna?"

Brandon let out a sigh. He missed her. He missed her a great deal, but didn't know how to admit it.

"No. No, not for a few weeks now. She sent me an e-mail stating that she was sorry."

"Is that all that she said?"

Vaughn sounded concerned. It was the same concern that a father would give to a son.

"Huh? Oh, no. She also said that she was in therapy for her issues and that she was giving her life to God or something."

"God, huh? It sounds like she's serious about turning her life around."

"Maybe. Who knows? I guess."

"Do you miss her, Brandon?"

Vaughn's concern was clear. In so many ways he could tell that Brandon was hurting. He wasn't distracted, and he was still on top of his game, but it was clear that he was hurting.

"She was loose. She and I not seeing each other is probably the best thing."

"That's not what I asked you, son. I asked you if you missed her."

His tone was sharp but sincere, tempered with concern for his protégé.

"Brandon, do you miss her?"

Brandon looked out the window. There was nothing to see that far in the air, but he did miss her. He saw her in the clouds, in his mind, and in his dreams. He missed her like the flower missed the rain.

"Yeah, boss. I do."

"Then call her, son."

Vaughn had no idea what was compelling him to tell Brandon to give Jayna a second chance. After all, he agreed with the breakup. It was clear that his concern was the same as a father for a son. Vaughn also thought about how empty he would feel if he were to lose Korie. There was also Korie's influence on him. What if Jayna was the one for Brandon? What if she was meant to be his wife? Vaughn didn't agree with Jayna's lifestyle. He especially didn't like the way Brandon had been embarrassed. He also knew, deep down, no matter what Jayna's transgression was, he had no right to judge her.

"Call her, Brandon."

"After everything that she did? After the way that she embarrassed me?"

"Yes."

"How do I bounce back from something like that? How do I just let her back into my life?"

"I don't know. But let me ask you another question. Do you love her?"

"How does a man fall in love with a woman who has bedded so many men? How does a man love a woman who brings that level of shame to the relationship?"

Vaughn laughed a little again. He looked at his protégé.

"Once again, you didn't answer my question. So let me ask you again. In fact, let me rephrase the question. Before you found out about her past, did you love her?"

"You know I did. That's why I got her the ring."

"Because you loved her, and it felt right."

"Well, yeah. It felt right then."

"And now?"

"And now, I don't know."

"You don't know or you do know and you're pissed off about it?"

"What? I don't follow."

"Did you love her and stopped loving her after finding out? Or do you love her still and because your pride is hurt, you're pissed off?"

"I don't know."

"You know."

"Then I guess I'm in denial."

"You need closure with this issue, son."

"How do I get that?"

"I don't know. Maybe try the same thing that she's trying."

"You mean go to church?"

"Maybe. When was the last time you were in church, Brandon?"

"Shit, a while."

"How long?"

"I don't know. I think I was eleven the last time I was in church."

Vaughn laughed.

"Okay, boss man, when was the last time that you were in church?"

Vaughn stopped laughing.

"I was in church just last week."

"Vaughn, we loaned that church money that we were in last week. When was the last time you were in church for services?"

"I don't know, but I wasn't eleven."

"No, but I'm betting you have been away from church more years than I have."

"You may be right. But we're not talking about me. You need to get closure on this matter. You need to go see her."

"Okay, when?"

"I don't know. But definitely not until we get back to the States."

"What do I say to her?"

"I don't know, son."

"You're a lot of help, you know that, old man?"

"Who you calling old?"

The two men laughed and had a few more drinks before watching an in-flight movie. Brandon watched the movie and tried to pay attention, but he could only think of one thing.

What do I say to her the next time that I see her?

Chapter Thirty-five

During the two weeks that Vaughn was gone, Korie and Darren did everything under the sun. They went to see plays, they went to Bulls games, they went to clubs, and of course they made love like teenagers, two or three times a day. Korie forgot how insatiable she could be. She forgot what it was like to make love every day for a week. She forgot what it was like to wake up tired, but a good kind of tired from long bouts of lovemaking. Darren cooked at her place, he brought movies over, and they went everywhere together hand in hand as they did years ago.

Korie was supposed to be weighing her options. She was supposed to be thinking about what both men brought to the table. Instead, she was enjoying Darren's company and everything he had to offer.

Everything.

She found herself lost in time. The way that they were now was the way that things should have been years ago. He loved her. He was happy with her. Now that he was successful, he wanted to give her the world as he had promised years ago. He even wanted to start having those babies that she wanted years ago. And she wanted to have babies.

She wanted to have his babies.

At the beginning of the second week, Korie got to see Darren's place for the first time. She was in awe of the condo that he had on Lake Shore Drive. His place

reminded her of Eddie Murphy's condo in the movie
Boomerang. Darren had hardwood floors, stainless
steel appliances, fresh flowers, and the entire place had
modern art pieces and the furniture was all first class.
The condo was decorated the exact same way Korie
would have done it had she been the interior designer.

The living room had two modular leather sofas. One
was white with black pillows and the other was black
with white pillows. Both sat on a large white area rug
with smoked glass tables in front of them. The walls
were adorned with African American art and the living room was accented by a picture-window view of
Lake Michigan. He had a full bar, soft music playing
overhead, recessed lighting in the ceiling, and what appeared to be aluminum ceiling fans from the Modern
Fan Company. He had a fabulous bedroom, a study,
and a bathroom with a Jacuzzi. His condo was on the
fifteenth floor. The enclosed balcony overlooked the
city and had two chairs and a table where two people
could dine and watch the fireworks in the summertime
or simply overlook the lake and the evening sky on a
romantic night.

The balcony also had a speaker system and windows
that opened outward so the balcony could take in the
evening air. Simply put, his place was incredible. Korie
walked out onto the balcony and overlooked her city.
Chicago was beautiful at night. She took a few minutes
to take it all in. She closed her eyes and took in the
evening air from the balcony and wondered if she and
Darren could continue to pick up where they left off.
She wondered could things be better the second time
around. Just as she went deeper in thought, she felt
two hands hug her around her waist. She smiled as she
took in his cologne.

"You're not wearing your ring," he said smoothly in
her ear.

"I know. All of this is so sudden." She shook her head as if she were still trying to awaken from some dream. "This . . . situation. It's so hard."

"It doesn't have to be."

"But it is." She turned to face him.

"Because he has money?"

"What?"

"Vaughn. We're talking about Vaughn now, right?"

Darren walked back into the condo and made himself and Korie drinks. He had rum and Coke and she had a seven and seven. He sat on the white couch. Korie sat on the black couch. She took a sip of her drink.

"It's not about the money."

"Then what is it?"

"He cares for me."

"Yeah, well, I love you."

"You didn't love me enough to stay five years ago."

"I did, but that wasn't what was best for us. Now, while it may be true that I messed up and true that I regret my decision, I only regret it because I lost you. Not because of everything else. My leaving was the best thing that could have happened for us, career-wise. I mean, look at you. Look at all that you've accomplished. Look at me and tell me you think we would be here if we stayed together five years ago."

"Okay, we wouldn't have. I admit that. But would things have been so bad?"

"Bad? No. Chances are we would have had at least two kids by now, you would have been laid off from your job, and I would still have had my job. No private practice. No condo on Lake Shore Drive. We would have made it. We would be okay. But that's just the thing, Korie, we would just be okay. We deserve more than that. We deserve better than that. So do our children."

"We don't even have kids yet."

"Listen to yourself."

"What?"

"You said yet. You want to have babies with me. You want this. You want to pick up where we left off and I know you want to see how far our relationship can go. Deep down, Korie, you want this. Deep down you know this is where you belong."

"Then what is holding me back, Darren?"

"Vaughn has millions. He's a man of means. He took you to Tokyo. What's fucked up about that is taking you to Tokyo was my idea, only I didn't know that it was you he was taking. He loves you. I get that. You like him, though. Every conversation that we had you talked about the fact that you like him. Not once have you told me that you loved him. Not once have you said you were in love with him. You said you were seeing someone. You said it was serious, but you never used the word love."

"I haven't told you that I love you, either."

She said it to defend herself. She said it to throw him off balance. It didn't work. It was like trying to knock down a wall with a sponge. He had a sip of his drink and then placed it on the table and walked over to her.

"Stand up."

Korie stood up and looked at him face-to-face.

"You haven't told me that you love me, but you don't have to. I see it in your eyes. I see it in your smile. I feel it when I hold your hand. I feel it when I'm near you. I feel it when I'm inside of you. Look me in the eyes and tell me that you don't love me. Look me in the eyes and tell me that you ever stopped loving me. Tell me that you don't want this. Tell me that your heart and spirit aren't telling you that things can be better the second time around. Korie, I love you. Tell me that you don't still love me."

She looked in his face and all she saw was sincerity. She looked in his eyes and saw nothing but unbridled love. She knew. He knew. They were meant to be together. He may have broken her heart when he left, but her soul was healed with his return. This time, it would be different. This time it would be better. Tears streamed down her face as she looked at him. Tears welled up in his eyes as he looked at her.

"Baby, tell me you don't still love me," he said smoothly.

"I can't. I do still love you."

"Then marry me."

They kissed.

"I will. I will marry you."

They kissed. He picked her up and carried her to his bedroom, where they made love well into the night.

Chapter Thirty-six

DeVaughn and Brandon closed their deal. In the corporate world they were like an educated, yet urban Batman and Robin. They closed the deal in record time. It only took four days to convince their competitors to fold, and another two to draw up the proper contracts. Brandon wanted to hurry up and get home. He wanted to meet with Jayna and speak with her. He wasn't sure about what he would say, but he assumed that DeVaughn was right. One way or the other, they needed closure.

Both men wanted to get home, but both men wanted to experience Germany as well. It was their first time there, and from what they understood, there was in fact plenty to do.

The concierge at the hotel where they stayed explained that Germany was one of the most beautiful places in the world. The concierge also stated that Germany had some of the most beautiful women in the world. Seeing that Vaughn and Brandon were of African American descent, the concierge told them that Germany had beautiful women of all nationalities, including black women.

Vaughn smiled at the suggestion but declined. Brandon, who was still trying to put Jayna out of his mind, was intrigued. After some talk, Brandon reluctantly convinced Vaughn to go to a nightclub in Germany their sixth night there. That night they ate, drank, and enjoyed themselves in the VIP section of one of the most expensive clubs in the country.

Women watched them; men watched them and the jealousy in the air from seeing two African American men, whom they referred to as caffers, live like kings, incensed some of the clubs patrons. Vaughn watched the people that were watching him. He was not unfamiliar with jealousy. It was something that he dealt with his whole life. Brandon simply shrugged them off as haters. He figured that haters were a worldwide problem. Brandon took two women back to his hotel room that night. He did it in an effort to forget about Jayna.

He failed.

No matter what he did, it seemed that Jayna was a permanent fixture in his heart.

During the next few days, the two men visited Stuttgart to visit the Mercedes home office and Munich to visit the BMW home office. Vaughn rented a top-of-the-line Mercedes. Brandon rented a top-of-the-line BMW. The two men decided to make their last four days a working vacation and although they came together, they had separate activities during the remainder of their stay.

Brandon needed a distraction. He needed time to get himself together, time to reflect on what, if anything, he would say to Jayna. She hurt him. Worse yet, she embarrassed him. Still, he loved her. He tried to tell himself that her past was simply that: Her past. He tried to tell himself what she did was not his concern, and should have no bearing on how he felt for her.

He felt that she was promiscuous, a whore, and a loose woman. The thing that burned at him most was the fact that she didn't have to be. She was a successful businesswoman who had no need to bed a man for anything other than companionship. Yet here she was sexing men like it was a hobby or a race.

He then thought about all the women he bedded over the years and wondered to himself why it was okay for him to do it, but not okay for her? He was considered in many circles to be a playboy. He thought, couldn't she just be considered a playgirl? He looked for reasons to forgive her and then wondered to himself why he would even consider such a thing.

Because I love her, he thought.

Brandon went to Berlin's Pergamon Museum to look at antique art. He went to a number of galleries, where he saw pictures that he and Jayna had talked about while looking in art magazines at home in the United States. Germany was one of three places Jayna said that she wanted to see before she died, along with France and Africa.

He visited the Charlottenburg Palace on the east side of Berlin. It was the largest surviving palace in the capital, built for Sophie Charlotte, wife of Prussia's King Friedrich I, in the late 1600s. While there, he then wondered if he could simply just go home and tell Jayna that he loved her. He wondered if perhaps the two of them could run away somewhere and get married. They could marry somewhere like here. Somewhere like the very palace he was visiting.

But running away was not the answer.

And Brandon was not a runner.

Like everything else in his life, he had to tackle this issue head-on. He needed to examine how was it that he could come to love a woman so deeply who hurt him so bad. She wasn't malicious. It wasn't her intent to hurt him. In fact, she was trying to get help.

But how do you marry a woman who has slept with many men that you know?

He was torn. He was conflicted. Worse yet, he still loved her. He needed time to think. He thought to himself where better to think than halfway across the world? Brandon ventured to the Harz Mountains, the Black Forest in Schwarzwald, and the Bavarian Alps. He went walking, skiing, and watched people training for the winter games. He bought a camera and took pictures of everything he saw. The trips he took were magnificent. The views he saw were breathtaking. He saw sights that some people would never see in a lifetime. All he could think was one thing: I wish she was here to see these things with me.

The next day he took a one-day cruise on the river; the day after that he rode a historic steam train in Saxony; and another on the coast of Mecklenburg. He went to a theme park in Friedberg, a soccer match in Hamburg, and a number of vineyards. He found beauty in every stop, romance in every stop, and with each stop he thought how wonderful it would be if she were with him. He imagined himself holding her hand, her passionate embrace, and he even thought about the intoxicating scent of her perfume. He missed her. He needed to go home. He needed her back in his life.

He was incomplete without her.

He loved her, flaws and all.

Vaughn's last days in Germany were quite different. He was in his hotel room having a sip of brandy and deep in thought his first day of his working vacation. He phoned Korie every day that he was gone. He missed her; he missed her a great deal. However, it seemed that to a degree that the tables had somehow been turned on him. He would phone her and tell her that he missed her, but these days she was always busy. She would talk to him anywhere between ten and twenty minutes, but the conversations seemed as if they were changing.

He wondered in the back of his mind if she were upset with him because of his work schedule. He wondered was she mad that he left the country. He also thought, how much money is too much? He made millions of dollars. He made his company billions. He would never want for anything and neither would his children.

Children he didn't have.

Children who would be heirs to his empire.

His wife died before they could have children. He never thought about having children with anyone other than his wife. He gave that idea up when she died. That is, until Korie.

Vaughn needed an heir.

He wanted to have a baby.

He wanted Korie to have his baby.

If his wife were alive she would be too old to have children now. He always assumed when he married again, if he married again, that his wife would most likely be too old to conceive.

Korie was young. Korie was fertile and Korie would make a great mother. He sat in his hotel room and thought about his future. He thought about who would carry on his family name. He thought about marriage. He was ready. He made up his mind that he would ask Korie to be his wife.

He stopped sipping his brandy long enough to go into the bathroom and relieve himself. His view of Germany from his hotel was breathtaking.

She should be here, he thought.

He was just about to get dressed when there was a knock at his door. Vaughn assumed that it was Brandon. It was his last day in Germany and he assumed that Brandon wanted to know what time they would be meeting at the airport tomorrow morning.

He opened the door and on the other side was a distinguished-looking older gentleman. He looked like the actor Willem Dafoe. He had distinct glasses on, round John Lennon–like spectacles. He wore what looked like a 3,000-dollar custom-made suit, and with him was a briefcase in hand.

"Can I help you?" Vaughn asked.

"May I come in?" the man said with a heavy German accent.

"That depends. Who are you?"

"I am a dealer, Mr. Harris. The concierge suggested that I stop by to see you."

"The concierge?"

"Yes, sir. You are DeVaughn Harris, are you not?"

" I am."

"Then I am in the right place. May I?"

Vaughn stepped aside so that the man could enter. He walked into the vast hotel room that could double for an apartment. He sat at the table in the foyer of the hotel room area and opened his briefcase.

"Hold on. What exactly is in the briefcase?"

"Something better than drugs."

"I didn't ask for anything. I especially didn't ask for anything better than drugs."

"But in the States, you do use Elite Escorts, do you not?"

"Double E, so that's what this is about. Listen, I no longer need the services of your company, I told you all that."

"I am not with double E, sir."

"No, then who?"

"I'm a private dealer."

"Then how do you know about my history with double E?"

"I make it my business to know when men of means leave one of my competitors."

"One of your competitors? So you have . . . products in the States as well."

"I do. I'm global."

"And your name is . . ."

"Here is my card."

The man who looked like Willem Dafoe handed Vaughn a black card with gold numbers on it. There was no name, only the silhouette of a woman. He pulled two catalogs from his briefcase. One for the United States, one was global. Vaughn looked at the man and laughed a bit. It took balls to come to his hotel room like this. Aside from that, Vaughn was impressed. Damned impressed.

"So what else is in the briefcase?"

"Models. There are portfolios of beautiful models, worth every penny."

"Well, like I said, I am no longer in need of your services. But just for shits and giggles, how much?"

"Five thousand American dollars, for one night."

"That's a lot more than double E."

"My workers are that much more than the workers at double E."

"That's a pretty arrogant statement."

"Yes it is. Do you know who Alannah Xavier is?"

"No. I'm afraid I don't."

"Well, she is a German model. She is Negro. Like you. She's very beautiful. More beautiful than America's Halle Berry. I have a girl who looks just like her, just for you."

"Right, look, Mr . . . What is your name?"

"Adler. Adler Bergan."

"Well, Mr. Bergan, I think I'm going to ask you to leave."

"May I leave the catalogs?"

"No. Please take your catalogs."

"Mr. Harris, please. I tell you what . . . keep the catalogs. Let me send someone to you this evening, for free. Call it a onetime special for new customers. I think you will be especially pleased with the worker on page thirty-three. Again, she is more beautiful than Halle Berry. I will send her at six o' clock."

"No, Mr. Bergan. But thank you, though." Vaughn escorted him to the door.

"I shall send her anyway. If you send her away, I understand."

The man headed toward the door and Vaughn politely smiled at him as he closed the door. He was impressed with the man, but he was also offended by his audacity. Vaughn went to the shower and planned his last day in Germany. He had a lot to do, including returning the rental car. He looked at the clock and it said 2:00. He showered, threw on some clothes, and grabbed his hotel key as he headed toward the door.

Then he saw it.

He looked at the catalog. It was sitting there on the nightstand.

It was sitting there like cocaine.

He looked at it like an addict.

He walked over to the catalog, which was bound in leather. He looked at the gold leaf pages that adorned its exterior. He picked it up. It had quite a bit of weight to it. The book was valuable looking. It looked like the type of book you would find in a German library. Someone went through a lot of trouble to make the book look impressive. Someone spent a great deal of money. Vaughn held the catalog. He measured its weight in his arm. He ran his fingers alongside the leather.

The book was impressive.

He opened it up.

What he saw was equally impressive.

He turned the pages, one at a time. The book was filled with women. Each was beautiful in her own right. Each woman was flawless. Some were tall, some were short. The book contained women of every ethnicity. They were black, white, Asian, German, and even a few Americans. Based on what he saw, these "workers" were more impressive than the workers for double E. They were enchanting.

"Finer than Halle Berry, huh?"

Vaughn turned to page thirty-three.

"Damn, he ain't never lied."

Vaughn ran his fingers alongside the photos of the woman on page thirty-three. She was synonymous with the word stunning. Her name in the book was Eve. Vaughn immediately knew why. She was clearly God's work of art. He looked at the picture and then looked at the clock on the wall. It was a look of guilt. It was the look a recovering addict had right before he relapsed. Vaughn reached into his chest pocket and phoned Brandon on his cell.

"Hey, Brandon, it's me. Listen, I'll meet you tomorrow in the lobby at nine. We will take off at ten. No, no, everything is fine. I won't be able to hit the club with you this evening. No, I have plans. Business plans. No, nothing I need your help with. Enjoy your last night in Germany. Listen, I will see you tomorrow. Okay then . . . bye."

Vaughn looked at the clock, then at his watch. He took the Mercedes back to the dealer where he rented it. He then came back and ordered room service after scouring around Germany in search of little blue pills.

***

At 6:00 there was a knock at the door to the hotel room. Vaughn took in a deep breath as he opened the door. On the other side was a woman who was the spitting image of the model Alannah Xavier. She stood six feet tall. She had a tiny waist, perky and firm breasts, and legs that went on forever. And that was just her front. Her makeup was flawless as well as her smile.

"Ju are De-Vawn Harris, no?" Her English was a little choppy, but her voice was smooth, like that of an angel.

"I am," Vaughn stated.

"May I come in?"

Vaughn smiled. "You may."

She walked into the hotel room, which housekeeping had cleaned while he was away. She walked in and Vaughn continued to examine her. Her backside was nice, very nice. Her perfume was intoxicating and not too strong, as many women wore it. He looked at her backside as she walked in and noticed no panty line. That meant either thongs or commando.

Her dress was peach. It matched her complexion perfectly, as did the peach-colored stilettos that she wore. The dress looked as if it were designed by Elie Saab. It fit her like a second skin, but the material was so light and so delicate that it hugged her curves perfectly. It was a one-sleeved minidress with chiffon and tulle cutouts from the lower hips to the sleeve. She wore no stockings, and her bare legs looked perfect. She walked in and had a seat on the couch.

"Adler told me that I was in for a treat, but I had no idea that you would be shock-o-lat like me."

"Shockolate? Oh, you mean chocolate." Vaughn smiled. "I guess you don't get too many black customers, now, do you?"

"Black, no. Very few."

"Well, I guess that's a shame. So, you do like chocolate men, I take it."

"Yes. Shock-o-lat men are nice."

"Hmm. I never heard anyone say chocolate before.
Why not 'black' or 'African American'?"

"Hmn. Why not shock-o-lat?"

Vaughn smiled again. "Okay. Okay, why not chocolate. So, do you want something to eat? I can order
room service."

"No. I don't want any food. But tank you, tho."

"Hmm. This is going to be interesting. Can I have the
pleasure of your name?"

She stood up right where she was and slowly peeled
off her dress. She left no mystery in why she was there.
She dropped her dress to the floor and stood there with
nothing but heels on and her smile. She was breathtaking and she definitely had Vaughn's attention. She
walked over to him and wrapped her arms around him.
Her delicate, manicured hands caressed his aged face
and his throbbing manhood. He took his pills minutes before she knocked on the door. His erection was
throbbing and his heart was beating fast like a drum
at an African festival of the hunt. She whispered her
name into his ear as she sucked his earlobe.

"My real name is Irina."

"Irina. That's a nice name."

"It's Russian," she said softly as her lips found his.
"Do you want to know what it means?"

"I do," Vaughn stated softly as he kissed her back.

"It means absolute peace."

Irina kissed Vaughn on the lips while undoing his
pants. She tore open his 500-dollar dress shirt and
buttons flew everywhere. Her head slowly went down.
Soon after, he felt the warmth of her mouth. He looked
at her; he watched her. Her pouty lips took him in like

a coffee-colored treat. He watched her work her magic. She took all of him in. There was no gagging, no resistance, just sweet, slow, warmth. She worked him fluidly, like a thing of art. She worked him, massaged him, and worshipped the thing that lay between his legs. Initially, he thought the response was just the Viagra, but she had an affect on him. With her looks alone, she aroused him.

Generally when he took the blue pills, it took him a long time to climax. It took him a long time to come. Within minutes he was filling her with his warmth. Within minutes, he was spent and embarrassed at how quickly she was able to make him go there.

She didn't shy away from his treat. She took all that it had to give and worked him well past climax. His heart raced. It raced like it had never raced before. His breathing changed to panting. His chest and body glistened with sweat. His jaw opened but no sound came out. She was too much for him. When sound returned, he sounded like a marathon runner at the end of a race who no longer had adrenaline to support him. She saw his predicament. She saw that he was overwhelmed with her skill, so she slowed down. She never stopped, but she slowed down enough for him to gather himself.

He was deaf with ecstasy. He couldn't hear her or the music. The only thing he could hear was the resounding beating of his heart. Minutes later his heart didn't race as hard. She took his hand and guided him to the bed. He was exhausted. He could only think one thing.

No more. No more, he thought it, but he didn't say it.

He didn't need to. His limp manhood said it all.

He watched her as she made her way to the bathroom. She smiled at him as she walked away. He watched her. He could do nothing else. She was that good. He had bedded women all around the world and no one gave him head as she had done just now. He saw her tear open the plastic to a toothbrush in the bathroom. She held it up as if to ask was it okay that she brushed her teeth. Vaughn could only nod yes.

Again she smiled at him. The next thing that Vaughn knew was sleep. It was two hours later when he slowly began to waken. He smiled as again he felt warmth between his legs. He looked down and the beautiful ebony goddess was still with him. She was waking him up as every man wishes to be awakened, by the warmth of the mouth of a beautiful woman.

Irina began bringing Vaughn's penis back to life. She massaged it, deep-throated it, and gave it the attention it needed. Blood rushed to Vaughn's manhood again and again he was ready to go. Irina mounted him. The warmth of her vagina was better than the warmth of her mouth.

Vaughn watched her as she mounted him. He watched the smiles, the tenderness, and the passion in her face as she forced his member inside of her. She rode him slowly. She contorted her body in waves to take all of him in her. She placed her hands on his chest as she rocked back and forth and made her beautiful backside slowly bounce up and down. Her juices rushed out of her sweet, warm vagina and onto him. She slid with the natural fluids back and forth. She let out gentle moans, as did he, as they began to make love. He placed his hands on her ass and began to squeeze. Her ass was soft, tender, and ample. He watched her as she looked at him lovingly. He watched her face, her smile, and her perky nipples as she rode him.

She took her time.

She made love to him.

She made him feel like a man.

It was like using cocaine for the first time.

Or crack.

It was earth-shattering, amazing sex. It was the best feeling a man could feel with a woman. It was intoxicating. But like any other drug, it could be deadly.

Vaughn cheated on Korie, something that he thought he would never do.

Vaughn relapsed. He relapsed with a drug called Irina.

For the rest of the night she brought him absolute peace.

It was worth every penny.

Chapter Thirty-seven

Korie felt guilty.

She awoke from another bout of sex at Darren's place and her body ached . . . in a good way. She got up, got dressed, and left his place. He was still sleeping the sleep of the dead. Last night they went at it as if they each had something to prove. Korie had won last night's bout of sex. It was Darren who cried uncle last night, although the night before it was Korie who screamed "no more."

It had been a great two weeks. It had been years since Korie had been this tired. But today was the day that Vaughn was due to come back home. Chances are he would want sex. Korie couldn't accommodate him for two reasons. One, she planned on breaking up with him. She told Darren that she would marry him. Two, she was worn out and her vagina was swollen.

She had one major dilemma. How would she tell him?

She needed to talk to someone. Korie phoned Jayna.

Vaughn and Brandon flew home in silence on the plane. Both men were deep in thought. Brandon was wondering what he would say to Jayna and Vaughn was wondering where his relationship stood with Korie. He was back to paying for the company of escorts again.

At least he thought he was. And if he wasn't, he was having thoughts that he never should have as a customer of escorts. Vaughn wondered what it would be like to have a woman like Irina as his partner.

Irina wasn't Korie. She was something else. She was something else altogether different. She was paid company. What's worse is that she was worth every penny. Irina was the type of women who sought out men like Vaughn. It seemed that men like Vaughn chose women like Irina, young, beautiful, and sexy to be the woman of choice to have on their arms when they went out. More and more Vaughn was beginning to wonder if that was the natural order of things.

Irina was flawless.

But Vaughn liked Korie's flaws.

Irina was the perfect size.

Korie had to work her way down to the size that she was now.

Irina looked every bit like an international model.

Korie looked like a model for a Gap commercial.

Irina swallowed.

Korie didn't.

In most cases with men, the last thing would have made Irina the undisputed winner. But Korie still had a lot going in her favor. She was strong, independent, and she would make a good mother to Vaughn's children, his heirs. Irina would simply be his companion and spend his money. He enjoyed his tryst with Irina. But he was done with her. He was going home to ask Korie to be his bride. He made up his mind that Irina would be his last fling as a single man.

He just hoped that he had the willpower to stay away from escorts once he got home. It was the same willpower that drug addicts wished for when they said they were going to stop using.

Chapter Thirty-eight

"He did what?" Jayna said.

"Darren asked me to marry him."

"And what did you say?" Jayna looked attentively at her best friend, already knowing the answer.

"I said yes."

"And what about Vaughn?"

"That's just the thing, Jay . . . I don't know."

"I thought things were going so well between the two of you."

"They are. I mean, they were."

"Then what are you doing, Korie?"

"I still love him. I still love Darren."

"Even after all he's put you through?"

"Even after all he's put me through, yes."

"Shit."

Jayna sat back in the living room chair at Korie's place with a confused look on her face.

"I know, right."

"When do you plan on telling Vaughn?"

"He should be home by now. He's heading over here to pick me up. I'm going to tell him in a few hours."

"Do you want me to stay here with you?"

"What? No. No, I got this."

"Are you sure this is what you want to do?"

"No. I mean, I love Darren. But I'm not sure that I want to give up the life that I have with Vaughn. I do like him. I like him a lot. But Darren and I have history."

"A tainted history. What about what you used to say about not going backward and always looking forward?"

"I'm looking forward. I'm looking forward to my relationship with Darren."

"Okay, hear me out. Just listen. What if he leaves again? What if things are perfect between you and Darren simply because they are new again? What happens if you give Darren another chance and he leaves you or disappoints you, or isn't the man who you thought he was? Won't you then be kicking yourself in the ass for leaving a man like DeVaughn Harris? I'd like to say that men like him come by a few times in a lifetime, but hell, they don't."

"What are you saying, Jayna?"

"I'm saying that he had his chance and he blew it. I'm saying, think about all this."

"You never liked Darren to begin with. The two of you never got along."

"Maybe so, but one thing has nothing to do with the other. I want what's best for you. Now, if you say that's Darren, then, girl, I got you and I support your decision one hundred percent. But, Korie, if you have any doubt, give it time."

"I guess you're right. I have been rushing things. My heart says jump right in there with Darren, but my mind says that Vaughn is the one."

"What changed in these past few weeks?"

"Sex."

"Sex?" Jayna looked confused.

"Yeah, I think I just got caught up in how Darren made me feel versus how Vaughn makes me feel."

"So, Vaughn doesn't satisfy you at all?"

"No, he does, just not as often as I would like."

"Darren will be that way in a few years. All men eventually lose their sex drive. It's at that point that many realize what they have. Sex isn't everything."

"Says the woman who has a phone full of numbers."

"Not anymore. I'm a changed woman, a new woman."

"Well, good for you."

The two women hugged and Jayna went home.

Korie sat on her couch deep in thought about her next move.

Chapter Thirty-nine

Jayna was surprised to hear a knock at her door. She had just finished packing. She put in a vacation request and decided that she needed a distraction from her breakup with Brandon. It had been well over a few months and she still found herself thinking about him regularly. Her therapist suggested that she treat herself, and the best place she figured she could do it was Hawaii. Jayna had never been to Hawaii before and as far as she was concerned, Hawaii might just be the thing that she needed. She didn't tell anyone that she was leaving, not even Korie. She was still stunned at Korie's news about Darren proposing.

Jayna had just packed her last bag when she heard the knock at the door. On her cocktail table were magazines about Hawaii, her ticket, and her purse. She usually didn't entertain company at her place and these days she was seeing no one, so the knocking was unexpected. She opened the door and was surprised at what she saw on the other side.

Brandon was standing there. He wasn't smiling, but he wasn't frowning, either. Most of all, he was there. Jayna was speechless. He was the last person in the world she expected to be at her door.

"Can I come in?"

"Uh, yeah. Sure."

Brandon walked in and had a seat on the couch. He looked at the magazines and brochures while he sat.

"Going somewhere?" he asked calmly.

"Uh, yeah. I'm going to Hawaii."

"Business?"

"Personal. I need to clear my head, so I'm going out there to relax and perhaps become stress and drama-free."

"Stress from work?"

"Stress from you."

She didn't mean for it to come out that way, but it did. It was said. It needed to be said. She wasn't trying to argue. Her tone wasn't malicious. She said what she said matter-of-factly.

"I'm stressing you out? I haven't been here."

"You haven't been here, but you have been here and here." Jayna pointed to her heart and her head.

"I'm sorry."

"No, I'm sorry. I'm sorry that my past, such as it was, had the affect that it did on our relationship. If I could have done things differently, I would have. If I could go back in time and change things, I would. But I can't. And I can only say sorry so many ways."

"So are you running to Hawaii?"

"No. I'm done running from my past and my problems. I'm going to Hawaii."

"Do you want some company?"

That threw Jayna completely off. It was about as unexpected as his arrival.

"I'm sorry, what did you say?"

"I said, do you want some company."

"For what? To be your booty call or something?" Jayna placed her hand on her hip.

"No. No, nothing like that. You see, I came here to talk to you. Vaughn and I both had to make a stop first before I came here and before he went to see Korie, but I came over here with a purpose."

"Oh, and what would that be?"

"Well, I came to ask you to move to L.A. with me."

"I'm sorry—what?"

"I came to ask that you move with me, to L.A. I'm asking that you relocate. I'm asking you to be with me again. I'm asking for your forgiveness."

"Wait, you—you're asking me—for my—forgiveness?"

"Yeah, you see, no matter how I try to fight it, I can't stop thinking about you. I can't stop loving you. It's the damndest thing. Now, don't get me wrong, you hurt me. You embarrassed me. But that didn't change things. I mean, it did. I was very mad about everything. Actually, I'm still pretty mad about everything. But what makes me even madder is the fact that I still love you. And I can't see me being without you."

"What are you saying?" Tears streamed down Jayna's face.

"I'm saying that I asked my boss if I could take over the L.A. office so we could have a fresh start."

"A fresh start?"

"Don't take this the wrong way, but I think we both could use a change of scenery."

They both laughed. Then they hugged. Jayna felt so at home in Brandon's arms.

"What did Mr. Harris say about you moving to L.A. to head up that office?"

"He said no. He said that he didn't need me to head up the L.A. office. He said he needed me at the corporate headquarters here in Chicago."

Jayna looked at him. She looked stunned. She couldn't believe that he came back. Worse yet, she couldn't believe that he was possibly giving up his career for her.

"And what did you say?" She had a look of worry on her face.

"I told him I couldn't stay in Chicago. I told him I wanted to remain with the company and the headquarters, but I couldn't stay in Chicago."

"And what did he say?"

"He said, 'Brandon, you're like a son to me. I understand what you are going through and one day you will be running all of this, so I see no reason why we can't move the corporate headquarters to L.A.'"

Jayna had an excited look in her eyes.

"You mean he's willing to move the company to keep you?"

"He is."

"Wow. Baby, I am so happy for you!"

"I miss you calling me 'baby'."

"I miss calling you 'baby'."

"So you will relocate?"

"Be your girlfriend again in L.A.? I think I can do that."

"No, not my girlfriend."

Jayna looked puzzled. Then Brandon retrieved a small box from his pocket.

"I mean . . . as my wife."

He got down on one knee. Jayna's eyes were filled with tears.

"Jayna, will you marry me?"

She got down on both knees with him. Tears filled her eyes.

"What about my past?"

"It's in the past."

"How would people view you?"

"I don't know. I guess we'll figure that out in Hawaii. We can begin sorting things out there. You still haven't answered me yet."

"This is all so sudden."

"It is. But it's also the right thing to do. So, what do you say? Will you be my wife?"

"Yes. Yes, Brandon, I will marry you."

They hugged, they cried, and then they got ready to leave for Hawaii.

"Wait a minute. You said that you and Vaughn needed to make a stop. Was that stop to the same place?"

Brandon smiled. "It was. He should be proposing to your girlfriend shortly after he gets there."

Oh my God, Jayna thought.

Chapter Forty

Korie had just opened the door for Vaughn when her cell phone began buzzing. She invited him in and then rushed to the bathroom as if she had to pee. She was checking her phone to make sure that it wasn't Darren who was calling. She looked down at the screen and was surprised to read a text from Jayna.

BRANDON JUST PROPOSED TO ME. VAUGHN IS ABOUT TO PROPOSE TO YOU! OMG! OMG! OMG! MAKE THE RIGHT DECISION.

Korie looked at the screen and read it a few times before texting back.

R U SURE? she responded.

Her heart was beating fast in her chest and she felt light-headed. Seconds later, her phone buzzed again.

DEFINTELY SURE. BRANDON TOLD ME. HE AND I ARE LEAVING FOR HAWAII IN A FEW MINUTES.

"Is everything okay in there?" Vaughn asked.

"Everything's fine; I'll be out in a few, make yourself at home. How was the trip?"

"It was okay, how were things here?" Vaughn asked through the door.

"Busy. Things were pretty busy while you were away."

Korie began texting back.

HAWAII? WTF? WHY R U GOING TO HAWAII?

"They must have been busy. I hardly heard from you while I was away," Vaughn said.

"Sorry about that. I figured if anyone would understand it would be you."

Korie's phone buzzed again,

I WAS GOING TO CLEAR MY HEAD AND JUST GET AWAY FOR AWHILE, BUT NOW I GUESS I'M GOING THERE TO GET MARRIED!

"I understand. That's one of the things that I love about you . . . your independence."

"How was the deal, did you close it?"

"I sure did."

"Congratulations."

"Korie, are you sure you are okay?"

"Yes. I, um, ate something that didn't agree with me. Why don't you just have a seat in the living room? I'll be right out, okay?"

"Okay."

She started typing on her phone and texting Jayna again.

HEIFER, YOU CAN'T GET MARRIED IN HAWAII. WE NEED TO PLAN YOUR WEDDING! YOU CAN'T ELOPE! WE'RE BEST FRIENDS. GO TO HAWAII AND BRING UR ASS BACK!

Minutes later Korie's phone buzzed again.

K. WHAT ARE YOU GOING TO SAY TO VAUGHN?

Korie texted back.

DUNNO.

Her phone buzzed again.

MARRY HIM...

...WHAT ABOUT DARREN?

...IF HE REALLY LOVES U, HE WILL C THAT HE IS ONLY IN
UR WAY...

...I STILL LOVE HIM.

...YOU CAN GROW TO LOVE VAUGHN.

...BUT DARREN ALREADY PROPOSED. I ALREADY HAVE HIS
RING.

WHAT DO I DO?

...K, I GOTTA GO. I HOPE U DO THE RT THING. LOVE U

Korie walked out of the bathroom after washing her hands. Vaughn had been walking around the living room patiently waiting for Korie to surface.

"So, how have you been?"

"I've been okay, how are you?"

"I'm good. I'm good. So, listen, I was wondering if I could talk to you about something?"

"Sure."

Korie tried to remain cool, calm, and collected. Her heart was beating fast in her chest at the prospect of Vaughn proposing. What would she say? She already had accepted Darren's proposal. It didn't help that Vaughn seemed to be approaching the whole matter like a business merger.

"Korie, I have something to say. Listen, I haven't felt the way that I feel for you in a long time; a very long time. Now, I've been around the block a few times. In that, I mean I have some mileage on me. I've been all over the globe and if there is one thing that I know, it's that love is both a luxury and a necessity. In other words, it's rare, its valuable, and it's needed. Now, a lot of people know that love is a luxury but they can't find it. Others know that they need it, but can't find it. Some people marry just for the sake of being married and in that, they hope that they'll grow into love. I think if you find love, true love, once, then you're good. Twice, and you're blessed. Korie, I came over here to tell you that I think I have been blessed; blessed that I've found you. What I'm trying to say is that I love you and I want you to marry me and I want to have a whole lot of babies, in that order.

"Now I, know that I'm a lot older than you. I know that I may not always be able to fulfill your physical needs. But I know this. If you let me, girl, I will love you like no other man will. Not only that, but all that is mine is yours. I'm not asking for a prenup. I'm not asking for any drama, I won't cheat on you and, again, if you give me a chance, I will give you the world. I want you to wear this ring and I want us to marry anywhere on the globe that you want to do it. I want to marry you and I want our wedding to be the mother of all weddings. No restrictions and money is no object. What do you say?"

Korie was speechless. Vaughn laid everything out and he was basically offering her the world and all it had to offer. She would never have to work again, she would never want for anything, and anything that she desired she could have; beginning with the mother of all weddings. She was speechless. She thought she knew what she wanted. She thought what she wanted was Darren and a life with him. All that seemed to go out the window when Vaughn played his hand.

"The wedding of my dreams?"

"The wedding of your dreams."

"Anywhere on the globe?"

"Paris. Rome. London. That spot you liked in Tokyo, anywhere."

"My friends can't just fly anywhere like that."

"No, but I can fly them in, if need be."

"You're serious, aren't you?"

"I love you. You make me feel brand new. You make me feel like a man should feel. You make me want to be a better man. And you know what? Not a day or a moment goes by that I don't think of you. I want you to marry me. I want you to have my children. I don't want you to want for anything. What do you say?"

"I guess there isn't anything left to say . . . except yes."

Chapter Forty-one

Korie felt guilty.

She felt guilty for sleeping with two men at once. She felt guilty for leading one man on. She felt guilty because of the things that she would do over the next week. She accepted two proposals when she should have only accepted one. She fooled around with two men when she should have only been with one. Finally, she gave one man her heart and let the other back in.

She should have never let the second man back in.

He had his chance. He blew it.

She thought about the sex. It was something that she had been struggling with since day one. Sure, she couldn't have sex all day, every single day, but did she need to? Was sex that important? Also, would she have sex everyday with Darren, or just everyday that the relationship was new? Accepting Darren's ring was a mistake. Like Jayna said, sex tended to cloud a woman's judgment. Had Darren not returned, Korie would have married Vaughn, hands down.

That was another thing: Was Darren a godsend or someone the devil sent back into her life? It's funny how when a woman just began to get over a man or just began to get herself together, that same man who broke her heart would pop his ass up again, acting like he was a changed man. Darren should have changed while he had her. Men needed to hold on to good women when they were blessed to have one. Korie thought to herself that she might still love Darren, but she was going to give Vaughn a chance. She was going to give love with him a chance. She needed time to get herself together; time to see where this thing with Vaughn might go. If anything, if Darren really loved her, he could wait. He could wait another five years, just as she had for him.

She moved in with Vaughn. She didn't tell Darren right away. Just as it was going to be hard to tell Vaughn no, it would be equally hard telling Darren. She didn't know how she would tell him. How do you tell someone that you are moving on without them, while things look like they're perfect?

She told Darren that she was busy with work and she moved in with Vaughn in one day. She took her clothes and her jewelry. Everything else she had thrown in the trash. She paid her lease up for the remainder of the year, just in case things didn't work out. She had the utilities cut off.

She phoned Jayna and told her of her decision. Vaughn proposed on a Monday. Korie put Darren off for as many days as she could via phone and it was Thursday that he received his ring back. She sent Darren's ring back to him by express mail, sending back the ring and a note. She thought a note would be the most appropriate way to tell him. She also decided that if she were going to marry Vaughn, there should be no secrets between them. She needed to tell her fiancée about her ex-boyfriend. Her note to Darren read as follows:

I'm sorry. I am truly, truly sorry. I don't know how to say this. But it appears that we had our chance at love and that time has passed. I don't regret the past two weeks. They have been wonderful. But you left. In a way, you abandoned ship. I understand that I might not be the woman I am today had we stayed together, but we didn't. Maybe I was meant to be the woman that I am now, the way that I am now and perhaps it was meant for me to get to this place in my life via the journey I had with you. I love you. I do. But again, our time has passed. I can't chance you walking out on us again. I can't chance you leaving me again. You say that you love me. You say that you never stopped loving me. But love wasn't enough to stop you from walking out on me like you did five years ago. It hurts, but I have to say good-bye. I have to at least see if what I have with Vaughn is real or not. I have to give my relationship with him a chance. He loves me. I love him. Just as I began to fall in love with him, you popped up and changed everything in my life. I used to pray to God to send you back into my life. I don't know how to say this, but I think maybe it was the devil that answered. Darren, I can't marry you. If things don't work out between Vaughn and me, you will be the first person that I call. I waited five years for you. That's five years too long. Again, I'm sorry.

With love,
Korie

Darren was crushed. His heart was broken. He looked at the ring and couldn't believe what Korie was saying. He received the ring at work, and minutes after he received it, he drove to her apartment. He used his key to let himself in and all traces of Korie were gone.

He jumped back in his car. Panic set in as the thought of losing his one true love burned in his head. It then dawned on him to go to Vaughn's house. He did. He drove like a madman and onto the shoulder of the expressway to get to Vaughn's Wilmette mansion. He raced to the gate of the grand home and rang the bell. No one answered. There were no cars in the driveway and no sign of Vaughn anywhere. He dialed Vaughn's cell phone.

"Hello?" Vaughn said.

"Uh, hi Vaughn. It's Darren. I—well, I need to speak with you."

"Go ahead. Say what you have to say."

Vaughn sounded upset. He sounded annoyed.

"I need to tell you something. It's hard for me to say, but there is something that you have to know."

"You mean about you and Korie?"

Darren was speechless.

"Your silence makes me think that you're stunned or surprised. She told me everything."

"Everything?"

"Everything. I can't believe that you proposed to her. I can't believe that you would pursue her knowing that I was with her!"

"Vaughn, you have to understand, I was with her first. I didn't know that the woman you were in love with was my ex. Is she with you? I need to speak to her."

"You're kidding me, right? There is no way in hell that I would put you on the phone with my fiancée."

"Fiancée? Vaughn, man, she's not going to marry you."

"Yeah, well, she already said that she would. In fact, I plan on marrying her shortly after the wheels on the plane touch down."

"I don't believe you."

"Believe it."

"She's going to marry me."

"Maybe you should be sitting around waiting for FedEx. Your ring should have come back to you by now."

"It did. That changes nothing."

"That's where you're wrong. It changes everything."

Darren's heart was racing and he couldn't believe what he was hearing. He couldn't believe that Korie told Vaughn everything. Just then, as he was heading back south on the expressway he heard another man in the background on the phone.

"Wheels up in twenty minutes, Mr. Harris."

Wheels up? They're at the airport.

Darren sped to O'Hare Airport. He opened up the engine on his 100,000 dollar car and raced to the largest airport in Chicago.

"Vaughn, please, let me talk to her! You all are making a mistake."

"You're the one making the mistake. I can't believe you! I can't believe how you betrayed my trust. I can't believe how much business I threw your way! Nigga, I made you!"

"You helped me, but you never made me. I would have been a success one way or the other. Vaughn, I know that you love her and man, I can respect that, but she's not meant for you. In my heart I know."

Vaughn hung up. With the disconnection he was slowly beginning to lose hope.

It was as if Vaughn disconnecting him was his way of disconnecting her from him as well.

Darren weaved in and out of traffic. He raced to the airport and risked getting arrested by driving onto a private, restricted road. He had his car going smoothly at 100 MPH. He headed to the airplane hangar with

Vaughn's company logo on the side. He got to the airport in thirteen minutes.

Thank God for his luxury sports car, although in truth it was Vaughn's money that paid for it. He pulled into the hangar and his car came to a screeching halt as it blocked the private jet that was just about to start taxiing out to the runway. The plane put its brakes on, almost hitting Darren's car, which was still running. Darren stood there defiantly. He wanted his woman back. He made up his mind that he would get his woman back. He didn't mind a storybook ending. He didn't mind admitting that he fucked up. He just wanted the plane to stop and for her to open the airplane door and come back to him. All would be forgiven. He didn't care that she accepted another man's proposal. He didn't care that she gave him his ring back. All he wanted was for her to come back to him.

Minutes later, the door to the plane opened. Rather than Korie stepping out, Vaughn stepped out at the top of the plane stairs and looked at Darren, furious. He had a look of fire in his eyes. The old lion was ready to once again bare his teeth. The airplane cued down its engine. It was clear that one way or the other, they would be delayed.

"You have some fucking nerve coming here," Vaughn said.

"Yeah, well, like I was trying to say, I'm sorry. I love her. Vaughn, I can't let you take her."

"Can't let me? Nigga, no one tells me what to do! Ever! No one stops me, ever! Now I admire your taste. Hell, I even admire the fact that you have the balls to come here, but I'm only going to tell you this once. Take your low-budget bargain-basement ass back to the hood or the middle-income suburb that you came from! Get the fuck off of my property!"

Just then, a gentle, manicured hand patted Vaughn's shoulder from behind. It was a hand that was delicate and strong all at once. It was a hand that was reassuring.

Korie surfaced. She whispered in his ear. Darren couldn't hear her from the distance between them. His heart skipped a beat as he saw her. Once again his spirit was filled with hope. She spoke to Vaughn, making an attempt to calm him down. Darren couldn't hear what she was saying, but clearly she was calming down Vaughn, who looked as if any minute now he would have a heart attack. That's how angry he looked. It did take balls to come here. It did take heart to tell another man that you desired and came for his woman, but Darren was not backing away. He would have to be killed or taken away in cuffs if they wanted him to go. Korie knew Darren. She had to know that he had no plans on letting her walk out of his life again.

He believed that she must have finally realized her mistake and was coming to her senses. He opened the passenger door to his car so she could get in. He then leaned on the front of his car with a look of confidence, arrogance. He waited for Korie to return to him. He was sorry for the ordeal that he was putting Vaughn through. He liked the older man. He admired him. But on this matter there could be no compromise. Darren came back for his lady.

Vaughn listened to Korie. She was able to calm him down and although he occasionally looked in Darren's direction, he listened to her. They hugged and somehow she convinced him to go inside the plane. Before going, he pointed at his watch as he went inside. He tapped it three times before going in. He was insistent. Darren still couldn't hear what was being said, but it was clear that Vaughn was telling her that they had a schedule to keep.

Darren thought, *she's not going with you.* Just get your ass on the plane and leave. He said a slight prayer to God. Thank you for sending her back to me.

Korie went to Darren.

Vaughn went inside the plane.

Korie had on a form-fitting satin dress that hugged her body and accentuated her ass. Her high heels matched her dress and she wore sheer black stockings. In her ears were two diamonds and on her hand was the ring that Vaughn gave her. It was a ring that put the rock Darren gave her to shame. Her makeup was flawless. Her hair was down and she looked so good that she could take a man's breath away. As she walked in his direction he thought about how lucky he was to have her back in his life. He thought about how breathtaking she looked. He gave her a look that said he would never let her go again. It was a look that said he fucked up, but for the rest of their lives he would try and make it right again.

He expected Korie to jump right in and for them to drive together in any direction. He stood by the passenger door, confidently, arrogantly. That is, until he saw the look in her eyes. It was a look that shook him to his core. It was a look that said I can't go with you.

He had a look of confusion.

The engines of the plane started up again.

The sounds of police sirens were in the backfield.

Korie walked over to him.

She hugged him.

She slowly kissed him on the cheek.

He took in her Issey Miyake perfume.

She took in his Chrome cologne.

He hugged her tightly, in a manner that said he would never let her go; like a child being pulled from his parent or like siblings being separated in foster care. He held onto her and hugged her for dear life, for love.

Tears streamed from his eyes. He held her as if he could never let go. He held her like he would never see her again.

She hugged him back tightly.

Tears were streaming from her eyes as well.

Only . . . she let go.

"I'm sorry" was the only thing he heard her say.

"It's not over," he responded. "It's not over."

"I'm getting married in seven days," he heard her say.

"You're supposed to marry me. I love you. I love you. I love you."

Over and over he said I love you.

Even when the cuffs were placed on his wrists.

Even as she walked away.

Even when Vaughn took her hand and led her back into the plane.

Even when the plane began to taxi away.

Even when he was placed in the back of the squad car.

Korie watched from the plane window as they took her first love away. She cried although Vaughn was sitting right across from her.

"Are you okay?" Vaughn asked.

"I'm okay," she said.

"This is the right thing. I love you."

"I know," Korie said.

"I know this was hard for you. But if you give me a chance, I will never hurt you, and I'll never let you down. From this point on, no secrets. We can't start a marriage with secrets."

"I agree. I confessed everything to you about Darren after you proposed to me. Do you have anything that you want to confess besides what happened in Germany?"

"No. That was it. That was the last time. I'm done. I'm ready to spend the rest of my life with you. That was our agreement."

"And if you break that agreement?"

"That's where the prenup comes in."

"I thought you didn't want a prenup."

"I didn't. But it seems like the smartest way to keep everyone honest."

"And I can hold you to the terms?"

"Of course, I'm a man of my word. If I cheat, you get fifty million dollars. If you cheat, you get nothing. If in five years you decide that you no longer want to be with me, then our divorce settlement will be ten million dollars, not a penny more. It's a win-win situation. All I'm asking for is the same chance that you gave him. I still have a hard time believing that shortly after accepting my proposal, you rejected it."

"It was all a lot to take in. I admit that I have fallen in love with you, but I never stopped loving him. I'm conflicted."

"I understand. For a long time I was conflicted too, especially regarding getting married after the death of my wife."

"And now?"

"And now, like I said, I'm no longer conflicted. I'm committed."

"Everything is happening so fast. Everything seems so . . . chaotic."

"I know, I know. But we have a nine-hour flight ahead of us and the rest of our lives to make sense of it all."

Korie and Vaughn sat in silence for awhile as the company jet headed toward Hawaii. As the squad car took Darren away, he watched the plane just as it began to take off.

Chapter Forty-two

Hours later Darren made bail. When he got home Karen was there in front waiting for him. He looked at her as he had never seen her before. He looked at her as his girlfriend.

She had no idea what happened earlier that day. But clearly she could see that her man was hurting about something. She never questioned him about it. She simply took his hand, guided him inside, and gave him a massage to try and rub the pain away. When that didn't work they made love and she tried to sex his pain away. She was a good woman. She was a good woman who Gucci made the mistake of letting go. It was a mistake that he too had made and was still hurting from.

Darren thought that he would give Karen 100 percent of him. He decided to be her man and perhaps one day her husband. In the meanwhile he also decided that he would be a father figure to Jacob. It was wrong. It was especially wrong considering he knew the pain and anguish that Gucci was going through after losing her. Gucci deserved her. Darren didn't. He had never been fair to her. To tell the truth, he used her. He needed to send her back to Gucci. He needed to tell her that she really needed to be with her baby's father. He wanted to tell her these things, but he couldn't bring himself to be alone.

Hours after he and Karen fell asleep, his doorbell rang. He sprang from bed in hopes that perhaps it was

Korie. Even now, he still thought of her. His body was with Karen, but his heart still belonged to Korie Dillon. He walked quickly to the door and on the other side was Stephanie.

"We need to talk," she said.

"About what?" he asked.

"About us." Stephanie walked in. She looked as if she had been crying all night.

"Who's at the door?" Karen asked as she surfaced from the bedroom in just Darren's pajama top.

Chapter Forty-three

Korie and Vaughn arrived nine hours later in Hawaii. It was still afternoon there with the time change. They were both exhausted as they stepped off the plane. Brandon and Jayna were at the airport waiting for them and Korie told Vaughn that she would meet him in the hotel room. She and Jayna went to the lobby and Korie filled Jayna in on everything that happened.

"So, Darren caused a scene like that at the airport?" Jayna asked.

"He did. He still loves me, and I think I still love him."

"Then why are you here?"

Korie was thrown off by Jayna's response, considering how much she despised Darren.

"I'm here because I owe Vaughn a chance. And, he made me an offer I couldn't refuse."

Korie outlined the agreement that she and Vaughn came to.

"So this is about money?" Jayna was really confused.

"No, it's not about money. It's about risk. I was thinking about everything that you said. I was thinking about what would happen if I did roll the dice again on love. I was also thinking about what would happen if Darren and I weren't meant to be together and what would happen if he did in fact leave me again. I don't think that he would, but I didn't expect him to leave the first time. If I gave him a chance and things didn't work out, I would kick myself in the behind for all that I would have lost. I love Vaughn. I don't know when it happened, but I love him. I know this sounds weird coming from me, but I think—hell, I know—that I love both men. Darren had his chance. It's time that I let the next man have a shot at loving me. I'm finally at a place in my life where I feel that I deserve the best that life has to offer. Vaughn is offering the very best and I need to see where this journey ends. He and I may only be married for five years, or it may be forever. In either case, for the first time in a long time, I won't be on the losing end of love."

"That makes sense. Korie, I'm happy for you."

The two women hugged.

"So where is this church where you want to have this double wedding?"

"It's not too far from here. Do you want to see it?"

"Sure."

Rather than go to her room, Korie and Jayna took a taxi to the church. Korie called Vaughn and told him that they were going to see the church and Vaughn and Brandon stated they would meet them there later. Clearly, Vaughn and Brandon had catching up to do as well. When Korie got out of the car she covered her mouth in fear as she walked into the foyer. Tears welled up in her eyes as she had a moment of déjà vu.

Jayna saw the fear in Korie's eyes and became concerned.

"Korie, what's wrong?"

"This church . . . this is the church in my dream."

"What dream?"

Korie sat in the nearest bench and told Jayna about the dream she had weeks before Darren came back into her life. Mysteriously, she knew every inch of the church and could tell Jayna what was behind every door before they opened them.

Jayna was spooked as well.

"Korie, I'm sure it's just a coincidence." Jayna tried to sound confident, but she wasn't.

"It's no coincidence, Jay. I think Darren's coming. He's coming to stop this wedding."

"Korie it was just a dream."

"We'll see."

Notes